NO WHISK NO REWARD

DONNER BAKERY BOOK #3

ELLIE KAY

WWW.SMARTYPANTSROMANCE.COM

COPYRIGHT

DEDICATION

For Laura. My biggest supporter since 07.07.07 <3

CHAPTER 1

"*I* really hope I am not lost. Please don't let me be lost."

I was talking to myself. I was doing that a lot lately.

Talking to myself had become a habit over the last couple of weeks and that was because I was more often than not alone.

I'd recently quit, or as I prefer to think of it, self-terminated my employment, at a high-end restaurant in Seattle called Paradigm, for reasons following a disastrous appearance on a televised baking competition called *No Whisk, No Reward*.

As it turns out, I have a pretty epic case of camera shyness and/stage fright.

Information that would have been useful to me prior to allowing myself to be goaded into auditioning, but I digress.

Long story short, I quit my job and was heading east to Boston where my best friend and fellow Culinary Institute of America graduate Anna was going to be opening up her own bakery which she planned to call Yeast Affection. I thought it was hilarious and suited Anna's irreverent personality perfectly, but I had doubts about whether Bostonians would find it as punny as we did.

Either way, with three months left on an employment contract with a restaurant in Back Bay, Anna didn't need me until the new year, so I decided to take a cross country sabbatical, stopping at many culinary points of interest along the way.

I thought that I would spend a lot more time weaving in and around any state with a bakery or restaurant with enough of a reputation to make me curious enough to stop in, but as it turned out, I hated driving in the dark. Also, gas, food, and lodging were more expensive than I had initially anticipated, and after just two weeks on the road, I realized that I was becoming quite lonely.

As a social person, I quickly learned that solitary travel was not for me and fleeting encounters with locals in small towns was not enough to sustain my need for human interaction.

Sometimes when I felt especially forlorn, and I had exhausted my vocal cords singing along to one of my many carefully curated playlists, I would talk to Paul Newman.

Or more precisely a laminated picture of him that I took with me everywhere as a good luck charm of sorts.

He kept me company, gave me advice, and sometimes when I really needed cheering up, he'd indulge me by running lines from his movies with me. My favorite movie to quote was *Cat on a Hot Tin Roof.*

For ten or so minutes, I forgot my troubles and I was Maggie the Cat, imploring Brick Politt to impregnate me.

Some people drink, some people do drugs, but my port of choice in a storm of loneliness was having an imaginary back and forth with a silver screen legend of yesteryear, and I'd be damned if I would apologize for it.

As I started to come to grips with the almost certain possibility that I had no idea how to get off the road I was on, I tried not to panic or engage my blue-eyed guardian angel just yet.

It felt as though I'd been winding down a never-ending mountain road for almost an hour, though in reality, it had probably only been fifteen minutes.

I kept a conservative speed so that I would not miss any possible turn offs or gaps through the trees that might reveal a hint of civilization out in the distance. Then I'd at least know if I was going in the right direction!

It was dusk now, getting close to dark and I needed to at least find my way back onto the highway.

I gripped the steering wheel firmly and leaned toward the windshield watching the thick canopy of trees pass by for what seemed like an age as George Michael cordially requested that I rouse him from slumber before I go-go'ed.

Had I not been so concerned about my whereabouts, I might have taken a moment to appreciate the beauty of the fire-hued, fall foliage.

Red, yellow, and orange leaves made the woods look like dying summer embers, and as I affixed a watchful eye on the road ahead, leaves fell like fiery rain and scattered across the asphalt like sparks.

The steering wheel seemed like it had been permanently hooked to the right as the car descended along the mountain road in what felt like a never-ending spiral.

Every so often I would cast my eyes to the phone in its dashboard mount to see if cell reception had been restored so I could use GPS to track where the hell I was. Each shift in the dimming light made me more and more anxious to find my way off this road.

Up ahead an old, gnarled tree arched its branches across the road only to realize I had already passed beneath that distinctive bit of forestry already.

"Oh wonderful," I squeaked, my voice straining through my tight throat. "I'm going in circles. How is that even possible? That's it. I'm gone, I'm dead. This is the Hotel California of forests. I'm in the Blair Witch woods, just point me to the corner and get it over with," I moaned, peering down momentarily at the radio to turn off the music as though the quiet might help me see better.

When my eyes flickered back to the road, it had straightened out ahead of me and the blinding brightness of approaching headlights alerted me to the fact that I had veered on the wrong side of it.

"Shit!" I yanked the steering wheel fully to the right as a big, black truck came into view and time seemed to slow down as the moment played out before me with the kind of clarity that only a near-death experience can bring.

The driver laid on their horn and both of our tires screeched as we simultaneously slammed on our brakes, maneuvering our cars away from each other and narrowly escaping a crash, which was just as well because that truck would have easily leveled my '95 Honda Civic with me inside it.

My car stopped abruptly, causing me to lurch forward and then reel back against my seat from the sharp stop. Then silence.

A horror reel of all the possible ways it could have ended differently played in my mind as my white knuckles clutched at the steering wheel.

I forced thoughts of my gruesome demise from my mind and shifted my eyes up to glance in the rearview mirror and saw that the other car had also stopped.

Shock immediately gave way to embarrassment and I knew I should get out of the car and make sure that whoever was in the truck was okay and apologize for my lapse in focus.

I also briefly considered that being a female and alone on a remote mountain road, it might be wiser for me to just put the car in drive and take off without opening myself up to the possibility of being abducted.

Society told me not to generalize but I honestly doubted that I'd find a woman driving a big, honking truck like that.

My eyes lowered to beneath the truck's back tires and I told myself that if it was sporting a pair of those truck testicles that seemed to be so popular amongst young redneck men then I would be absolutely justified in making a run for it.

Nothing untoward dangled between the back "legs" of the truck but it still did little to ease my nerves about confronting the driver.

I acknowledged and fully accepted that I deserved to be scolded and if that was their intention then I'd dutifully take it on the chin, promise that it would not happen again, reiterate my regret, and then be on my way.

But the longer the moment dragged on, the more my imagination began to run away with all manner of horrific scenarios that involved more sadistic means of punishment.

"I really need to stop listening to true crime podcasts," I told myself trying desperately to find enough rationality and aplomb to get out of my car and express my repentance to the other driver.

I was still shaking, though I tried to convince myself that it was from the shock of the near head-on collision I'd narrowly avoided, and not the fact that any moment a mountain man wielding a chainsaw in one hand and the head of his last victim in the other might exit the cabin of his vehicle and come lumbering toward me with the inhuman speed of the T-1000.

My eyes flickered to my phone again.

No reception still.

"Shit."

I swallowed and looked up at the laminated picture of Paul Newman clasped to a nylon lanyard that hung from my rearview mirror the way rosary beads hung from other people's mirrors.

"Mr. Newman, if you're up there ..." I began, my voice small and breathless as I appealed to the spirit of Paul Newman the way that others appealed to God. "If you get me out of this, I swear I will go back to your Sockarooni sauce, chocolate sandwich cookies, and microwave popcorn. It's just that ... well, the other brands were discounted, and I needed to watch my spending," I explained trying to justify my lapse in brand loyalty. "I see now that everything has a price, but if you please get me out of this next ten minutes unscathed, I *swear* I won't stray again. I mean, not that I can commit to feeding myself exclusively with your products, but ... you know what I mean. Amen."

I lowered my chin from my "prayer" in reverence for a moment and then sighed, lifting my eyes back to the rearview mirror.

The driver's side door of the truck swung open and my shoulders immediately knotted with tension.

I took a long, deep inhalation and held it watching as a pair of jean-clad legs with brown boots stepped out onto the road.

His body exited facing away from me and in the low light, I struggled to make out any level of detail other than the fact that he didn't seem to be holding a gun or chainsaw.

"It's fine. This is fine. Everything is fine," I babbled nervously to myself.

His muted, olive-green T-shirt clad back straightened and his long arm grasped the driver's side door as he rose to his full height.

He was big, broad, and imposing even from a distance and I made a strangled whimpering sound as I watched him start to turn around.

Tension made my eyes water and I choked out an exhalation; unable to hold in my breath any longer as I mentally weighed the merits of contrition and asking for forgiveness against not being kidnapped, driven to a house with a hidden torture bunker, and killed in backwater nowhere.

"Oh God, he's massive," I said as his six-foot-three-ish frame turned around and my eyes involuntarily lowered from the rearview mirror as I reached to unclasp my seatbelt.

My heart thundered with a concerning amount of force within my chest cavity.

I liked to credit myself as being quite a brave person, but I was brave in the sense that I was down for bungee jumping, approaching an attractive man at a club and asking him to dance, or even confronting people in public who were harassing others or being obnoxious or distasteful.

At that moment however, my bravery cup runneth bone ass dry and I wrestled only with my sense of self-preservation.

And then he started walking. *Toward me!*

"You know what, buddy, you're not going to get the chance to kill me because I am going to have a heart attack," I declared as though I were somehow one-upping him by beating him to his murderous punch.

I unfastened the clasp of my seatbelt and it retreated with a zip as I looked in the mirror again, the heat rising in my cheeks and neck as I watched him get closer.

"Please don't be a murderer, please don't be a murderer," I chanted as I reached to my left with shaking hands to release the latch on my door.

I hesitated before pushing it out slowly, not in any hurry for a lambasting, nor my imminent demise.

The first sound that filtered through the air outside the car—other than my own heartbeat—was crickets chirping and the crunching of his boots along the gravel as he approached.

His pace was purposeful and steady, but not necessarily urgent or hard against the road.

I tried to swallow as I twisted my body to lift my legs out of the car and place them down on the road.

My Converse sneakers met the dirt and I leaned my weight onto them feeling my knees shake as I exited the cabin.

As I stood upright, I heard the man's crunching steps come to a stop behind me some ten to fifteen feet behind where my car had screeched to a halt.

Unable to prolong the inevitable any further, I spun on my feet and turned to face the music.

The first thing I noticed was his scowl.

His eyebrows were low and furrowed, with two parallel lines etched between his eyes as he glared at me. My chest tightened.

It was too dark to make out what color his eyes were and his lips encircled by a thick, full beard were pressed into a straight, flat line.

The way his hands gripped his narrow hips emphasized the broadness of his chest and strapping width of his shoulders in contrast, and his chest rose and fell with his measured breathing.

"You alright?" he barked, his voice firm and gravelly, sounding harsh like his concern was merely a formality before getting to what he really wanted to say.

His shirt fit him well enough that his stomach muscles drew inwards and tensed at his words which did not escape my attention. Were it not for the deep frown on his face and displeased demeanor, I would have thought him incredibly attractive.

7

Again, I went through the motions of swallowing, but my mouth was too dry to have the desired effect.

All the moisture in my body seemed to pool in my palms as I wiped them against my jeans.

"I-I'm fine ... are you? Okay, I mean?"

I struggled through a clumsy response and his eyes narrowed at me.

There was a quality about the way they glinted, even in that darkness that told me his eyes were light colored, though I couldn't tell if they were blue or green.

The more I looked at him, the more I struggled to keep a grasp on the circumstances that had brought us to this moment.

"You been drinkin'?" he asked sternly.

I started at his directness and suddenly I remembered.

Oh yeah, I almost killed us.

He had every reason to believe I was driving incapacitated and I let the surprise of his brusqueness pass before shaking my head.

"No, I—"

"Fall asleep at the wheel?" he interrupted me tersely and immediately my cheeks, neck, and ears erupted into flames of embarrassment.

Through my mortification, my ears picked up the drawn-out syllables of a southern drawl. Possibly from years of watching movies, I had a slight tendency to romanticize anyone with a southern accent. This absurd facet of my subconscious decided right then and there that I wanted this accented giant to like me and I rushed to defend my actions.

"No, I swear it was nothing like that, I just ... I'm not from around here and ..."

I saw his chin tilt upward as he regarded me with something akin to cautious curiosity from under his heavy-lidded eyes, so I forged on with my weak excuse.

"I have been driving perfectly for like seven hours, then the *one* second I veer off to the left, there's another car coming right toward me!" I explained ending with a nervous, shaky laugh, my arm lifting from my side and falling back against my thigh with a slap.

He didn't laugh, but the severity of his expression downgraded from arctic to glacial as he continued to stare at me.

I cleared my throat and looked down at the road between us repentantly.

"I'm really sorry, I'll be more attentive from now on, I promise it won't happen again," I said crossing my heart and hoping the sincerity I tried to impart in my tone and expression would be enough to unlock myself from the pit bull-like grip of his castigation.

His glower held for a few more seconds and I held my breath as I waited until finally his chin lowered and his eyes dropped to the ground as he sighed.

"Don't worry about it, just … be more careful," he grumbled, as though he was disappointed that I'd not been more indignant and combative.

He glanced back at me for a moment and my heart rate picked up again for a different reason.

He was really gorgeous. And that southern accent? *Oh God, yes.*

He turned to go back to his truck and it was then that I remembered that I was still lost, and it was now completely dark.

"Uh … sir … before you go," I called after him and he stopped and glanced at me over his shoulder.

He then turned his body fully around and brushed his palm across his bearded jaw.

Holy shit, he is otherworldly attractive, I thought, noticing how even the voice inside my head sounded breathless.

His hands were back on his hips and his knee was cocked to the side in a stance that translated universally as, *I don't have time for this.*

Carrying on because I didn't have a choice, I cleared my throat and drew my eyebrows together pleadingly.

"So … not that you owe me your help given that I almost just killed you, but … I think I've just spent the better part of an hour driving in a circle so if you could please just tell me how to get off this mountain or somewhere with cell reception, I would be really, really grateful," I said clasping my fingers together pleadingly.

His expression was inscrutable as he stood there staring at me for what seemed like forever. I didn't get the sense that he was considering my question so much as he was considering me, and what to make of me.

Once again finding myself in the vise-like hold of his stare, I shifted on my feet uneasily and was about to tell him to forget it when he finally spoke.

"Where are you headed?" he asked, his question still concise but softer and without the same brusqueness as before.

"Well, for now … anywhere there's a hotel, motel, bed and breakfast, or guest house for rent would be nice, but … if you can get me out of here, I am sure I'll come across something."

His eyebrows furrowed again like my answer confused him.

"Where specifically were you trying to get to?" he asked again, his voice re-adopting the directness from earlier.

I cleared my throat. He was intimidating.

"Boston," I replied realizing how ridiculous that sounded considering where I was.

"Might I suggest you delay any further traveling until tomorrow," he stated prosaically. "You're not going to make that trip tonight," he said looking at me with something akin to condescension.

I lifted my chin and squared my shoulders finding some gumption before responding. "Well, sir, that is exactly why I asked after accommodations," I replied with a slight edge in my tone.

He observed me for a moment longer before nudging his chin in the direction I'd been traveling in.

"I'm going to turn my truck around and pull out ahead of you, follow me until I've stopped."

"Where are you leading me?" I asked my tone laced with a hint of cautious reticence.

"I know a place you can stay the night. It's in town so you won't have to go out of your way to find breakfast in the morning, there's a supermarket if you need supplies, and it's pretty much a straight shot back onto the highway."

I paused at his words and stared at him in surprise, not sure why he was suddenly being so helpful since I seemed to have done nothing but annoy him for the past five minutes.

Ultimately though, I decided not to look a gift horse in the mouth and quickly reminded myself to be grateful for the abetting shift in his mood.

"Thank you! That sounds ..." I struggled to find an adequate superlative to finish the thought and his lips hitched up at the corner of his mouth as though it took some effort on his part to do it.

"You're welcome," he said with a nod and then turned and headed back to his truck.

I watched him and took a moment to observe his gait as he walked away from me.

He had a physical kind of confidence that made his stride more like a saunter.

His hips shifted from left to right in an easy swagger some men wield effortlessly yet it was obvious from the tightness of his shoulders that he was still frustrated from our exchange.

"Good Lord ... you sir, are going straight into the spank bank," I muttered under my breath before the sound of his truck door slamming shut shook me from my objectifying thoughts.

I got back into my car and put it in drive, waiting and watching in my rearview mirror as he easily maneuvered his huge truck through a perfect three-point-turn and pulled out ahead of me.

He stopped for a beat as though signaling to me that he was ready to proceed, and I lowered my handbrake and pressed my foot on the gas to follow as he started to drive away.

Ten minutes later, he veered right onto what I thought was a runaway truck ramp and then made a sharp right at the end of it onto an unpaved road obscured by overgrown trees.

I tensed a little as the branches scraped the sides of my car and thought of my kidneys as my poor, mature-aged vehicle jostled roughly down the jagged road for about a quarter mile.

As we rounded a bend, I caught a glimpse up ahead where the road smoothed out and joined back up to what looked like a highway and my shoulders relaxed as I sighed with relief.

I glanced over to my cell phone and saw the signal indicator flash back to life letting me know that I was now once again back in the land of cell reception.

I glanced up at the lanyard on my rearview mirror and smiled.

"Thank you," I whispered to my blue-eyed guardian angel.

CHAPTER 2

*M*r. Frowny Brows wasn't unfriendly per se, but neither was the wall of a squash court and as such, my attempts to engage him in conversation kept bouncing off his cool exterior while I was left running from one end of the metaphoric court to the other, trying to keep a rally going.

Maybe the energy that had accumulated in my body over the past eight hours of driving was responsible for the projectile of interrogational vomit that I proceeded to subject him to as we walked along the street toward a cluster of low-rise buildings in what looked like the town center. I was a woman and he was an unnervingly attractive man, so naturally, I wanted to become better acquainted with him, despite the sentiment not feeling entirely mutual.

He took my inquiries in stride and didn't expressly request that I stop from asking them so my compulsion to unrelentingly question him went unchecked.

"So, have you lived here long?"

"Sort of."

"You work nearby?"

"Kind of."

"What do you do for work?"

"A few different things," he replied vaguely, which only served to further pique my curiosity.

"Like a handyman?" I asked conjuring an image of him in my mind wearing a tool belt which I did not hate.

"Sometimes."

'Sometimes?' What the hell does 'sometimes' mean?

"So, where's the place where you said the breakfast was good?" I asked, looking around for an eatery of some kind but not spotting anything nearby.

"I don't recall recommending anything, but you'll probably want to head to Daisy's Nut House."

"Do you go there?"

"Yep."

"What do you recommend?"

"Anything on the breakfast menu is pretty good, I guess, but they're known for their doughnuts and pie."

"Ooh! I like doughnuts and pie. You have a favorite?"

"I don't have much of a sweet tooth," he stated, which I didn't personally understand given my profession, but I wasn't about to judge him too harshly on it.

"Ah, so you're a breakfast guy?"

"I'm an everything guy," he said casting me a brief sideways smile at the mention of food. Finally! Something that prompted a reaction from him that registered at the detectible end of enthusiastic.

Seeing the quick upturn of his lips made my feet tingle and my response was to immediately giggle. I was going for warmth, but it more likely came across as awkwardly flirtatious. I was obviously out of practice when it came to interacting with people I considered attractive.

"Yeah, me too. Food's great."

Food's great? Smooth.

I shook my head at myself and did a little gallop to catch up when I noticed I'd fallen behind.

By the light of the irregularly spaced street lights we were passing, I could make out his features a little more clearly.

He was even better up close which most certainly contributed to my ungainly manner.

He had dark brown hair which was short, straight, and all messed up as though he only brushed it with his fingers when someone pissed him off, and flecks of either gray or blond through his beard, which turned silvery when it caught the light.

His eyes were somewhere between blue and green and I had a hunch that they became more of one or the other depending on what he was wearing or what mood he was in. They were framed by thick, expressive brows and his skin looked like it was holding onto the summer just passed, all golden brown and sun-kissed.

"So, what do people do around here? For fun I mean," I asked when I was done ogling him, hoping he hadn't noticed me doing it.

"Hmm." He shrugged. "The usual stuff, I guess. Go to bars, eat, go dancing."

I saw an opportunity at the mention of "dancing" to try and wedge a conversational crow-bar between the metal doors of this guys' personality elevator, jump inside his cabin, and push the top floor button.

People's responses to dancing usually elicited some kind of response one way or the other and I figured since I'd earned myself a smile, maybe he was a little more comfortable around me now.

"Do you dance?" I asked, narrowing my eyes at him as though I had a suspicion he did.

"No," he scoffed, hanging his head bashfully as though the mere thought of being associated with having ever moved to the sound of music was just crazy. I pressed on, undeterred.

"I *love* to dance!"

"No kidding," he responded, making little effort to keep the sarcasm from his response, but I got another smile, wry as it was.

I had to gallop beside him in an effort to keep up with his long strides and simply let his detachedness roll off my shoulders.

"Yeah! I did a flash mob one time," I volunteered, thinking that was a neat little tidbit to share with a stranger who surely already thought I was a sandwich short of a picnic.

"A what?" he asked as we came to a stop on the sidewalk and turned to face me, giving me my first opportunity to really take in the details of his face, which up until now had been obscured by darkness or blurred by the motion of trying to keep up with him.

Once again pinned by that stare, I noticed a scar on the left side of his top lip and just how red his lips were as his tongue came out to brush across the scar before he rolled his lips back into his mouth.

"A flash mob," I explained as he continued to frown at me like he didn't know what I was talking about. "You know, when a group of people do a surprise dance routine in a public place, like a mall, a park, or a crosswalk?"

His expression turned nonplussed and practically screamed *"why the hell would anyone do that?"*

"Right," he said instead, placing his hands on his hips and cocking his knee again.

I cleared my throat, hitching my backpack strap back up onto my shoulder as I fidgeted under his scrutiny.

"So … what song was the dance routine to?"

My eyes shot up from the ground, surprised by his question.

I wasn't sure if his expression suggested that he was especially interested, however, he seemed like the kind of guy who couldn't abide by only knowing half the story.

Despite my awareness of his level of interest, I still somehow managed to overcompensate in my response.

"I know its cliché, but it was Halloween and we did Michael Jackson's *"Thriller"* … you know with the …" I proceeded to claw my fingers and sway them from left to right through the air to exhibit one of the more recognizable moves in choreography.

He held up a staying hand. "Yeah I know the dance, you don't have to demonstrate," he remarked, the smile threating to make a reappearance once again as he tried to keep his amusement in check.

I cleared my throat and decided a swift change of topic was in order.

"What's your name by the way?" I asked, holding out my hand

between us and his eyes glanced down at it as though he would be making some kind of commitment by shaking it.

"Joel," he replied eventually, and then proceeded to engulf my entire hand with his, prompting what I swear was a second sexual awakening. It reminded me vaguely of the time in my life that I started to appreciate how different a man's hand felt compared to a woman's.

When I began to recognize how solid and strong they were and how it made me feel weird in my tummy, but I wasn't sure how or why.

Now that I was older, I knew why.

Yep. I was attracted to this guy.

"Hi Joel, it's nice to meet you. I'm Sophie," I managed to reply, trying to look less mesmerized by his eyes than I was, and more like I was simply maintaining polite eye contact.

"Pleased to make your acquaintance," he drawled in that luscious accent as he returned my gaze, albeit through a much cooler filter than I most assuredly viewed him through.

I could have sworn we had a moment where the handshake went on for one pump too many but before I could think too much about it, he dropped my hand and gestured behind me with a quick point of his finger.

"You can stay here for the night. Room's not taken."

I turned to look over my shoulder to where he'd indicated but only saw a shopfront for a used bookstore.

"In the bookstore?" I asked, confused.

"No, above it," he explained. "The top floor is split into two studio apartments. I live in one, and the other is a rental. It's available right now. Come on," he said cocking his head for me to follow and immediately began walking toward a blue door that sat nestled between the entrance of the book shop and the conjoined hair salon beside it.

I had questions, but he walked fast and was already fishing a set of keys out of the pocket of his jeans to unlock the door before I had time to ask them.

"Hey, wait," I called out after him as he got to work unlocking two deadlocks that were inches apart from one another on the door.

"What kind of rate are we talking for the room? I don't have a lot of mon—"

"Don't worry about it," he interjected, pushing on the door so that it swung open on its hinges to where I could see nothing but an ascending flight of wooden steps.

I peered up the steps and caught sight of the landing at the top which broke off into opposite directions, before turning my attention back to him.

"What do you mean, 'don't worry about it?' I can't stay in your rental for nothing," I insisted folding my arms across my chest and frowning with disapproval.

"Look, you're going to be on your way in the morning, so it's hardly worth my time and effort to go through the whole booking process for the amount of money I would end up charging. You need a place to stay, I have one, and I'm late to be somewhere. Do you want it or don't you?" he replied, hitting on only the main points of his argument which were frankly hard to argue with, in my current predicament.

I should have been annoyed at his impatience, but he'd just said so many words in that sweet, sweet southern drawl that I needed a moment to collect myself.

I considered his offer for a moment, regarding him with a scrutinizing glower as though I wasn't sure whether or not I could trust his too-good-to-be-true offer.

He returned my glare with a practiced look of indifference, but I swear he was fighting a smile.

"Can I see the room first?" I inquired finally, still probably sounding unsure, but in reality, after eight hours on the road, I would have settled for anything so long as it was safe, clean, and *not* the back seat of my car.

It was also possible that I was just delaying the inevitable because I didn't want this interaction to end yet. I didn't know where he was going but I wasn't making any apologies for making him late. Joel wasn't giving me much, I admit, but every little smile that threatened to pull at those lips left me wanting to see the real thing, if only to confirm my suspicions that it would be spectacular.

Without a verbal response, he pushed himself off the doorjamb and proceeded to cross the threshold inside the building to start making his way up the narrow wooden stairs.

When he was an appropriate distance ahead of me I followed, keeping my eyes fixed on his back as he climbed each step and the way his hips swung as he did.

His footfalls were heavy in the narrow passageway of the stairs and his large frame took up almost the entire width of space between the two walls.

When we reached the landing at the top, I saw one door to the left and another to the right.

"Wait here," he instructed, turning to the door on the right and using his keys to unlock it before disappearing inside the apartment and closing the door before I could try to subtly peek inside.

I stood on the dimly lit landing and glanced around trying to make deductive observations about what I could potentially expect inside the rental apartment.

There was little to glean from the wooden staircase and landing that was losing its polish but otherwise unremarkable. The absence of staining or blood was a relief, I figured.

There was no mold or rising smell, which also boded well; even though the cream colored, embossed wallpaper was beginning to bubble and peel off and every now and then the dim light that emanated from the singular sconce on the wall would flicker off and on.

There was a green, locked metal box mounted to the wall outside his door and a welcome mat at the doorway of the rental, but not outside his own.

Shortly after I had made that observation, his door opened, and he reappeared, closing it quickly behind him before taking long strides past me to the rental suite.

He quickly unlocked it and nudged it open on its hinges, reaching inside to feel around on the wall for the light switch.

When he found it, the lights inside flickered on and he gestured for me to precede him as we made our way inside the apartment, so I could inspect it.

At first glance, it was nothing special and it didn't take Sherlock Holmes to surmise that it had been furnished by a man.

It was a small space with only three distinct rooms that I could immediately see, but as I walked around, I noticed that it had some really nice structural points of interest, like the exposed brick wall in the living room and the wooden beams that crisscrossed along the ceiling up above.

The wooden flooring on the inside was much better maintained than out in the hall, and the few pieces of furniture that there were looked modern and clean.

In the bedroom which was also the living room, there was a big bed pressed up against the wall, with a window that looked out onto the street. The dark gray sheets it was covered in were neat and pulled tightly across the surface of the mattress.

There was a navy blue, two-seat sofa in front of the entertainment unit which consisted of a modest sized flat screen TV, a cable box, wireless router, and modem.

The walls were devoid of any artwork, but there was a palm in the corner of the room parallel to the bed adding some much-needed life to the space.

The room smelled pleasant and all the surfaces were clean, so I turned back to him and started to attempt to negotiate a deal that I would have felt more comfortable with.

"This is great, but I need to insist that you at least let me give you—"

I was instantly silenced as he tossed the keys through the air, shutting down my speech function abruptly in order to fully engage the hand-eye coordination required to catch them.

"Tomorrow morning, when you leave, strip the bed and leave any used towels on the floor of the bathroom. You can leave the suite keys in the green box beside my door on your way out. If any urgent matters should arise that require my immediate attention, there's a number you can reach me at by the phone in the kitchen on an info sheet which also includes the Wi-Fi password. You have yourself a pleasant evening, Miss Sophie."

Before I could comprehend and absorb his instructions, the front door shut and he was gone, leaving me slack-jawed with my fist balled, frozen in place where I'd caught the apartment keys.

"O … kaaay," I said to nobody, frowning and looking around the now empty apartment, wondering what the catch was.

I lowered my arm and looked around the space, which felt much larger now that Joel was no longer in it.

My first thoughts naturally veered into true crime territory because I'd spent countless hours listening to podcasts on the road. My most recent one involved a very detailed recounting of a serial killer at the World's Fair, so I promptly began a search for trap doors, hidden passages and since technology had progressed since the World's Fair, I also included hidden cameras in my search.

After finding none and deciding I was paranoid, I decided that I had two choices. I could stay up all night worrying that I had been lured into an H.H. Holmes style murder house and get zero rest, or I could just relax, eat something, have a shower, and get a good night's sleep before heading back out on the road the following morning.

In the end, the allure of cooking myself a real meal was a prospect too tempting to resist, so I brushed all my serial killer thoughts aside, gathered up my purse, and went in search of the nearest supermarket.

CHAPTER 3

*a*fter a quick search on my phone, I acquired directions to the nearest supermarket called the Piggly Wiggly and headed there for provisions.

As I meandered through the mostly deserted aisles, trying to decide what I was in the mood for, I felt my cell phone vibrating from within my pocket.

I fished it out, inspected the screen and immediately groaned aloud because it was a number I didn't recognize, which meant that I knew *exactly* who it was.

John Moxie was the executive producer of *No Whisk, No Reward* and he had been calling me multiple times a day, every day, for the past two weeks.

I had answered his calls the first few times and indulged his initial attempts to entice me to participate in what he liked to refer to as, "*the perfect opportunity to restore your reputation,*" which was actually a best-of-the-worst episode where contestants who had bombed out of previous seasons were given another chance to compete against each other for redemption.

After my polite declinations to participate eventually devolved into not-so-polite refusals, I started to realize that people who worked in the entertainment industry had a particular aversion to taking no for an answer. Nothing I said or did seemed to deter him from haranguing me about it.

At my wits end, I stopped answering the phone, but then he started calling from different numbers, which I fell for the first couple of times, before quickly growing wise to his game.

Normally, I wouldn't have answered but I still had some residual adrenaline from getting lost and the subsequent near-death experience that followed, and he was the perfect punching bag to let out my pent-up anxiety.

"Mr. Moxie," I answered, allowing my tone to express how I felt about his call.

"Did you miss me?" he asked with that disingenuous, salesman-like quality to his voice that I had grown accustomed to when conversing with him.

"I miss the time in my life where you didn't have my cell number."

"You don't mean *thaaaaat*," he said as though he refused to believe it, and I cocked an eyebrow as though he could see my expression.

"Oh, I do, I really, really do. Like from the bottom, top, and both sides of my beating heart."

"Look I don't blame you after how things went down on the show, but I think you'll change your mind when I tell you about what the network is willing to do to entice you to come back for the *Double the Whisk, Double the Reward* episode."

"We've gone over this *ad nauseam*," I sighed wearily, rubbing my forehead as I walked along the aisle.

"Just let me pitch you the incentive and then you tell me that you don't want to participate."

"And if I don't, you'll leave me alone?" My tone implying that his response would be a promise.

"Let's not get ahead of ourselves," he replied evening out his tone enough to make it clear that he wasn't prepared to give up on me any time soon.

Though I couldn't imagine anything would be enticing enough to convince me to embarrass myself on national television for a second time, I would have been lying if I said I wasn't curious to see what was on the table.

The potential to make $300,000, which was almost double the show's regular winnings, was tempting, but all I had to do was remember the fallout from my last disastrous appearance to feel secure in the knowledge that nothing John Moxie said or did would convince me to agree to any terms.

My mind flashed with memories of how things had changed for me at the restaurant I worked at, post-show.

Paradigm was a high-end restaurant in Seattle, Washington where musicians, actors, sports personalities, and politicians frequented, and despite its pretentiousness, being able to have such a prestigious establishment on my resumé, gave me some serious clout. At least it used to.

Until one day John Moxie came to Paradigm for dinner and created a buzz amongst my co-workers in the kitchen by actively recruiting some of the staff to participate on his popular, prime time television show *No Whisk, No Reward.*

Most of the buzz in the kitchen amongst the predominantly male staff was little more than braggadocios peacocking about how they'd "smash the competition," but when I was singled out by John Moxie for a dessert he'd ordered that I had made, I naïvely let myself get talked into signing up for the show.

Suffice it to say, I did not do well. More precisely I was knocked out of the first round for fucking up a simple crème pâtissière that I had scrambled in a flustered stupor.

After the show, I started noticing the head chef Julian Lefebvre loitering around my work station more than usual and suddenly nothing I did was good enough.

"Your crème pâtissière is too tick."

"Your crème pâtissière is too tin."

"What temperature did you temper ze shock-lat? It's not shiny. MORE SHINY!"

"More height on ze soufflé, it's flat. IT'S FLAT!"

Up until my appearance on the show, I had a good working relationship with Julian, which was to say he left me alone to do my work.

I understood that he felt like my performance on the show reflected poorly on the reputation of the restaurant, but his sudden vigilance over my work, and determination to find fault in everything I did, only served to make me doubt that I had ever done anything right in the first place.

My confidence was shaken and a commercial kitchen environment in the competitive upscale market was not exactly conducive to fostering the kind of team spirit where people stood up for one another. I was essentially left to the wolves until eventually, I couldn't even crack an egg without worrying that I had done it wrong.

Over time, the bright lighting in the restaurant during rush hour made me nervous and forget the most basic techniques. I tried to force myself to be rational and tell myself that I wasn't in a studio, I was in the same restaurant I had worked in for years, but the thought of people watching me all the time made me feel incredibly anxious.

Eventually, I decided that it was no way to live, and after a fortuitously timed conversation where my best friend Anna broke the news to me that she was finally ready to open her own bakery, I quit my job at Paradigm, broke my lease, and hit the road bound for Boston to help her develop her products in a less stressful environment.

"Well go on then, but I have to warn you, you're wasting your time," I sighed into the phone while perusing items that were appropriate for feeding a single person for one night only.

"Come on, Sophie! What's my motto?"

"Pester people to within an inch of their sanity?"

"Be *open!*"

"Just cut to the chase, John, I have shit to do," I lied, just wanting this phone call to be over.

"Okay, okay. Here it is. If you agree to come back for the *Double the Whisk, Double the Reward* episode, not only has the studio increased the prize money, but they have also agreed to let each contestant bring along a friend or family member. Additionally, they are also organizing to have a celebrity mentor *of your choosing*, subject to availability, there to help guide you through the competition. Doesn't that sound neat?"

I came to a stop by the potato chips and briefly considered John's proposal.

"Neat? That doesn't sound neat, it sounds like a nightmare!"

"*What?*" John hollered incredulously into the phone as though he couldn't believe I didn't immediately agree to participate.

"You remember why I did so badly in the first place right?"

"Yeah, yeah so you had a smidge of stage fright, the studio has already agreed to having a coach present—"

"Oh good, so after I burn, scramble, or split something, and Gordon Ramsay tells me what an incompetent twat I am, a counselor will be there to stop me from sticking my head in the oven. Sounds like a party, what time should I be there?" I asked sarcastically.

"Sophie, honey! This is your shot at redemption! Don't you know what this could do for your career if you nail this? I mean the prize money bumped up to three hundred thousand dollars alone should be enough of an incentive, you could open your own bakery!"

I felt a twinge inside at the mention of opening my own bakery. It had been a goal of mine ever since I graduated from culinary school and three hundred grand would certainly clear the path for such a goal.

Despite the sweetened pot, the tension that had built up in my body just thinking about getting back in front of those cameras was enough to make me double down on my position and stick to my guns.

"Sure, sure, to the victor go the spoils, while the rest of us are left to salvage what's left of our tattered reputations, which by the way, in this industry is *much* harder for a woman to do than a man."

"I agree. Really, I'm on your side, but, Sophie, just like the show says, n—"

"Don't. You. Dare!" I interrupted, preempting his next words. "I *know* what you're about to say, and if you do, I'm gonna hang up on y—"

"No risk, no reward!"

I growled and stabbed at my phone with my finger, ending the call before cocking my arm as though I were about to pitch the device right down the snack aisle, until I caught sight of an employee stacking bags of pretzels and looking at me wide-eyed.

I took a moment to regain my composure, relaxed my stance, and lowered my arm. As I glided by, I smiled and affixed a mask of equanimity to counter the embarrassed flush that was quickly rising in my cheeks.

"Good evening." I nodded courteously as I passed by, making as cool and efficient an exit from the aisle as I could manage while feeling their eyes on me until I was out of sight.

From the safety of the baking aisle, I leaned against one of the shelves and sighed deeply, rubbing my tired, stinging eyes and losing the motivation to cook more every passing moment.

Needing to hear a familiar voice and seeking guidance, I dialed Anna's number, thinking it had been a couple of days since we'd last spoken and I should probably check in to let her know I was alive and well.

"Who is this?" she asked immediately after answering the phone and instantly I smiled because I knew what she was doing.

"It's Sophie, you jackass," I replied my voice full of affection for her.

"Sorry, I don't know anyone by that name. I used to, but that was a long time ago. I thought we were friends but … she stopped calling and writing, so I have learned to move on and forget about her. God, it's almost too painful to talk about."

"It's been two days."

"Which is the equivalent of five friendship years. Where are you? Who's seen you? What has become of you?"

"I'm in Tennessee," I replied attempting to adopt the local drawl in my response and immediately cringed at how awful it sounded.

"Was that your southern accent?" she asked sounding equal parts quizzical and appalled.

"It's actually harder to emulate that I thought," I admitted thoughtfully.

"Well, don't let any locals hear you attempting it or you'll be run out of town."

I laughed, but it lacked enthusiasm and she could immediately tell.

"What is it? What's wrong? Is everything okay?"

"Yeah, I'm fine. Just getting sick of being on the road. It's lonely," I admitted, even though that wasn't the sole source of my gloomy mood.

"Aw, if only there were a solution to your problem," she cooed, feigning sympathy. "Oh yeah! There is. Hurry up and get your keister to Boston already."

"I know, I am," I assured her, "but it's not just that … John Moxie called me again."

"Ugh. Still trying to up the ante? What's he offering now?"

There was no sense in lying or playing down my conflicting emotions, I knew I could be honest with Anna.

"They doubled the prize money and there's a bunch of other stuff too. I'm not gonna lie, I could use three hundred thousand dollars right now," I lamented, thinking of my depleted finances. Just because I had worked at a high-end restaurant, didn't mean I had been paid accordingly.

"So, what's holding you back?" she asked recognizing that there was an impending "but."

"I should have nailed it. I could have nailed it. Even now, after everything that happened, I *still* think I can. Baking and creating is not the issue. The problem is finding a way to make sure that I don't get completely paralyzed by the sight of lights and huge cameras. Everyone keeps telling me that I just need to learn to block it all out, but I can't, and I just … I can't screw this up twice. I'll never be able to look myself in the mirror again."

"You are so hard on yourself," Anna stated, her soft voice full of pity and frustration on my behalf.

It was not the first time I'd heard that. From her or others. I was not good at bouncing back from the sting of a mistake.

"Because I know what I can do," I responded, getting to the heart of the matter as succinctly as possible. "I'm just too chickenshit to try and prove it."

I heard Anna sigh on the other end of the phone.

29

"You know I support you no matter what you decide right?"

"Yeah, I know."

"And you also know that you have a job waiting for you the second I am ready to open the doors to Yeast Affection, right?"

"Yes."

"But I really would love to see you take a second crack at that show. I am glad to hear you say you're confident in your abilities, because, honey, you are an amazing pastry chef. Let me ask you this. What do you think you need in order to get to a place where the studio environment doesn't freak you out?"

I took a moment to ponder the question and the only solution I could come up with was impractical and not feasible.

"I don't know, spend a week or two working in a studio. Like I can make that happen," I scoffed.

"Oh Sophie," she murmured sympathetically. "You know I'm working on marrying Chris Hemsworth so I can make that happen for you, right?"

"I know." I laughed softly. 'You're the best friend money can buy, you know that?" I joked absentmindedly rolling a jar around in my hand.

"Yeah, yeah, I know. Now put the Nutella back, you know it gives you underground chin zits," Anna said causing me to freeze in place, for a moment before whirling around to look for her and wonder how she could possibly know what I was doing in that moment.

"Dude! What the fuck? Are you watching me right now?"

"*Dude,*" she replied echoing my tone. "What kind of friend would I be if I didn't know that every time you get down about something, you bury your feelings under half a pound of chocolate hazelnut spread?"

"I know, but—" I started to say, still floored by her innate under-standing of my emotional eating habits.

"Put the jar back, you always regret it," she interrupted with the all-knowing wisdom of a mother. "Now, go find the pasta sauce aisle, get yourself a jar of that sweet, sweet Sockarooni sauce and come up with a new recipe for your as yet unpublished cookbook entitled *101 Recipes using Sockarooni Sauce.*"

"Okay, now you're making fun of me," I said shifting my weight to my right leg and placing my hand on my hip just in case she really was able to see me somehow.

"No! I swear! As Paul Newman is our god and witness, I have never in my life met anyone more dedicated to finding as many possible uses for a singular food product as you are with Sockarooni Sauce. I tip my hat to you," she insisted though I still detected a hint of amused sarcasm in her tone.

"It's a good sauce," I insisted, still sounding slightly defensive, but taking her advice and returning the Nutella to the shelf before starting to make my way over to the pasta aisle. "And as a matter of fact, I *do* actually really need to pick up a jar," I explained, finding renewed purpose as I began making my way to the pasta aisle.

"You only say that when he gets you out of a jam, what happened?" she asked, her voice adopting a knowing tone once more.

"It was no big deal, I almost got into a little accident tonight, but it's fine, no harm done."

"No big deal? Soph, your car is held together by duct tape, hope, and the sticky remnants of spilled coffee, I don't like you driving around in that thing. It's a ticking time bomb."

"There's nothing wrong with my car, she might not be pretty, but she does a bang-up job."

The line went quiet until I realized that I might not have inspired much confidence with my turn of phrase. "Okay that was the wrong expression to use, but she runs fine, honestly. When I get to Boston and I've settled in, I'll think about trading her in, I promise."

"For what? A cup of coffee at the car dealership?"

"Hey," I cautioned, stung by her hostility toward my so far reliable steel steed.

"And not even a latte, like … shitty drip coffee."

"You want to buy me a Camaro?" I challenged.

"Only if you promise to make out with me in the back seat," she responded with a smile in her voice.

I laughed despite her insults toward my car, which I felt compelled to defend the same way some people are compelled to defend a family member in spite of bad behavior.

"Alright, enough bashing my car," I chuckled, finding the familiar jar of bright, red sauce and placing it in my shopping basket.

"So where are you staying tonight? Somewhere luxe, I suppose because you're so fabulous."

Right as she said that, I caught a glimpse of my reflection in a glass door passing by the frozen food section.

My long dark hair was scraped indelicately into a pile on top of my head, and not in an effortless, cute kind of way. No, I had more of a *does she have a place to stay and food to eat,* kind of aesthetic going on, which was accentuated by the tired, purple rings and reddened whites surrounding my hazel eyes, brought on from the many long hours of staring out of the windshield and into the glare of the fall sun.

I looked so haggard as I tried in vain to at least smooth the flyaways from sticking out at the sides of my head.

"Well," I began, "it's a funny story, actually. The guy I almost caused an accident with, he has a rental suite in the town," I explained. "He's letting me stay there for the night. For free."

"Mm-hmm," Anna said, her hummed response dripping with distrust.

"I already checked every square inch of the place, it seems legit. Besides, he didn't really seem like a weirdo."

"Yeah, that's what people said about Ted Bundy," she responded prosaically.

"No, really. He was actually really good looking."

"Yeah. That's what people said about Ted Bundy."

"Knock it off! I'm already too scared to drive alone at night."

"Sorry, I just hate you being out there by yourself, I know you're a full-grown adult and all but … wait, exactly *how* hot was he?"

"Like … probably the most attractive guy I have seen in a long time."

"Did you talk to him?"

"Yes. I did *all* the talking," I replied, recalling our basically one-sided exchange as I reached for a package of cookies bearing the likeness of none other than Mr. Newman.

Nearby, the same store employee from earlier was now stacking snacks just a few feet away.

"That's okay, you don't need him to talk, you're just passing through town. There for one night only, you know what I'm saying?" she offered suggestively followed by a flirtatious laugh.

Anna's allusion prompted a momentary explicit visual in my brain that despite it only lasting a second, was enough to cause a temporary seizure of my motor function, which sent the package of cookies tumbling out of my hands and onto the floor at my feet.

The sound of the cookies being obliterated inside the plastic packaging made the store clerk stop what they were doing and turn toward me.

Our eyes met in a wordless stand-off.

You dropped the Newman-O's.

Yes. Sorry. It was an accident.

You broke it, you bought it, lady.

Yes. Of course. You're right.

Without a word, the store clerk and I nodded at each other in mutual understanding and I slowly bent over, retrieved the crushed package of cookies and placed them in my basket before once again escaping over to the next aisle which was blessedly empty.

"Hey! You still there?" Anna asked after I'd been silent for too long.

"Yes. Sorry. What were you saying?"

"I was just saying, you should invite him over for a little southern hospitality. *Bow chicka—*"

"Please don't finish, you know I hate that stupid onomatopoeia. I don't know why, but it just makes me cringe," I said with a shudder, hoping for a swift change of subject.

"Maybe it's because you need some *bow chika wow—*"

"Okay," I interrupted shaking my head and trying not to laugh. "This conversation is over, I'm hanging up now."

"Alright, alright," Anna chuckled as though she had accomplished her goal of riling me up. "I'll let you go, but you have to promise me that you'll text me tomorrow morning and let me know you're okay. Promise?"

"I promise, I promise," I assured her.

After hanging up I felt as though the desire to make something homemade had abandoned me and all I had to show for the last thirty minutes in the supermarket was a package full of cookie shards and a jar of sacrificial pasta sauce in exchange for the protection afforded to me by my self-appointed guardian angel.

My indecision resulted in me purchasing a jar of sauce that would be luggage for the rest of the trip, the cookies, and a can of chicken noodle soup.

I paid for my items, left the Piggly Wiggly, and made my way back to the apartment for a quiet night in.

CHAPTER 4

The next morning, I enjoyed a scalding hot shower, gathered up my belongings, stripped the bed, and made sure I'd left the apartment as spotless as I'd found it.

I dropped the keys in the green box by Joel's door along with a thank you note and stood outside his door for a moment pressing my ear against it to see if I could hear anything from inside his apartment like the creeper that I was.

I shook my head at myself in an attempt to reboot my senses, making my way downstairs to load my stuff into the car and set about trying to find somewhere to grab some breakfast.

I recalled Joel's recommendation and after a quick Google search, it appeared that Daisy's Nut House was about all there was for breakfast in the near vicinity anyway.

There was one other option called the Donner Bakery which had stellar reviews, but it was out of the way, so I decided on Daisy's and followed the GPS directions, arriving a short time later in search of food and coffee.

I parked my car at the diner and made my way inside where I briefly considered taking a seat and having an in-house meal, but I was too anxious to get back on the road, so opted for takeout instead.

I spotted the takeout counter at the other end of the diner and as I made my way over to join the queue, I found myself sweeping the patrons for a familiar brooding, brown-haired, blue-eyed, bearded mountain man.

It was busy in the diner, but I figured someone as imposing as him would stand out fairly easily, so when I didn't see him in there, I turned my attention back to the interior of the diner.

There was a display behind the cashier along the back wall with rows and rows of various kinds of doughnuts and I noticed that people seemed to be buying them by at least the dozen or more.

I shuffled along in the line and found myself getting lost in a fantasy that I had conjured in my mind in bed the night before.

It involved me naked in bed and a malfunctioning fire alarm going off in the middle of the night only to have Joel bursting through the door in nothing but a pair of boxer shorts.

My eyes must have been burning a hole in the doughnut display because a voice from behind me broke me out of my thoughts.

"If you're having trouble deciding, may I recommend the apple cider cruller or the blueberry fritter?"

I turned and looked over my shoulder to address the man who I assumed was talking to me, but only saw a white T-shirt clad chest.

I tilted my chin skyward and peered up at him as he regarded me with a countenance that was completely devoid of any discernible expression.

"Pardon?" I asked, looking up into olive-green eyes rimmed with thick, long lashes that women paid good money to emulate.

His eyes narrowed almost imperceptibly before he gestured with his bushy, bearded chin toward the display.

"Visitors to our fair locale can find the selection of doughnuts here overwhelming. The apple cider cruller and blueberry fritter are the bestsellers, particularly for this time of year, and chances are you'll be happy with your purchase if you go with one of those options. Not that you'll be unhappy with any other option you might be inclined to go with, but sometimes it's easier to make a decision when a local resident is able to advise on what's good."

His expression remained neutral as he spoke, but something about him made me smile instead of backing away slowly.

Despite his cool demeanor, I'd been through enough small towns by now to recognize with a fair amount of confidence what was happening.

He was obviously a local, he'd never seen me around before, and he was curious.

Once again charmed, by the smooth sound of a southern accent, I offered him a polite smile.

"Far be it from me to go against the advice of a local. It's always nice when someone is willing to give you a recommendation. I think I will go with the apple cider. Thank you."

"That's a good choice." He nodded as though he approved of my decision before we both went back to staring at the menu board.

My turn came around and I ordered a coffee to-go and the apple cider cruller.

As I waited for my coffee to be made, I stood out of the way by a window and was soon joined by the man who had spoken to me earlier.

He wasn't looking at me, but I felt curiosity coming off him in waves.

I was sensitive to these sorts of interactions, so I was not the least bit surprised, when he turned to me and asked, "New in town, or just passing through?"

"Just passing through," I replied, and he nodded in recognition before casting his eyes upward like he was either thinking or staring off into space.

My order came up, and I collected my coffee cup and the paper bag containing my doughnut.

As I started toward the exit, I bid him goodbye with a smile and lift of my eyebrows and he reciprocated with a cordial nod of his head as I left the diner to make my way to the parking lot.

While I walked to my car, I noticed a group of about four men loitering around the edge of the parking lot on motorcycles, and one of them nodded hello.

I ignored him and promptly got into my car, placing the doughnut on my lap and the coffee in the cup holder to my left.

I turned the keys in the ignition and instantly winced as it sputtered and screeched in a way that I immediately knew wasn't normal.

"Don't you even think about it," I warned my car as though it would be motivated to make the extra effort if it heard the tone in my voice.

I tried again and cringed at the sound it made, pulling my hand away from the keys and throwing myself against the seat in frustration.

I sat for a moment, took a breath, and looked up at my lanyard and the blue eyes of my silver screen guardian angel.

"What do you say? Help me out?"

Mr. Newman stared back at me, his expression neutral, but I felt comforted by it nonetheless.

I let the words hang in the air a moment, then tried turning over the engine one last time, but the same horrible grinding, metallic sound rang out jarringly through the air.

My wrist reflexively snapped to turn the ignition off, and I covered my face with my hands seeing nothing but dollar signs floating through the darkness behind my eyelids.

A firm tap on my window made me jump out of my skin and I shrieked loudly as I turned to the right, expecting to see one of the bikers, but instead noticed the man from inside the café peering at me through the passenger side window.

He waved from behind the glass pane as I placed my hand over my heart and took a moment to catch my breath before opening the door to step out and greet him.

He held up his hands submissively.

"Didn't mean to startle you, miss, and I'm not following you, I am happily attached," he said holding up his hand to display his ring.

"Oh, no it's fine," I assured him, shaking my head as though I were trying to shake off the fright. "You just gave me a little fright is all."

"I'm parked behind you and was happening by when I heard you try and start your car," he explained. "I'm an auto mechanic."

Well, what are the chances?

I glanced at the car behind mine and must have made a face of some kind because he humbly offered, "She runs better than she looks," in reference to the dated looking sedan painted in primer gray.

"I don't want to trouble you," I offered, shading my eyes from the glare of the morning sun as I peered up at him from beneath the cap of my hand.

"You're having car trouble. I am qualified to assist," he stated as though there were no other facts to be considered.

I hesitated for a moment thinking primarily about the cost, but then he spoke and gestured with his chin toward the front of the car. "Pop the hood. Let's see what the damage is." He made his way to the front of my car, placing his coffee on the roof as he passed.

Grateful, I reached below my dash for the release hatch and squeezed it, the hood clicking loudly as it unlocked. As he lifted the hood, I walked around to meet him.

"Thank you for helping me out, Mr. ..." I paused holding out my hand to him.

He looked down at it for a moment and then accepted and shook it.

"Cletus."

"Mr. Cletus."

"No, no. Winston," he corrected me, but I still wasn't sure if that was his first name or last name.

"Winston Cletus?"

"Cletus is my first name, Winston is my surname," he explained.

"Oh, I see. Sorry about that," I said with an awkward laugh.

"I realize I made that more difficult than it needed to be, I was distracted by the possible causes of your car trouble here," he explained as he affixed the metal stand to keep the hood upright.

"Are you the only mechanic in town?" I inquired curiously as he lowered his upper body to hunch over the engine.

"Not precisely. I part own one with my brothers ..." he explained and then stopped short. I couldn't tell if he got distracted again or if I needed to prompt him for the rest.

I decided to press for more. Just in case I could get a better deal.

"And the other?"

"Well," he said, pulling aside a handful of wires and twisting something that seemed loose. "Let's just say it's a good thing you ran into me and not the fella that runs the other place," he replied, dashing any hopes I had of haggling before straightening back up to his full height. "Why don't you give it another crank for me? See if I can't tell where the trouble spot is."

I didn't have time to think too deeply on his allusion as I walked back around to the driver's side and lowered my upper body inside the cabin to try starting the engine as he'd requested.

Just like before, the metallic, grinding noise that followed made me cringe.

"That's good!" I heard him call out from around the front of my car as I let the keys flick back to the off position but left them hanging in the ignition.

As I walked back around to his side, Cletus stood upright and placed one hand on his hip, stroking his beard with the other.

"It's hard to say precisely what the problem is, but I suspect your starter gear is worn out and needs replacing."

"How much might that be?" I asked bracing myself for his response, but he just shrugged.

"Not sure exactly, depends on the availability of the part for these older models. Also depends on whether or not I'm correct on the cause of the problem. I'd need to get it to the garage to know for sure."

I sighed dejectedly and he nodded solemnly as though he understood my plight.

"Is there any chance you can give me an estimate on the towing and diagnostic assessment before you do anything? I'm running a little low on cash."

He looked at me for a moment, and I could practically hear the cogs of his mind turning as I presumed he was attempting to evaluate if I was telling the truth or using the excuse of financial hardship as a means to get a better deal.

Before he could respond, his phone rang, and he looked between his left and right pockets as if trying to work out where the ringing was coming from. He reached into the right pocket and retrieved the device before inspecting the screen to see who was calling.

"If you wouldn't mind excusing me for a moment," he said politely before turning and walking away out of earshot.

My stomach knotted thinking about the potential expense ahead of me and ducked into my car to retrieve my coffee and doughnut so I could once again begin ingesting my feelings while lamenting the fact that I had never cultivated a healthier outlet such as running or weight lifting.

I placed my coffee on the roof of my car and reached into the paper bag to break off a piece of the doughnut and shove it in my mouth.

I didn't have too much of a sweet tooth anymore as a direct result of choosing a career path lined with sugar, and even though I did like doughnuts every now and then, I was more of a croissant kind of girl.

Just then, Cletus began making his way back over and I took a sip of coffee to wash down the chunk of doughnut that I hadn't chewed well enough to go down right.

He laid the metal stand that was holding up the hood of the car down before guiding the hood to drop closed and turned to me, placing one hand on his hip.

"We'll tow your vehicle free of charge and if the diagnostics take less than twenty minutes, I'll charge you a flat twenty. Cost of labor and any replacement parts won't be subject to any discounts though. Best I can do." His words were delivered in a business-like manner that grossly belied the extent of his generosity.

My eyes widened, and my jaw dropped.

"Are you serious?"

"As a rabid raccoon," he responded deadpan with a decisive nod of his head. "My brother will be along with the truck shortly. And don't thank me yet, if I'm right and it is, in fact, your starter gear, then that could be a costly fix," he warned.

"Oh," I said dolefully, but not wanting to seem ungrateful, I smiled and sighed. "Well nonetheless, I appreciate you coming over to help."

Cletus tightened his lips into a line, giving me as close to a smile as he seemed to be capable of and collected his coffee from the roof of my vehicle.

"How do you like the doughnut?" he inquired, which I recognized as an attempt to change the subject. Gratitude seemed to make him uncomfortable.

I let him off the hook and looked down at my breakfast.

"Well, as far as doughnuts go, it's pretty good. Nice, light texture, not overwhelmingly sweet and the apple cider flavor comes through nicely. Though, if I were making these, I'd cook it for just a tad longer at a slightly higher temperature to get the outside nice and crisp—"

"Are you by chance a pastry chef?" he interrupted, and I looked up from the doughnut I was reviewing to find him staring at me with a renewed interest.

"I … yes. Sorry, was I rambling about texture and technique? I am prone to do that."

"It's quite alright, my wife is inclined to do the same. She is also a baker and owns an extraordinary bakery here in Green Valley, you'd be remiss to not visit while you're here."

"Is it the Donner Bakery?" I asked, recalling the results of my earlier internet search for breakfast.

"That's right. One and the same."

"Get outta town," I exclaimed incredulously.

"I will not, I live here," he responded without irony, making me laugh at his dry delivery.

"Can I have the address? I'd love to check it out," I requested, pulling my phone from my back pocket and fixing to take down the details.

"I can do you one better and take you by there on the way to the garage," he offered, just as an approaching tow truck took his attention from over my shoulder.

"I don't want to be any trouble," I insisted.

"It's no sacrifice to drop in on my wife at work," he bargained, as the tow truck pulled up alongside us and before I could respond, Cletus was making his way over into the street to direct the driver into position.

When the tow truck stopped, the driver got out and made his way over to Cletus.

Both men were handsome in very different ways. Cletus had sun-streaked, unruly dark blond hair, and was barrel chested while the other was redheaded, leaner, and all smiles.

"What the hell is this?" the redhead asked, mimicking the hand gestures Cletus was making as he directed him in the truck. "You directing air traffic or something? This ain't the Nashville International Airport."

I tried not to laugh at the jovial ribbing and good-natured exuberance of the redhead so I looked down at my feet so as not to appear to be eavesdropping.

"Hush, Beauford, would a mite of professionalism kill you?" Cletus admonished him quietly before gesturing toward me with his hand.

"This here, is … is …" he paused when he realized that he didn't know my name, nor had he asked for it.

"Sophie. Sophie Copeland," I responded as I stepped over to his brother and held out my hand.

He took it without hesitation and smiled warmly while I tried and failed to not stare at him. Good looks appeared to run in the family, but Beauford's eyes were blue, his hair was red, and his beard was more groomed that Cletus's.

"Nice to meet you, Miss Copeland, my name's Beau," he offered, closing both hands over mine.

"Please, call me Sophie."

"Sophie it is then," he agreed with a nod of his head. "Do you have anything in the car you want to grab before we winch her up to the truck?" He gestured toward my car.

"Ah. Well, I have most of my belongings in the trunk."

"Not to worry, you can grab whatever you need at the garage and we'll get you all sorted with a loaner until we can get this baby back to you. Whereabouts are you staying while you're in town?"

"She's just passing through," Cletus replied on my behalf.

"Oh well, might I suggest trying to find a room for the night? I know a couple of places if you need a recommendation."

"Oh, that's okay," I smiled, my mind immediately recalling that I had stored Joel's number in my phone. "I think I know of a place."

CHAPTER 5

here were worse places to be seated than inside a tow truck, sandwiched between two attractive, southern brothers bickering harmlessly over just about any topic that came up as we made our way to the Donner Bakery.

After just a few moments of observation, I came to the conclusion that Cletus was the more reserved, knowledgeable, sardonic type, while Beau was the friendlier, more conversational extrovert who could charm the pants of just about anyone.

It quickly became apparent that their brotherly rapport was hard for them to curb, even in front of customers such as myself.

I didn't mind. Quite the opposite in fact. I found their good-natured ribbing to be quite entertaining and it also made me feel more comfortable around them, as though I were reconnecting with old childhood friends.

"So, what brings you through Green Valley?" Beau inquired curiously, turning his attention to me once it became clear there would be no resolution today on the subject of whether "Don't Stop Believing" by Journey was a more impactful rock anthem than "Livin' on a Prayer" by Bon Jovi.

"I'm on my way to Boston. My best friend is currently working on opening up a new bakery there, and she asked me to help her out," I explained succinctly.

"Ah, so you're a baker," Beau stated. I immediately recognized that the question was rhetorical, but Cletus couldn't help himself.

"No, dummy, she's a lion tamer," he quipped before tossing back the last of his coffee.

"She could be." Beau shrugged as though it were totally plausible. "She might have been working at a zoo this whole time and decided she'd had a passion for baking cakes instead."

"Somehow I don't think lion taming is an available occupation at the zoo."

"Not *technically*, but to some degree, they would have to condition the lion to learn specific behaviors around enclosure maintenance and feeding time," Beau argued.

"You're grasping, Beauford," Cletus informed his brother before retrieving his phone from his pocket as I stared straight ahead and tried not to laugh.

"So much for professionalism," Beau retorted tossing me a wry smile.

"Anyway, where are you from?" Beau inquired with friendly curiosity.

"Seattle, Washington. I left a couple of weeks ago and I've slowly been making my way across the country," I explained not really thinking much about how my answer might elicit even more curiosity.

"Sick of rain?" Beau asked, his choice of words reading as a gentler way of asking, "*why did you leave?*"

The real reason why I had left Seattle flashed through my mind like a condensed movie reel and it was way too long a story to get into now. Also, I didn't want to invite the assumption that I was bad at my job after telling them what I did for a living.

In the end, I decided to spare them the gory details of my baking show fiasco and settled on a half-truth instead.

"I definitely wasn't sad to leave it behind, but I had always wanted

NO WHISK NO REWARD

to do a cross country bakery tour. I think I've stopped at more than twenty-five bakeries on my travels so far," I responded cheerily as though I were impressed with my own efforts.

"That's a lot of baked goods," Cletus said absent-mindedly tapping on his phone.

"Anything stand out as exceptionally good?" Beau inquired as the scenery passed by us in a whoosh of brown and green.

I always found questions like that hard to answer due to my years having worked as a pastry chef in high-end establishments.

We were trained to find fault in just about everything including our own work. The heart of a true pastry chef and its penchant for quality and perfection could never be satisfied, and that very characteristic tended to peg a lot of us as "food snobs."

Of course, I didn't consider myself to be a food snob. My fondness for Paul Newman's jarred sauces was evidence enough of that, but I was also adamant that there would never be a substitute for sourcing the highest quality ingredients and using techniques that interfered as little as possible with them in order to let those ingredients speak for themselves.

Instead of trying to explain all that, I simply nodded and offered an understated, "Yeah, there were a few."

"Well prepare yourself to experience the gold standard," Beau stated proudly as we rounded a bend that straightened up ahead to a view of a structure which I assumed was the bakery even though I couldn't make out any level of detail yet. "My sister in-law's bakery is the pride of Green Valley."

Cletus didn't utter a word, which I interpreted as being the first thing that Beau had said that he actually agreed with.

"I'm excited to get in there and try s—Oh my God! Is that the line?" I exclaimed, fixing my eyes on the queue of people curving along the side of the building and out onto the street.

"Don't worry, today you're Cletus's special guest, you get to go through the back entrance."

The Donner Bakery, I could now see was a true jewel of an establishment in Green Valley. It was a pretty town anyway, but this particular building really stood out.

It looked exactly as though a tornado had lifted a true Parisian bakery right off its foundations and flung it *Wizard of Oz* style all the way over to small-town Tennessee.

There were two picture windows on either side of the front entrance with *The Donner Bakery* stenciled in a bronze-gold drop shadow lettering with smaller text beneath it that read *Home of the World Famous Banana Cake Queen.*

The claim made little impact on me and passed by like another face in the bakery crowd.

I had become jaded by such assertions, learning over the years to come to interpret the cheap marketing ploy as meaning *"mediocre at best, but the best you'll get around here."*

Perhaps I just had a case of baked goods fatigue, but I pushed the cynical thoughts from my mind and reminded myself to be optimistic and open-minded, especially since cakes tended to be successfully interchangeable with pizza in the analogy that even the bad ones were still pretty good.

As Beau slowly pulled the truck up to the side of the road near the parking lot to let us out, I noted once again the line of people spilling out the front doors and winding all way around the corner.

"Here we are," Beau announced stopping in a spot where we could safely alight from the vehicle.

Cletus climbed out of the car first and I turned to Beau in the driver's seat.

"Thanks for the ride, and for taking care of my car," I said. He smiled and winked at me.

"No trouble at all, I'm gonna drop her off at the garage real quick, and then I'll come right back here with that loaner, so you can get around until you get her back."

"Then how will you get back to the garage?" I inquired. "And Cletus left his car back at Daisy's," I added realizing I was just thinking out loud now.

Beau chuckled and waved off my concern.

"Don't worry none about any of that, we have ways and means of getting around, Miss Sophie," he assured me and I could have just sat right there in that truck and listened to him talk all day.

"You best be going now, Cletus is not one to wait around too long," he said snapping me from my dream-like state and gently urging me to get out of the car.

"Oh right," I said shuffling along the bench seat to exit the truck.

"Watch your feet, ma'am, it's a bit of a drop," he cautioned me, but I made it out of the truck without incident and closed the door to allow Beau to be on his way.

By the time I turned around, Cletus was already making his way toward what I assumed was the back entrance of the bakery.

People watched us as though they were wondering if there was a shorter line on another side of the building, but none of them wanted to lose their spot to find out. I felt a little guilty to be skipping the queue.

I also suspected that since his wife owned the place, Cletus probably had free run of the property and didn't need to bother with front entrances.

As I continued to follow along behind him, I continued to inspect the bakery, which was beautiful and felt warm and welcoming.

There was a seating area outside with tables packed in as tightly as possible, so as to fit as many patrons as they could. I observed that every single one of the green and ivory striped chairs with wicker backrests was occupied by someone slicing or biting into some form of dessert or savory treat with gusto and joyful enthusiasm.

The awnings that jutted out from the roof were striped green and ivory to match the chairs and raised flower beds embellished with elaborate fall themed arrangements skirted the perimeter of the building.

Jack-o'-lanterns and pumpkins from the Halloween just past, and carved wooden turkeys for the impending Thanksgiving holiday encapsulated the seated guests and separated them from the sidewalk as people came from every direction to join the ever-growing line.

I felt a smile pulling at my lips as the unmistakable scent of almost everything that I considered to be good in life—freshly baked bread, cookies, and cakes—sailed across on the chilly autumnal breeze to greet me and my shoulders lifted as I inhaled deeply.

Warmth spread through my body as a sense of being "home" flooded my senses, and suddenly the urge to create took a hold of me.

"These custard almond buns are proof that God exists," I overheard an enthusiastic customer garble with a full mouth as he walked by me, and just like that, I plummeted back down to earth with a thud that would have broken my metaphoric tailbone.

I felt my stomach lurch at the mention of the word "custard" and the involuntary flashes of my televised nightmare.

I shoved it to the back of my mind as I had trained myself to do and picked up my pace to catch up to Cletus who was now out of sight, around the corner of the building.

I caught up to him just as he opened a door from the back entrance and then stepped aside, gesturing for me to precede him.

As I crossed the threshold, the feeling of warmth of familiarity found me once more.

The sight of industrial metal benches, ovens, and sinks might have appeared clinical to some, but to me, they were as warm as flannel sheets and hot cocoa.

Busy, bustling staff floated around the kitchen in a dance that I knew well, their arms laden with trays of muffins right out from the oven, fresh baguettes that smelled incredible, and at one of the benches was an assembly line of three people, passing along cake after cake to be iced, decorated, and either boxed up or sliced into generous portions for the front display.

It was positively Willy Wonka-esque.

I looked over to Cletus who gestured with his head for me to follow him before starting to make his way toward a doorway which I assumed contained an office of some sort.

I was careful to give a wide berth to anyone moving through the space and balancing any sort of cake or tray in order to avoid any unfortunate mishaps, but as I followed Cletus I found myself smiling.

I missed this environment. It was so active and lively, and everyone was so focused and useful.

I'd love to work in a place like this, I thought to myself as I followed Cletus through the doorway.

"Oh, hey you," a sweet voice greeted from inside the office which was currently blocked by Cletus's body.

"Hey, yourself," he replied sounding gentler than I had thus far heard him speak.

That must be his lady love, I concluded judging by the tender shift of his tone.

"What brings you here?" she inquired not sounding unhappy to see him, just curious.

I had anticipated that he would initiate the customary introduction, but instead, Cletus crossed the threshold of the doorway and stepped to the left to reveal my presence to the woman inside.

Then he said nothing.

I was waiting for an introduction, or at least an invitation to join them inside the office, but the two of them just stood there staring at me, and I suddenly forgot how I had gotten there and what I was even doing there in the first place.

"Uh ... hello there," I said, offering a small wave, but before the woman in the office could respond, I felt someone brush by my side to squeeze their way into the office.

"Jenn, we have a problem," a young woman with fiery red hair and bright green eyes informed her.

"What is it?" she asked, her attention focused intently on her employee. "Don't tell me it's that Scotia Simmons again, I can't deal with her today."

"No. Well, she was here earlier, but she didn't fuss this time. What happened is, we ran out of butter so I sent Joy to go get some more, but she got the lightly salted European kind instead of the grass-fed unsalted and now we have a batch of Black Forest cake batter that we can't use. Should we toss it?"

No! I screamed internally knowing that even a batter made with salted butter could still produce an amazing result if balanced with other ingredients correctly. The sweet and salty flavor combination was one of my favorites and I knew I could make it work.

Jenn sighed as her shoulders slumped while she considered the problem.

She thought for a moment and then shook her head regretfully.

"Turf it," she ordered, much to my chagrin.

"You sure?"

"I will not put out an inferior cake, Tempest, you know that. Get rid of the batter and start over with the right butter."

I couldn't hold my tongue any longer. My confidence with custard might have taken a hit in recent times, but I had just enough of it left to *know* I could fix this problem and prevent the bakery from losing money.

"Oh no, please, don't do that," I said pleadingly and suddenly there were three pairs of eyes on me, looking at me as though they had no idea where I had come from, so I hurried to try and offer my alternative solution.

"I'm sorry to speak out of turn, but as a fellow baker and pastry chef professional, I feel compelled to try and offer an alternative solution for the batter, which I'd be loathed to see go to waste," I said imploring them to consider my input, even though I had no right to give it.

"An alternative?" I took a step toward Jennifer and held out my hands enthusiastically, ready to give my pitch now that she was open to hearing it.

"Yes. One that benefits the bakery. So that you're not throwing money or food down the drain," I continued.

"Go on," she urged with a polite smile.

"Perhaps you could go ahead and bake the cakes, but instead of assembling the Black Forest cakes you mentioned, you could make a sweet and salty kind instead? You could sell the cakes by the slice for a reduced price and maybe you could even have a little fun with it! Maybe call it … I don't know … garbage cake: cakes that didn't make the cut or something silly like that. Customers like novelty and will appreciate the show of humor from such a refined establishment," I said twisting my hands together and wincing, realizing that I had gone on for much too long and told a bakery owner, who was clearly more successful than me, how to suck eggs.

The room was excruciatingly quiet, at least to my ears, and I felt like it took an age before Jennifer exchanged a wordless glance with Cletus, who nodded at her before she turned her attention back to me.

"What was your name again?" she inquired, and I looked over at Cletus who didn't speak but raised one eyebrow at me as though to say, "go ahead."

I approached Jennifer's desk and held out my hand.

"My name is Sophie. Sophie Copeland."

Jennifer accepted my hand and smiled warmly as she shook it.

"Nice to meet you, Sophie, I'm Jennifer Winston."

"It's a pleasure to meet you," I offered feeling oddly humbled. "Cletus speaks very highly of you."

"Ah well, he's biased," she replied modestly.

"Your bakery is very beautiful, I can't wait to join that line and try some of your goods," I said looking over my shoulder in that general direction.

"Oh, no need for that, did you have your eye on anything in particular?" she asked.

"Well I'd be lying if I said I wasn't intrigued about the banana cake, but Cletus said that the croissants are also exceptional. Croissants are my favorite."

"Tempest, would you mind dashing out to the store to fetch Miss Copeland a slice of the banana cake and a croissant?"

I immediately pulled on the flap of my shoulder bag for my wallet.

"Please," Jennifer said, holding up a staying hand. "It's on the house, I insist. Won't you have a seat," she offered, gesturing to the chair in front of her desk and I tentatively lowered myself into it as she did the same.

"Thank you," I said, pulling my hand from my bag.

"First things first," Jenn started in a very businesslike tone which made me feel as though I was about to get an earful for usurping her authority in front of a subordinate and I braced myself for the impact. It wouldn't be the first time my stupid mouth got me into trouble.

"I *love* the idea of garbage cake," she said, and I felt like a weight was lifted off my shoulders.

"You do?" I asked, leaning slightly forward in my seat as a smile spread across her face. I noticed the incredible color of her eyes, which were an incredible violet-hued shade of blue.

"I do. And you're right about food waste. I normally wouldn't consider tossing a batch of batter, but I simply do not have the extra hands to improvise. We just lost a couple of employees so we're a little short-staffed right now and I hate to put any extra burden on the team when they're already working so hard to keep up with demand."

Her response shocked me for the simple fact that I didn't think I'd ever worked anywhere where the highest-ranking person cared much for how much work their employees could handle.

"I could do it," I blurted without thinking. "I mean, I'd be happy to help with the assembly of the garbage cakes if you were okay with it? I'm a graduate from the Culinary Institute of America, so I am qualified."

"You'd do that?" Jennifer asked with an incredulous giggle.

"Of course, I mean it would give me something to do while I wait for Beau to arrive with my loaner car," I explained as Jennifer frowned curiously.

"Loaner car?"

"Oh yes. I should probably explain. I am on my way to Boston to stay with a friend of mine who owns a bakery there. It's currently being renovated for the grand opening. I was passing through Green Valley, but I ran into some car trouble and Cletus just happened to be passing by and kindly stopped to help," I explained gesturing toward him as he listened intently, or at least appeared to be. "Anyway, it looks like I'm stuck here for at least the night and I'd love to make myself useful. You know, to earn my cake and croissant." I shrugged.

"Have you worked in a commercial kitchen before?" Jennifer inquired.

"Oh yes. After I graduated from the New York campus eight years ago, I moved to Seattle where I have worked at three restaurants over that time including Paradigm," I said pulling out the big guns.

"Paradigm. Isn't that Julian Lefebvre's restaurant?" Jennifer asked intrigued, which didn't surprise me. Julian was well known and highly celebrated in the restaurant industry.

"Yes, that's right," I affirmed with a nod of my head.

"Wow," Jennifer said on a breath and I smiled politely even though a bitter flavor began to form at the back of my tongue at the mention of his name.

"What was he like?" she asked leaning forward with interest.

"It was a great opportunity and I got a lot of good experience," I said, but my tone was forced and Jennifer could tell, raising one eyebrow as though to urge me to continue. "He would have thrown out the cake batter," I added as Jennifer nodded in understanding.

"I see," she said quietly. "When did you say your friend was opening her bakery?"

"February," I replied noticing another subtle exchange between husband and wife.

Just then my phone rang, and I was going to ignore it, but Jennifer flicked her hand in my direction and encouraged me to answer it.

"You can go ahead and get that, I'm going to pop into the kitchen real quick and get you a spot where you can get going on those garbage cakes," she said rising from her seat and then looking up toward the ceiling. "Garbage cake," she said thoughtfully and then laughed. "I like it!"

"Thank you," I laughed as she and Cletus both left the office and I quickly rummaged to find my phone.

I didn't recognize the number but answered anyway risking a call from John Moxie when it might be a report from Beau on my car.

"Hello," I answered already cringing at the possibility of hearing John's voice.

"Hello, Miss Copeland?"

"Yes, Beau it's me," I said just as Tempest reappeared with a paper bag with my croissant and a plastic container with my banana cake.

I thanked her silently and she promptly left the room.

"Are you sitting down?" Beau inquired, and a sinking feeling immediately came over me.

"Oh no, Beau, please don't say that," I pleaded.

What followed was a lot of words I didn't understand which I presumed were car parts, concluding with, "Around eight hundred dollars."

"Eight … wha … huh … what? Eight hundred dollars? That's more than my car is worth," I exclaimed.

"I didn't want to say it, but you're not wrong, Miss Copeland."

"Well … I guess it's time to get back to prostituting," I joked before realizing how wildly inappropriate it was, but luckily Beau laughed heartily on the other end. "Ugh, I'm so glad you recognized that was a joke."

"Of course. Look, I feel for you, so I'm gonna come down to the bakery with the loaner so you can still get around until you decide how you'd like us to proceed, does that sound good?"

Oh God, Beau could make the end of the world sound like a multiple orgasm with that southern accent and smooth delivery, but, it didn't change the fact that I was still in quite the pickle. I had two choices which were to either write off my beloved Honda Civic and buy a new car which would surely drain the rest of my savings, or I could get her fixed and use up *almost* all my savings.

"Yes, thank you, Beau, I really appreciate your help," I said though my words were probably slightly muffled seeing as my head was in my hands.

"No problem, I'll be along soon. You just hang tight."

I hung up the phone and leaned back against the chair as thoughts of my predicament ran rife through my mind.

No Whisk, No Reward was offering a three hundred thousand dollar cash prize to the winner which was sounding mighty tempting right about now, but all I had to do was remember the look on the judges' face when they ate my scrambled crème pâtissière and any temptation there might have been turned instantly to vapor.

"I take it the diagnostic did not go well," I heard Cletus's voice behind me as he and Jennifer re-entered the room.

"Nope. You were right, it was the starter gear."

"Hmm," Cletus nodded solemnly as I eyed the container of cake in front of me.

"Miss Copeland," Jennifer began, "I have a business proposition for you."

CHAPTER 6

*U*pon completion of five perfect three-layered Garbage Cakes, I had secured a paid three-month contract at the Donner Bakery where I would work six days a week until New Years Day.

Beau had arrived with a loaner vehicle that he'd graciously offered to let me keep until I made a decision on whether or not I would replace my car, or travel the remainder of the journey to Boston by bus.

Before I thought any deeper on that, I had other, more pressing matters to attend to.

Being the diligent and responsible guest that I was, I had saved my rental suite host's phone number into my contacts list in case of an emergency and I didn't feel bad or weird about it because he had left it on the fridge along with the Wi-Fi password, so really it was Joel's fault.

I was equal part eager and anxious to have such a good excuse to talk to him again, but before I could even think about that, I had to call Anna and let her know that my arrival into Boston would be delayed. By now, it was more of a courtesy than anything else. Every time I spoke to her, there were new issues postponing the opening of her bakery, and I knew she would understand that the potential for me to make some much needed cash was not something I should pass up.

"You're alive. That is fantastic. I'm thrilled," she greeted me after answering.

"I have good news, bad news, and news that we're both going to feel very differently about," I informed her.

"I'm already on the edge of my seat," she responded sounding distracted. I carried on knowing she was probably busy dealing with contractors and paperwork.

"Is this a bad time?" I inquired, not wanting to monopolize her time if she had other, more pressing matters to attend to.

"No, no," she assured me, "just dealing with contractor crap. They keep finding issues with the building and everything keeps getting delayed by another couple of weeks. Yesterday, they discovered that none of the electrical wiring is to code, so I have to have electricians rewire the entire shop." Her frayed nerves started to become detectable in her voice.

"Dude, that sucks. I'm sorry. Is there anything I can do?" I asked, knowing she would refuse any kind of assistance but doing my duty as her friend to ask regardless.

"No, just get here already so I can weep betwixt your ample bosom."

I cringed a little at her response and not only because I hated the word "bosom." I felt slightly guilty, but forged on, knowing that ripping off the Band-Aid was the best tactic in this situation.

"Yeah, about that ..." I began.

"Uh-oh," she groaned, preempting more bad news.

"Not *uh-oh*," I insisted echoing her tone. "It's more like ... *Oh!*" I softened the impending blow modulating the *"oh"* with an upswing to make it sound less foreboding.

"So, the bad news is, today, after eight wonderful years together, my Honda Civic gave up the ghost—"

"I thought you said it was bad news," Anna replied somehow finding a way to sound simultaneously confused and enthusiastic.

"Hence, the part of the story where you and I have conflicting emotions. Anyway. My car's gone. She's toast. The good news is that the mechanic who looked at my car has a wife who owns this incredible bakery here in Green Valley and they just lost a couple of members of staff, so they offered me a couple months of work to make some extra cash."

"Wait a minute, Green Valley? Is that the Donner Bakery by any chance?" Anna asked with a sudden, renewed interest.

"Yes!" I exclaimed, "Yes, that's it. You know it?"

"Uh yeah, apparently every time someone eats the banana cake there, they start hallucinating rainbows and unicorns."

"I'm not surprised. That banana cake is no joke, I have no idea how she manages that texture with a butter base, it should be heavy, but it's not. She must whip that butter for days," I raved knowing that Anna would understand my reference. "Anyway, it's exceptionally good and totally worth the hype."

"Wow, it must be if *you're* saying that," Anna responded, knowing how hard I was to impress. "She used to have a YouTube channel, but she stopped posting to it shortly after making a pretty dramatic image shift from a full-on Stepford bot to … well … a more regular kind of girl."

"Jennifer Winston?" I asked incredulously, not really able to reconcile the girl I had just interacted with as a Stepford bot.

"Yeah that's her," Anna confirmed as I tried to imagine it, but quickly decided it was irrelevant. Besides, Jennifer must have been barely an adult when she started the bakery, so I felt that a shift in image would have been inevitable and completely understandable.

"Huh … well anyway, my employment contract with the bakery is up in the new year, and since it doesn't look like Yeast Affection will be up and running before then anyway, I thought I'd stick around and try and earn some extra money. Will you still love me if I took just a smidge longer?"

"No," came her immediate and brisk response. Despite her delivery, I smiled.

"Liar," I challenged.

61

"Okay fine, but only because I am glad you're finally rid of that horrible car."

I rolled my eyes and sighed into the phone.

"Yeah, your wish came true and so did my financial nightmare."

"Well I know you don't want to hear this, but you do have an opportunity to make three hundred thousand dollars. You know that, right? You could buy a brand new car *and* open up your own bakery with that kind of money … but not near mine, I don't need you competing with Yeast Affection."

Those were the same motivations which had led me to participate on the show in the first place, and while I still deeply desired those things, I had become too gun shy to even entertain the fantasy of having them anymore.

"I know. I am thinking about it," I assured her with a bright tone, though the subject caused a familiar heaviness inside my chest. Anna blessedly changed the subject.

"So, you have a place to stay there yet?"

"Not yet, I'm working on it, I wanted to call you first and—"

"Ooh, sorry to interrupt, but can I call you back later? Rob, my hot vegan contractor is calling and I'm like, one phone conversation away from entangling him in my alluring womanly web."

"Sure, fine," I snorted. "Ditch me for Tofurkey."

"Never! Don't you ditch me for Ted Bundy and I won't ditch you for Tofurkey! Okay, I gotta go, I'll talk to you later," she said in a rush.

"Okay, okay!" I managed to laugh before hearing the line go silent.

After ending the call, I took a few moments to gather my thoughts before navigating to Joel's contact information. I sat staring at his phone number on my screen and tried to acquire the mind-set I needed to negotiate a short-term lease, but all I could think about was the way he suppressed his smile in front of me and the way his blue-green eyes twinkled, giving him away.

Having his number stored in my phone was good. Having an excuse to actually use it was even better.

He had a rental suite, I needed a place to stay, and I had his number. As far as I was concerned, the stars were aligned, but I cautioned myself against being too eager.

As easy as it would have been to get swept up by the prospect of seeing him every day and maybe even coaxing a smile out of him, I instead deferred to my better sense and reminded myself that I didn't know him yet, so it was in my best interest to approach the situation cautiously. Though I prided myself on being a fairly good judge of character, I wasn't so naïve as to assume that I was always right about the book based solely on the cover.

Damn, that book had a nice cover though.

If Joel were a book, he'd be the old fashioned, leather-bound kind. All sturdy and robust on the outside, with rough page edges that were just begging to be opened up to reveal the story inside.

I was surprised by the magnitude of my interest in him, given how little of himself he seemed willing to share, but I rationalized it by telling myself that chemistry was weird sometimes, and couldn't always be explained.

All I knew was that, I had fallen asleep last night fantasizing about calling him for trivialities that I would never feel justified enough to follow through on in real life.

A broken light bulb or wobbly table might have been good enough for some women to lure him over, but I had way too much pride for such a cheap and transparent approach. I was quite capable of changing a light bulb or sliding a piece of cardboard under a table leg to level it myself, thank you very much. He had already helped me out of two jams that I had gotten myself into and I didn't need him thinking that I was completely helpless.

The more I thought about his demeanor from our brief interaction, the more I found myself coming to the conclusion that despite his curtness, Joel was one of those guys who protected a soft heart with a tough to crack exterior. Apparently, that combination was irresistible to me.

Joel had been in a hurry when he had come across me last night and could have declined to help me find my way off the mountain road, but he didn't.

He didn't need to lead me on the twenty-minute drive, in the opposite direction from which he was initially heading, to take me back into town, but he did.

He also didn't have to tell me that he had a rental suite, let alone allow me to stay in it free of charge for the night.

In the end, I was left with the impression that he was actually one of those guys who ultimately couldn't help but do the right thing even while grumbling about it the whole time.

In my mind, somewhere out there Joel was begrudgingly jump-starting an old lady's car while lecturing her about leaving her lights on, or politely but impatiently suggesting to the woman who had flagged him down on the side of the road to help deliver her baby that he really needed to be somewhere, and could she possibly speed things up by pushing just a little harder?

If nothing else, the phone call would at least give me another few minutes to enjoy the sound of his lush and lazy Sunday afternoon drawl, even if it was just to tell me that he was busy and I was interrupting.

God knew, I possessed a particular predilection toward poking sleeping bears, and boy did Joel make my poking finger itch.

There was just something about his cool, reserved nature that felt completely superficial to my usually very finely tuned bullshit meter, and once I got that notion in my head, I couldn't stop thinking about what was underneath that he was trying to hide. Or maybe even protect.

I wasn't so naïve as to assume that it was entirely possible that he acted like a dick, because he actually *was* a dick. But now that I had gotten all worked up about it, I *needed* to know the truth and was fairly confident that I wouldn't need a lot of time with him to work it out.

I could hear Anna in my head berating me for overanalyzing.

"Jeez Louise, just call him! You don't have to marry the guy, just fuck him a few times!"

"Okay, let's just start by calling him and asking about the lease first, shall we?" I responded aloud to the specter of my best friend as I sat in the driver's seat of the loaner car that the Winstons had graciously allowed me to use.

By now, I had succeeded in stalling for about ten minutes and needed to be prepared for the possibility that the apartment might not be available. I quit putting it off and finally pressed the call button.

The desire to engage in another interaction with him tempered my nerves as I lifted the phone to my ear and listened to it ringing, bracing myself for him to pick up.

It rang and rang and just when I thought it was about to ring out or go to voicemail, he answered, and my breath halted when I heard his unmistakably gruff, southern drawl come pouring out like hot honey through the line to say, "This is Joel."

It was then that I knew, beyond a shadow of a doubt that I was in trouble because the amount of effort required to swallow down my heart at the mere sound of his voice, which was even more delicious than I remembered, was bringing on a sudden and severe case of heartburn and indigestion.

"Hi, Joel," I greeted, probably sounding like he should know it was me.

"Who's this?" he inquired, sounding equal parts cautious and curious.

God, his voice is sexy. Okay, calm your farm, Sophie, just breathe and talk. All you have to do is say words, you've been training for moments like this your whole life.

"Hi, Joel, it's Sophie. Sophie Copeland. I stayed in your rental apartment last night," I said still sounding a little strangled but I nonetheless figuratively patted myself on the back for constructing and delivering a full sentence.

"Miss Copeland. What can I do for you?" he inquired and though I wouldn't say he sounded particularly friendly, his delivery was a touch guarded but I also detected a note of curiosity there too.

"Well it's kind of a long story, but it seems as though I'm going to be in town for a little while and I was calling to see if your apartment might be available. Perhaps as a short-term lease?"

Look at you. Making sense and being articulate, I thought as I continued to congratulate myself for every menial verbal accomplishment.

There was a short pause before his next words, causing my face to grimace in anticipation of an unfavorable response. I kept getting ahead of myself. I needed to relax, or I wasn't going to make it out of the Donner Bakery parking lot.

"That shouldn't be a problem, Miss Copeland, did you want to come by the shop to talk about the particulars or would you like me to come and meet you somewhere?"

With effort, I refrained from doing a jig in the car seat.

Ooh. So many options.

My eyes went to my lanyard and I looked up at Paul Newman, or Mr. Newman as I liked to address him, seeking guidance as I always did when there were decisions to be made.

I know it sounded crazy, but even though his expression was relatively neutral, whenever I looked at him hard enough, there was always a hint of something there. A smile if he thought it was okay to proceed or a scowl if he disapproved of my intentions.

I'm sure if I shared that particular snippet of information about myself with anybody other than Anna, they would politely suggest that I seek professional help. But I didn't need to pay a therapist to tell me that deep down, I knew Mr. Newman's supposed changes in countenance were simply illusory manifestations of my own conscience guiding my decisions. It was just way easier to blame him when things went wrong, because as I had learned from my failed television appearance, it was easier to forgive others than it was to forgive myself.

"I could meet you after work?" I suggested. "I'll buy you a beer as a thank you for the freebie last night. Would that be alright?"

I congratulated myself on how friendly and calm I sounded, while also taking precautions by suggesting we meet in public because Mr. Newman's expression was especially indistinct in that moment. He was practically shrugging at me and saying, "I don't know, kid. Whatever you think."

As a result, I decided to err on the side of caution, since I still didn't know anything about Joel other than the fact that I wanted to find out what he looked like first thing in the morning. I was willing to bet he looked like sleepy-eyed, bearded perfection and that his voice was even deeper and raspier—

"Hello? You still there?"

Shit! I missed what he said!

"Oh … sorry, you cut out for a second there. I missed what you said."

Nice save. Another pat on the back.

"Sorry about that. Old phone," he offered apologetically. "Is this better? Can you hear me now?"

I was dying. The shift in his tone from cautious to courteous had me melting down against my seat.

"Yes, sorry. I can hear you just fine," I said and sunk my teeth into my knuckles to keep from bursting at the sound of his voice.

"I was just suggesting that maybe you could meet me at Genie's? It's a bar not too far from town."

"Sure, that sounds great. What time should I be there?"

"Do you have time now?"

"Now?" I asked, peering down at my torn jeans and croissant crumb be-speckled NASA T-shirt.

"Yeah."

"Yeah sure, I can do now, I'll head right over," I said raising my arm and sniffing to see how my deodorant was holding up.

"Alright then, see you shortly, Miss Copeland," he said sounding … almost friendly.

As soon as I hung up the phone, I collapsed over on to the passenger side from the effort required to maintain the conversation.

Okay. Calm down. Breathe. The apartment is available, that's the main thing. It's all over.

Only it wasn't all over because now I was meeting him *in person*. The prospect both excited and unsettled me seeing as I was a little out of practice in these kinds of situations, and by these kinds of situations, I meant trying to act normal in front of an attractive man.

The only men I had associated with other than the once-in-a-blue-moon and usually awkward one-night stands, were the ones who worked alongside me at the restaurant and *none* of them looked like Joel.

After sitting back upright in my seat and affixing my seat belt, I took a breath and looked up at my lanyard dangling from the rearview mirror.

"What do you think?" I asked Mr. Newman.

After a few minutes of silence, I nodded in agreement.

"You're right. Don't get ahead of myself. One step at a time," I stated decidedly before turning the keys in the ignition and pulling the car out onto the road.

Vibrating with anticipation as I drove along, I reached for the radio hoping that some music would help to focus my scattered thoughts and was ecstatic when I heard the unmistakable synth and marimba of one of my favorite songs filtering out of the speakers.

Cranking the volume, I took a deep breath and let the soothing melody of "Africa" by Toto wash over me and steady my thoughts as I focused on singing along to the lyrics.

About halfway through the first chorus, I heard a low, rumbling sound and spotted about six motorcycles in my rearview mirror.

I tried not to pay attention, but the closer they got, the more they drowned out my music, until it barely registered in my ears.

"Oh, for crying out loud, just pass already! You're ruining my song!" I exclaimed in frustration as they zoomed by me and it wasn't until the end of the second chorus that I could hear it again.

"God, I hate bikers," I sputtered with contempt wishing I had the means to start the song over again but trying nonetheless to enjoy the rest of it as I allowed Google Maps to guide me to Genie's.

CHAPTER 7

I arrived at Genie's just before five and managed to remain somewhat calm by focusing on all the questions I should ask that were pertinent to the short-term lease and how much he was going to charge me to stay in his rental.

Even though his tone had been decidedly more pleasant than it was the night before, I still had no basis or expectation as to what he would be like to negotiate with.

As I got out of the car and made my way across the parking lot, I thought it best to do away with any expectations, focus on qualifying myself as a suitable tenant and let Joel be responsible for being a suitable landlord.

On my way toward the entrance, I recognized his black truck parked in the lot but refrained from veering into stalker territory by peeking inside for the purpose of gaining a modicum more insight into Joel. Was the interior of his car messy, disorganized, and full of trash? That might be a turnoff. Or was it completely clean with one of those pine tree-shaped air fresheners hanging from the rearview mirror?

With a sigh for my unfulfilled curiosity, I headed straight toward the entrance, hearing loud music and chatter coming from inside.

I opened the door to the bar and was immediately met with the scent of beer, barbecue, and wood.

The long bar was lined with barstools and stretched out along the wooden dance floor toward a separate section with pool tables, a jukebox, and a stage where I supposed a band performed, though there wasn't one there now. Inside, it was completely shut off from daylight, but soft, warm lights lit up the space offering an inviting ambience to the bar.

As I glanced around, I spotted Joel up on a raised platform with booth seating and smaller tables, sitting alone at the very last booth.

He was dressed casually in a light gray T-shirt underneath a dark green and blue flannel with the sleeves rolled up to his elbows—*hello, forearms!*—and a black baseball cap pulled low over his eyes. He was using his thumbnail to pick at the label of an empty beer bottle which made me worry that I'd kept him waiting.

I did allow myself a brief moment to observe him.

Just to make sure that I hadn't imagined how gorgeous he was.

I hadn't. In fact, I might have underestimated it.

Sitting alone at the booth, he was a big shape in a small space and I couldn't help but notice how lonely he looked.

All around him were people in groups, talking, laughing, and hollering but there he was, tucked away, alone in the farthest possible corner of the room.

The thought occurred to me that a guy like that should be turning away women by the dozen, but I also didn't want to make any assumptions about his personal affairs. I was here for a very specific reason and considered any extra intel I could get to be a bonus.

Shifting my thoughts from his forearms to a more business appropriate mindset, I made my way purposefully past the bar, across the dance floor, and toward the steps leading up to the booths.

Don't trip on the steps. Don't trip on the steps, I chanted to myself, knowing how prone I was to such fumblings when I was nervous, but managed to make it up the handful of steps without incident.

Just as I was congratulating myself a bald guy who was seated at a table with a group of his friends slid backward in his chair without checking behind him first.

His seat connected with my left hip, shoving me directly into a member of the waitstaff who was carrying a tray laden with frosty steins of beer and steaming racks of saucy ribs.

Time slowed, as it does in moments of shock and horror, and I found myself staring directly into the horrified, contorted countenance of the waiter, his mouth and eyes both formed into perfect Os.

Joel is seeing all of this.

Why me?

Of course, this would happen to me.

How am I able to have such fully formed thoughts in such a short space of time?

Okay, this is happening, let's just get it over with.

I closed my eyes and braced for impact.

There was a collective gasp that rang out from the table and I shrieked as I felt the cold splash of beer soaking through my clothes and the warm slide of saucy meat against my entire upper body.

As Mr. Newman is my witness, after the initial racket of plates and glass hitting the floor, there was no sound that followed other than the metallic peal of the tray spinning against the wooden floor until finally it slowed and fell on its side with one last resonating clang.

After a short, loaded pause, a wave of hollers, howling laughter, and *ooohs,* converged upon me in a veritable tsunami.

"Mother fuck!" was my contribution as I stood with my hands in the air, dripping with sauce and beer.

"Oh! Oh, my Lord, miss, I am *so* sorry!" the waiter offered, as people continued to point and laugh.

"It was my fault. I'm sorry!" the little bald-headed man insisted, snatching up as many napkins as he could from his table.

"Did you see that? That chick just got annihilated by a rack of ribs!"

I glanced over my shoulder where four young guys were laughing considerably harder than everyone else.

I tossed them a scowl before turning my attention back to the people who were trying to help.

"It's fine, it's fine. I'm fine," I insisted, attempting to reassure everyone who was echoing sentiments of concern for my physical wellbeing. My pride on the other hand ...

"Did it burn?"

"Let me get you some towels"

"Here let me help—"

I was so stupefied by the commotion that I hadn't realized that someone's hands were swiping and pressing napkins against my breasts. Worse still, my brain was still too scrambled to register the personal intrusion as wrong until a flurry of motion snapped me to back to attention.

The next thing I knew, the bald man who had knocked me over, was being pushed back against his table and Joel was towering over him with a fistful of his shirt.

"Hey, asshole, what the hell do you think you're doing?" he growled, as some of the laughter in the room dissipated into hushed chatter.

The little bald guy held up his hands submissively as other members of his party rose from their seats in anticipation, readying themselves to intervene in case the situation escalated.

From the veil of undiluted terror in the eyes of Joel's quarry, I felt quite confident that it wouldn't.

"Whoa, Joel," the bald guy sputtered nervously. "Hey take it easy, friend. I was just trying to help," he peered wide-eyed up into Joel's intimidating, glacial glower.

"You could stand to be a little less handsy with your help, *friend*," Joel responded in a deceptively calm voice.

The target of his ire nodded in understanding, and once Joel was satisfied that the guy was sufficiently unsettled within an inch of his bowel control, Joel finally unhanded him.

I glanced around the room at the other patrons who were watching with intense interest and decided that the show had gone on long enough.

I took a tentative step toward Joel and placed my hand on his upper arm.

At my touch, he turned to me and my breath caught at the glacial focus of his eyes.

I swallowed and tried to smile reassuringly.

"I'm fine," I insisted, watching as his fierce expression softened slightly. "Come on, let's go sit down," I suggested, letting go of his arm and gesturing toward the booth.

Joel took one last hard look at the bald guy who was still watching him cautiously to make sure he wasn't about to come back for more, and then turned and followed me over to the booth he'd been sitting at.

"That was epically calamitous!" I heard a disembodied voice snicker from somewhere behind me and I was so tightly wound that my head snapped around looking for the source and bracing to give whoever it was a piece of my mind.

Before I could unload, I felt the gentle grasp of fingers close around the crook of my elbow and I turned to find Joel, shaking his head.

"Don't worry about it. Ignore it. Come on, let me get you a beer," he offered, his voice soft and cajoling, his fingers grazing down my arm.

Taken aback by this new side of him, I peered up at him and watched as his lips turned up into a soft smile.

"You okay?" he asked, his eyebrows furrowing with concern.

It was a subdued smile, but it changed his whole face and sent a sweet, soothing warmth all over me as I let my shoulders drop and looked down at my soiled clothing.

"Yeah, I'm fine just embarrassed." Peeling the fabric of my soaked T-shirt away from my skin by the hem.

"Here," he said shrugging his flannel off his shoulders. "There's washrooms down the steps and back past the pool tables," he explained, holding out his shirt with one hand and gesturing in the direction of the bathroom with the other.

Though I was still taking some time to come back to my senses, I did have enough presence of mind to know that I was not about to let an opportunity to wear one of his shirts go by and accepted it gratefully.

Just as I was about to thank him, the manager of the bar approached our table in full damage control mode.

"Ma'am, please allow me to extend my most sincere apologies for this unfortunate accident. We'd be happy to provide you and your company with any food or drinks you wish free of charge," he offered looking very nervous indeed.

I glanced toward Joel who inconspicuously cocked an eyebrow and shrugged.

"Thank you, I appreciate that but that's not necessary. It was just an accident," I reasoned but I could tell Mr. Manager was about to insist by the way his mouth opened to talk before I'd even finished speaking.

"Please, ma'am, I must insist. Can we start you off with a round of beverages? One of our servers will come by to take your order once you've had a chance to settle in and look at the menu."

Seeing that the offer was not up for negotiation, I relented, secretly pleased by the money I would save.

"Well alright then, thank you. I guess I'll have a beer," I requested, and the manager nodded before turning and regarding Joel with an unease that made me narrow my eyes curiously.

Joel requested the same and as the manager scurried away, I noticed that the attention of the room was still on us.

"Why is everyone still staring at me?" I asked self-consciously. "Seriously, the show's over."

"They're not staring at you, they're staring at me," Joel replied with a resigned quality.

Before I could ask what he meant, he nudged his chin toward the shirt in my hand.

"Go on, get cleaned up. You'll feel better."

The balmy, gentle delivery of his instruction sent heat right to my cheeks and I figured a moment alone to recompose myself was not a bad idea.

"Yeah okay, I'll be right back."

After I was done scrubbing barbecue sauce and beer off my jeans, chest, arms, and the ends of my hair, I put on Joel's shirt.

It was way too big on me, but after a little finessing I managed to make it look intentional by further rolling up the sleeves and tying the bottom into a knot.

The flannel had a scent to it that was not distinct like soap or cologne or body odor. It just smelled like ... him.

As I made my way back to the table on high alert for any sudden movements, I kept noticing people casting me sideways glances.

It didn't really bother me, but it caught my attention as I neared our booth just as one of the waitresses dropped off our beers.

When Joel spotted me, he rose from his seat, and the gentlemanly gesture made me smile as I approached him.

"Good timing," he greeted, his eyes giving me a once over in his shirt as I slid into the seat across from his. "Feel better?" he inquired, his lips twitching as he tried not to laugh at my expense.

"It's not funny," I insisted trying to be serious, but I'd never seen him smile this broadly before and it was completely and utterly contagious. "Okay it's a little funny," I conceded as we both allowed ourselves to laugh at the situation.

"Some might describe it as epically calamitous," Joel quipped tipping the neck of his beer toward me.

"Oh God, no. This is going to be a thing now isn't it?" I asked with a groan and was rewarded with a wide, toothy smile.

"Well, you did make one hell of a memorable entrance," he laughed with amusement.

"It was kind of a showstopper." I nodded in agreement. "And let me tell ya, I would roll around in a kiddie pool of barbecue sauce all day long if it meant I get to eat for free," I said raising the bottle of beer to my lips.

"Now there's an interesting late-night cable television pitch," he joked leaning casually against the wall at his side and I laughed, glad to see that he had a sense of humor.

"Thanks for the shirt, by the way, I think it probably looks better on me than you, what do you think?" I asked stroking my fingers across the fabric of his flannel.

"Don't get any ideas about the shirt, I know where you live," he cautioned playfully which jogged my memory on the whole reason I had met him here in the first place.

"Oh yeah, you're gonna be my new landlord. That's so weird."

"Why is that weird?" he asked, his eyebrows knotting together curiously.

"I don't know." I sighed, rubbing my forehead wearily wondering how to succinctly explain the chain of events that had occurred that day to lead me here. "It's just been a very interesting day," was all I said in the end.

"So why the decision to stay in Green Valley, if you don't mind me asking," he inquired, lifting his baseball cap to run his hands through his hair before affixing it back over his head.

"Well it's kind of a funny story," I began with a sigh. "My car actually decided to crap out on me this morning," I explained.

"What do you mean it crapped out on you? Did you want me to take a look at it for you?"

I narrowed my eyes at him curiously.

"You can fix cars?"

"Yeah, I'm an auto mechanic," he shrugged as though that detail should have been obvious.

"I thought you said you were a handyman," I said confused.

"I didn't say that, I said that I do a few different things, which is true, but I also own an auto shop," he explained.

I cocked my head, trying not to jump to conclusions as I remembered what Cletus had said about being lucky I hadn't run into "the other guy" earlier that morning.

"Hmm," I said, leaning back against my seat as I struggled to reconcile what Cletus had implied about Joel with the guy sitting in front of me.

Nothing about Joel struck me as particularly alarming, but I realized I didn't know him enough to completely discount Cletus's appraisal of him.

"Anyway, thank you for the offer but it's not necessary, I already had someone look at it," I said as Joel's body visibly wilted and he rolled his eyes.

"Let me guess. The Winston brothers," he stated as though the mere mention of their name left an acrid, bitter taste in his mouth.

I cocked an eyebrow questioningly at him as I swallowed another sip of beer. "Yeah. Is there some beef there you want to tell me about?"

"Not really," he replied shaking his head. "Just be careful. They have a tendency to make up car parts in order to charge customers more money for repairs, so if they tell you your doohickey has come loose from the thingamajig, I recommend you Google it to make sure they're not ripping you off."

"Isn't that par for the course with auto mechanics?" I asked, implying that they were all the same.

"Not all of 'em," he replied pointedly before taking another long sip of beer.

"Well it doesn't matter anyway," I said with a mournful sigh. "My car would have cost more money to fix that it was worth, so now I have to buy a new one. You happen to know anyone who can give me a good deal?" I asked perking up in my seat with a hopeful smile.

He grinned at me and began picking at the label of his new bottle of beer.

"That depends, what are you in the market for?"

"Oh, you know, a 1969 Camaro Z28 in dark green should do the job," I joked as Joel raised his eyebrows with interest.

"You're a Camaro girl, really?" he asked, surprised.

"Yeah, is that weird?" I asked curiously.

"Not weird, just … interesting." He smiled, his eyes narrowing with curiosity and the slight pause made me wonder if that was really what he'd intended to say. "Wait how did you get here?" Joel inquired realizing he'd missed a detail.

"The *dastardly* Winston brothers hooked me up with a loaner," I said making fun of Joel's distaste for them, while simultaneously hinting at how they had been very generous to me and I had no cause to speak ill of them.

"The Dodge Neon?" he grumbled, his curled lip once again expressing his disapproval.

"Beats walking everywhere.," I shrugged. "What's the deal? Why do you hate the Winston brothers so much?"

"I don't hate them, I just don't like them is all," he said shrugging as though the two things were mutually exclusive. "Anyway," he said in the way that I knew meant he was about to change the subject, "back to you, and why you're hanging your hat in Green Valley."

"Well," I began, "while he was looking at my car, it came up in conversation that I am a pastry chef, and since his wife owns a bakery, he took me to meet her. I guess they lost a couple of staff members recently, so anyway, one thing led to another and I agreed to a short term contract to help them out over the next couple of months," I said summarizing the events of the morning.

"That's kinda cool," he said to my surprise, sounding decidedly more approving. "I might not be the biggest fan of the Winstons, but Jennifer Donner Winston is a good girl. I got no cause to speak ill of her, besides her terrible taste in men," he added, and I briefly considered that he might have carried a flame for Jennifer but didn't dare ask.

"Yeah, she's an amazing woman." I nodded in agreement. "And that bakery is beautiful, I'm excited to work there and start baking again, I miss it." I sighed forlornly.

"So, you're a baker, huh?"

"I am." I nodded. "Well, if I am being picky about the title, I'm technically a pastry chef, but there's nothing wrong with being called a baker."

"Where are you from? You sound kind of East Coast," he said narrowing his eyes as though he were trying to place my accent.

"I was born in New York, but I've moved around a lot. Most recently I was in Washington and after this, I'll be heading to Boston to help my best friend open her new bakery," I explained as he nodded while listening intently. "How about you?" I asked.

"Green Valley, born and raised," he replied scratching the side of his head as though he were somehow embarrassed by that.

"You're lucky, it's a beautiful place," I offered, watching closely to see how he responded to my hinting that there was nothing wrong with having lived in one place his whole life.

"Yeah, it's alright," came his lackluster response.

"Have you thought about living somewhere else?" I asked, reading the subtext behind his flat responses.

"All the time," he said with an emphatic nod of his head.

"So why don't you?" I continued, curious to see what he'd say.

"It's … complicated," was all he offered in return and as badly as I wanted him to elaborate, I decided to respect the boundary that he was very clearly placing between us.

"Fair enough," I said glancing down and watching his thumbnail scraping at the label of the beer bottle once again. "Well if you ever find yourself in Boston one day, you gotta come check out my friend's bakery after it opens. It's called Yeast Affection," I explained watching as his lips turned into an uncertain smile.

"Yeast Affection? That's what she's calling her bakery?"

"Yeah," I nodded, "It's a pun, you know like yeast infection, but instead of an affliction it's an affinity for yeasty baked goods."

"Yeah no, I got it. I just don't know if your customers will be tempted by the reference to the affliction part."

"Yeah, I kind of worried about that too," I admitted. "But then, that's just my friend Anna's sense of humor. She's irreverent and always aims to offend people just a little, which is kind of what I love so much about her. If she was here right now, she would probably tell you that she doesn't actually use biological waste in her recipes and she's not the babysitter of other people's irrationalities."

"She sounds like a firecracker," Joel replied which made me happy to hear because she was. In the best kind of way.

"She is amazing," I confirmed. "And I am very excited to help her in her venture which I know she will be super successful at."

"What about you, any plans to open up your own bakery?" Joel inquired.

There were a lot of layers to the complete response to that question and I was simply plumb out of the energy required to do so.

"Uh, sure. One day, I guess," I said fumbling my way through a vague response.

Just then a waitress approached our table and I might have been imagining it, but she seemed a little tense as she offered to take our food order.

Joel once again gestured for me to go first as I tried to ignore the weird vibe that suddenly seemed to be hanging over everyone at the table. I glanced at Joel who stared passively back at me as the waitress' eyes remained fixed on her notepad. I hadn't had a chance to look at the menu, and knew that if I had, I would have chosen the most affordable option, but seeing as how everything was on the house, I decided to indulge.

"You know, some of that barbecue sauce flew into my mouth earlier and it tasted really good, so I think I'll get the ribs, please?" I said which made Joel snicker.

"That sounds good, I'll have the same, and another beer, please," Joel requested swaying his empty bottle between his fingers.

"Oh, me also, please," I added quickly as the waitress scrawled our order down, cleared our table of empty beer bottles and their shredded labels and hurried off to get our order in.

While we ate, Joel and I talked about a range of benign subjects, including, movies, music, and books.

Things turned slightly more existential when the conversation switched to space, prompted by my lamenting about the fact that I would have to discard my now sauce soiled NASA shirt.

During the hour and a half that we ate and drank, there was not one moment that Joel set off any alarm bells or displayed any behavior that I felt warranted Cletus's cautioning me against him.

Though I remained open to the possibility that Joel still might be involved in something shady, I resolved instead to simply respond to the person in front of me.

We worked out a fair price for rent and Joel said he would draw up the lease as soon as possible and let me know when it was completed so I could sign it and have my own copy, which I thought was about as legitimate as anyone could hope for.

When we were done, we drove our respective cars back into town where I would be given back the set of keys to the apartment.

After I pulled into the spot in front of the used bookstore I would soon be living above, I climbed out of the car and went to the trunk to begin unloading my two suitcases and one storage container which amounted to all of my worldly belongings.

"Here, let me give you a hand carrying all this up," Joel offered, appearing at my side before easily lifting a suitcase in one hand and grabbing the plastic storage container with the other.

"Thank you," I said gratefully as I shrugged on my backpack and reached for the remaining suitcase while trying not to notice the ease with which he carried the two hefty items.

We made it up the stairs and Joel retrieved the suite keys for me as we stood together on the landing preparing to retire to our respective apartments.

"Thank you for helping me with my stuff and for agreeing to let me stay here," I offered feeling very conscious of his eyes on me as he slid his hands into his pockets and flattened his lips into something of a smile.

"You're welcome, if you need anything, you have my number or if I'm home feel free to knock on my door," he returned.

"I'll get this back to you as soon as I can," I promised, tugging at the tail at the end of his knotted shirt.

"No hurry," he assured me waving it off with his hand. "Thanks for the epically calamitous company," he said with a smirk and I rolled my eyes with a sigh.

"You're never gonna let me live that down, are you?" I asked watching him shake his head before I was even done asking.

"Nope sorry," he said turning to go and unlock his door.

"Great," I grumbled watching him for a moment as he opened his door and then turned back to me.

"Good evening, Miss Sophie. Have a good night."

"You too, Joel," I responded feeling a little breathless at the sound of my name from his lips, and watching him disappear into his apartment and close his door.

As I stood out in the hallway, I thought back and tried to recall one thing I could have faulted him for but came up empty.

Joel had piqued my curiosity though and once that happened, I tended to become a little inquisitive. Or nosy, as some people who knew me preferred to call it.

I wanted to know what the deal was with Joel and the Winston brothers and I was probably going to get myself in trouble trying to find out.

CHAPTER 8

*I*f you were to ask your average baked goods enthusiast what they envisaged working in a small-town bakery to be like, I am willing to bet that a lot of them imagine it to be quite the quaint affair.

Your slightly more realistic folks might cite the early starts as being a bit of a bummer, but for the most part, most people think of coming to work and eating cakes, pies, and baguettes all day. Behind the counter, there would be shelves of house-made jams, pickles, and spreads, and every day a puppy comes to steal a sausage from a rotund middle-aged man named Bob who is spending the morning making pigs-in-a-blanket.

The reality of working in a bakery is quite different.

On my first day at the Donner Bakery a few days later, I woke at three AM, and fought against the urge to go back to sleep for the entire thirty minutes that it took me to shower, dress, and get into my car.

Glancing at Mr. Newman hanging from the rearview mirror of the Neon, I prayed that bottomless coffee was a condition stated within the terms of my employment.

There was nobody on the road at that hour and it felt creepy driving in the dark through a town I wasn't entirely familiar with yet.

There was so much space in between everything, and trees lined the road almost the entire way making me feel like something could pop out of them at any moment.

I took comfort in the fact that the prospect of seeing Bigfoot was more of a concern for me than the fact that it was my first day in a new bakery. I felt confident that I had been baptized by enough oven fires and overbearing personalities to know that I could handle whatever was thrown my way.

I arrived at the Donner Bakery at 3:45 AM. A little early and eager perhaps and sans grainy camera phone footage of Sasquatch, but I was anxious to get to work.

I took a breath and knocked on the back door, waiting until a moment later Jennifer Winston appeared in a gray T-shirt, jeans, and big smile.

She was so beautiful, even at that ungodly hour and I found myself unable to help zeroing in on her incredible violet-colored eyes. They were completely mesmerizing.

"Good morning, Sophie, and welcome to your first day. Come on in." She grinned widely, pushing the door open and stepping aside to let me cross the threshold into the bakery.

I could already smell good things happening in there and it made me even more anxious to get started.

"Thank you. Am I the first one here?" I inquired noting the lack of clattering sounds coming from inside.

"Yes, but the zombie crew will be along shortly," she advised. "In the meantime, why don't I show you where you can put your stuff and give you a quick tour of everything," Jennifer offered waving her hand in a gesture for me to follow her.

"Sounds good," I agreed and fell into step alongside her as we walked toward the back office where I'd first met her.

"You excited to get started? Lockers are right here, just pick one and keep the key pinned to your T-shirt until you need it," she instructed.

I chose the nearest locker and crammed my backpack inside before locking it and securing the key on a safety pin to the hem on my T-shirt.

"I have been itching to get started ever since coming to your bakery last week. This place is amazing," I gushed, genuinely wishing all bakeries were like this.

"Thank you. That's very kind and I'm glad to hear it, because we're going to have plenty for you to do," she said lowering her chin slightly as though it were more of a warning than a promise.

I didn't mind a bit. I was used to environments that pushed me hard, so I welcomed the challenge and was anxious to show Jennifer what I could do.

As I was shown the lay of the land, Jennifer imparted some useful hints pertaining to particular idiosyncrasies in her kitchen that everyone needed to be aware of, and I was careful to make note of everything she mentioned.

"This oven on the left runs slightly hotter than the one on the right, so drop the temperature by twenty degrees when baking in there. We only have one blast chiller so it's first come, first served. I will take care of your paperwork and payroll, so if you have any questions, feel free to ask. Only use the industrial mixer with the blue stripe of electrical tape across the top because the other one doesn't work right now, but Cletus is working on it."

"I think that's all for now, but if I think of anything else, I'll let you know," she said leaning casually on one of the industrial metal benches.

"I think I can handle that," I said with a confident nod, and then noticed Jennifer looked like she wanted to say something but was hesitating.

"Before I put you to work, can I ask you something?"

I considered myself to be a fairly open book, but questions like that still made me nervous.

"Sure."

"I just wondered if your leaving Paradigm had anything to do with your appearance on that television show?"

My stomach dropped down to my feet and my shoulders tightened at the prospect that someone like Jennifer had witnessed the most humiliating experience of my life.

I immediately lowered my eyes and cleared my throat.

It was a complicated answer.

"Indirectly, I suppose," I said realizing that I was being cryptic, but the question caught me off guard and my mind scattered like an intrusion of cockroaches after a light coming on.

"Oh, my goodness, look at you," Jennifer said reaching forward to rub my arm comfortingly. "All the color just drained right out of your face," she said sympathetically. "You've got nothing to worry about, this doesn't change anything about your employment here. The spotlight is not for everyone and I know you're going to do a great job."

Grateful to her for being so understanding, I felt my shoulders drop with relief.

"Thank you. And yes, what happened on that show ..." I trailed off searching for an explanation which I still felt like I had to give, "was not at all a reflection of my capabilities. I promise."

I crossed my heart, knowing I still sounded like I was begging to have my life spared, but Jennifer just waved her hand and smiled.

"I'm not worried," she assured me before leaning in as though she were about to tell me a secret. "One time my momma told me about plans to put me in a TV commercial and I passed right out cold." She shared with me, which her confidence went a long way to making me feel as though she genuinely understood.

"I suppose I just underestimated how much that kind of environment would affect me, and I let the pressure get to me," I attempted to explain. "I wish I had never let myself get talked into doing it," I admitted thinking about how things had changed as a result of the whole debacle. "Now if I could just get the producer of the show to stop calling me to come back."

"Get out! He is?" Jennifer asked scrunching her nose in disapproval.

"Yep. Calls me just about every day, trying to get me to agree to a 'best of the worst' special they're filming early next year."

"Well how could you say no to that?" she asked in an ironic tone that made me laugh.

"I'm not anxious to make the same mistake twice."

"I don't blame you, I would feel the exact same way. Now, how do you feel about pumping out some croissants?" she asked, her voice shifting to a purposeful tone.

"It's my very favorite thing to make," I replied, and Jennifer smiled at my enthusiastic response.

"Good, let's get to work then."

I was immediately put to work laminating ten sheets of croissant dough which yielded twenty-five pastries per sheet, while other employees slowly started to filter in just after five AM.

Tempest Cassidy, a fiery, little redhead with the greenest eyes I think I'd ever seen, who I recognized from my first visit to the bakery informed me that the two hundred and fifty croissants I was working on "should see us through to lunchtime." I both marveled at and relished at the sheer volume of product leaving the kitchen.

Soon, croissants were followed by various fruit Danishes, then individual assorted tarts and cannoli while cakes seemed to be the task reserved for the most senior employees.

I didn't mind feeling as though I needed to earn my stripes before being entrusted with that task, especially after tasting the quality of the cakes that the Donner Bakery produced. When I tried Jennifer's banana cake, I told her that they should preserve one and put it in its own exhibit at the Smithsonian in Washington, D.C. and still felt like I had understated how good it was.

It was clear that Jennifer was a stickler for quality ingredients, an attribute which I could not respect more, and I was as proud, if not more so, to be working here than I had been working at Paradigm.

As the morning wore on, I was working up both a sweat and an appetite, but I was in my element. I didn't even notice that I had yet to be formally introduced to most of the people who were working around me with equal focus until Tempest reappeared in front of the bench where I was piping ricotta mixture into cannoli shells, dipping the ends in crushed pistachios, and gradually building a cannoli castle.

"How's your first day going so far?" she asked, her tone dry, but not unfriendly.

"Good! Productive. I've missed this," I said placing another tubular delight atop the pile.

"Well, the novelty will wear off come Thanksgiving when the special orders start rolling in like an avalanche. You're gonna be up to your neck in batter and buttercream, my friend," she informed me as though I didn't know what I had signed up for, but I just smiled and cocked my head.

"'*If it only reaches your neck, then you can still breathe.*' That's what my old boss used to say," I said knowing it sounded obnoxious, so I followed it up with an eye roll.

"Oh yeah, you come from one of those fancy city restaurants with a bunch of dudes who act like laying a sprig of parsley on top of a piece of fish will save the world. What was that like?" she asked.

"Just exactly as you described," I confirmed with a laugh at the accuracy of her valuation.

"Don't get me wrong, there's nothing wrong with taking pride in your work," Tempest began as though she worried she might have offended me.

"It's okay, I understand," I assured her. "But this right here is much more my pace and it's nice to work with some ladies for a change."

"Well we're sure glad for the extra hands, you've already made a huge dent in the workload, just save some work for the rest of us okay?" she requested, before offering me a smile and tapping the table.

"You got it," I said nodding my head in agreement.

Just then, a dark-haired, wide-eyed woman approached us and gasped theatrically.

"You must be Sophie! It's so nice to meet you," she said grabbing me by the shoulders and pulling me with a yank right into her with an "oomph" before wrapping me up in a tight hug.

"Oh! Okay," I said, my eyes finding Tempest whose eyebrows were raised not in surprise, but more like she was saying, "Yep. She's a hugger."

My gloved hands were caked in ricotta and pistachio, so I tapped her back with the insides of my wrists to reciprocate the gesture.

She grasped onto my shoulders once more as she peeled herself off me and smiled widely.

"My name's Joy, and I am super excited to be working with you. We're gonna be friends, I can already tell by your kind eyes. Don't go anywhere, I'm going to put my bag in my locker, get my apron on, and then I'll be right back, okay?"

"Okay," I replied because I feared it was the only response she would accept and then in a puff of perfume, she was gone.

I turned to Tempest who was fighting a smile with her eyebrow cocked.

"She's always like that isn't she?" I asked knowingly, having encountered her ilk before.

"Mm-hmm. Yes, ma'am, that one doesn't have an off switch," she confirmed with a nod of her head.

"Good to know," I managed to reply just as Joy came bounding toward me once again while tying her apron behind her back.

"So, where are you from? How long are you staying in Green Valley? I heard you worked at a super fancy restaurant before you came here, is that true? Because if it is, I bet you ten bucks Jenn is gonna want you over at the Donner Lodge."

I struggled to decide which of Joy's questions to address first, but in the end, I decided the last one should suffice.

"What's the Donner Lodge?" I asked curiously.

"Oh my, you haven't seen it yet? It's just right next door," Joy informed me pointing over her shoulder. "I should take you around the grounds after work one day. Oh, my stars, I just love the Donner Lodge, it's so beautiful there," Joy said dreamily. "I'm gonna have my wedding there some day."

She didn't really answer the question, but I didn't mind. I got the gist from what little I was able to parse from her enthusiastic response.

"Where are you staying while you're in town?" Tempest inquired curiously as I worked with her to move the now completed trays of cannoli while Joy got to work mixing a batch of Swiss meringue buttercream in preparation for a three-person cake assembly line.

"Right in the town center, above a bookstore. I met a guy who has a rental apartment and he's letting me stay there," I explained while simultaneously fantasizing about said guy.

"Oh yeah? What's his name?" Joy inquired. "I bet I know *hiiiim,*" she sang and I smiled, not doubting that she probably did. It was hard to imagine any lady in town not being familiar with Joel and not just because it was a small town. He kind of stood out. At least to me.

Surely every woman and maybe even a few men knew all about Joel. A rugged, brooding Southerner who says something shitty before doing the right thing, because he can't help himself? Of course, they knew him.

"Joel. Joel Barnes," I replied taking the initiative to pull over the tray of naked cakes to be trimmed, leveled, and prepped for icing.

I'd just sliced my way through the first cake when I noticed how silent they'd become and glanced up to find them both looking at me with expressions that I couldn't quite place.

"I'm sorry, should I not be touching the cakes?" I asked holding up my hands.

"Joel Barnes?" Joy parroted, and I narrowed my eyes.

"Yeah. You know him?" I asked, half expecting she would say he was her ex something or other.

She didn't respond, except to look to Tempest who also didn't seem to know what to say at first either.

"You mean the auto mechanic, right?" Tempest eventually asked, as though there might be more than one Joel Barnes in town and his occupation was what made him distinguishable from the other.

"Yeah, why? Is there more than one?"

"No," Tempest scoffed as though realizing she'd asked a silly question. "It's just …"

She paused and turned back to Joy, and that worried me because Tempest Cassidy did not give off the vibe like she held back.

"Okay, now you're freaking me out. If there's something I should be aware of, then I'd like you to tell me."

"Oh, it's nothing," Joy insisted. "It's nothing. I'm sure it's fine it's just … well … Joel and the Winstons don't really care for one another," Joy explained, and I got the sense that she was trying to be tactful in her delivery.

"Yeah, I kind of got that impression from both him and Cletus. Anyone know why?" I asked curiously.

"Nobody really knows," Tempest shrugged, doling globs of strawberry jam onto the layers of cake that I was handing to her. "But I suspect it's got something to do with the Winstons taking all his auto repair customers."

"Oh well … that makes sense, I guess," seeing how that could certainly cause tension in a small town with only so many cars to be fixed and two mechanics to choose from.

"I think it's got something to do with those Iron Wraiths," Joy speculated, standing on tiptoes to peer into the mixing bowl while waiting for the icing to be whipped to the desired consistency.

"Iron what?" I asked, placing a scrap of cake from the offcuts into my mouth for a taste, and just like everything else I'd sampled here, it was heavenly and dissolved in my mouth like a dream.

"They're a biker gang here in Green Valley."

"Seriously, a biker gang? In this tiny town?" I asked incredulously.

"Yes, ma'am. Their HQ is here, but they have chapters all over Tennessee," Tempest explained, using an offset spatula to spread the jam across the middle layer of cake.

"And Joel's one of them," I inquired feeling the pit of stomach twist at the prospect of living across a short hallway from him.

"I don't know for sure, it's kind of hard to say," Tempest paused before looking around to make sure nobody else was listening and then lowered her voice. "Sometimes folks around town have said they've seen Joel talking to some of them. Nobody knows what about, but I can tell you one thing for certain, the Winstons don't want anything to do with the Wraiths or anyone associated with them."

"No respectable person goes around letting the community believe they're mixed up in all that mess. That's why people don't care too much for him," Joy informed me, and I felt myself deflating like a balloon at the possibility that Joel would be a part of something like that.

"Except for Beau. Sometimes he hangs out with Drill and Catfish. Or at least, he used to," Joy explained, which didn't make any sense to me.

"Beau? I don't understand, why would he do that if—"

"It's all very complicated," Tempest interrupted waving her hand as though it were too lengthy a discussion to start now. "I'm sure you've got nothing to worry about. Just something to be aware of," she added in an obvious attempt to allay my fears.

"Yeah, you know I'm sure he's just quiet," Joy said, flapping her hand. "He kind of always has been but ever since his b—"

"Joy," Tempest interjected, "don't go blabbing about other people's business. You don't want to be like Scotia Simmons, do you?"

"No." Joy sighed, leaving me to wonder about what she was about to say before Tempest stopped her.

"So anyway," Joy continued, swiftly changing the subject, "I think you should let us take you out for a drink on Friday." She grinned, bumping her hip to mine and wagging her eyebrows.

"Yes! We can celebrate your first week at the bakery and give you a real Green Valley welcome. What do you think, Joy? Genie's?" Tempest asked looking past me to Joy.

"Oh, I've been to Genie's!" I exclaimed glad to talk about something that I actually knew about. "Got my boobs good and slathered in barbecue ribs and beer, and then they gave me my dinner and drinks for free."

Both women looked at me curiously, squinting their eyes.

"You sure that was Genie's and not the Dragon?" Joy asked me.

"No, it was definitely Genie's. I met Joel there to talk about my short-term lease," I explained watching them closely for a reaction.

"He's getting you to sign a lease? Well, that's good," Tempest said as though she were impressed by how aboveboard it was as I sighed inwardly, wondering what the hell I'd gotten myself into.

CHAPTER 9

$\mathcal{T}$he one good thing about a 3:45 AM start time was the noon clock out.

I had done a little exploring in the couple of days before I officially started at the Donner Bakery and was eager to see what else the town had to offer.

That was, of course, if I could drink enough coffee to keep me awake.

I was not as accustomed to early starts as I was to late finishes, but wasn't overly concerned about it, knowing I'd adapt to the hours quickly enough. Plus, I liked the idea of having a whole day ahead of me to do whatever I wanted.

By the time I had hung up my apron and collected my personal items, I could hear the swarm of customers out in the shopfront either waiting for their turn to order their favorite staples and indulgences or to pick up their special orders.

I hadn't eaten anything all morning aside from the odd nibble of offcut cake and I was starving, so I decided to drive to Daisy's for something slightly more substantial than cake.

I fished my phone from out of my bag and saw that John Moxie had phoned four times.

The usual wave of conflicting emotions sent me bobbing in a sea of indecision.

I was still tempted by the thought of three hundred thousand dollars, but sure enough, the lurch in my stomach as I remembered the slop of dog vomit that I had put up for consideration to the judges the last time was enough to make me shake my head in dismissal at the idea.

No. No. Not happening, I told myself swiping my finger across the screen to delete the notifications.

"Sophie."

I heard my name being called and turned to find Jennifer peeking out from behind the office door by the lockers.

"Do you have time for a quick chat before you leave?" she inquired.

"Yes, of course," I replied, hoisting my bag up onto my shoulder and pocketing my phone as I made my way over to her office.

"I just wanted to check in and see how you feel after your first day," she asked motioning for me to take a seat in the chair in front of her desk.

"Good! I think it went pretty well," I replied feeling accomplished and energized despite the early start, "Although, I think how *you* feel is the more important question," I added giving Jennifer the opportunity to offer me her feedback. She was my boss after all.

"I am very pleased with how your first day turned out," she said as though it were an understatement. "It's very clear you know your way around a batch of croissants, so I am very grateful that you decided to stay in Green Valley for a little while to help us out," she said with such a genuine warmth that the praise felt almost uncomfortable because I wasn't used to receiving it.

"Thank you," I smiled knowing that my response was inadequate, but not knowing what else to say.

"In fact, I was hoping to run something by you, if you have a moment?"

"Oh, of course," I replied, my expression turning curious.

"Well it's just, I'd love to develop some new items for the bakery and once a week, me and a couple of the other girls come back after hours and run a little test kitchen session. We basically just drink wine, experiment with new recipes, and have a laugh, but I wanted to see if you were interested in joining us for the next one?"

I was taken aback once again by the invite because Jennifer was my boss and in all my years working in the hospitality industry, I had never had a superior extend an invite to hang out for shits and giggles.

As wonderful as the idea of hanging out in a kitchen with co-workers sounded, the part that really appealed to me was the test kitchen part. I had been itching for access to a kitchen to try out some new ideas since I had left Paradigm, so this was the perfect opportunity for me to do so while also having some fun.

"Yes, I'd love too," I replied enthusiastically. "That sounds like fun."

"Good. We meet here on Thursday nights after closing. Just knock on the door and one of us will let you in."

After accepting Jennifer's offer and a few minutes of friendly chit-chat, I was back in my courtesy car heading to Daisy's Nut House for something to eat.

It was raining outside and the cold, damp, late autumn air chilled me right through my spring jacket. As far as I had seen, there wasn't a store nearby to buy something warmer, so I reminded myself to layer up if I was going to make it through to the new year.

I parked my car outside the diner and ignored another of John Moxie's incoming calls as I made my way inside, eager for something hot to eat and caffeinated to drink.

It was nearing one o'clock in the afternoon, and the lunch rush still appeared to be in full swing as I looked around for a lone seat at the bench but couldn't spot one.

That's when I saw Joel sitting alone in a booth by a large window, eating a sandwich, and reading a newspaper.

Oh. Hello, conflicted feelings. You're looking extra conflicting today. Did you do something with your hair?

His gorgeous brown hair was a mess and the sleeves of his gray shirt were pushed up revealing his forearms which looked even thicker than I remembered them being, as he worked to fold the gigantic pages of the newspaper into neat manageable folds.

This man was seriously hotter than a melting ice-cream analogy.

And also, possibly involved with a crime organization! I reminded myself as I continued to stand uselessly trying to find somewhere to sit.

I tried not to stare, but it was impossible not to smile at the indelicate way he shoved the corner of his sandwich into his mouth and then proceeded to chew as though it might try to escape.

He picked up his coffee and was mid-sip when his eyes rose up from the rim of his cup and saw me standing by the entrance staring at him.

Busted.

"Take a seat wherever you can find one, hon, I'll be along shortly to take your order," a lady with a nameplate that read Janice, instructed me as she hurried by with a tray of coffee and doughnuts.

I looked back over at Joel who was watching me and gestured to the empty seat across from his.

My mind immediately went to Joy and Tempest's reaction when they found out he was my landlord, but I quickly reminded myself that he'd done nothing to warrant any rudeness on my part.

Despite their apprehension, I figured this was a good opportunity to try and get more insight into whether I thought their response carried any weight.

Plus, I really needed coffee.

I made my way over, feeling his eyes on me as I crisscrossed around tables while trying to be ever vigilant of any sudden movements from other patrons.

My good sense will not be thwarted by your blue-green eyes and frowny brows, you magnificent biker beast.

"Good afternoon," he greeted in a smooth as hot honey drawl. I was glad that I was already halfway into the seat because I felt my knees completely give out.

Traitor knees.

My armor of detachedness was not as hefty as I'd hoped.

"Taking a break from work?" I inquired, proud of my cool, even tone.

"Yep, just grabbing something to eat. You?"

"I'm done for today," I replied reaching for a menu and unfolding it as though it were just as informative as his newspaper.

"Nice. Got any plans?"

"Not really, I was going to check out the bookstore downstairs, but that's about—"

I was interrupted by the feeling of fingers gently stroking my cheek and looked up to find him reaching across the table, his eyes focused on a spot as he gently swiped at something on my face.

"Sorry, you got flour or something on your cheek it was driving me crazy," he said before pulling away and leaning back coolly against his seat.

I'm gonna get thwarted, aren't I?

"Thank you," I said wiping the spot with my jacket sleeve which I could have passed off as catching anything he'd missed, but really it was to overpower the lingering sensation of his surprisingly gentle touch.

"Well if you're not doing anything, you should come by the garage. I have something there I think you'd be interested in."

Is he ...

I cocked an eyebrow at him and put down the menu, the edges of which were beginning to shake due to my quaking hands.

"You want to show me something at your garage?"

"What do you think I'm talking about?" he inquired, catching on to the fact that I clearly thought he was being suggestive.

"I'm not sure, but you should probably be specific to avoid any misunderstandings," I explained pointedly, folding my arms on the tabletop.

"Yeah, but that would spoil the surprise and I want to see your face when you see it." He smirked. "I think it's interesting that's where your mind went though," he added looking smug as hell. He was even more sexy when he was teasing me.

"Please, you're *clearly* flirting with me," I said in an attempt to shift the focus back to him, and I was mostly feigning arrogance, though it was obvious that there was at least a little mutual flirting going on.

"You think so?" he asked innocently.

"Really?" I scoffed. "*Sophie, come sit with me. Oh, Sophie, you have flour on your face, let me gently caress your cheek with my big, manly hands. Why don't you come to my garage so I can 'show you something'?*" I said impersonating him and punctuating the last three words with air bunnies.

Joel laughed as he crossed his arms over his chest and hung his head as though he'd been caught out and even though I knew we were joking around, I also believed that most jokes held some element of truth to them.

"You think I have big manly hands?" He grinned with amusement.

This was a very interesting shift in dynamic and I could feel myself being swept along in the most effortless of ways.

"Fine. I'll come to your garage, but try and control your feelings for me okay? I know it's hard," I requested haughtily as Joel's body continued to tremble with laughter.

I love it when he laughs ... no! No, you don't. His laugh is the laugh of a thwarting biker!

"I'll do my best." He chuckled holding up his palms submissively and just as I was thinking how well the banter had served to neutralize how nervous he made me, he added, "No promises though."

Hi. I work with the department of thwarters for the state. I'm here to serve you your thwarting papers. You've been thwarted.

Just then, Janice appeared at our table.

"Sorry for the wait, folks, you ready to order hon?"

"Ah ..." I looked at Joel who seemed to know that I was having trouble assembling my thoughts.

"You're good, we're not in a rush," he assured me.

"Can I have a cup of coffee and the farmer's feast breakfast wrap?"

"Home fries or shredded hash browns?"

"Shredded please, extra crispy," I requested, glancing up and noticing how closely Joel was watching me.

I turned back to Janice to avoid extended eye contact and held up the menu for her to collect.

"What about you, Joel?" she asked, but he shook his head and held up his hand.

"I think I'm good, just the check when you have a moment. Together is fine," he replied and I was so transfixed with the way he said the words that it almost escaped my attention that he was intending to pay for my meal.

"Comin' up, Joel," she said as I noted the way she interacted easily with him.

"Thank you, darlin'," he offered as she walked away.

Oh no! Why'd he have to say the 'D' word with that southern accent? I lamented, wilting into myself as I felt my heart taking over my head more each passing moment.

This was too easy, I needed to take a harder line with this guy.

I glanced up at him and though his expression was neutral, his features were so striking that every time he looked at me, I could only stand to return his gaze for a few seconds before buckling under the force of his presence.

What was it with this guy? Biker? I hadn't seen him on a bike. He didn't wear leathers or a patch.

I was going to obsess about this. I could already tell.

"So ..." I began when the din in the diner wasn't enough to quash the rising awkwardness as we sat silently. "What's new in the world of auto repairs?"

I was now officially Ralph Wiggum-ing him. *So, do you like ... stuff?*

My phone, though it was on silent, began vibrating and sliding across the table.

I didn't need to look at it, because I knew who it was, but it caught Joel's attention.

"You going to answer that?" he inquired when I made no move to reach for it.

"No, I'm happy to let my voicemail get this one," I responded cryptically.

"Clingy ex-boyfriend?" Joel guessed, and I scoffed at his response though I did get a little jolt from the slight bitterness in his words.

"No. Definitely not," I affirmed with a resolute lift of my eyebrows. "Television producer, but it's uh … it's a long story," I said, not sure I wanted to get into any matters pertaining to John Moxie right now.

I knew Joel was curious, but thankfully he refrained from seeking further information.

Janice arrived and placed my plate of food in front of me and a steaming cup of coffee which I reached for with the fervor of a cheese-addicted mouse.

I was aware of his attention on me as I poured sugar and cream into my coffee and a thought occurred to me then, to ask him about the night we met.

"So," I said using a spoon to stir up my coffee, "that night when you helped me off that weird road—" I began and was surprised when Joel immediately shifted in his seat and interrupted to apologize.

"Yeah, look, I'm really sorry about that, it's just … I was late to meet someone and …" He trailed off and I narrowed my eyes at him.

"Clingy ex-girlfriend?" I echoed his earlier question.

His response was identical to mine. "No. Definitely not."

I nodded in understanding and swore I saw a hint of guilt in his eyes as though he wanted to tell me, but couldn't. "It's a long story."

I wanted to press but refrained, based on the fact that it wouldn't be fair to make him explain when I had been as equally obscure in my response.

Conversation was sparse over the next fifteen minutes as I rushed to try and finish my food, anxious to see whatever it was he wanted to show me.

As I tried to suppress my hiccups from eating too fast, Joel insisted on paying for our food and soon we were ready to leave.

As we were walking toward our respective vehicles, Joel stopped me suddenly with his hand on my arm and I turned to him.

"You know, if you're not comfortable coming to my garage, I can just bring it into town when I come home later and—"

"No, no," I interrupted, impressed that he'd been self-aware enough to know how inviting me back to his garage might have come across. "It's fine really," I assured him. I couldn't explain it but I trusted that his intentions were innocuous. "Besides you've got me all curious now, I have to know what it is."

"Okay good, because I think you're going to really like it," he said with a knowing quality in his voice which made me wonder how he could be so sure about what I liked.

Leaving me intrigued, we both got into our respective cars, and Joel pulled out of the Nut House parking lot, with me following closely behind.

The first thing I noticed when we pulled into the garage parking lot was how big it was and the second thing I noticed was how run down it looked.

It was a nice garage, but years of harsh weather had dulled the light blue paint of the three-building structure, all the signs were rusted to the point where you could barely read them anymore, and one of the windows had been busted and boarded up, some time ago by the looks of the weather-stained wood.

I got out of my car and hated to think it, but it was no wonder people preferred to take their cars to the Winston brothers.

Comparatively speaking this was the "*Hotel California*" compared to the Winston's Shangri-La.

I was careful not to look like I was critiquing the state of the place as Joel got out of his truck and waved me over.

"This way," he said sifting through his keys until he found the one he was looking for.

We came to the third structure of the conjoined, three-part building, which had a much smaller sliding garage door than the larger middle structure which I guessed was where the actual shop was.

Joel crouched down and unlocked the garage door before sliding it upward, just enough for him to get himself back into a standing position.

"You ready?" he asked, glancing at me over his shoulder.

"I was born ready, baby," I responded through my chattering teeth.

I was freezing my ass off and crossed my arms over my chest to guard against the cold.

"You sure about that?" he asked with a twinkle in those eyes and proceeded to lift the garage door all the way up to reveal what we had driven here for him to show me.

There, parked inside the garage was a *pristine* 1969 Camaro Z28.

I felt my face fall free of all expression and my arms slackened and fell at my sides as my mouth gaped open when I saw her shiny, chrome majesty.

She was painted in burgundy red, with white racing stripes from front to back and chrome hubcaps so shiny, you could probably see every pore of your skin in them.

My eyes went to Joel who was waiting for my appraisal.

"What do you think?" Joel asked, watching me closely.

I was struggling to find words. My mouth fell open, but nothing came out except for a disbelieving scoff.

"I have a feeling you already know what I think," I said dreamily, stuffing my arms back under my arms so I wouldn't be tempted to reach out and touch her. I knew guys with cars not as grand as this one, who couldn't bear to have a single fingerprint on the paint job, but this was the only car that I felt warranted such obsessive care and I was careful to be respectful of that.

"Is this yours?" I asked peering up at Joel who nodded and stuffed his hands in his pockets with shy pride.

"She is," he said, his eyes sweeping over her as though my appreciation for her had become contagious.

"She is otherworldly," I sighed taking a few steps in Joel's direction to take in a different angle.

"You want to take her for a spin?" he asked producing a set of keys from his pocket, and my eyes snapped to his to see if he was serious. "You know how to drive stick, right?"

"Are you kidding? You'd really let me drive her?" I asked incredulously.

"Yeah," he shrugged as though it was no big deal. "Seems a shame not to share her with a fellow Camaro lover."

I looked back at the car apprehensively, not sure if I was ready for the responsibility of handling such an obviously cherished vehicle.

Oh, I wanted to drive her. I desperately wanted to get her out onto the open road and open her up to see what she could do, but I wasn't sure if I trusted myself enough to take it that far.

"I don't know," I said with uncertainty.

"Here, catch," Joel said, sending the car keys sailing through the air just as he had done with his apartment keys the first night I met him.

Terrified at the prospect of the keys landing on the car and nicking the paint, I gasped and reached out my hands to catch them shooting him a look after they landed safely in my palms.

"You really need to stop throwing keys at me," I informed him.

"You think too much. Right here, you have the car of your dreams waiting to be ridden hard and put away wet"—*Lord have mercy on my gutter-minded soul!*—"and all you can say is 'I don't know'?"

Joel was incredulous as he eyed me with his eyebrows raised.

"I just don't want to do anything to damage her," I explained.

"You won't," he replied with a confidence I didn't share before nudging his chin toward the driver's side. "Get in, let's go," he ordered leaving no room for negotiations as he opened the passenger's side door and got into the car.

Oh, my Newman. This is really happening. Okay.

I opened the driver's side door and slowly lowered myself into the seat, enjoying every second of the descent into a machine I'd dreamed about for over a decade.

Taking a moment to observe the lush, white leather interior and mahogany dash, there wasn't so much as a speck of dust to be found anywhere. She was very obviously well looked after.

"I can't believe you're letting me drive her."

"Neither can I after witnessing your driving skills," came Joel's retort and we both laughed as I flung out my arm to reprimand him for his jibe only to have my knuckles bounce off the unyielding roundness of his bicep.

Ridiculous arm muscles are ridiculous.

I let out a breath and smiled, turning to Joel who was waiting for me to kick into action.

"I just need a minute here. I might never get this opportunity again and I want to commit every detail to memory."

"Drink it in, I don't have anywhere to be. I knew you'd love her. As soon as you told me you loved Camaros I knew I had to show her to you." He smiled with a glimmer of pride in his eyes and once again I had to unhook myself from his gaze and look away.

"Nobody else cares for Camaros in Green Valley?" I inquired though I was mostly joking.

"Nobody I care to spend time with."

I couldn't help but wonder if he was referring to the Winston brothers, but didn't ask.

"I'll take it as a compliment," I said instead.

"It was intended as one," he replied, his candor catching me off guard.

Oh yeah. Yep, he's flirting.

I was of two minds about how I felt about that but decided the best way to get him to show me his true colors was to let me take his prized car out for a joyride and see if we were still friendly afterward.

With that in mind, I inserted the key into the ignition but paused before turning it.

"Oh, I almost forgot," I said reaching into my bag and retrieving my Mr. Newman lanyard which I kept on my person at all time, even when I was out of my car. "Do you mind?" I asked holding it up toward the rearview mirror but waiting for his permission before doing the honors.

"What is that?" he asked, taking the picture and inspecting it. "Why do you carry around a picture of the salad dressing guy?"

The salad dressing guy?

I turned to stare at him for what seemed like an inordinate amount of time.

"What?" He shrugged, the corner of his lips quirking, and I couldn't tell if he was just trying to rile me up or not. "Is it like a good luck charm?"

"Sort of. It's like Thor's hammer. It's not the source of my power, it just helps me focus, it helps me think, make decisions, and stay calm."

He nodded in understanding though his eyes twinkled with what looked like suppressed amusement and I felt suddenly self-conscious about it. I reached for the lanyard again. "It's silly, never mind."

"Wait," he said grasping the fabric loop as I tugged on the other end. "I'm sorry. I wasn't making fun of it. I wasn't. Lord knows people have hung weirder shit than this on their cars. I get it … it's just … cute."

Cute?

His voice was gentle and insistent and the earnest way he made eye contact made me feel certain beyond a shadow of a doubt that he meant it, but cute?

I sat held in place by his eyes, completely unable to recall, in that moment, all the rumors about him that I was supposed to be so cautious of.

I needed a mood shift. The air turned heavy around this guy in no time flat and I still didn't know enough about him to feel okay with being swept along by the tide.

"Okay fine, just … don't call him the salad dressing guy, jeez have some respect," I scolded him playfully.

I felt relief when he laughed and rolled his eyes. I reminded myself to breathe which I found challenging in a small enclosed space with his all-consuming presence.

There was definitely some kind of hum between us. I felt it the first time I met him, which at the time, had been easy to write off as a passing fancy. But each time since then, it became a little more pronounced until I couldn't deny its presence.

My good sense made a timely appearance then, reminding me of all the reasons why I should take more care to put a tight lid on this developing flirtation, no matter how harmless it might seem.

There was the issue of his apparent aversion the Winston brothers which could be awkward for me considering I was now working for one of their wives. And there was the secondary issue of my time in Green Valley being finite.

But now was not the time to dwell on such matters.

If I got nothing else out of Joel Barnes, I was going to take advantage of having the steering wheel of a 1969 Chevy Camaro Z28 at my fingertips.

"Okay, here we go," I said, taking a breath before reaching below the dash to turn the key in the ignition. My eardrums rattled and powerful vibrations rippled all through my body as she roared thunderously to life and an irrepressible smile stretched across my face.

"Listen to her purr," I marveled glancing briefly at Joel who seemed to be enjoying my reactions.

I put her in gear and then slowly released the clutch, feeling her emergence from the garage like a dragon coming out of her lair.

I steered her carefully out of the parking lot and onto the road, attempting not to get too excited with her while also reminding myself to seize this moment while I had it.

As we drove along, I could feel her heft, and how the tires seemed to stick to the road like Velcro.

"Damn, she's heavy," I remarked feeling ourselves sway at her mercy as we went around a bend.

"Yeah, that's what makes these cars a bit tricky to handle. It takes some practice if you really want to have fun with them," Joel explained as we neared an intersection.

"Uh, I don't really know where I'm going," I said, looking to him for direction.

"Just keep following the road until we come to the highway ... then you can really open her up," he said with a lopsided grin.

"You're being so calm, I can't believe you're so calm right now. I can't believe I'm driving a Camaro, I feel like Vin Diesel would be so proud of me."

"Do you think Vin Diesel rides the clutch?" he replied sarcastically, and I immediately removed my foot from the pedal.

"I'm not," I lied, not sure how he could tell that I was. He laughed, seeing through my ruse and turned back toward the windscreen as we sat in silence while he allowed me to become acquainted with the car.

"There's the ramp onto the highway," he instructed, pointing up ahead.

I followed it on, and gradually switched gears until we were cruising along at the pace I felt comfortable I could handle but craving more.

I was barely even tapping what she could do, and if a car could be bored, I thought that's what she must be feeling under my control.

You took me out for this? I could practically hear her say, but I was too aware of my inexperience to take any chances, especially since she wasn't mine.

"How does she feel?" Joel asked as I bit my lip while concentrating on the completely deserted road ahead of us.

"Like we need some time to get to know each other," I responded before glancing over at him beside me. "But I am *dying* to see what she can really do."

CHAPTER 10

"Alright, Miss Sophie, so far you've nailed a burnout and a doughnut, now it's time to kick it up a notch with a J-turn, you ready?"

I wasn't. I had actually nearly lost my bowel function during the doughnut, but I figured carpe diem and all that.

"Sure," I said unconvincingly, hearing my voice crack with nerves.

My heart was beating alarmingly fast from the previous maneuvers that Joel had talked me through, so sure that I was going to mess up and ruin this beautiful piece of modern, driveable art.

"You're doing just fine, don't be nervous," he assured me with a confident smile. "It's really easy, all you're going to do is throw her in reverse and floor it until you have enough momentum. Get your left hand into position at about 4:30," he explained tapping the spot on the steering wheel which I obediently gripped. "Keep your right hand on the gearshift. Then you're gonna let up on the gas and crank the wheel as fast as you can. Once you're at about ninety degrees, you're going to let the steering wheel turn through your fingers until we've done a complete one-eighty turn. That's it, that's all there is to it."

He made it sound like nothing, and though I understood his instructions, I couldn't get the idea out of my head that I would mess up the timing or get confused and spin out of control.

"Don't think too much. Get out of your head. Repeat the instructions back to me," he said leaning forward slightly to catch my eyes.

"Put her in reverse, let her get some momentum, hands in position, let go of the gas, and crank the wheel, then let her straighten up when she hits ninety degrees."

"You've totally got this," he scoffed as though he were instructing me on a task as benign as folding a towel or cracking an egg. Like the idea that there might be a consequence if things went wrong didn't even occur to him.

Every time I started to put the car in reverse, my muscles locked up and I could feel Joel's eyes on me, waiting for me to break out of my fear-induced paralysis.

"Maybe, you could do one first," I suggested.

"No," he said with a gentle, but firm manner. "You have all the information you need, you just have to clear your mind of everything except the instructions. You got this, I am not in any way, shape, or form concerned that you're going to mess this up."

"I appreciate the vote of confidence, but I tend to save my best fuck-ups for moments just like this," I snorted and then instantly regretted it.

"What do you mean?" he asked curiously, but I shook my head dismissively. Now wasn't the time to rehash my *No Whisk, No Reward* failure.

"It's nothing just … damn my heart is beating so fast," I laughed nervously, and before I knew what I was doing I took his hand and pressed it right over my heart.

Well done, Sophie, just make him grab your tit. For Newman's sake, what is wrong with you?

Joel blinked slowly, his smile soft and sympathetic as my heart thundered under his palm.

"S-sorry," I sputtered. "That was a weird thing to do," I said letting go of his hand, but instead of removing it, he shifted his hand to my shoulder.

"Hey," he said softly, "take a breath and relax. You got nothing to be scared of, I promise. If I feel like you're gonna spin out, I'll reach over and grab the wheel. I got you."

His tender encouragement made my whole body melt and as I looked over at him I started feeling my body fight against trying to lean toward him.

Oh no, no, no. That's not happening. Quick, do the J-turn before you embarrass yourself. Or at least spare the embarrassment for a fucked-up J-turn.

"Okay, Barnes, hold onto your potatoes, because I'm about to do a J-turn."

"Show me what you got, Copeland."

I took exactly one second to switch my brain off from everything, including how goddamn sexy Joel Barnes was, shifted the stick into reverse, and floored it.

I was barely present for what transpired over the next few seconds, except for my vision blurring as the car spun, and the sound of my own voice screaming "Oh my God! Oh my God! Oh my God!" over and over again.

Somehow, the next thing I knew, we were facing 180 degrees in the opposite direction and a thick cloud of dust was sailing around us on all sides of the car.

The inside of the car was silent except for my panting, but when I looked over at Joel he wore a wide, proud smile.

"Did I just do a fucking J-turn?"

"Yeah, you damn did." Joel laughed as my mouth dropped open in a smile and my eyes widened.

"I did a J-Turn in a *Camaro,*" I exclaimed with irrepressible joy, bouncing in my seat as though I had accomplished some kind of miracle.

Joel laughed indulgently at my enthusiasm and nudged his chin toward the windshield.

"What do you think? You want to switch and let me show you what else she can do, or are you good for the da—"

He had barely finished the sentence before I scrambled to get out of the driver's side.

"More reckless driving! More!"

Over the next hour or so Joel tore down a deserted stretch of highway, showing off his incredible car handling skills to within an inch of my bowel control.

Without breaking a sweat, he commandeered the Camaro through snaking twists and turbocharged turns that had me clutching at whatever my hands could find to hold onto, including his thigh at one point. By the time he decided he'd shown off enough, I was hoarse from all the wild scream/laughing and tuckered out from a level of excitement I hadn't experienced in … well, ever.

Despite the hair-raising maneuvers, I felt completely safe in Joel's experienced hands and not for one moment did I fear that he might be carelessly pushing his own known limits and risk losing control. He just shredded down that highway, cool as you like, with a laser-like focus and a faint smile on his lips determined to give me the ride of my life.

As we headed back into town, I was a puddle in the passenger's seat beside him, wearing a smile I couldn't wipe off my face.

Joel kept looking at me and laughing at my boneless, speed-induced drunkenness.

"How was that? Did you have fun?" he asked, and I loved the way he sounded when he said it.

"That was incredible. Where did you learn to drive like that?" I asked turning toward him slightly in my seat, so I could just look at him.

"Just being a meathead in my younger days, I guess," he said casually. Even though we were still going pretty fast, it definitely felt more subdued after the crazy stunts Joel had performed.

"Will we get to go out again?" I asked, holding my hands together and giving him my best pleading expression.

"We have to." He shrugged like we had no choice. "We gotta build up your speed on those J-turns."

"I still can't believe I did that. I still can't believe you trusted me enough to. That was seriously the most fun I've had since … psshhh … I don't even know when," I said trying to remember when I last experienced something so thoroughly exhilarating.

"Maybe I can teach you a couple more tricks before the winter sets in," he suggested. "We gotta get you ready for the day when you finally get your own Camaro." I sighed, fantasizing at the thought.

"One day I am going to have a Camaro just like this," I vowed running my hand along the mahogany dash in reverence.

"Maybe I can bequeath you mine," he suggested in jest.

"Sure, you can do that. Just go ahead and update your will and you definitely will *not* die a sudden and mysterious death," I said in a monotonous tone that suggested I had ulterior motives. When Joel laughed that time, I really noticed the deep, rich rumble that emanated from within his chest.

"You have a lovely laugh," I complimented him. "You should laugh all the time." I avoided eye contact when I said it, because once it was out of my mouth, I realized it probably sounded flirty and perhaps and a little intimate.

"That's a nice compliment, thank you," he said graciously.

"Also, your accent is really," I almost said "sexy" but quickly changed it to, "charming."

"Charming, really?" he asked, brows furrowing skeptically. "I think I sound like trash, but thank you, I'll take it."

He's so humble.

"I have a thing for southern accents," I explained wondering why was I suddenly incapable of keeping thoughts like that inside of my head, where they should stay.

"Well you're in the right place for that," he returned. Thankfully it didn't seem like he had read too much into it.

"So, when we first met, I asked you about what people do around here for fun and you said they go out to eat, drink, and dance," I began with the intention to try and get him to open up a little more.

"Yup, that's about the extent of things to do around here," he said before tilting his head thoughtfully. "Well … there's hiking. There's a lot of trails around here," he suggested which made me grumble and curl my lip.

"Not a hiker?" he asked tossing me a sideways glance.

"Nope. *Way* too much nature out there. And bears," I added with a fearful expression in my eyes.

"Yes, ma'am, there are a lot of bears in the mountains."

"So, I was looking on the internet for stuff in Green Valley and I found the bar you and I met at," I said, tapping my finger as though I was going to start listing things off.

"That's right, Genie's, they have dancing, darts, and pool tables."

"Okay, and the Pink Pony, which is very clearly a titty bar," I said tapping my second finger.

"Which you probably wouldn't care for much," he guessed.

"Why not? Because I'm a woman?" I challenged, as Joel turned to regard me with an uncertain expression.

"I don't know, I guess." He shrugged looking like he was worried he might have said the wrong thing.

"Au contraire, my friend, I happen to very much support a well-managed establishment which provides a fair, safe, and clean environment for adult performers, which all the reviews online say the Pink Pony does, so maybe I *will* check it out," I informed him.

"Alright no need to get your panties in a twist, I just wasn't aware that it was ... you know ... your thing," he said in a tone that I needed to let sink in before I realized what he was implying.

"Oh no, I am not gay," I clarified. "Although sometimes I wish I was, because I think it would easier to find a partner if I was," I said twisting my lips to the side with disappointment.

"Yeah, tell me about it," Joel grumbled in a response that now had me looking at him in confusion.

"What?" he asked.

"Nothing, I guess I just ..." I realized that I had misjudged him the same way he'd misjudged me.

"Go on, finish the sentence, it's okay," he encouraged me with a laugh.

"Well now I feel terrible, but I just thought, you know since you're

... a white, straight man in a small town, that you might be ..." I fumbled my way through the entire explanation before finally blowing out a frustrated breath.

"A homophobe?"

I cringed at myself and looked over at Joel sheepishly.

"Well ... yeah. Sorry," I said cringing softly as he smiled reassuringly at me.

"Don't apologize, it's quite alright. Now, let's get back to your list."

"Oh right," I said remembering what we were talking about before we got sidetracked. "Someone said something about a Dragon Bar."

"Don't go anywhere near there," he practically ordered, and I noted his sudden and very serious expression.

"Why? Is it gross?" I asked curiously.

"It's not *gross,* it's dangerous. It's the local biker hangout. You don't want to go anywhere near there, trust me."

I considered what Joel had just said, trying to reconcile it with what Tempest and Joy had told me about Joel being mixed up with them.

"Have you ever been there?" I asked sounding casually curious even though I was totally fishing for more information.

"No," Joel scoffed and shook his head as though what I'd just asked was ridiculous.

"Oh, I see. It's just, a couple of girls at work were telling me about how much the Winstons hate the Iron Wraiths and since you and the Winstons don't care for one another, I just ..." I watched his eyes cloud over more with each passing second, "... came to what is *clearly* the wrong conclusion," I finished sheepishly.

"Yep," Joel grunted, his expression firm and his disposition tense.

I couldn't work it out entirely but given his reaction to the mere suggestion that he might be an Iron Wraith, I thought it safe to assume at this point that he wasn't one of them.

"I need to apologize, again don't I?" I asked gently, feeling as though I had offended him.

"No need," he said curtly, reminding me of the first night I'd met him and how short he'd been with me.

A few minutes of awkward silence passed between us until Joel's mouth opened and he yawned, covering his mouth as a rumbly growl emanated from behind his palm.

"Pardon me," he said absently to himself.

"Late night?" I inquired conversationally, trying to get him talking again and vowing not to mention the Wraiths again.

"Yeah, just working," he replied, which was an answer I did not expect.

I wanted to ask more, but I didn't want to interrogate him, so instead, I decided to invite him to Genie's at the end of the week.

"So, a couple of girls at work are taking me out for drinks on Friday night. I'd love it if you came along."

I don't know why I invited him, considering I was supposed to be cautious but the more time I spent with him, the less I started to believe that I had anything to worry about.

"Thank you, I appreciate the invite, but I don't want to impose," he offered politely.

"It's not really an imposition if I'm inviting you, is it?" I challenged, not wanting to let him off the hook.

"I guess not," he smiled briefly before looking down at his hands. "Still, I don't think it's a good idea. Hanging around with me is liable to start gossip and I don't want you to have to deal with all of that."

"Well, first off, I appreciate your concern for my reputation, but I'm not really one of those people who has hang-ups about what others think about me, and second of all why would people start gossiping about me, just because I'm hanging out with you?"

"Just stupid small-town stuff," Joel responded, his vague answer not really giving me much to go on.

"I'm not worried," I assured him. "Besides, I'm only here for like eight weeks and then I'll be leaving all that gossip in a cloud of dust behind me. Come on, come with us, it will be fun," I said reaching over to touch his arm and gently shake him in a cajoling fashion.

Finally, Joel smiled a genuine smile even though he shook his head uncertainly.

"I don't know," he said undecidedly. "Who are your friends from work? Anyone I know?"

"Tempest Cassidy and Joy Jones," I responded, hoping he didn't have any beef with them.

"Tempest Cassidy?" Joel asked incredulously.

"Yeah, why?" I asked wondering why everyone in this town said everybody else's name as though they were asking, "Really? Them?"

"Nothin' just … You're so different than her … personality wise I mean," he explained.

"Yeah, I know, she kinda scares me a little, which I think is the reason why I like her so much," I replied, and Joel seemed to be amused with my explanation.

"What?" I asked waiting for him to explain what was so funny, though I was glad to see him laughing again even if it was at my expense.

"Nothing it's just … I don't think I've ever met anyone quite like you before."

"I'll take that as a compliment."

"Good, it was meant as one." He grinned, casting me a quick glance from the driver's seat before turning his attention back to the road.

"So, does that mean you'll come with us?" I asked him again, not wanting to let him off the hook and not sure why it was so important to me that he be there.

"I'll think about it," came his noncommittal response and I supposed that would have to suffice for now.

"Okay, well I guess that will have to do for now, but just so you know, I have your phone number so I'll probably just text you incessantly until you agree to come," I informed him, but he smiled like he really didn't seem to mind.

"Thanks for taking me for my first ever ride in a Camaro," I said, and Joel turned to glance at me wide-eyed.

"Your first time in a Camaro? This is the first time?" he asked incredulously.

"Yeah," I confirmed with a nod.

"How can you be so obsessed with them if you've never even been in one before now?"

"Well," I began on a sigh, staring thoughtfully out into the distance as though I were recalling some life-changing memory. "You see, Joel, it all started with *2 Fast 2 Furious ...*"

CHAPTER 11

*A*s far as small towns went, Green Valley was one of the happier locales that I had visited on my travels over the past few weeks. Aesthetically, it was a pretty town, where people took pride in their houses and made an effort at every opportunity to promote the rich history of the area as well capitalize on its proximity to the Great Smoky Mountains.

I personally wasn't much of a nature enthusiast, but you had to have a heart of stone not to be moved by the sight of the mountains in the distance shrouded by the foggy clouds of mist, that inspired the range's name.

During the fall, the endless sea of elevated spruce trees wore a frosty, silver tinge but on clear days, they glowed with the breathtaking pinks and oranges of the sunrise and sunset. Hues that made you want to become a recluse and spend your life chasing an endless autumn, floating around from cabin to cabin, snuggled up with a never-ending supply of books and hot chocolate somewhere in the midst of all that incredible foliage.

Perhaps it was just the propinquity to the holiday season, but I got the sense that locals went to a lot of effort to ensure that its residents had ample opportunity to get together for social gatherings. There were weekend markets at the local elementary school, entertainment events at the community center, and all around town, I spotted posters appealing to residents to sign up as vendors for the inaugural Green Valley Christmas Market.

Yet despite all that, ever since being informed of Green Valley's insidious underbelly, there was an ever-present hint of something a little darker and more dangerous than just bears and mountain lions despite all that natural wonder and charm. I wasn't so naïve to think that Green Valley was a perfectly quaint, sleepy little town. Even though everyone did, in fact, know everyone's name, after just one week, I already had gained insight into who were the gossip mongers, the deadbeats, and now the local biker gang that marred the otherwise peaceful town.

Thanks to Joy and Tempest, who'd educated me on the existence of the Iron Wraiths, I started to notice them a lot more in my comings and goings. Like a word you'd never heard before and then suddenly you start hearing it everywhere.

It was nothing as overt as a procession of deafening Harleys or street brawls in broad daylight, but now that their presence had been brought to my attention, I was more aware of the distant rumble of a motorcycle or the occasional presence of an imposing form wearing riding leathers and a patch at the Piggly Wiggly stocking up on frozen burritos and boxes of beer.

They certainly seemed to have an air about them, walking around with that *answer to nobody* brand of arrogance that seemed both ridiculous and dramatic at the same time. But I guess people either feared or revered that kind of thing.

I tried to reconcile the bikers I saw around town with the rumors that Joy and Tempest had shared with me at work. Although I knew it wasn't completely outside the realm of possibility that Joel could somehow be associated with them, it just didn't seem to gel in any way that I could make sense of and I was beginning to fixate on my inability to get to the bottom of it.

It was true he had more or less denied being a member of the locally infamous club, but the more I thought about it, the more I wondered if he had only been *technically* honest.

I recalled on my first day when Joy had mentioned that Joel didn't wear riding leathers or a club patch, but that didn't mean that he wasn't involved with them some other way.

I thought about coming right out and asking him if he was involved with the Wraiths in *any* capacity, but I wasn't sure that he was comfortable enough with me yet, despite the obvious mutual flirtation during our last few encounters. I also wasn't naïve enough to confuse sexual attraction with being truly intimate and honest with someone. He didn't owe me the truth even though I hoped he felt he could be honest with me.

I was also cognizant of the fact that I was basically in Green Valley for less than eight weeks. Even though that was plenty of time for a lot of things to happen, I knew the time would pass by in a blip and I wasn't so sure that it was a great idea to become attached to Joel or allow him to become attached to me.

The problem was that every time I was near him, I felt this inescapable draw toward him like we were connecting on some unspoken, unseen level that I had not experienced with a guy before. It was really hard not to get carried away by it.

It had been a few days since our joyride in the Camaro and I hadn't seen him around all that much, but I texted him on a regular basis just as I had threatened to do in an attempt to get him to join me, Tempest, and Joy at Genie's.

Joy and Tempest indulged my having invited him along, after I explained to them that seeing him in a social setting, interacting with others, might give us more of an insight into whether or not he was into anything shady. What I really hoped for, was for them to see that he was actually a polite, kind man who seemed to just need a little help connecting with others.

He was on my mind when I arrived at work on Friday morning and entered the bakery to find a very flustered Jennifer scurrying around with Blithe Tanner, who appeared equally, if not more, ruffled.

"What's going on?" I asked, furrowing my brow as I cautiously approached.

"Oh." Blithe laughed nervously. "Just a last-minute order for five hundred assorted cupcakes, you know how it is," she said trying to make it sound like a joke, but her voice shook.

"What do you need to me do?" I asked immediately pushing thoughts of Joel from my mind as I took purposeful strides across the kitchen toward the lockers to put away my belongings.

"If you can start on as many of the breads and pastries as you can until the others get here, that would be great, otherwise we won't have anything to open the store with," Jennifer requested with a calm, but firm resoluteness to her voice as she leaned forward, using her entire bodyweight to cut into an industrial sized slab of butter with a wire.

"I'm on it," I responded, making my way to the proofing cabinets to begin work.

When Joy and Tempest arrived, I'd just put baguettes and loaves of sourdough bread into the oven and was busy laminating sheets of pastry for the croissants and Danishes.

"What's all this? What's happening?" Tempest inquired, noticing that everyone was rushing around with very focused, determined expressions.

"We got a last-minute special order for five hundred assorted cupcakes for a special event taking place at the Donner Lodge. We need all hands on deck and we need cake for the store, can you and Joy take care of that?" Blithe requested so politely I shook my head slightly at her grace under pressure.

What a departure from the brash, surly restaurant environment I was used to.

Some days I felt like working at the Donner Bakery was like enjoying a visit to the local spa compared to the testosterone-fueled, impetuous arrogance of Paradigm.

"Yes, ma'am, Joy, you and me. Cake conga line. Let's do this," she said snapping her fingers and pointing to the steel benches where the cake assembly team usually worked.

"Ooh, I love a good conga line!" Joy exclaimed to nobody's surprise.

"Can we get some music going in here? What is this, a funeral?" Jennifer asked piping strawberry jam into the center of cupcake after cupcake with all the speed and efficiency of any professional chef I'd ever worked with. That woman could really motor.

Someone somewhere flicked on the radio and though it wasn't loud, it did enough to liven up the mood at that ungodly hour and gave everyone an extra pep in their step as they hauled ass with extra motivation to accomplish in eight hours what they would normally need twelve to thirteen hours to complete.

I was portioning, notching, and rolling croissant dough at a nearby bench when I heard Joy and Tempest start a conversation that sounded very interesting indeed.

"I heard Simone and Roscoe are here for Thanksgiving," Tempest mentioned quietly.

"I can't believe they would want to come back here after everything that happened," Joy whispered back incredulously as she slowly shook her head.

"Well, it's their home. Nobody has the right to make you too afraid to come back home," Tempest reasoned with a shrug.

"I know nobody has the *right* to, but I wouldn't dream of sticking around here for one minute longer after what happened to that poor guy. I can't imagine what his recovery was like."

"No, you never really heal from something like that," Tempest agreed.

"What about Billy Winston? Taking off like that and leaving Dani Payton without a word. I did not think he was like that."

"Their relationship was sketchy anyway, and besides, I heard that Dani was still making time for Catfish Hickson."

"Somehow, I think that's over now after his cohorts almost killed her sister," Joy said sounding doubtful about it.

"Well you never know. Look at Bethany Winston, who woulda thought a woman like that would end up with a dog like Darrell Winston."

This was getting too complicated to keep up with so instead of just tuning out and minding my own business, I leaned back, and stage whispered, "What are we whispering about?"

"Oh." Joy giggled, when she turned over her shoulder and saw it was just me. "Just talking about how Roscoe, Simone, and Dani are back in town for Thanksgiving is all."

"Oh, nice." I paused for a moment before asking, "And who are they?"

Joy laughed and shook her head.

"Oh my, Sophie. You know sometimes I forget that you're not from here and that you don't know who everyone is."

"Oh well thank you, I'll take that as a compliment," I said continuing to form croissant after croissant.

"Roscoe is Cletus's baby brother and Simone and Dani are the daughters of Daisy Payton," Tempest explained as I made the connection in my mind.

"Oh, you mean like Daisy's Nut House, Daisy?"

"One and the same. The Paytons are kind of a big deal around here, though you'd never know it to meet them. Really good, salt of the earth type of folks. They have a brother too, Poe, but I haven't seen him in town now that I'm thinking on it," Joy said, staring up at the ceiling as if trying to recall whether or not she'd seen him around.

"Anyway," she said after a moment, "the Paytons and the Olivers were kind of the backbone of Green Valley back in the day. The Winston's momma was an Oliver," she explained as I attempted to connect the dots.

"Okay, so Winston is the last name of this Darrell character who married Bethany, who we don't like? Right?" I asked trying to see if I had it straight in my head.

"No, ma'am, that Darrell Winston is a boil on the ass of Green Valley. He was a senior ranking member of the Iron Wraiths for decades," Tempest explained, and my eyes flew open in shock.

"Stop it! Are you kidding me?"

"*Shhh*," both women cautioned me as I cringed and mouthed the word *sorry,* looking around to make sure I hadn't drawn any attention to us.

"Nope. Serious as syphilis," Joy confirmed continuing on where we'd left off.

"I thought you said the Winstons didn't want anything to do with the Wraiths," I stated, recalling our earlier conversation on the subject.

"Okay, here are the basics of what you need to know," Tempest said ready to break it down for me. "You got the Paytons and the Olivers. Forget the Paytons for now, we'll come back to 'em. Bethany Oliver, Cletus's momma, married Darrell Winston. Classic tale of good girl meets bad boy, you get the picture. So, they have a bunch of babies—"

"Seven to be exact," Joy added with her eyebrows raised and mine followed suit.

"Wait, Cletus has six siblings?" I asked incredulously, not able to imagine what that house must have been like.

"I know right? Poor Bethany, rest her soul. Anyway, so fast forward to all the kids being grown up. Simone, the youngest Payton is cozy with Roscoe who is the Winston's youngest, and not too long ago, Daniella, the middle Payton, was engaged to Cletus's brother Billy. It's a long story, but Billy was a Tennessee state congressman and most people weren't really buying them as a couple. Pretty much everybody knew it was because Dani wanted to get into politics. Still does probably. Anyway, that didn't last long."

"This is like a television series! What happened after that? I heard you saying something about how someone almost killed Simone and Roscoe?"

"Oh, you don't know the half of it," Joy said with a deep rumble of a laugh, her eyes wide as she blew out a breath to indicate that there was so much more to the story than I could possibly know. Before I could ask any questions, Tempest took a hold of the helm and steered our focus back on course.

"That's another story, for another time. We'll fill you in later, but right now we got work to do if we have any hope of getting this order fulfilled and having anything to serve to our customers."

I felt disappointed to have to move along right when it was getting good, but I knew Tempest was right.

Before leaving them, I leaned closer to them over the bench and whispered, "Don't forget, I invited Joel to drinks tonight. I hope you don't mind."

I watched their faces carefully and could see them both tensing a little.

"I don't mind, but are you sure it's a good idea?" Tempest asked, frowning with concern.

"Why wouldn't it be?" I asked, wanting them to give me a solid reason why I should doubt my own judgment. I was getting to a place where I was starting to need more than hearsay to justify everyone's insistence that I be careful with Joel.

"Well you know, it's just that he's kind of ..." Joy began to say but couldn't seem to finish the sentence.

"Shy? Reserved? Withdrawn?" I asked, helping her thought along, but all she did was twist her face and look skyward as though my suggestions hadn't quite fit and she was working on a more accurate alternative.

I decided that it didn't even matter.

"I assure you both that I am being very careful, just as you've advised, but he has been nothing but kind to me since I have arrived and so far, neither he, nor anyone else has given me a good, solid reason as to why I shouldn't ... hang out with him."

I caught them glancing toward one another briefly which made me hurry to explain further.

"I just mean, you know ... I'm not so delicate that if this blows up in my face I won't be able to move on with my life. I'm just here temporarily, I'm not going to marry the guy." I snorted, shaking my head as though the idea was preposterous.

"Okay," they said in unison and I lifted my chin to find them both staring back at me with raised eyebrows and pursed lips.

"Just be nice to him, please? Unless he expressly gives you a reason not to be, can you both please promise to be civil?"

"Alright, fine," Tempest agreed, albeit begrudgingly. "But one false move on his part …" She held a finger up in the air, her green eyes expressing that she was very clearly issuing a warning.

"If he gives you an excuse, then by all means, have at him," I agreed waving my hand through the air, though I wondered what Tempest might consider an "excuse."

We refocused and returned our attention back to stocking the bakery knowing that opening hours were nipping right at our heels and that a line of customers would already have started forming outside.

By eleven that morning, there were stacks of pink boxes lined up by the door just in time to be picked up by a staff member at The Donner Lodge who would deliver them right to the resort. Forty-one of them to be exact.

I had taken over the cake assembly, trimming, filling, and frosting the four-layer carrot cake with cream cheese frosting. Joy and Tempest got to work on restocking muffins and tarts. Blithe was out front, taking care of service with a couple other members of staff. I glanced around, trying to spot Jennifer. I found her standing by the back door talking to a breathtakingly gorgeous woman who had a presence that made it hard not to stare.

Just as I was wondering who she was, Tempest passed behind me with a stack of dirty muffin tins and whispered, "Speak of the devil. That's Dani Payton," and hurried off to drop the muffin tins in one of the nearby industrial sinks.

As Jennifer and Daniella sailed by my bench, talking in hushed tones to one another, I busied myself applying a crumb layer of frosting to one of the eight cakes that I had to dress before getting started on the berry stack and compassion cakes, which I would have to complete before leaving.

"Oh, my goodness, Jenn, your team works so fast. Look at how quickly you're icing that cake."

I looked up, right into the engrossed face of Daniella Payton who was inspecting my efficient cake dressing skills with her mouth open in awe.

"Yes, Sophie, in particular, is very proficient, being quite an accomplished pastry chef from Washington state. She spent five years working at Paradigm with chef Julian Lefebvre." Daniella's eyes widened in surprise as everyone's did when someone mentioned my ex-boss' name.

"Wow, that is very impressive," Daniella offered. "Hello, Sophie, nice to meet you. I'm Daniella Payton," she introduced herself, holding out her hand to me which I immediately accepted.

"It's nice to meet you too. Your mom makes wicked doughnuts," I said, and she laughed graciously at my awkward compliment.

"Well thank you very much. Wow, you worked with Julian Lefebvre, I can't imagine how much invaluable experience you must have gained under his employ. That's quite impressive," she offered which always prompted mixed feelings, but I pushed aside the less pleasant ones and focused instead on my usual, complimentary response.

"It was a great working experience, I'm proud of what I was able to accomplish there. Have you been to Paradigm?" I inquired, continuing to work as I maintained the conversation.

"I haven't been to Paradigm. I don't get out west all that much, but I have always wanted to go. I *did* have the pleasure of attending one of Chef Lefebvre's pop-up restaurants in New York a few years back, and it was just extraordinary. I am still dreaming about it," Daniella swooned as I felt the same odd sense of pride tinged with bitterness thinking about how things ended with my old boss.

"Oh well, I'm sure he'd be pleased to hear how much you enjoyed it," I said still offering platitudes on his behalf because it was way too awkward to tell people what really happened. Despite the fact that I didn't leave on the best terms, it was still a bridge that I was not prepared to burn.

"Well," Daniella said turning to Jennifer and gesturing to me with her hands, "Jennifer, it looks like you're in good hands here," she said before turning her attention back to me. "Sophie, it was a pleasure to meet you, I'm going to get out of your hair so you can continue making these incredible cakes."

"Oh well, thanks for stopping by, it was a pleasure to meet you too."

When she was gone, all I could think about was how her presence continued to linger even when she was no longer within sight.

She had the kind of gravitas that you would usually associate with people in very powerful positions, and I could very much see her not only pursuing, but also succeeding in the political endeavors that Joy and Tempest had mentioned earlier.

I would not be the least bit surprised if I turned on the television one day and saw her addressing the nation.

Sometimes you didn't need to know a person in order to be able to sense certain things about them, and you had to be deaf and blind not to see that Daniella Payton was a force of nature.

I didn't have siblings, but my mind dwelled on what Joy had said about Daniella being involved with an Iron Wraith who had almost killed her sister. All I could do was speculate on the reasons why.

I was careful not to judge Daniella, seeing how I was not privy to the intricacies of the Payton family dynamic or any other family dynamic for that matter. What I did know was that relationships, just like the people that built and broke them, were complicated.

Speaking of complicated, as I absentmindedly powered through my work, my mind inevitably returned to Joel and I felt a smile tug at my lips.

Despite texting with him fairly regularly that week, he seemed to keep avoiding answering when I mentioned Genie's and I was determined to keep my promise to pester him about it until he did.

I retrieved my phone and began sending him a text.

Me: What time will you be escorting me to Genie's tonight? Can we take your Camaro? Can I drive it? You said I could. Also, just so you know, if you don't let me, it doesn't make you a bad person, it just makes you kind of a person who says they're going to do something, and then you don't.

I was not above using guilt to get him to relent.

I pocketed my phone because he usually took a while to respond, but after only a few minutes, I felt my phone vibrating in my back pocket.

I retrieved it and inspected the screen. His response was succinct and did not answer most of my questions, but it made me smile nonetheless because it answered the most important one. The one I was most invested in him responding to.

Joel: See you at seven.

CHAPTER 12

*J*oel, Tempest, Joy, and I were huddled together in a booth at Genie's Country Western Bar to celebrate the successful completion of my first week at the Donner Bakery.

Joy and Tempest had promised to be on their best behavior, which by their approximation, apparently meant sitting awkwardly and making little to no attempt to involve Joel in conversation. In fact, they were barely talking.

Joel was doing his part to try and engage them despite it being clear, to me at least, that he regretted agreeing to come. He asked how our work week had been and whether or not we had plans for the weekend, but all he received in response was a lot of shrugging and monosyllabic responses.

I, of course, allowing the discomfiting exchange to get to me, managed to overcompensate by talking for ten minutes straight about how I had thought about going hiking, but then remembered that I hated hiking, and nature. So, I decided instead, that I was going to binge watch something but couldn't decide on what. Then I was thinking about going to Nashville but didn't want to go alone, which finally prompted a response from Joy.

"Can you believe I have never been to Nashville? I've been to Memphis, Knoxville, and Chattanooga, but never to Nashville."

"Well that does it, hand in your Tennesseean card, right now," Tempest joked, holding her palm out to Joy who swatted her away.

"Shush and go get me another drink," Joy commanded playfully. Tempest raised her eyebrows and planted her palms down on the table, preparing to leave to oblige her friend's request.

"Gladly," she snorted as though she couldn't wait to get away and rose from her seat.

"I'll join you," I told her, seeing an opportunity to have a private word with her.

Ignoring the barely veiled terror in Joy's eyes at the prospect of being left alone with Joel, I trusted her to be more civil with him in a quiet moment alone than I did Tempest.

The two of us made our way to the bar in silence and as we waited for the bartender, I stared at her profile waiting for her to stop deliberately avoiding my gaze.

I was determined to burn a hole in the side of her face with laser eyes until she acknowledged me.

Finally, her eyes narrowed and slid to the side.

"What?" she asked tempestuously, but I brushed it off, intending to remind her of the promise she'd made.

"Don't you give me that, Tempest, you know what."

"I don't like him." She shrugged as though that were all there was to it.

Here we go.

"Why not?" I asked taking care to sound more curious than confronting.

"I don't know, I just don't."

I took a moment to compose my response even though I had a pet peeve about people who harbored negativity toward something without being able to clearly express why. I wasn't angry at Tempest. She was being a friend and looking out for me. But I considered Joel to be a friend too and I wanted them to get along.

"Do you mind if we unpack that a little?" I inquired planting my butt on the barstool that I was standing by to let her know that I planned on settling into this conversation for as long as was necessary.

I was relieved when she followed suit and sat down too.

"I pack light, honey, there's nothing more to it than he just rubs me the wrong way."

Once again, I took a moment to try and arrange my thoughts to construct a response that would get her to open up to me, instead of trying to create conflict or invalidate her point of view.

"I am sorry he makes you uncomfortable. Can you be more specific? Maybe you've seen something that I missed, or heard something about him that I don't know?" I suggested trying to guide her to explain her rationale.

Now it was Tempest's turn to contemplate and compose her thoughts. After a while, she hung her head and sighed.

"Okay so I don't have anything tangible, but what if I'm right, Sophie? What if he turns out to be trouble?" she asked, her brow laced with worry and my heart softened and grew one size bigger when I saw how important my well-being was to her.

"If he turns out to be trouble, then he'll be dust-covered trouble after I haul ass outta town in a few weeks. I'm not planning on marrying the guy. Can you just be cool? If he gives you an excuse, you have my blessing to raise hell, but until then, can you please just make an effort?" I pleaded, my body slackening as I placed my palms together to beg.

"I'm trying, but, Sophie," she said turning toward me to give me her full attention, "you don't know how dangerous the Iron Wraiths are. If he's mixed up with them, then you could find yourself in deep trouble, really quick and I don't want to see that happen."

I didn't know enough about Joel to know if the rumors about him were true, but I absolutely trusted that Tempest knew what she was talking about when it came to how dangerous the Wraiths were.

I sighed and turned my attention to the booths and was pleasantly surprised to see Joel and Joy engaged in what looked like a fairly amiable conversation.

"I asked him if he was a Wraith," I informed her, watching him smile politely at Joy as she talked while he shredded the label on the bottle of beer he was drinking.

"What, and you think he'd tell you if he was?" she replied skeptically.

"Yes," I said confidently. "If he was a member of the Iron Wraiths, he would be hanging out with the Iron Wraiths, wearing their patch and shit like that, right?" I reasoned, but Tempest just shrugged.

"I guess."

"I don't think he's a Wraith," I said again with more certainty. "It doesn't mean I don't think there could be a connection there, but I can't assume there's one until I know better," I reasoned.

When I looked back at Tempest, she was smirking.

"You're just giving him all that latitude because you think he's hot," she said wryly.

I scrunched my nose, like I couldn't argue.

"He is kind of hot though. Can you at least give me that?"

Finally, Tempest laughed and turned to look at him under the veil of objectification, rather than cautious skepticism.

She turned to me and rolled her eyes.

"Yeah alright, he's pretty hot," she conceded and I laughed until suddenly she brought her palm down on the bar top hard, causing me to gasp in fright as she screamed at the bartender.

"Hey! Can we get some drinks anytime soon or what?"

"That's a lot of shots right there! You trying to get us hospitalized?" Joy asked when she saw Tempest and I heading back to the booth with one tray full of beers and another full of shots.

"We're celebrating! What's a celebration without a couple drinks?" Tempest asked, and I was relieved to find her demeanor much more friendly than earlier.

Joel immediately pulled out his wallet and was about to pull out some money, when Tempest stopped him.

"Forget it, Barnes," she said waving him off. "You can get the next one."

In spite of her generosity, her words had an edge to them, but I recognized that this was Tempest being a good friend and making an effort.

We decided that since some of us were trying to get to know each other better, a drinking game would help to grease everyone's wheels and loosen up the tension.

After just ten minutes of Truth or Drink, Joy was already two of four shots down and I was starting to think that maybe she was a cheap drunk.

"My turn! My turn!" she declared drumming the top of the table. "What was your first impression of the person sitting to your immediate left?"

Everyone turned to look at the person sitting in the spot she had indicated, which for me was Joel.

Joel looked at Tempest, Tempest to Joy, and Joy to me.

"I always thought Tempest could kick my ass," Joel divulged first, looking to Tempest who grinned pridefully at his assessment.

"Ha! Well thank you, I'll take that as a compliment." She beamed proudly.

"Good, it was meant as one," he admitted which made my heart flutter because I didn't get the sense that he was saying that just to win her over.

"Well, you keep thinking that," she added only half joking before turning to Joy and giving her a once over before responding with, "I thought Joy was one of those obnoxiously virtuous, Stepford types, who secretly has a whole closet full of BDSM gear."

Joy was in the middle of sipping her beer when Tempest offered her evaluation and I half expected her to spit out her sip, but instead she raised her eyebrows and said with a shrug, "not a *whole* closet full."

A chorus of *oooohhhhs* swept over the table followed by some laughter before Joy turned to me.

"My first impression of you was that I thought you were way too cool to be friends with me. You know. Big city girl with her fancy restaurant career," she said. I noticed her words had started to become a little looser in pronunciation toward the end of the sentence.

"Are you drunk already?" I asked her, narrowing my eyes at her.

She looked like she might deny it at first, but then she covered her mouth in a girlish giggle and held her index and thumb an inch apart.

"A little." She giggled sheepishly.

"Pace yourself, Joy, we just got started," Tempest cautioned her before sipping her beer.

"Your turn! You have to tell us what you thought of Joel when you first met him," Joy commanded pointing at me from across the table.

I turned to Joel, who raised his eyebrows expectantly and I laughed as I recalled our first encounter.

"I legitimately thought you were going to kill me for almost crashing into you."

"I almost did," he confirmed though he was laughing now too.

"What? What happened?" Joy asked, narrowing her eyes at us as though she didn't understand what we were laughing about.

"Mr. Frowny Brows over here almost grounded me and sent me to my room after I almost drove my car into his on the night we met. I can laugh about it now, because we didn't actually crash, and I know you a bit better now, but holy shit, you were intimidating."

"Intimidating?" he asked incredulously as though he genuinely didn't see himself that way.

"Are you kidding? I thought I was going to have a heart attack."

"More likely as a result of almost being crushed to death by a two-ton truck," he volleyed in defense and I waved him off.

"Whatever, you still are and always will be Mr. Frowny Brows to me."

"Alright you two, that's enough, it's my turn to ask a question," Tempest said, drawing our attention back to the circle. "If you could go back in time and do one thing in your life differently, what would you change?"

A thoughtful hush fell over the table as everyone considered the question.

Joy was the first to share her thoughts.

"I think if I could have my time over, I would have gone to college."

"Why didn't you?" Tempest inquired peering at her friend curiously.

"Well Momma was struggling to keep the house and I didn't want to go away and leave her to muddle through alone, so I got a job right out of high school, so I could help her out with the bills and mortgage. I don't regret it, but if I had my time over, I'd probably want to try and find another solution, so I could have gone to school," she said.

"You can still do that," I reminded her gently, and she nodded in that sad indulgent way that people did which really meant, *I could, but I'm probably not going to.*

"I know," she smiled with a shrug before turning to her friend. "What about you?"

Tempest puffed out her cheeks and stared up at the ceiling thoughtfully for a moment, before scratching her head, almost seeming guilty about what she was about to say.

"I know I shouldn't say this, because I have worked really hard to curb my anger and resentment issues, but I wish I had kicked Asher and Mindy's ass when I had the chance."

"I wouldn't have blamed you. Those adulterous swine," Joy spat with contempt on her friend's behalf before sipping her beer with a scowl.

"Who? What?" I asked, lost.

Tempest waved her hand as though it wasn't worth the lengthy response. "Just the time when I walked in on my ex-husband in bed with someone else. I should have kicked their asses when I had the chance," she explained concisely. "Anyway. Next."

Everyone turned to me so, I guessed that it was my turn and I already knew what I wanted to say.

"If I could go back and do my time again, I never would have gone on that stupid show *No Whisk, No Reward.* Easy answer."

"You were on a TV show?" Joel asked, more animated about the idea than the reality it deserved.

"Yeah what happened there?" Tempest inquired curiously, having heard rumbling about it from around the kitchen.

"What happened is that I basically suffered a full-scale stage fright meltdown and served up a scrambled egg custard mille-feuille to Filipe Armand, one of the most brutal judges in food television history, thus ruining my career as a successful pastry chef," I explained.

"A scrambled egg what?" Joel asked furrowing his brow, and I was happy that instead of commenting on my failure, his focus seemed to be on the dessert.

"A mille-feuille. It's basically just a dessert made up of thin layers of pastry separated by crème pâtissière or custard," Tempest informed him.

"Yeah, I mean, obviously I tried to sex it up a little, but ... in the end, it didn't work out quite the way I'd planned. I was too nervous."

"What was it? The pressure?" Joel pressed, his face twisted with curiosity. "Because you don't really strike me as the nervous type."

"I'm normally not, but ..." I tried to figure out how to explain what happened. "I guess I just freaked out when I made it to the studio and saw how bright the lights were and how big those cameras are. And then there're the three intimidating judges who just come and stand there and watch everything you do like you're fucking everything up. Then I actually made a mistake and ... well, it just snowballed," I explained, getting toward the end of my willingness to discuss the topic much further, but Joel narrowed his eyes at me as though he was trying to work something out.

"Is that why the television producer was calling you when we were at Daisy's the other day?"

"Yeah," I confirmed. "He's trying to get me to come back for a double or nothing, best of the worst special."

"Double or nothing? How much are they offering?" Tempest inquired with renewed curiosity.

"Three hundred grand," I replied sipping my beer, and waiting for the "advice" that inevitably followed when I told people how much money was involved.

"Three hundred grand? Are you *sure* you don't want another crack at that?" Joy asked cringing at the thought that I would let an opportunity like that pass me by.

"Why?" I shrugged. "To hammer the last nail in the coffin of my career?" I asked bitterly.

"I think the more likely answer is that you would win and use the money to open up your own bakery." Joel shrugged offering his optimistic perspective.

"Yeah, Sophie, we've seen you in the kitchen. Baking is not the problem," Tempest said leaning forward with interest.

"I know that," I said and then stopped my mouth from saying anything further by sipping my beer. "Now can we talk about something else?"

"Okay we will, but you at least have to tell us more about your dessert, what did you have planned?" Joy demanded and since I figured if anyone would appreciate what I was trying to accomplish it would be two fellow bakers and it was still a recipe that I was proud of and I wanted to share it.

"I called it Chestnuts Roasting On an Open Fire," I reluctantly divulged, though the name of it brought a little smile to my face.

"What are the elements?" Joy asked curiously. "Besides chestnuts, obviously."

"It's basically three alternating layers of thin puff pastry, a smoked crème pâtissière infused with roasted chestnut puree, and chestnut chocolate praline crumble. Then on top, I place a super thin, glassy sheet of chestnut butter toffee and a row of scorched, caramel dipped chestnuts ... oh and some chocolate curls to look like burnt logs."

"*Whooooaaaaaa,*" Tempest and Joy chorused in unison as Joel's eyes seemed to glaze over, not quite able to picture it.

Joy and Tempest promptly began talking over one another.

"Can you make that for us on test kitchen night?"

"That would be perfect as like a limited-edition holiday special at the bakery!"

"You should tell Jenn your idea!"

"Okay, okay," I said waving my hand as though I were a mother bear, pawing at her two cubs whose excitability was getting out of hand. "Moving on. Joel, your turn. Spill," I ordered, anxious for the spotlight to be placed on someone else.

Joel eyed the shot glasses and for a moment, I thought he was going to take one, but then he surprised me by answering the question.

"I would have sold the garage after Dad died, instead of keeping it and I would have stayed in Nashville with the construction company I was with."

"I'm sorry about your dad. He was a really sweet man," Tempest offered sympathetically, and Joy nodded in agreement.

"Yeah, he fixed my bike for me after I crashed down a hill. It was just like *The Karate Kid*, you know when Mr. Miyagi fixes Daniel's bike? I think my momma might have had a crush on him," Joy said which made Joel laugh a little.

"I didn't know you worked in construction," I added, seeing the way his body language seemed to curl inward more and more as the conversation about his father went on, so I tried to shift the focus from his dad to the construction job he'd left behind.

"Yeah it was the best job I ever had," he said looking down at his hands that were shredding the label off another bottle of beer. "Working outside all day, building houses that people made into homes. It felt meaningful."

I don't know why but I glanced at Tempest who was staring at Joel as though she were looking at him with new eyes. I could feel myself getting further and further away from feeling as though he was some-body I should be wary of.

"Why can't you sell the garage now and get back into it?" Joy asked curiously, and Joel just shook his head as though it weren't an option.

"It's complicated," was all he was willing to impart before he cleared his throat uncomfortably. "Anyway, I guess it's my turn to ask a question," he said raising one eyebrow at me questioningly.

"Sure." I shrugged and watched as his big hand came to his face and he began sliding his palm up and down the side of his face thoughtfully.

I watched the action and my fingers ached to touch him there. To feel the abrasiveness of his beard under the soft palm of my hand.

He was starting to look more relaxed, his eyelids a touch heavier than they were when we'd first arrived, and I couldn't help but think he was the kind of guy who would lean into my touch.

"Alright," he said, sitting up straighter when he thought of the perfect question. "You find yourself in a threesome with your first crush and the current object of your desire, who are they?"

I got the distinct impression by the way he stared directly at me when he asked the question, that he knew exactly what he was doing, and I wasn't sure how to feel about it.

I could feel myself getting swept along by this mutual flirtation between us and it seemed to be gaining momentum the more time I spent with him.

The caution that I was supposed to be exercising when it came to Joel was now something that I had to remind myself of, rather than it being my first consideration like it was supposed to be.

I was starting to feel the urge to kiss first and ask questions later.

I had two options. Take the shot and risk lowering my guard further once the alcohol kicked in or answer the question.

I waited to see if he would answer first.

"Oh Lord," Joy breathed and eyed her shot, placing her hand over it and letting it hover there while she decided if she wanted to share.

"It's not like everyone doesn't already know the answer," Tempest goaded her.

"Joel doesn't," Joy responded eyeing him as though he might betray the circle of drunken trust.

"I don't know either," I piped in raising my hand. "And now I am curious, so you have to tell us."

Joy took a moment before reaching for a shot.

"I'm not taking the shot because I don't intend to answer the question, it's to numb the pain of the reality that it will never happen," she explained. "So here goes. First crush: Cletus Winston. Current object of my desire: Cletus Winston," she admitted before tossing back the liquor.

Joel frowned in disapproval as my eyes widened in surprise.

"Yeah, big shock there," Tempest quipped sarcastically, but I was shocked, having had no idea how intense Joy's feelings for Cletus were. I sympathized with her, watching as she closed her eyes and gently placed a hand on her chest.

"You know how sometimes you can just look at someone and just *know* they would break you in two in bed?" she murmured dreamily.

"That sure ain't what I see when I look at Cletus Winston," Tempest added from the corner of her mouth.

"Amen," Joel added. "Ugh. That's in my mind now," he groaned shaking his head as though to wipe the thought free.

I turned to Tempest who shrugged as though her response was no big secret either.

"First crush: Jonathan Taylor Thomas. Current object of my desire: My man, Cage Erickson. Now you," she said pinning me with a hard stare. "Go!"

Put on the spot, I lost my nerve and took the shot, not because I didn't want anyone knowing that technically, my first crush was Leonardo from the *Teenage Mutant Ninja Turtles.*

It was more that my current crush was sitting about two feet away and I had a feeling he was fishing.

When I lowered my glass down, I could feel Joel's eyes on me and I felt that by drinking, I had still told him everything he needed to know without having said a word.

"Joel," Tempest said raising her eyebrows expectantly at him as if to say, *"well she chickened out, are you going to as well?"*

He pressed his fingers to a shot glass and turned it around on the tabletop while he thought about it for a moment.

"I know I am going to regret telling you this, but my first crush," he began, his lips hitching up at the corners, "was Scotia Simmons."

"WHAT?" Tempest and Joy exclaimed in unison, but I had no idea who that was.

"Scotia Simmons? That gossipmonger?" Joy spat, thumping her fists on the table in disbelief.

"She wasn't always like that," Joel reasoned. "Besides, I was ten and she was a looker back in the day." He shrugged one shoulder to justify himself.

"And the *current* object of your desire?" Tempest prompted impatiently with the subtlety of a jackhammer.

"Nancy Grace?" Joy quipped sarcastically, her lips curled in disapproval.

"No. Closer to home than that," Tempest replied, narrowing her eyes at him knowingly.

I kicked my leg out from under the table connecting with her shin, but instead of taking the hint, Tempest yelped and jumped in her seat.

"Ow! What was that for?"

"What was what for?" Joy asked, wondering what had promoted Tempest's sudden outburst.

I shook my head at Tempest subtly, warning her with my eyes that if she said another word, we were going to take it outside.

Her eyes narrowed challengingly at me and her lips curled into a sly smile.

Where the hell was this coming from?

Just as she opened her mouth to speak, Joy gasped and held her finger to her lips to silence us.

"What? What is it? Are you gonna puke?" Tempest asked side-eyeing her as she prepared to clear a path.

"No! Listen!" Joy shrieked pointing to the air as though we would be able to see the sound.

"Alright, folks," the DJ announced from his booth. "Let's kick off the Friday night festivities with Cadillac Ranch! Line dancers assemble!"

"Let me out! Let me out!" Joy shrieked clamoring to get out of the booth and I could have kissed her for the distraction as Tempest rushed to get out of her way.

"Alright, alright! Hold your horses!" Tempest grumbled making way for Joy to free herself from the table.

"Come on!" she exclaimed, surprising everyone, but mostly Joel by reaching over and taking his wrist, attempting to pull his giant frame up from his seat.

"No, no. Trust me, it's in the best interest of anyone within a ten-foot radius that I *don't* dance."

"Just for one song!" Joy bargained, groaning with effort as she leaned back on her heels and used all her body weight to try and get him up.

"Go on," I encouraged, pushing on his shoulder encouragingly. "Just one song. Tempest and I will join you in a minute."

Joel was still frowning with reluctance but tossed back two of his shots as though he needed them before he finally relented.

"Alright fine, it's your funeral," he warned Joy before allowing her to lead him to the front row of people on the dance floor.

Some guys were very comfortable on the dance floor and could move with relative ease so long as they had some basic instructions because they knew it was all in good fun.

Joel was not one of those men.

His movements were rigid and constantly a beat behind everyone else, his brow furrowed with all the focus and determination of a heart surgeon working on a presidential patient.

His big, galumphing body worked against him especially when he was supposed to bend his knee to tap his heel and some of the more sympathetic dancers around him made their own movements more defined, so he could follow along.

"Are you witnessing this?" I heard Tempest ask at my side.

I turned to her, reminded of her meddling earlier and sat back against my seat.

"What was that about before?" I inquired, confused. "An hour ago, Joel was the harbinger of doom and now you're playing cupid?"

"What do you mean?" Tempest shrugged in false innocence.

I leaned forward and placed my hands atop the table.

"Hey, I am trying to be good here, as per *your* advice, remember?"

"I know, and your neck veins are popping out from the effort. I'm starting to feel sorry for you," Tempest said, poking fun at me with a thoroughly amused expression, before turning back to glance at Joel failing on the dance floor. "Lord knows why. What is wrong with him?"

I turned back to the dance floor where the scene had devolved into Joy giving him verbal instructions for each step. He seemed to get the hang of it for a few bars before forgetting a step and then falling behind again and scrambling to catch up.

"Good Lord, it's like watching a car wreck."

"He's a horrible dancer," I agreed but even to my ears, my words were completely at odds with the tone in which I'd said them.

"Uh-oh," I heard Tempest groan. I turned to look at her, realizing that I had been grinning like a loon watching him with my hands pressed to my cheeks.

"What?" I asked casually dropping my hands back to my sides and trying to appear less like I had just found the father of my future children.

"You know what," she accused while side-eyeing me with a half-cocked grin before making an obscene gesture with her hands.

"Hey, hey, hey!" I squawked. "Knock that off before he sees you," I scolded her and reached over the table to separate her hands.

I narrowed my eyes at her and could detect the faint whiff of rum on her breath and looked down to find all four of her shot glasses empty.

"We dancing, or what?" she asked, reaching for my remaining shots, three of which were still full, as I laughed and moved two of them away from her.

"You can have one," I obliged, doling out one drink to her and placing the two remaining in each of my hands. I knocked them both back and shuddered at the spiky, burning sensation as the alcohol blazed its way down my throat.

I gathered up Joel and Joy's last shots before sliding out of the booth and nudging my head toward the dance floor.

"Come on."

"More drinking!" she exclaimed slamming her palm down on the table.

"Okay but *with* dancing!" I bargained with her, sensing that if she didn't start moving her body, she would be on the floor in twenty minutes. "Here," I said passing her the bottle of beer which was still half full. "Drink this and get your ass up. Let's go!"

"Alright fine!" she finally agreed and slid out of the bench, following me down onto the dance floor where I handed Joel and Joy their last shots of rum which they accepted gratefully.

Tempest and I joined the line and I could feel the pleasant buzz of the alcohol starting to loosen my limbs.

The four of us danced, laughed, and periodically took turns grabbing Joel by the back of his shirt to prevent him from trying to slink away while we weren't watching.

Every so often one of us would disappear and return with a round of shots or beer, and the dancing helped to keep our drunkenness on an even keel.

After the three of us ladies broke into an impromptu and incongruous display of the Zorba dance paired with a country version of the song "Footloose," the song ended with no fadeout causing the crowd to start to jeer.

"No! Boo! No slow dancing!" Tempest shouted in the general direction of whoever was responsible for the music.

"Yeah! More fast dancing!" Joy shouted throwing her arm around Tempest's neck as the two of them laughed and swayed unsteadily.

"I think those two are going to need a ride home," Joel stated placing his hands on his hips like a police officer getting ready to lecture a bunch of rowdy teenagers. Even through the haze of my intoxication, I added his sense of responsibility to my friends to the ever-growing list of ways Joel had demonstrated how un-biker like his behavior was.

"Yes, sir, I concur with your conclusion," I slurred offering him a lazy salute. His eyes came to mine and narrowed slightly realizing, I was likely only a hair less drunk than my friends.

"How're you holding up, Fancy Pants? You still with me?" he asked turning his body toward me as a slow bluesy tune started to play over the speakers.

"I'm quite drunk," I informed him placing my hands on my hips, to mirror his stance. "But I am really good at hiding it."

"You think so?" Joel asked with a cocked eyebrow and a wry smile, but I was plastered so irony escaped me.

"Yup," I said holding out my arms in front of me like a zombie. "Come on, let's slow dance," I said rolling my wrists toward me, motioning for him to approach.

Joel smiled and lowered his hands to his sides as he took the few short steps over until he was standing before me and then just stood there like he didn't know what to do.

"What are you doing? Put your arms around me, what are you? Fifteen?" I asked, taking his wrists and guiding them around my waist, as he laughed at my drunken bossiness.

"There, how's that?" he asked pulling me right up against him and sliding his hands down onto the narrow strip of uncovered skin at the small of my back.

"This is good. This is nice," I mumbled nuzzling my cheek against his chest and hooking my arms up underneath his arms to rest on his back.

"Any minute now, I'm going to be holding you up," Joel guessed, probably eluding to the fact that I was gradually melting against him and eventually my legs would give out and he would need to catch me.

"Hmm," I hummed in response but even I wasn't sure what I was trying to communicate by it.

I could smell his detergent and the faintest hint of something else spicy and woodsy and closed my eyes as we began swaying in time with the music.

I could feel the pad of his thumb, stroking tiny lines across my skin and now that things had slowed down, the heat of his body seemed to dial up my level of inebriation until I was practically asleep on him.

"When was the last time you slow danced?" I asked him, wondering briefly about other women who'd found their way into his arms.

His eyes blinked upward as he tried to recall and shook his head like he couldn't remember.

"I don't know … a long, long time ago," was the best he was able to offer.

147

"Do you miss slow dancing with someone?"

His eyes searched between mine, the glacial spikes of blue and green ensuring I was in no danger of drifting into unconsciousness, though I might have if I had been in anyone else's arms.

I was suddenly aware of the pad of his thumb sliding across the highest point of my cheekbone toward my temple and he nodded slowly in response to my question.

"Did you have fun tonight? I know you didn't really want to come, but are you glad you did?"

Joel breathed a soft laugh and his eyes blinked slowly as his hand returned around the curve of my waist.

"I don't remember the last time I had this much fun," he admitted and once again I felt something bloom inside my chest cavity. I got the sense that Joel was a man who was hiding a lot of loneliness and I felt obliged to show him that it didn't always have to be that way.

"I think we should go dancing every Friday night," I drunkenly suggested and smiled as I watched Joel's lips press into a straight line at the thought.

"Let's not get carried away now.'

As much I didn't want to, I was just about to suggest that we get going, and Joel seemed to have the same thought. He tilted his head as he scrutinized my lack of sobriety and his focus on me only made me feel more off-kilter. I begrudgingly peeled myself off him and made an attempt to demonstrate that I still had my faculties about me, by looking at my watch.

"Shoot, we should get going, I have work in a few hours."

"You work Saturdays?" he inquired as though it were a shame.

"Yeah," I sighed, acting as though it were, even though I was no stranger to a full weeks work schedule.

"Best be on our way then," he agreed, "there's probably just enough time to get these girls home and get you back home for a shower before you have to head into work. I'll drive you to the bakery today," he stated rather than asked.

I was about to protest, which he anticipated, and cut me off at the pass.

"That's not open to negotiation. You're too drunk," he added with a finality that made me close my mouth and drop the issue.

"What about you? You drank too."

"Yeah, but I'm bigger than you, I can take more," he replied tucking a lock of hair that had fallen over my eyes behind my ear.

"That is true. You're quite a big man," I said nonsensically. "Okay fine. I accept," I said gratefully, glancing past him and sighing when I saw what Joy and Tempest were up to.

"You want to go take care of that?" Joel asked with an amused grin. Joy was pole dancing with a mop handle that she'd found god knows where, while Tempest was sitting on the floor laughing too hard to stand.

"Sure," I laughed shaking my head and I went off to collect my friends.

CHAPTER 13

$\mathcal{T}$he push to make it through the workday, remain professional, and not puke into a mixing bowl of sickly-sweet icing was an excruciating ordeal, that drained every last ounce of my energy, but at least I was not alone.

Every now and then, I would glance over at Tempest who was roughly the same shade of seafoam green that I was, with a matching sheen of cold sweat across her brow.

"I'm never drinking again," she mumbled to me as we met side by side to begin our cake assembly line, which was moving a little slower than usual.

"Ugh, me neither," I agreed. "Until next week," I added knowing that I wasn't about to give up on alcohol for too long.

"Why? What's happening next week?" Tempest asked, her voice sounding like it was sticking at the back of her throat.

"Nothing specific, I'll probably just be ready to start drinking again by then," I explained knowing that even a mean hangover wouldn't be enough to discourage me from any future libations.

"Oh." Tempest chuckled making an attempt to laugh, but her expression quickly fell into a grimace as she clutched the edge of the bench and took a couple of deep breaths to work through her nausea.

Once composed, she began the process of leveling and sectioning the cakes, passing them along to me to fill, apply the crumb layer, and then frost before passing it along to Joy to be decorated.

"You're awfully quiet this morning," Tempest observed, peering past me over to Joy, who was not her usual, bubbly self and I got the sense it wasn't just from the hangover.

"I'm just tired," she said, dismissing Tempest's concern with a subtle shake of her head.

A few moments of silence passed between the three of us until finally Joy sighed and looked at us, her eyes filling up with worry as she whispered, "Did I say too much about Cletus last night? I mean did I say anything …" she paused and looked around before turning back to us, closing her eyes and wilting forward a little, "inappropriate?"

"Oh honey," Tempest said reaching around me to touch Joy's arm comfortingly. "You didn't say anything we didn't already know. You know we're not going to say anything, you're in our three-person circle of trust, okay?"

"Okay." Joy nodded tilting her head back as she tried to blink back the tears in her eyes. "It's just, I said it all in front of Joel and—"

"Don't you worry about him. The last person on earth Joel Barnes is gonna flap his gums to is Cletus Winston," I assured her, dismissing her concern with a wave of my hand.

"What is the beef between them anyway, I feel as though that rivalry has been going on for years," said Tempest, her voice rough and quiet as Joy took a break from piping to chug some water, which was exactly what Tempest and I should have been doing.

"I don't know, he hasn't told me yet, but I'm gonna get it out of him," I declared, confident that if I was patient enough with him, that I could get to the bottom of the tension between Joel and the Winstons.

"You know, Joel is so different than I thought he'd be," Joy observed as she gathered up the piping bag again and went back to work on her cake.

"What did you think he'd be like?" I asked curiously, eager to get their perspective now that they had spent some time with him.

"I don't know, he just always looks ornery and unapproachable.

What did you call him again? Mister Frowny Brows? Anyway, once you get underneath all that, he's not bad. I think we might have been wrong about him being in with the Wraiths," she said decidedly.

My shoulders loosened a little from how tense they had become when the conversation turned to Joel, and I was pleased that Joy felt that way.

"Hmm." Tempest shrugged as though she might not agree and the muscles in my shoulders coiled again.

"You still think he is?" I asked, wondering how she could possibly continue to think that after last night.

Before she could respond Joy jumped in. "Maybe he isn't, but I think his brother definitely was. You know, before he passed," she said glancing up to find Tempest glaring at her.

Wait, what?

"I'm sorry, it just slipped out. I'm so tired." She sighed resigned to Tempest's ire, instead of begging for forgiveness like she normally would have.

I did not have the capacity to handle surprise and my stomach lurched involuntarily at hearing this new information.

"Wait," I said holding my finger up to halt either of them from proceeding.

I pressed my finger to my lips as my stomach started to rumble and braced myself for what felt like an impending disaster. "Oh God, I think I'm gonna—"

Just then, a positively uncivilized belch tore forth from my mouth as Tempest, Joy, and several others turned to me wide-eyed.

"I am so sorry," I announced regretfully to the room, "but trust me, that was *way* better than the alternative." Tempest and Joy grumbled their mutual disgust under their breath.

"Joel had a brother? I didn't know that, why didn't I know that?" I whispered, getting back to the topic at hand. "How did he die?"

"Motorcycle accident," Joy replied, her eyes softening with sympathy.

"So, he *was* a biker?" I asked wondering how there could be any ambiguity surrounding whether or not Joel's brother was a Wraith.

"Not necessarily," Tempest began to explain. "I mean he rode a motorcycle, but he always had. Even before rumors started going around that he was involved with them. Also, I don't know much about how they operate, but bikers are usually pretty hardcore about representation, so the fact that he didn't wear a patch or anything like that makes his involvement unclear."

"I don't understand why Joel wouldn't have told me that he had a brother. I mean, not that I'd asked, but you'd think it would have come up by now," I said, working through my thoughts aloud.

"Maybe because then he'd have to tell you the truth," Tempest suggested, which made too much sense to dismiss the possibility that she might be right.

"It's clear he's into you, maybe he thinks it will scare you away," Joy added.

This was getting way too complicated, I needed to change the subject.

"Anyway, I have a new recipe I want to try out for our test kitchen on Thursday," I said hoping to move things along.

"Ooh, what is it?" Joy inquired taking the bait all too easy, for which I was grateful.

"It's an Earl Grey cupcake with lemon curd and Swiss meringue swirl icing on top and the Swiss meringue is torched. I call them the Smoky Mountain cupcakes."

"That sounds like a worthy inclusion for the spring," Tempest offered, yanking muffins out of their tins which had cooled just enough to come out without falling apart.

"You're so creative, no wonder you were picked for a baking competition," Joy said working on a cake at half her usual speed.

"Yeah, that turned out great for me," I scoffed getting to work on some cannoli.

"Oh, I forgot to tell you, I went online and found the episode with you in it," Joy informed me, causing an immediate frown to form across my face.

"I did too, I was curious to see if it was as bad as you made it out to be," Tempest added with as much of a smirk as she could muster in her current state.

"Oh good, well now you know that I wasn't exaggerating," I said, cringing into another dimension at the thought of them having seen it.

"I mean you didn't do great, but … that one judge, that Filipe guy," Tempest began, referring to Filipe Armand, who reveled in his reputation for being the harshest, most intimidating critic. "He was just a sack of dog shit to you, I would have thrown a knife at his head if he had said to me what he said to you."

"Yeah that comment about you having not progressed beyond the Easy-Bake Oven was a bit over top," Joy agreed causing my stomach to turn over with uneasiness.

"I tell ya what though," Tempest said pointing at me from across the bench with a spatula. "Had you nailed that dessert, you would have won for sure. Those other contestants weren't as creative as you," she offered but I had long conditioned myself to accept compliments on the experience as merely an obligatory kindness, so her words had little impact.

"Yeah, the guy who won it made nothin' but a froufrou, over-the-top banana split in my opinion," Joy offered sounding dismissive and annoyed on my behalf.

"Thanks for the words of encouragement, ladies, I appreciate it," I said offering them as much of a smile as I could muster and hoping that the conversation had run its course.

"I think you should do the follow up episode," Tempest declared with a shrug.

"Me too," Joy added in agreement as I trained my features to remain neutral.

"I'll think about it," I replied robotically, not really caring if I sounded like I was just telling them what they wanted to hear.

"Good, because three hundred thousand dollars is a lot of money, and someone like you should be running their own bakery instead of always coasting safely beneath the surface of their own potential and letting other bakery owners benefit from their talent."

My eyes went to Tempest whose attention never strayed from the rack of muffins she was working on.

"Amen," Joy agreed, equally focused on her task as I looked down to find that I was dipping an unfilled cannoli shell into the crushed pistachios.

I had heard variations of what Tempest had just declared, but I had never heard it said quite like that and I would be lying if I said it didn't make an impact.

It seemed the only person who couldn't see my potential was me.

Of course, I had a dream to run my own bakery. I had folders and folders on my laptop, brimming with pictures of bakery interiors, kitchen layouts and designs, recipes, and even a fully written business plan.

I thought about it all the time, but whenever I started thinking about actually doing it, there was always a nameless, faceless block there.

After Tempest's candid declaration that I should have my own bakery by now, I was starting to recognize that the nameless, faceless block that was getting in my way was me.

Nobody else but me.

I sighed, attempting to push thoughts of the show and the prize money out of my mind to focus completely on the cannoli instead.

It was my last task before I would be free to go home where I planned to go straight to bed and fall into oblivion.

Then I remembered that Joel had dropped me off and I wondered how in the heck I was going to get home.

"Hey, do you guys have Uber here?" I asked Joy, who was still too hungover to be polite.

"You're kidding right, city girl?"

"Alright, I was just asking," I said, recoiling from the intensity of her glower as she said it.

I wracked my brain trying to think of an alternative mode of transportation and just when I resigned to either having to hitchhike or walk, my phone vibrated with an incoming text message.

It was Joel, and I couldn't hide the smile that took over my face when I saw his name light up my screen.

Joel: Need a ride home?

My heart danced inside my chest as I bit my lip and typed up my response.

Me: I will love you forever if you can please just get.me.home. *sleepy emoji*

I looked up from the screen and saw Tempest looking at me with a raised eyebrow.

"What? It's a friend," I exclaimed, figuring that I wasn't technically lying.

"Mm-hmm," she hummed and tapped her finger to her nose twice while giving me a knowing look.

My phone buzzed again and I turned away from her to read it, which probably didn't help to convince her that I was engaged in an innocent friendly conversation with the very person she suspected that it was.

Joel: Hang tight, I'm on my way.

"Oh my God, everything he says makes me want to die," I said to myself under my breath, clutching my phone to my chest and sighing.

"Hey," Tempest said from directly behind me causing me to yelp in surprise and spin to face her while barely keeping a grasp on my phone

"Don't do that! Holy shit, I cannot handle being snuck up on right now," I scolded her, which only seemed to amuse her.

"Sorry," she said, not sounding sorry at all. "I just wanted to make sure that we're cool."

I furrowed my brow in confusion because I didn't know what she was talking about.

"Of course, we're cool, why wouldn't we be cool?" I asked her, trying to recall what might have given her the impression that we were at odds.

"It's just, I know you really like Joel and I've made no secret of how skeptical I am of him and I just want to make sure that you know it's only because I'm looking out for you."

Tempest had this no muss, no fuss directness about her, even when saying the sweetest things. I smiled at her and pulled her into a hug.

"Tempest Cassidy, you are one of if not my most favorite person in Green Valley, you know that?" I said, feeling her tap my shoulder.

"Yeah, yeah, I know," she groaned before I decided to let her go.

I gave her a grin before moving in close once more to whisper, "Don't tell Joy I said that. Of course, I love her too, but … I just think you're really cool."

"Alright you can stop blowing smoke up my ass, go get yourself a croissant from the front display and get out of here, you're making me nauseous," she grumbled making me laugh as she rushed to get away from me.

I gathered my belongings and took her advice, swiping a croissant before leaving the bakery to go and wait for Joel out front.

CHAPTER 14

*W*hen Joel pulled up in his black truck, the relief I felt as he approached was akin to finding an oasis in the desert.

I opened the passenger side door as Joel turned his head to greet me.

"*Take Me Home, Country Roads*" by John Denver was playing on the radio.

"Headin' my way?" he asked me with that beguiling southern accent, and in my sleep-deprived, exhausted state, I was forced to call upon a secret hidden reserve, stored somewhere deep inside, to stop myself from actually swooning.

"My baseball cap wearing, knight in shining pickup truck," I declared after taking some effort to climb gracelessly into the cabin of his truck.

"Let's get you home, you're a mess," he teased, knowing I didn't have the energy to retaliate.

"Thank you for coming to get me," I offered instead, nestling back against the seat and curling my body toward the window.

The Donner Bakery wasn't even out of sight in the rearview when my thoughts began to jumble and turn into nonsense. After a few half-hearted attempts to remain awake, I gave into my fatigue, leaned my head against the window and fell asleep.

I was awoken too soon after by the sensation of something warm sliding down my cheek, and as my eyes fluttered open, I heard Joel's voice talking to me softly.

"We're home," he informed me softly, and I turned into his palm as I resisted opening my eyes.

"Come on now," he cajoled. "You're just one flight of stairs away from your bed," he urged stroking my face with the back of his fingers.

I sighed and opened my eyes, finding myself looking directly into his glacial colored eyes.

"You have such pretty eyes," I mumbled somewhere between wakefulness and sleep.

"So do you," he responded trying to divert attention away from him by returning the compliment.

"They're just boring and brown most of the time," I argued, blinking slowly as his eyes moved along the lines of my face down to my mouth.

"They're not boring brown, they're hazel like ..." He blinked up at the roof of the truck, trying to recall something akin to the color of my eyes, which amused me enough to bring me into wakefulness.

"Like swamp water," I suggested, "or a baby's soiled diaper perhaps." I offered and then froze as he leaned his body over to hover over mine.

He was so close I could feel his warmth all over my face and his eyes stayed fixed on mine as he lingered there.

The blood in my body whirred and heat prickled my skin as the air seemed to clump around me and gain mass, making it difficult to breathe.

My eyes fell to his lips and I watched them part.

"You're delirious," he murmured, before yanking on the truck door handle at my side and opening my door for me, before easing back into his seat and visibly sighing.

I reeled from the sudden, gaping distance between us and wondered what he was thinking.

"You're not coming inside?" I asked when I realized he wasn't making any attempt to get out of the truck.

"No, I gotta get back to the garage. You should get some sleep anyway," he responded sounding every bit as distant as he had on the night I first met him.

I was about to ask if I had done something wrong when his phone began to vibrate.

He had placed it in the cupholder, and I glanced down at it when it started to ring.

Before Joel had a chance to pick it, up, I caught a glimpse of the name that displayed on the screen and swallowed when I saw it read *Catfish Hickson.*

Joel's eyes came to mine and I waited for an explanation, trying not to jump to conclusions.

"You going to answer it?" I prompted him, when he made no move to take the call, and I could hear my words come out sounding tight and challenging.

I was doing my best not to allow myself to indulge in one of the million doubts converging on my mind, but the fact that he wasn't rushing to explain was unsettling.

His eyes were clouded over and dark as he avoided my gaze.

"Promise you'll give me a chance to come by later and explain," he requested, and I furrowed my brow in confusion.

"Why don't you just tell me now?"

"I can't," he replied shortly and suddenly I felt like all the progress I'd made getting Joel to open up had gone out the window and I was back to the short, terse version of him I'd met that night on the mountain road.

"Why not?" I asked, stubbornly refusing to make any move to leave his truck.

Joel didn't answer for a minute, and finally, his phone stopped vibrating against the plastic cupholder, plunging the inside of the cabin into a void-like silence that stretched on for some time.

"Just go on upstairs," he instructed finally. "I'll explain everything when I get home later."

"Are we in danger, can you at least tell me that?" I asked feeling entitled to know at least that much.

I must have looked terrified, because Joel took a moment to compose himself and turned to me, his eyes soft and earnest.

"I promise you, you're not in danger. I want to keep it that way, so please go upstairs, get some sleep and I'll come around later on and explain everything. I promise."

I noted that he only made a point to reassure me of my own safety, but I decided to oblige him and wait for a fuller explanation.

"Everything?" I asked pointedly narrowing my eyes, and he nodded in agreement.

"Everything, I promise. Now get out of here, I have to go."

Then he blindsided me by leaning toward me, cupping the back of my neck in his hand and pulling me toward him so he could press his lips over mine.

He lingered there for a moment but before my brain and body had the chance to register what was happening, he pulled away and pressed on the orange button to release my seat belt.

"Go on," he ordered me once more with gentle authority and turned back to the windshield.

Reeling, and struggling to catch one of the million fleeting thoughts going through my mind, I got out of the truck.

My eyes swept the moderately peopled street as I walked toward the entrance of the building and that's when I spotted a guy leaning against a motorcycle at the end of the block. I hurried inside and made doubly sure that both the locks were engaged before racing up the stairs and locking myself in my apartment, hurrying to the window to see if I could spot the biker guy again.

I zeroed in on him still waiting in the same spot as Joel's truck approached him.

The imposing-looking form pushed off his bike and began to make his way around to the driver's side of Joel's truck as I watched from a sliver of space between the blinds.

I wished I could hear what was being said. The whole exchange only lasted about two or three minutes before Joel sped off and the biker mounted his bike and took off in the opposite direction.

I sighed and rubbed my head wearily, too tired to trust my own judgment based on what had just happened.

Opting to avoid torturing myself, I lay down on the bed, and curled up on my side, but I was suddenly finding it difficult to keep my eyes closed and my foot wagged restlessly against the mattress as my nerves coiled.

Was this how I was supposed to feel for the next few hours until Joel came back?

Would he come back?

I sat upright in bed at the dark thought, and scolded myself for being irrational as I reached for my phone to call Anna so she could either put my mind at ease or yell at me for being willfully obtuse to every sign that Joel was, in fact, mixed up with the local biker gang.

I dialed her number and felt relief when she answered.

"What are your thoughts on Ariana Grande?" she greeted as though she'd given a lot of consideration to the question and wanted to know my opinion.

Some tension loosened in my body and I smiled, albeit half-heartedly.

"Ah, let's see." I sighed, grateful for the distraction of being engaged in one of her silly games, "Ariana … Ariana Richards from *Jurassic Park …*"

"Ooh, clever girl …"

"And some kind of overly sweet, caffeinated beverage from Starbucks in the grande size. Ariana Grande, there ya go. How's that?" I asked covering my eyes with my arm.

"Are we actually twins? Because, dude, that's exactly what I think about Ariana Grande too. Wait, try and guess what I'm thinking right now."

"Something sexual about Channing Tatum?" I guessed because that's what she was usually thinking about.

"Right track, wrong train. I've moved onto Chris Hemsworth, but it's not your fault, I don't think I sent out the requisite memo on the switch in management over my lady parts," she informed me, saying "lady parts" in a suggestive tone.

"Noted. I'm cataloging that info away for future twin quizzing."

"How's it going, buddy? What's happening?" she asked, and I could tell from the way she said it that she already knew I needed to talk.

"Oh … you know, just hungover and resisting the urge to eat an entire potful of homemade pasta and ragù."

"Okay, first off, why can't you just call it spaghetti like a normal person?"

"Because I'm not normal, and it's not spaghetti, we've talked about this," I replied with a sigh, genuinely annoyed at her for continuing the deny the difference.

"Why do you want to eat all that pasta? You only binge eat spaghetti when you're one step below a jar of Nutella, what happened?"

"Do you have time for an info dump session?" I asked, shifting into a sitting position as I prepared myself to tell her what I'd just witnessed.

"Sure, go ahead. Oh! Wait! I need to get my shaker weight," she announced and the line went silent for several moments while she went to retrieve it. "Okay, go ahead," she said as I took a deep breath in preparation of explaining what had just occurred and all the events leading up to it.

"Urgh, okay here goes. So, some of the girls I work with at the bakery had a strange response when I told them that Joel, my landlord, who owns a *1969 Camaro*, offered me his apartment to stay in, and when I asked what the problem was, they alluded to rumors that he might be part of the local biker gang."

"How can there be a biker gang? Isn't there only like ten people in that town?" she asked incredulously.

"Anna," I sighed impatiently.

"Okay, okay, I'm sorry. Also, no. Bikers are bad. Stay away from him," she cautioned me, which is exactly what I thought she'd say but hoping to give her the whole story before she came to that conclusion.

"No, wait," I rushed to explain. "He doesn't ride a bike. In fact, I don't even think he owns one, and he doesn't wear leather or patches or anything like that. He's super flirty with me and he's been nothing but helpful to me ever since I arrived."

Even to my own ears, I sounded too desperate to convince Anna of Joel's virtues and that's when I knew I was really in deep and worried about the possibility that I was going to have to accept that he was not as trustworthy as I initially thought. Still, I had to paint the whole picture for her before I could accept her judgment on the matter.

"Dude, he might not ride a motorbike, but he could be their accountant, he could be their computer hacker guy, he could be their drug mule," she rattled off and I felt myself becoming more deflated with each alternative suggestion. "I don't know, Soph," she said sounding dubious about the whole thing, and the fact that she'd stopped joking concerned me.

I blinked slowly with disappointment because I knew that it was possible that she was right.

"He could be one of those bikers who takes sick kids from the hospital out for rides in the countryside?" I suggested as in a last-ditch attempt to rationalize the situation to myself.

"Hey, here's an idea," Anna said, her voice perking up deceptively as though she had the answer. "Why don't you just *ask* him?"

"Well, I kind of did," I replied. "I asked him when he took me for a ride in his incredible Camaro. By the way, didn't I mention he has a 1969 Camaro Z28?"

"Yes. Let me tell you something okay, my dad's evil brother had a Camaro and he was a fucking nightmare. One Camaro does not a good man make."

"I bet your uncle had a 1980s model," I guessed. Nothing but silence on the other end of the line except for the *shake, shake, shake* of the shaker weight.

"Okay, I don't know how you knew that, but regardless, what difference does *that* make?"

"Come on, Anna, only cool people who are serious about being awesome go to the effort of acquiring and maintaining a 1960s era

Camaro, and a Z28 no less," I added but I was fully aware that I was grasping at straws.

"Oh yeah? I'll be sure to remind you of that when I come to visit you in prison once a month because you became a biker bitch in backwater Tennessee because your landlord is hot and drives a Camaro. Anyway, what did he say when you asked him?"

"He seemed kind of mad actually. Maybe even offended that I asked, and so I thought for sure he wasn't, so we went out with some friends last night and—"

"Friends? You're making new friends? Are you trying to phase me out?"

"Can I please just finish my story?" I asked, finding myself biting back some impatience.

"Tell me you love me first."

I sighed and rolled my eyes.

"Anna, please."

"Say it!" *Shake, shake, shake.*

"Oh my God, I can't believe you're staging an affection stand-off when I'm trying to tell you that I might be getting married to a criminal and having biker babies."

"I thought you said he wasn't a biker." *Shake, shake, shake.*

"Well he more or less told me that he wasn't, so I invited him out with some friends for drinks and we all had a really good time. I was still drunk when we got home, so he drove me to work and picked me up this afternoon and while he was dropping me off one of the bikers called him!" I said getting to the part of the story that I had been trying to get to since I called her.

"How do you know it was a biker?"

"Because I have been hearing people talk about this Catfish Hickson guy and that's the name that popped up on his phone when it rang."

"Catfish? His name is Catfish?" she asked incredulously. "That doesn't sound like a biker."

"Well if it was the guy who I saw hanging out across the street just a few minutes ago, then he might not sound like a biker, but he sure as fuck looks like one."

"Okay so … what more do you need to know here?" Anna asked with a serious edge in her tone that instantly made me nervous.

"He made me promise that I would give him a chance to explain why Catfish was calling him, so he's going to come around later to … I don't know … explain."

"So, what's the magic word here? What are we accepting as a legitimate explanation for all this nonsense?" she asked curiously.

"I don't know," I responded dejectedly. "I am too tired to be able to rationalize anything right now, that's why I called you, I was hoping you could get me there more efficiently."

"Well, you know that without all the information, I am going to default to the safest outcome for you, and unfortunately, in this case, I am leaning toward getting the heck outta there."

"Yeah … yeah me too," I lied.

"Alright, well get some rest and let me know what happens with the whole explanation thing later, okay?"

"I will. Thanks, Anna. You're a good friend you know that?"

"Of course, I know that. What do you think, I'm stupid?"

"I love you."

"Yeah, I love you too. Sweet dreams."

I hung up the phone and didn't even have the energy to parse through our conversation for the gems of wisdom that I required to make things any clearer, and before I knew it, my eyes were closing and I was drifting off to sleep.

CHAPTER 15

*W*hen I woke up, it took a few minutes for my mind to make the transition from the jumbled memory of my nonsensical dreams to the grounded solidness of reality.

Everything was dark inside the apartment and I still needed a moment to remember where I was.

As soon as I recalled my whereabouts, my thoughts instantly circled back to Joel and I felt a weight come over me when I remembered what had happened that afternoon.

Shit.

I had agreed to give him the opportunity to explain why Catfish Hickson was calling him and why he had agreed to meet with him, but I wasn't sure how much more of an explanation I needed.

I had seen the interaction with my own eyes and I couldn't imagine a scenario that would negate the underhandedness of Joel clearly being involved with the Wraiths after telling me he wasn't.

He'd lied. Right?

I felt so stupid and I hated making mistakes.

Anna always told me that I was too hard on myself and that I took my own shortcomings too much to heart. But hindsight and having the ability to go back and pick apart all the ways I should have known better, were my preferred methods of self-torture.

I'd done it with *No Whisk, No Reward,* and now I was doing it again with Joel.

I rolled over to switch on the lamp and gather up my phone from the bedside table.

It was 10:13 PM and I had four missed calls from numbers that I didn't recognize and one text message from Anna checking up on me.

I responded to let her know that I was fine, and that Joel and I hadn't talked yet before getting out of bed and walking to the kitchen to make myself a cup of tea.

A magnet affixed my Mr. Newman lanyard to the fridge and I stared at him while I waited for the kettle to boil.

"I'm not the snappiest piranha in the swamp of life, am I?" I inquired self-deprecatingly.

Mr. Newman looked back at me sympathetically.

Don't take it so hard, kid, we all make mistakes.

"There were enough signs to have avoided making a mistake, I just didn't want to see them. I appreciate the support though," I countered.

Hmm. Maybe, maybe not.

"What else do you need to know?"

As I recall, you were promised an explanation. Perhaps, we should reserve judgment until you've received it. What do you think?

I sighed and pinched at my bottom lip thoughtfully as a firm knock came from the front door.

I hesitated for a moment, before starting toward it.

You owe me another jar of Sockarooni, he taunted me.

I stopped and turned back to the fridge.

"For what? Getting me into more trouble?" I scoffed and shook my head as I made my way over to the front door.

I held the latch in my hand and took a steadying breath before unlocking it and pulling the door open.

There Joel stood. Looking like a dog left out in the rain and I almost gave in and grabbed him by the front of his shirt and pulled him inside the apartment.

"Hi," he greeted, and I could immediately see him searching my face for a clue as to what I might be thinking.

"Hello," I returned, okay with letting him see the doubt in my eyes and in my tone. I felt it was justified.

"Sorry I took so long, I ..." he paused and then shook his head. "It doesn't matter. Do you have time to talk?"

He seemed agitated or nervous but making an effort to remain on an even keel.

I widened the gap in the door and stood aside to invite him in.

"Do you want to go for a drive? I can't tell you what I need to tell you sitting still, I need to move to think," he explained gesturing to his temples by moving his fingers in a spinning motion and then breathed a laugh as though he were embarrassed about it.

I must have looked unsure because he sighed, and his eyes turned pleading.

"Please? You're the last person in the world I want looking at me like that."

"Like what?" I asked wondering how he interpreted my expression which I was trying to make as neutral as possible.

"The same way everyone else in Green Valley looks at me," he replied with a hint of bitterness in his voice. "Like I can't be trusted. Like I'm trash ... like I wanted any of this. Please, can we just get out of here and breathe for a minute? I'll tell you everything you want to know, I swear on my life. Whatever that's worth."

My heart hurt hearing him say that and maybe it was all too easy, but Mr. Newman was right. I wanted the explanation. I didn't like loose ends. I didn't want to be lying in bed five years from now wondering how things might have been different if I'd have listened to what he had to say.

"Okay," I said finally, "let me get my jacket."

* * *

Joel parked his Camaro in a small lot, which in the dark didn't seem to serve any purpose except maybe as an entrance to a hiking trail of some sort.

In the dark all I could see were trees and I didn't like the idea of being out in the woods at night even if I had a six-foot three man with me.

"Are you going to make me hike?" I inquired making sure my tone adequately expressed how enthusiastic I was about the idea, which wasn't much.

"No, it's just a short walk to the jetty on the lake. I come here to think," he explained, before reaching behind him to the backseat to collect a red, blue, and green tartan blanket. "Here take this, it's cold."

I accepted the blanket and we exited the car, making our way to the start of the trail.

The frigid air ate right on through to my bones, and I stopped to throw the blanket around my shoulders, falling a few steps behind Joel.

When he realized I was no longer beside him, he stopped to turn and held out his hand to me.

I hesitated briefly, not because I didn't trust him, but because I wasn't sure if it would still be appropriate after having heard what he had to say.

The feeling of his solid, strong hand closed tight around mine called to me like a siren song and I took it in spite of my reservations.

I'd come to crave the tiny promises of intimacy with him. His hand on my cheek, his touches at the small of my back, the way he gripped the back of my neck.

We walked along together, in silence, enjoying the still briskness of the fall air which served to draw me closer and closer into his side, seeking his body heat to guard against it.

"You still cold?" he asked me when he finally spoke, but I shook my head.

"I'm alright," I assured him as we walked along a little farther, until Joel suddenly veered off the path and started leading me through the trees.

"We're going into the trees?" I asked hoping that he knew where he was going.

"Not exactly, just cutting through to the shore," he explained as we traversed our way through shrubs, dirt, and fallen branches.

"You said there wouldn't be any hiking," I grumbled as he laughed and kept a tight hold of my hand in case I decided to run away when I realized I'd been hoodwinked.

"Not much farther," he promised.

After a few more minutes, we breached the trees and stepped out onto the packed dirt and sand of the lakeshore.

"Come on, there's the jetty just over there," he said pointing off to the right where I could see a structure jutting out onto the water which shimmered in the reflection of the moonlight.

"When my brother and I were kids, we used to come swimming here every day during the summer," Joel said as we walked onto the jetty. "The jetty goes right out to the deepest part of the lake and we used to jump off the end into the water every single day at noon, and go home at dinnertime, sunburnt and pruned to high heaven," he recalled smiling sadly at the memory.

"Every time we ever got into trouble for staying out too late as kids, it was because I let Nick talk me into staying for just five more minutes. He'd always say, 'Five more minutes. Just five more,' and before we knew it, it was dark, and my mom was out of her mind with worry," he said as our footsteps creaked along the aging planks of wood.

"Where's your mom now?" I asked gently, seeing as how it was the first time he'd mentioned her.

"Not sure. She took off when I was about nine or ten. I don't really remember much about it other than one day she was there and the next day she wasn't," he explained sounding somewhat distant about it, though it was unclear if that stemmed from resentment or simply being too young to remember her with much lingering fondness.

"Nick was two years older than me and looking back, I feel like the only time I *ever* got into trouble was because of something I let Nick talk me into," Joel said, his chin lowered to peer down at his feet as they casually kicked out in front of him as we strolled along.

173

"My brother was a good guy, but he had a big mouth and knack for finding trouble wherever he went."

I got the sense Joel was building toward something important so I listened attentively and patiently.

We reached the end of the walkway and Joel let go of my hand, lowering himself down to sit at the edge of the jetty with his feet dangling off the side. I followed his lead and sat beside him, pressing myself against him to try and leech some his warmth.

"You sure you're not too cold?" he asked again, and I shook my head.

"No, I'm sure. Tell me more about your brother," I encouraged, fearing that he might change his mind suddenly and stop talking. "What kind of trouble did he get into?" I inquired, shoving my hands into my jacket pockets and burrowing into his side.

"Mostly stupid stuff like underage drinking and smoking weed, trespassing on the fancy properties out at Cades Cove, sneaking out with girls, and getting into the occasional dustup," he recounted. "Nothing that serious, just things I look back on now and wonder if I should have seen it coming when he decided he was going to go behind my back and get our auto shop mixed up with the Iron Wraiths."

My stomach lurched and I pulled myself upright to look at Joel who had turned to me as though he'd anticipated my reaction.

I instantly had a hundred questions, but something he'd said stood out to me as particularly notable, so I started there.

"What do you mean, 'behind your back'?" I inquired.

"After my Dad passed, my brother and I inherited his garage. Back then we were the only one in Green Valley, so instead of selling it, my brother convinced me to leave my job in construction in Nashville and come back home to help him run it. Dad still had outstanding debts on the family home and the garage was a source of income, so I agreed to help him out temporarily until he either found someone else or sold the shop. Then a few years passed by and the Winston brothers opened their garage and from there, things just went to hell," he said shaking his head hopelessly.

174

"It was alright at first seeing as how they only seemed to be interested in custom and rare vehicles and there were plenty of shitty cars around Green Valley to keep Nick and I busy. Then slowly but surely, people in town started taking their cars to the Winston garage, and it didn't matter if it was a 1967 Ford Thunderbird or a 2009 VW Jetta."

"So, you started losing money?" I guessed, and Joel nodded solemnly.

"Nick said he ran into one of the twins and tried to negotiate a jurisdictional agreement," he explained shaking his head as though it weren't how he would have handled that situation. "Obviously, they weren't having it, and eventually, we had to sell our family house to pay for the remainder of the mortgage."

Joel was silent for quite a while before clearing his throat and continuing to recount to me the details of the story.

"You can guess where this is heading, right?" he said looking at me briefly with a humorless smirk.

"I think so, but why don't you tell me anyway?" I encouraged, getting the sense that he needed the catharsis of sharing all this with someone.

"At some point, I started noticing that things were beginning to ease financially. Just small things like bills getting paid and money not bleeding from our business account, which didn't make any sense to me because we were down to working on two or three cars a week, if we were lucky. I was suspicious, so one day I waited for Nick to leave the garage and I started going through the office and found the invoices for the cars we'd worked on that week. All of them had been doctored to make it look like the repairs were way more extensive than the work we'd actually done, and the cost of the repairs were increased after the fact. I knew then that something was up, so I confronted him with the invoices and that's when he told me that he had made an arrangement with the Iron Wraiths and was running a chop shop operation for them after closing hours for a cut of the money after they'd sold the parts."

"Then what happened?" I asked wanting to hear all of it in its entirety before I came to any conclusions.

"And then." Joel blew out a breath and shook his head as though he couldn't believe what he was about to say. "I somehow let him talk me into helping him," he admitted with what I could only describe as unimaginable regret in his tone.

"Five nights a week, the Wraiths would bring stolen cars into the garage after dark. Nick and I would break them down and load the parts into trucks to be sold on the black market and we would get a cut of the profit they made from the sales. He said it was a six-month arrangement and after that, we would sell the shop and I could go back to construction, so I thought there was an end in sight which is the only reason I was stupid enough to agree to it."

I could feel Joel becoming tightly wound but waited as he rode the waves of emotion.

"Then what happened?" I prompted after a moment.

"Exactly what I tried to tell Nick would happen. I told him there was no way they were going to just let us walk away after six months, and sure enough, they strung us along for almost two goddamn years. They even tried to get us to join the club, threatening to anonymously tip off the cops about our garage if we didn't patch in, and that's when I lost it. There was no way I was going to spend the rest of my life answering to the likes of Razor Dennings and Darrell Winston. So, I put my foot down. Nick and I got into a big fight over it, throwing chairs and shit at each other. And then I threatened to—" Joel stopped short as though it was becoming difficult to continue and I reached out to place my hand comfortingly on his thigh, knowing where his story was leading. "I told him he either needed to tell the Wraiths that we were out, or I was going to move back to Nashville and leave him there to deal with it. Nick looked at me and said, 'Joel, would you really turn your back on me? Your own brother?'"

Pausing at the painful memory Joel licked his lips and took a number of steadying breaths.

"The last thing I said to him was, 'You sound as manipulative as they do, why don't you just patch in and get it over with? I'm not following you down.'"

I felt the fibers of my heart straining against one another as the story neared its inevitable conclusion and couldn't fathom the unimaginable guilt that Joel's final words had caused him. I found Joel's hand and put it into my lap, because I knew the hardest part was coming, and that he would need to know that I wasn't going anywhere.

"About three years ago, just a couple days after our last fight, I was at the garage when I get a phone call from the Sheriff's office," Joel began and then stopped as I watched his Adam's apple bob in his throat before continuing. "They were calling to tell me that there had been an accident and Nick had been treated at the scene but died on the way to the hospital."

I had anticipated those words since he began sharing the story but hearing his voice quaver as he said the actual words wrenched my heart and I squeezed his hand tightly into mine, feeling him squeeze back.

The guilt that radiated off him was so heavy and palpable that it almost seemed to form itself into a separate entity that hung over him and now I understood why Joel had all but separated himself from everyone in Green Valley.

I wanted to tell him that I was sorry for the loss of his father and brother in too short a space of time, but it was too woefully inadequate a platitude to really express how I felt, so I stayed quiet until he felt ready to continue with the story.

"The police report said that Nick had lost control of his bike and slammed into a tree, but I knew better. I knew exactly what happened. I even went to the scene a week later and to this day, I have no idea how they missed that there were multiple sets of tire tracks on the road. I had heard people talk about how the Wraiths had killed people, but you never think it's more than just small-town gossip. And then it hits really close to home and your mind ..." He paused and shook his head and I could see his eyes were brimming now. "Your mind ain't right. I convinced myself that they had moles inside the Sheriff's office, I mean how else could there be no mention of secondary tire marks on the police report? They made sure I wouldn't talk to anyone about it and I was convinced that they were coming for me next, so I alienated myself from everyone because I didn't know who I could trust. Then one night, about two weeks after the accident, I get a call from Repo, one of the Wraith's captains at the time. He's wondering if I'm going to be available to get back to work any time soon."

"You gotta be kidding me?" I asked incredulously and Joel nodded.

"To which I politely as possible told him to go fuck himself." Joel snorted without humor.

"He more or less told me that I don't have a choice. I could either get back to the garage or copies of my invoices would be sent to the Sheriff and I'd go to prison on a laundry list of charges which he proceeded to list out like he was ever smart enough to go to law school," he says, shaking his head bitterly. "A while back there was a whole thing between the Winstons and the Wraiths, and I don't know what happened, but Razor Dennings who was the club president at the time, was arrested in some undercover operation. Repo took off nobody knows where he went, and Darrell Winston supposedly went turncoat on the Wraiths."

"That's good, right?" I asked, hoping it meant that the Wraiths had bigger fish to fry and that small potatoes like Joel would no longer hold their interest.

"I thought so," he said, his tone indicating that my hope was in vain. "Things were quiet for a little while after all that mess, nobody called me for months and I was ready to sell the shop and get the hell out of Green Valley."

"Until …" I prompted him understanding that if Joel's ordeal was over, then he most certainly wouldn't be here right now.

"Until Catfish Hickson decided he wanted to go hell for leather in a bid to try and take over the club presidency," Joel continued, and it felt like a door slamming shut in my face just to hear it. "Just when everyone thought the Iron Wraiths would be forced to disband or at least move their HQ out of Green Valley, Catfish stepped in declaring everything was business as usual."

"I suppose he came looking for you?" I guessed, and Joel nodded, sighing heavily.

"Though it's generally understood that he's not as psychotic as Razor Dennings, it doesn't make him any less dangerous as far as I'm concerned. Especially now. He can't afford to let the Wraiths look weak and risk being patched over by a rival club, so he's ramping up his efforts in order to get voted in as club president, or however their fucked-up system works," he spat dismissively as though the details were irrelevant. "The Wraiths are keeping a low profile right now because they can't afford anyone to come sniffing around, but Catfish has told me in no uncertain terms that he wants my garage back up and running as soon as possible. That's why Catfish came to see me today. That guy you saw me talking to. That was Catfish Hickson. He came to tell me that I need to hire someone who can help me start breaking down cars again, or he's going to assign recruits to come and do the work on my premises."

"What did you say?" I asked curiously.

"I stalled by telling him he needed to give me time to find some-one, but I can't stall on that for long," he said swiping his hand wearily across his forehead.

Joel sighed, his eyes staring unseeingly out at the water. He looked and sounded exhausted.

"I don't want to do this anymore, but every time I think there's an out it just closes up on me and I don't know what to do anymore. Honestly, at this point, I feel like going to jail would probably feel like a relief."

Hearing such despair in his words made my heart ache so much, I couldn't even entertain the idea that that was a possibility.

"Isn't there anybody in this town you could talk to? Someone who could … I don't know, find a contact within the Sheriff's office that you can trust?"

Joel shook his head hopelessly.

"I can't trust anybody, and nobody trusts me," he murmured icily and though I refused to accept that, I understood that he felt like he had exhausted every avenue and didn't want to be bright-sided with opti-mism. He just wanted someone to listen.

"What can I do?" I asked feeling his hand slip out of my grasp as he lifted his arm to drape it over my shoulders and pull me tighter against him.

"Nothing," he said shaking his head as he stroked my upper arm as though I were the one needing comforting. "Maybe just take me slow dancing a couple more times before you leave Green Valley?" he suggested with a sad smile.

CHAPTER 16

*A*fter we left the lake Joel and I went home and I made him watch *Cool Hand Luke.*

I had the foolish hope that Mr. Newman's portrayal of a dissenting nonconformist who refused to back down to anyone might spark a little fire inside Joel, and if not, then at least the infamous egg scene might make him laugh, which it did.

When it was over, we lay on my couch together staring up at my ceiling when a thought occurred to me.

"Did your brother live here?" I asked turning my neck toward him.

Joel nodded and distracted himself fiddling with the buttons on my pink and gray plaid shirt.

"Was it really a rental or did you just tell me that?"

"I had planned to list it as a rental, but I never could bring myself to," he mumbled, weary from the emotional toll that the retelling of his brother's death had on him.

"Can I see your apartment?" I asked suddenly, realizing that I had never been inside it before.

"Sure." He nodded with a tired smile.

We both stood from the couch and left my apartment without bothering to close it up.

Joel unlocked the door to his apartment and turned on the lights inside.

The layout was exactly the same as mine only Joel had a pull-out sofa in the spot where my bed was, and there were two huge bookshelves. One overflowed with books and the other was packed with vinyl records. In between the bookshelves was a sideboard with a record player on top of it, and I immediately made a beeline right toward it.

"Whoa," I said on a breath as I neared and saw that he had most recently listened to Sam Cooke.

"Can I look through your records?" I asked looking at him from over my shoulder as he crossed the apartment toward the kitchen.

"Sure, pick something and put it on."

I didn't need to be invited twice as I immediately pulled out a large stack from the bookshelf, sat on the floor in front of the record player and began leafing through them.

"Joel, this collection is incredible," I declared after going through only a handful.

"Thank you. A lot of these were my dad's but I've slowly added a bunch of my own," he explained as he came toward me with a takeout container. I craned my neck to inspect its contents.

"What is that?" I asked scrunching my nose at the completely unappetizing congealed ball of yellow lumps inside.

"It's mac and cheese," Joel replied lifting the box toward me and I recoiled.

"Yergh. No thank you. You don't cook, do you?" I asked, a conclusion I had come to after recalling the only time that I had seen him eat was when we were out together.

"Nope," he replied distractedly as he tried to shake the unyielding glob of mac and cheese that was too big to shove in his mouth off his fork.

"I can't even watch you eat that," I cringed, turning my attention back to the pile of records just as an idea occurred to me. "Hey, do you want me to teach you how to make something really good?"

"I don't really have anything to cook in my fridge, this is pretty much it."

He let go of the bottom of the container and the whole thing, food and all, hung off the end of his fork.

"No. Nuh-uh. You're not eating that. Wait here," I ordered placing the stack of records on the floor and leaping to my feet to make my way across the hall to raid my refrigerator.

After raiding my own supplies, I returned with a bag full of groceries and dumped them out on his kitchen counter.

"Come on," I called to him.

I felt him creep up behind me to inspect what I had brought, and I could hear he'd chosen *Rumours* by Fleetwood Mac to play on the record player.

"What are you making?" he inquired, as I tried not to pay attention to the warmth of his breath on my shoulder.

"I'm not making anything, you are," I informed him and promptly eased my way out from between him and the kitchen counter.

I crossed to the bench opposite and hoisted myself up onto it, raising my eyebrows at him with a grin.

Joel cocked an eyebrow at me as though I didn't know what I was in for.

"Let's see how long your patience lasts with my lack of aptitude in all matters concerning cooking."

I rolled my eyes and cocked my head to the side like I wasn't buying it.

"You're not getting out of this by pretending that you're too stupid to stir food in a couple of pots. Even the terminally incompetent can handle this recipe," I assured him. "Now, grab me a frying pan and a small saucepan."

"Ooh, I like it when you're bossy," Joel drawled suggestively which both aroused and annoyed me because I knew he was trying to distract me.

"The novelty will wear off if you don't follow my instructions," I cautioned not giving him any leeway and he rifled through the cupboards until he found what I'd requested.

For the next fifteen minutes, I guided Joel through how to make an easy tomato bisque using none other than Mr. Newman's eternally versatile Sockarooni sauce. With the few additions of ketchup, fresh basil, and heavy cream, Joel now had a pot of rich, creamy, satisfying soup bubbling away while I talked him through the Gruyère grilled cheese sandwiches that would accompany it.

"Once both sides of the sandwiches are done, we're gonna grate a little more cheese on the outside so that it forms a crust on the bread when we flip it over," I explained watchfully, as Joel did a perfectly fine job of assembling the meal.

It felt nice to focus on something other than the weight of Joel's situation and the million other questions and worries it stirred up in my mind.

While we waited for the grilled cheese sandwiches to brown in the pan, Joel turned and folded his arms over his chest, crossing one leg over the other.

"What's with the Paul Newman thing?" he inquired curiously, turning back to the pan every now and then to check that it wasn't burning.

"My mom's influence," I explained swinging my legs from side to side. "When I was growing up, we used to watch a lot of old movies together and I guess I just took a particular shining to him. Then when my mom died, I watched his movies a lot because it made me feel closer to her somehow. I know that sounds stupid," I added dismissively.

"That's not stupid," he offered with a compassionate and tender lilt to his voice that made me smile. "People deal with grief and loss in all kinds of different ways. Church, therapy, drugs, drink. If watching old time movies makes you feel close to your mom and like you're honoring her memory by doing that, then who's to say that's stupid?"

I promptly felt the stirring of my emotions building so I nudged my chin toward the pan.

"Those are probably ready to be turned now," I informed him, handing him a spatula and watching as he turned the sandwiches over.

I instructed him to sprinkle grated cheese on the outside of the sandwich and then, when the other side was done, he flipped it over to do the same to the other side until both sandwiches were crusted in crispy, browned cheese on the outside and flowing, gooey cheese in the middle.

"This sure beats the hell out of the rubber ball I was gonna eat," he mumbled with approval after taking a bite.

"Great job," I grinned at him offering him a high five, which he reciprocated before we took our plates into the living room to listen to more records.

We both found we had a penchant for long, indulgent guitar solos, dramatic key changes, and stadium anthems and so our choices gravitated to the realms of Dire Straits, Queen, Led Zeppelin, and Pink Floyd.

We spent the entire evening going through record after record, playing only our favorite songs from each album and still, we hadn't made a dent in his amazing collection.

As "Telegraph Road" by Dire Straits faded out, I could see Joel's eyes getting heavier and decided it was time to go.

"I'm gonna get going or I'm going to be a useless mess at work tomorrow," I informed him looking at my phone and seeing it was after one in the morning.

"I understand," he replied, his voice husky and inviting and starting to feel every bit as comforting to me as a Paul Newman movie or a jar of Sockarooni sauce.

"Thank you for sharing everything with me tonight," I offered, grateful to him for his trust, particularly after having heard how hard that was for him to give.

"Thank you for listening," he responded, his lips hooking into a tired, but grateful smile. "It goes without saying that I'd appreciate it if you kept it to yourself, right?"

"Of course," I assured him.

"Thanks ... sweet dreams, Sophie."

"Goodnight, Joel."

I was definitely starting to feel things for him beyond physical attraction and I knew that I needed to be careful now.

Thanksgiving was just around the corner and I was all too aware of how finite my time in Green Valley was. How was I just supposed to leave him there now, knowing what I did?

He was a grown man, yes, but everybody needs someone in their corner and Joel didn't have anybody.

I felt honored that he opened up to me but my heart felt his burden deeply.

I went to bed and the few hours of sleep I managed was restless and fitful.

* * *

At work the following week, I could think of nothing else except what Joel had shared with me. Between the confliction I felt about *Double the Whisk, Double the Reward* and worrying about Joel, I was less engaged with the group, and tended to sequester myself in quiet corners where I could obsessively mull over everything he'd told me.

I guess it must have been obvious that I was distracted because people kept asking me if I was okay, but how could I be, knowing what I knew?

How am I doing? Oh, just great. Yeah, I'm developing feelings for a guy who I plan on leaving behind in a few weeks, trapped in the clutches of a murderous crime organization, which I can't do anything about. I am also being hounded on a daily basis with the opportunity at a second chance to win a sum of money that could change my life, only I'm too much of a chickenshit to take it. How are you?

Joel had made me promise not to tell anyone about his situation, and I knew it wasn't my story to share, but any time his name was mentioned, even in passing, I had to remind myself to bite my tongue. Even if I thought that it might help people better understand why he was the way he was.

By Thursday, Tempest had decided that I'd had enough space and sidled up to me while I was finishing up a batch of eclairs.

"Here," she said holding out a croissant for me to eat and my stomach grumbled as though on cue.

I mustered as much of a smile as I could manage and accepted the baked good from her.

"You sure you're okay there, princess of pastry?" she asked watching me as I chewed a bite of croissant and nodded with approval at her impromptu nickname.

"Princess of pastry, I like that."

"Or maybe the countess of croissants?" She shrugged offering an alternative which I found equally pleasing.

"I do make a good fucking croissant though," I declared inspecting the impressive separation between the velvety layers between the walls of the crisp exterior.

"Yes, ma'am, and I've been watching you do it so that we can carry on producing them once you've left us for Beantown. Now, what is up with you this week? And don't say nothing because you haven't spoken but five words since Monday and I know you well enough to know that you can talk underwater with your mouth full of marbles."

I sighed and began pulling out the buttery innards from my croissant, playing with my food more than I was eating it.

"I guess. I'm just thinking a lot about the show and … how much I know I'll regret it if I don't do it, and how much I'll regret it if I do and it all goes to hell again."

I wasn't technically lying. I was thinking a lot about that too, but that's not what was causing the heaviness in my heart and my subdued mood.

"What if I told you that Joy and I have been thinking a lot about it too?" she asked cautiously, and I scoffed as I tossed her a cynical sideways glance.

"I would tell you both to get a life," I joked, but Tempest cocked her head at me and nudged my arm with her elbow.

"I am serious, what if there was a way that we could help you eliminate the performance anxiety aspect of appearing on the show?"

I was fixing to brush off her suggestion, but she held up her hand to cut me off at the pass.

"Sophie, I know you're about to argue, but just come with me on this journey for a second, alright? If we could help you work through your stage fright over the next couple of weeks, would that help you feel more comfortable accepting the offer to return to the show?"

"Sure." I shrugged. "Who wouldn't go for it if they knew they wouldn't crap their pants at the first sight of a red recording light?"

Tempest smiled as though my response pleased her and I narrowed my eyes at her suspiciously.

"Good," she said and turned to start walking away.

"Why? What are you planning?" I asked after her, realizing that it sounded like she and Joy were scheming.

"Nothing, I'm gonna go take over out front, I'll see you at the test kitchen tonight, okay, bye!" she shouted hastily at me from over her shoulder and disappeared to the front of the store.

* * *

In the hours between the end of my shift at the bakery, and the time I needed to return for test kitchen, I explored Green Valley and the surrounding areas to keep myself occupied.

Usually, a long drive with a kickass Nineties R&B playlist was enough to guide me back into a good headspace, but even "Motown-philly" by Boyz II Men couldn't pull me out of my weighted intro-spection.

When I arrived for test kitchen night, I felt like I had been hit by a three-mile-long procession of freightliners only to have them back up and run over me all over again.

Even though I was not particularly tickled by the idea of being around a bunch of people, even if they were my friends, I did feel like the distraction of perfecting my technique for Chestnuts Roasting on an Open Fire might be a benefit to my frame of mind.

When I knocked on the door at the back entrance, instead of being greeted by Jennifer, I was surprised when Joy appeared in her place.

"Oh, hey, Joy. You early?" I inquired seeing how she was usually the last one to arrive.

"No, Jenn had to go take care of something, so I offered to close the store and since I was already here, I just thought I'd stick around until you ladies arrived," she explained as I slid my bag underneath a bench and went to retrieve an apron.

"Does that mean Jenn won't be joining us?" I asked as I reached behind my body to knot my apron and Joy shook her head regretfully.

"No, I don't think she'll make this one, so it's just you, me, and Tempest today," she said making her way back to the door when she heard more knocking. "Ooh, that'll be Tempest now."

"Splendiferous," I declared to nobody in particular as I shuffled off to find some wine glasses.

"Good evening, friends," Tempest greeted us slinging a grocery bag onto the bench, while Joy got to work uncorking a bottle of wine. "How's our countess of croissants? Are you feeling better?"

"Oh no, you're not feeling well? I thought your skin looked a little pallid," Joy contributed, her eyes laced with sympathy as she began to pour the wine.

"Thanks, Joy," I replied as I picked up my glass of wine and drained it without a breath.

I placed the glass on the bench and poured myself another glass, promising myself that I would enjoy this glass more slowly and glanced up to find Tempest and Joy staring at me.

"What did he do?" Tempest asked, her voice hard and accusatory. Her assumption that Joel was at fault, caused my muscles to coil defensively.

"Why does everyone default to the worst-case scenario when it comes to him?" I asked rhetorically as I got to work on making some puff pastry, which I hoped would help channel some of my frustration.

"I don't get it. Everyone in town throws their unmentionables at Beau Winston despite it being universally acknowledged that he is fishing buddies with two known members of the Wraiths, but if there's a whiff of a rumor that Joel is involved with them, then everyone avoids him like the plague. Did it ever occur to anyone that he might have more cause to despise them than most?" I asked, beating a cold slab of butter with a rolling pin to within an inch of its life.

"Those Winston boys have plenty enough cause to despise the

Wraiths," Joy countered, but I didn't know how that was possible with the information I had become privy to.

"How so?" I asked, roughly slapping the flattened sheet of butter on top of a sheet of dough.

"Well, you know their daddy was like one of the top-ranking members, right?" Tempest asked, and I nodded.

"Yes, you mentioned that to me some time ago," I replied distractedly rolling out the pastry. "But I only got half the story because we had a last-minute special order to finish."

"Right." Tempest nodded, recalling where we'd left off. "Well I guess I did promise to fill you in on all the gory details, or at least the ones I know of, and seeing as how Jenn isn't here, I think now's as good a time as any." She sighed, taking a break from shredding a block of cheese to sip her wine.

"Damn, I don't even know where you'd start." Joy sighed, before taking a generous gulp from her own glass. "It's a pretty epic saga, I think we should just give you the CliffsNotes version," she decided, placing her glass back down as she turned her attention to Tempest.

"Okay sure, go ahead," I replied, anxious to hear the rest of the story.

"Okay so, the long and the short of it is, the Winston's mom, Bethany Oliver was a good girl, from a good family who went way back with the Payton family, who owns Daisy's Nut House and the Mill. Then Darrell Winston, a scumbag with charm to spare, who was already in deep with the Iron Wraiths, swept Bethany off her feet and they got married. As we explained prior, they had a bunch of kids, to whom Darrell was a nightmare of a father until Bethany told him to go take a hike. Several years later, one of the Winston boys, who you haven't met, Jethro, was recruited to the Iron Wraiths, but somehow managed to get out. I'm not sure how, so don't ask. More years later, poor Bethany got sick. Cancer and it was inoperable. She and Darrell got in a dispute over the estate, but she managed to secure it against him having any claim. So, what does Darrell Winston do? He and his biker buddies try to kidnap a couple of the older kids, but those

Winstons put up the fight of their lives and in the end, Darrell was sent off with his tail between his legs."

"Then what happened?" I asked, placing my rolling pin down to give Tempest my full attention.

"It's hard to say. I mean it's not easy to distinguish between rumors and truth in this town, but a little while ago, Roscoe, the youngest Winston, got involved with Simone Payton who was an undercover FBI agent, while his big brother Billy was engaged to Simone's sister, Daniella, the lady who came to visit Jenn at the bakery that one day. Anyway, so nobody knows exactly what happened, but there was a big shoot-out at Daisy's Nut House and Roscoe and Simone got shot."

"Oh my God," I said covering my mouth with my hands and closing my eyes in shock.

"They're both okay," Tempest rushed to assure me, "but Razor Dennings, who was the Iron Wraiths club president at the time, got super fucked up. He didn't die or anything—"

"Unfortunately," Joy added with a flicker of her eyebrows.

"But, the cops captured him and in a really strange turn of events, Darrell Winston suddenly decided to testify against Razor! Probably because he figured with Razor caught, the jig was up and wanted to negotiate some kind of plea deal. Anyway, Billy Winston disappeared suddenly after that, and nobody knows where he is, Duane who is Beau's twin, is living in Italy with his wife and kids, Jethro the eldest—"

"Yeah, can we go back to Jethro for a sec?" I asked, the mention of his name prompting something that Tempest had said which sparked my interest.

"So, Jethro was a recruit in the Iron Wraiths?"

"Correct."

"I know you said not to ask how he got out, but do you have any clue, any kind of inkling about how he managed to leave?"

Tempest just shrugged so I turned to Joy who didn't seem to know either.

"I can't help you there, but if I tell you something you gotta promise me that it won't leave this room," Joy said ominously.

I needed to take a moment to think about making that kind of promise, particularly if any of the information about to be shared was pertinent to Joel's situation. I respected Joy's friendship, but I would have done anything if I thought it would help Joel out of the quagmire of a situation he was currently struggling with.

"I'll try," I offered noncommittally which thankfully didn't seem to deter her from continuing.

"Good enough." She shrugged before continuing. "I heard that Cletus Winston is secretly some kind of vigilante superhero."

"Good Lord, Joy." Tempest sighed rolling her eyes.

"No, I swear, I heard he has more evidence against the Iron Wraiths than the police department does—"

"That's not technically accurate," a disembodied voice—which most certainly did not belong to a woman—boomed from behind us, and we all shrieked in surprise, spinning around to see who it belonged to.

CHAPTER 17

*C*letus Winston appeared from the back room, wiping off a wrench with a cloth.

I guessed he was there fixing the broken mixer, but I wondered how he'd been there the whole time without anyone seeming to realize it.

"You scared me into the afterlife!" Joy exclaimed clutching her chest and giggling nervously, until she remembered what we had been talking about.

"How long have you been standing there?" Tempest asked sheepishly.

"Long enough," he responded with a knowing nod that made Tempest and Joy shrink back with guilty expressions.

"Is that true?" I asked him, supposing too late that it was arrogant of me to expect Cletus would simply spill the beans and fess up as if I were his mother. The rules around social etiquette while attempting to persuade someone to reveal themselves as some kind of vigilante mastermind were not something I thought I'd ever have to consider.

"Is what true?" he asked trying the classic ignorance card, but I was a dog with a bone now and it was not going to work.

"The thing that compelled you to blow your eavesdropping cover,"

I replied, referring to his obvious decision to inject himself into our conversation.

"Do I *look* like a vigilante superhero?" he asked pointing to himself with an eyebrow cocked as though it were too preposterous an idea to entertain.

"Did Ed Gein *look* like someone who made a belt out of human nipples?" I countered. "When do people ever *look* like something that other people would never expect?"

"Touché," Cletus conceded. "However, that does not change the fact that it is simply not true and your preoccupation with serial killers is concerning," he said with his usual brand of composed stoicism, but something about his response didn't make sense.

"You didn't say it *wasn't* true when you walked in here, you said, it wasn't *technically* true," I replied placing special emphasis on the words which would drastically change his intent.

"I misspoke," Cletus replied with a shrug and practiced look of nonchalance bordering on bored.

"I don't believe you," I challenged, seeing Joy and Tempest glance back and forth between us as though they were at a final at Wimbledon.

"That's your prerogative."

"Cletus, if you have evidence against the Wraiths, why the hell wouldn't you use it? They're ruining people's lives," I appealed to him gesticulating passionately with my hands.

"I don't know what you're talking about and the Iron Wraiths are as good as done once Darrell testifies against Razor Dennings," he said keeping his infuriatingly calm composure.

"How long will that take?" I asked, knowing it wouldn't be soon enough to be of benefit to Joel's current predicament.

"It's hard to say, both sides will need time to put their case together for the legal proceeding so ... months, years, who knows?"

"So, Joel's just supposed to suffer at Catfish's hands in the meantime?" I asked, placing my hands on my hips and knowing that my voice was becoming shrill, but unable to control it.

"Suffering? By *willingly* using his garage to run their *illegal* chop shop operation?" Cletus volleyed, narrowing his eyes in the first sign that I might be getting somewhere with him.

"Not willingly! Joel *never* wanted to have anything to do with the Wraiths until you and your brothers practically bankrupted the Barnes Auto Shop by taking all their customers."

"What?" Cletus scoffed shaking his head as though he didn't believe it.

"Yeah, while you and your brothers were busy charming the pants off every man, woman, and dog in Green Valley, you were also putting Joel and Nick Barnes out of business."

"Strictly speaking, Sophie, it was probably Beau who was doing all the charming. I know you haven't met Duane, but trust me it wasn't him, and it most *certainly* wasn't me—"

"I don't think that's true," Joy piped up for the first time, raising her hand timidly as three heads snapped toward her.

She slowly lowered her hand and looked toward Tempest for assistance.

"I think we should probably leave these two to chat," Tempest said tentatively, reaching for Joy's hand as the two of them started toward the back door.

"Yeah, I have to go … pick up … milk," Joy said fumbling through a lie as the two women scurried hand in hand out of the bakery without taking anything other than their absolutely essential items.

When they were both gone, Cletus sighed and slowly approached me at the other side of the bench.

He towered over me, but I was not intimidated because, despite my possibly misplaced frustration toward him, I knew he was a good man, someone everyone in Green Valley respected. A truth which only made his refusal to help all the more exasperating.

He anchored his hands flat against the metal bench and regarded me with a slightly softer, but still firm, countenance.

"I didn't know about the Barnes's business struggling. They always kept to themselves, but if we had've known—"

"Joel told me that his brother tried to talk to one of your brothers about some kind of jurisdictional agreement and they didn't want to talk about it."

Cletus's eyes flickered around as though he was trying to work out who Nick might have spoken to or perhaps trying to think of a suitable response. I sighed and flicked my hand.

"Anyway, it doesn't matter now. It doesn't change Joel's current situation. It doesn't change the fact that Nick went to the Wraiths behind Joel's back and offered their shop to keep them from having to file bankruptcy. It doesn't change the rift it caused between them when Joel found out about it, or the fact that Nick was killed in an 'accident' on the way home from a meeting with the Wraiths when he tried to cut ties with them because his relationship with his brother was more important. Things were quiet for a while after that Razor character went into custody, but now Catfish is on Joel's ass, hassling him to get the garage back up and running. Joel bought a little bit of time, but it's running out."

Cletus listened intently to me as I recounted the details that Joel had shared with me, and though I felt bad for betraying his confidence, I needed more people to know how he was being manipulated and controlled by Catfish.

"I know you two have had your differences, but all Joel wants is to sell his garage and maybe move back to Nashville so he can get back into construction. That's what he really wants to do, he wants to build homes, not chop cars for the Iron Wraiths."

"Move back to Nashville?" Cletus asked me suddenly like he was confused.

"Yes," I said tentatively, not sure why that seemed to shock him. "That's where he was when his father passed. That's why he had to come back to Green Valley." Cletus continued to look at me as though what I was saying didn't make any sense.

"And you'll be off to Boston on New Year's Day?" Cletus asked as I raised my eyebrows at him, wondering why he sounded like he didn't know this already.

"Hmm," he hummed looking at me through narrow eyes.

"Anyway," I said not really understanding why he was more caught up on where Joel was going rather than how he was going to even get there.

"Please, is there anything you can do to help? There must be something you can do to help. You must know somebody in town who can do something. Wasn't your brother a congressman? Doesn't he have any contacts?"

"Billy no longer has any political associations," he stated regretfully.

"What about that Daniella lady, what was her name? Payton! Daniella Payton. Isn't she trying to get into politics, your family and her family go back a long way, there must be someone she knows? Can't you ask?"

Cletus was looking at me like his neck was permanently set to the left, and I expected that any minute he would start stroking his beard in thought.

I felt like I wasn't really getting anywhere, so I sighed and placed my elbows on the bench and buried my face in my hands for a moment before standing back upright and trying one last time.

"You're driving down the road. Up ahead, you see a car. As you get closer you realize that there is someone trapped inside, begging for help. Do you just drive by?"

"I realize you're trying to analogize Joel's situation, but in reality, take any first aid course and the number one rule, before you do anything, is to make sure that the environment around you is clear of any danger that could cause *yourself* any harm."

I was getting nowhere and his rationale was infuriatingly sound. I had nothing to counter with except to ask if his personal safety would still be the number one priority if it were Jenn trapped in the vehicle.

I refrained, recognizing the argument was too confronting and that it would infer a relationship with Joel that I wasn't sure we had. I knew I had come to care deeply for Joel, but love was not a term I threw around frivolously.

I silently stewed as Cletus looked at his watch, and then to me before saying, "I think perhaps we should call it a night on tonight's test kitchen."

"Sure," I said dejectedly, and walked over to collect my backpack before leaving the kitchen feeling angry and frustrated.

* * *

Most people lose their appetite when faced with overwhelming periods of stress and sorrow, but ever since I could remember, those emotions seemed to have the opposite effect on me.

When I was happy, which if I was honest, was most of the time, I was quite happy to only eat one meal a day, albeit a substantial one, particularly when I was working long hours in a commercial kitchen.

If, however, I was faced with a loss, or something that made me anxious or angry, it was like a second stomach awakened from a long winter and wouldn't stop screaming until each respective stomach had had their fill.

After what happened at the bakery with Cletus, I didn't want to go home because I didn't trust myself not to go knocking on Joel's door, so I headed over to Daisy's for something to eat.

"Hey, Sophie," Janice greeted me brightly as I walked into the diner, but her smile turned down a couple of notches when she saw my swollen, tired eyes and defeated countenance.

"Hey, Janice, how's it going?" I replied robotically, as I tried to hide my face behind the menu so as not to encourage too much conversation or Newman-forbid she ask me how I was.

"Good now that the dinner rush is over, coffee and a slice of day-old pie, hon?" she asked me. I smiled because it reminded me of when Anna used to say, *"There's too much good food out there, if you go to a place, and they know what you're going to order, it's time to switch it up and try something else."*

Seeing as how my options were limited, I decided that instead of switching up the place, I would switch up my order.

"No thanks, I think I'm gonna try something different today," I said scanning the menu for something that looked like it was capable of filling the canyon-sized cracks in my heart.

"Alrighty, what're you thinkin'?"

"Is it possible to get a larger slice of pie than usual?" I inquired.

"Sheesh, rough day?" Janice asked seeing that I meant business.

"I've had better," I admitted, "but I have definitely also had worse," I added, trying to mix being honest about how I felt with some semblance of perspective in hopes that the old adage of "fake it 'til you make it" held some truth.

"You know, there's a saying around here. *A piece of pie can make your troubles better, but two pieces can solve them.*"

"That sounds like the kind of sage wisdom I need to hear right now. Can I please have a Daisy Burger with extra cheese and fries on the side, an extra big piece of today's coconut cream pie, and a Coke?"

"Oh, shoot, Sophie, we just ran out of Coke. Our usual delivery was held up, so we won't have any 'til tomorrow. We have Diet, if you want that instead?"

"No, I don't drink diet. Aspartame is bad for you," I responded, completely oblivious to the irony of what had just come out of my mouth, and though Janice's forehead pinched with confusion, she refrained from saying anything for which I was very grateful for in that moment. "How about a root beer?"

"Now that we have. Comin' right up, hon," she said before leaving to place my order with the kitchen for what I hoped would provide me with the emotional ballast that I needed.

When my food arrived, I sat tucked away in the booth letting the cheeseburger wrap her greasy arms of comfort around my soul and the arteries of my heart, lost in the cyclone of thoughts that hadn't stopped since Joel's admission about his involvement with the Iron Wraiths and Cletus's refusal to do anything to help him.

My emotions had been looping back and forth between sadness for Joel's losses, despair at his entrapment within Green Valley, anger at the Wraiths, and worst of all helplessness. Not having the means to be able to help him find a way out of this mess, was the worst part and I thought about it constantly to the point where I thought I'd just burst.

"Excuse me, is anyone sitting here?"

I lifted my chin at the sound of the deep voice and felt a *whoosh* when I saw who it belonged to.

Oh shit, I thought training my expression so as not to give away my surprise to see him there, but also at him having approached me.

"Catfish" Hickson stood beside my booth waiting for a response, but I'd just placed a huge forkful of coconut cream pie in my mouth and had suddenly forgotten how to chew.

My mind was immediately rife with thoughts about what he was doing here and what he wanted from me.

I was a naturally curious person, so ordinarily, I would have just defaulted to coming right out and asking but seeing as how I'd never conversed with a criminal before, I thought it prudent to take a moment and read the terrain before diving into interrogating him.

He was still waiting for a response, but my mouth was still stuffed with the oversized bite of food that comically rounded out my right cheek and I had to remind myself that I should probably start chewing again if I had any hope of being able to find out what he wanted.

Seeing that I wasn't jumping out of my skin to oblige him, Catfish folded his large body forward and maneuvered into the seat across from mine.

Once settled, he appeared relaxed, but his eyes were focused in a way that alluded to his concealed intentions, even if I wasn't entirely sure what they were yet.

"I haven't had the pleasure yet, my name's Catfish," he began and held out his big hand across the table.

I gave his outstretched hand a cursory glance before reaffixing my eyes to his.

He raised his eyebrows and smiled when it was clear I wasn't going to reciprocate. He lowered his hand atop the table in front of him and I resolved to keep one eye on them at all times in case he made any sudden movements.

He studied me for a few moments like he was trying to figure me out, but when he finally spoke, he started talking about himself.

"You know who I am, don't you?" he asked me knowingly, his eyes glinting with good humor, but as he leaned toward the window casually, I couldn't shake how superficial that grin looked and wondered if people really fell for it.

"I think my reputation may have preceded me in this case, which is a shame," he said sighing regretfully. "I'm really a nice guy," he said holding up his hands submissively.

I finally managed to choke down most of my bite as I watched him passively, my brain running a mile a minute in time with my thundering heartbeat.

I was determined not to let him see that he was having such an effect on me.

What does he want? Why is he talking to me? Does he know who I am? Where I'm from? How did I get this much pie in my mouth? Did I unhinge my jaw or something? Holy shit, I feel like I've been working on this mouthful for twenty minutes.

My instincts were practically screaming to me that he was about as genuine as a used car salesman. He was too relaxed, smiling too warmly, and trying to be too charming. It only served to highlight how jarring it would be when he inevitably showed his true colors.

"You're awfully quiet. I don't bite, I promise," he assured me, noting the fact that I still hadn't said anything to him. I wondered if that made him uneasy, particularly given the way I was glaring at him.

This pie won't die. Why won't it just go down?

I reached for my drink while trying to maintain my facade of unmoved indifference despite my unsettledness.

Finally, with the help of a sip from my drink, the last of the burdensome coconutty, crumbly, mass of pie found its rightful path down past my throat and I took a moment to breathe before finally opening my mouth to talk.

"I had my mouth full of pie," I explained still trying to lick what felt like sawdust out of my gums.

"No problem. Take your time. I understand, it's easy to get carried away. Best pie in town. Best pie in the *country*," he said with all the pride of someone who had baked it himself.

Urgh, so fake, I grumbled mentally to myself.

"You want to tell me your name, sweetheart?" he asked.

I could see people falling easily for his particular brand of so-called easygoing charm. His voice was calm and warm, but I found it unsettling how he had barely blinked since sitting down. He was watching me with such unwavering focus, and my mind was a whirlpool trying to stay ahead of and anticipate what he was thinking.

I sighed and offered him a small smile which was about as on par with his in terms of sincerity.

"Why are you asking? You hitting on me?"

I tried to pass it off as both a joke and a hint for him to get to the point.

He laughed and lazily waved it off.

"No. Nothing like that. I just thought, with you being new in town and all, must be hard to make new friends."

What is he getting at? I wondered.

"Not at all," I said shaking my head. "Actually, the people here have been really friendly. So far," I contradicted him to hint at the fact that I knew his benevolence was an act. "I've already been given a lot of great pointers on what's good in town. Where to eat, where to drink … who to avoid," I added staring at him pointedly.

Catfish continued to stare at me unflinchingly, calm on the surface, but his eyes were too fixed, giving away the torrent beneath.

"Go on," he said nudging his chin toward me, his tone shifting *almost* imperceptibly to sound more authoritative. "Tell me your name," he requested once again.

A thought occurred to me and I narrowed my eyes at him.

"You're awfully anxious to know my name."

Stop poking the bear, Sophie.

"Anxious?" he said incredulously. "Nah, I don't get anxious."

"You sure?" I questioned narrowing my eyes again and tilting my head. "New girl comes into town out of nowhere, starts spending a lot of time with a guy that you've been blackmailing into doing *illegal* work for your motorcycle gang, and now you're here to introduce yourself and make sure I am making friends?" I asked incredulously. "Come on … my guess is that you're nervous that I'm an undercover cop," I said laying my theory out on the table.

I saw his eyes narrow almost imperceptibly and the hollow of his jaw became deeper as it tightened briefly. That little tell let me know that my hunch was exactly right.

"I heard you guys have been having a little trouble with them lately," I added in a stage whisper as I leaned across the table.

Poke. Jab.

I was anticipating his wrath, but instead, Catfish seemed to relax even more than he already seemed to be, and his smile returned as he rolled his eyes and shook his head as though he'd been let in on some kind of joke.

"No undercover cop goes around implying that they're an undercover cop," he stated after a moment, having come to the conclusion that I wasn't a threat. At least not in any lawful way.

"You're right, I am not an undercover cop," I confirmed, "and you don't need my name because you already have it. You've already had someone look into exactly who I am and where I am from, haven't you?" I asked knowingly.

"You watch too many TV shows," he said predictably.

"I'm more of a true crime podcast kind of a girl." I corrected. "Okay so now that you know I'm not a cop, what else do you need from me? Do you want to make sure I'm eating right and exercising?" I asked poking fun at his thinly veiled excuse to come over and begin a conversation.

Stop. Poking. The bear.

He surprised me again by throwing his head back and laughing as I watched him closely to make sure he wasn't about to reach into his vest pocket to take me by surprise with some kind of concealed weapon.

"Sassy." He chuckled instead as though I were delighting him. "I like 'em sassy," he said and then paused.

Suddenly his hand reached across the table and I flinched, sucking in a breath.

The action sent my heart racing like a racehorse on speed.

We both froze, our eyes locked, as his fingers slowly pinched the lip of my pie plate and I felt disappointed that I had let him see that he had me on edge.

"It's alright," he assured me gently. "Are you done? Mind if I have a bite?"

I slowly exhaled, but my shoulders were pinching with tension.

"Be my guest, I've lost my appetite all of a sudden," I said returning his glare with what I hoped came across as equal defiance, but I sure that I was visibly shaking.

"Why's that?" he asked furrowing his eyebrows with contrived curiosity.

"Just a weird, little quirk I have about hating being around people who bully others into doing their dirty work."

"You think I'm a bully? Come on now," Catfish asked, feigning shock. "I'm trying to *help* Joel. We're working together, this is a mutual agreement."

"Yeah, one in which he does as he's told or you kill him. Right?"

He didn't confirm or deny my accusation as he wiggled his fork through the pie crust.

"I can see why he likes you so much," he said bringing the fork to his lips to take a small bite of pie. "You've got balls. Usually, people are drawn to those who possess qualities they lack, you know what I mean?"

The implication that Joel was weak, tempered my fear and I immediately felt my hackles rise.

"Joel plays innocent but doesn't seem to mind benefiting from the work we give him," Catfish argued with his characteristically calm demeanor.

I should have bit my tongue, knowing that he was trying to incite a response, but I couldn't seem to keep my lips sealed.

"Is it the money he doesn't mind or the not being murdered part that motivates him more do you think?"

"Is that what he told you?" Catfish asked as though it were ridiculous.

"Well, you're welcome to give me your version of events, but the fact that you're patched into a criminal organization doesn't really do you a lot of favors in terms of credibility."

"This," he said pointing to the patch on his vest, "has nothing to do with crime and everything to do with family and brotherhood. I don't expect you or Joel to understand anything about that."

"You got me," I said raising my hand. "I'm an only child. Joel on the other hand probably had a pretty good idea about family and brotherhood before—well … you know."

My allusion to Nick seemed to make Catfish very uncomfortable and he shifted restlessly in his seat.

"I told him, and I'm telling you, I had nothing to do with that," he said sounding like he truly believed it.

"Maybe not you specifically, but your so-called brothers did," I countered, narrowing my eyes. "Call me crazy, but if I had a family member who was capable of murdering another human being, then I would bet that it wouldn't take much for them to forget about their 'loyalty' and come after me if it suited them."

He was simply bursting to defend the Wraiths now. I could see it in his hard stare and the way he licked his lips as an excuse to bare his teeth at me.

"You're a crazy little bitch you know that?" he spat harshly, but quietly so as not to draw attention to us. I smiled with false sympathy, tilting my head condescendingly.

"Don't be upset Catfish. In a few short weeks, I'll be out of Green Valley and you can go back to deluding yourself into thinking that terrorizing a small town and blackmailing its residents somehow makes you powerful. At least until you get old enough to realize that this pack of wild dogs you run with wouldn't hesitate to eat you alive if it served their interest even slightly more than yours. If you call that family, then you're the 'crazy bitch' not me," I stated prosaically even though I was barely able to hear my own words over the thunderous pounding of my heart.

His ire was palpable, but the restaurant was busy.

I am sure he had a whole lot he wanted to say in response, but he simply sat there glaring at me with an inferno raging behind his eyes.

After deciding that the bear had been sufficiently poked, I stood up from the booth and watched as his eyes watched me collect my belongings.

"Look," I said reaching for my backpack,"you came here to find out if I was a cop. I'm not. You happy? I'm a fucking pastry chef working temporarily at the Donner Bakery. I make shitty money baking cakes and pastries in the idealistic hope that it might help to brighten someone's day. If you Google me, you'll find a nice little video of me making an ass of myself on national television, and ever since then, I've spent more than too much time letting better men than you intimidate and underestimate me. So please, don't take it personally that your little bullying tactic didn't quite go as planned. It's totally me, not you, I'm just fresh out of fucks to give one more asshole who thinks he can get what he wants by swinging his dick," I said starting to walk away and then pointing at the remnants of my meal. "You got this, right? Tip Janice well, she's had a rough day," I instructed before attempting to make an exit from the diner without my knees giving out on me.

Once I was in my car, I tried not to think about what I'd just done, but thoughts of consequences whirred in my brain like am almighty stor.

I made it about four miles heading into the direction of town when what I had just done caught up with me, and I finally had to pull over to the side of the road to throw up.

When it was over, I got back in my car and numbly made the rest of the trip home to spend the remainder of the night staring out the window.

CHAPTER 18

I sat up all night wondering if my inability to keep my mouth shut had now put me in the crosshairs of the leader of the local biker gang. Did people kill other people for being sassy? It's not like I slapped him or threw my root beer in his face which did cross my mind, and would have been unspeakably satisfying, but let the record show that I showed some restraint.

Still, now I was paranoid. Was he going to come for me with his biker buddies? Should I kidnap Joel and leave Green Valley? Leave the United States? Go to England and start a new, secluded life as a papier-mâché crafter?

I wondered what my favorite comic book hero Smash-Girl would do in a situation like this. Smash Catfish presumably.

That's what made sense in my brain at one in the morning as I tossed and turned and moved between the bed, couch, and dining room table in a restless, never-ending loop. I tried all kinds of remedies to ease the knot in my stomach and the faster than usual thumping in my heart, but nothing worked.

Every noise made me jump including the detached sound of my own breathing. Every time I heard a car or any sort of movement outside, I leaped off of whatever furniture I was sitting on to go and peek out the window.

I'd had one encounter with Catfish and I was a wreck. I couldn't fathom what Joel's nerves must go through on a daily basis.

I debated back and forth for hours on whether or not to tell him about what happened with Catfish at Daisy's, but I didn't know how he would react and I didn't want to him to freak out, or worse, retaliate in some way. So instead I sat in my apartment and waited until it was time to pull myself up off the couch and get ready for work.

A hot shower helped me physically but mentally, I was all over the place.

I had missed calls from John Moxie to ignore, missed calls from Anna to return, a full day's work to contend with, and another night alone in my apartment wondering. Today was going to be rough and I knew it.

I arrived at the bakery at 3:45 AM as usual, and put myself straight to work, trying to avoid interacting with anyone as much as possible, which was especially difficult to do with Joy, who kept coming over and asking me how I was and if I needed to talk. I acknowledged that she was trying to be kind, but I just wanted to be left alone to finish out the day and then go home and lay in the fetal position on the couch until I either passed out from exhaustion or came up with the perfect foolproof plan that would save Joel and rid the town of Green Valley from its sinister underbelly.

"What's that smell?" I heard Blithe ask from across the kitchen and the second it hit my nose, I knew it was the tart shells that I had been blind baking and had completely forgotten to set a timer for.

"Oh no!" I exclaimed, running to the oven and yanking the door open. A thick cloud of acrid smoke burst forth.

I hadn't been thinking clearly all morning and apparently wasn't about to start now, as I reached into the oven to grab the tray of tart shells with my bare hand. Instantly, searing pain annihilated my fingertips and palm as I shrieked and recoiled, my other hand coming to protect its injured counterpart as I felt someone pull me back by my shoulders. Joy was leading me to a sink to run my hand under cold water and over my shoulder, I watched as Tempest gloved her hand and went in to retrieve the tray of singed pastry.

As icy mountain water soothed my hand, I watched Tempest extract the smoking tart shells before rushing them to the second industrial sized sink with the garbage disposal attached and switch on the faucet to let cold water sizzle the tray and shells until the plumes of smoke promptly dissipated.

"I'm sorry, I'm so sorry," I kept apologizing, and wanted to immediately get to work on a new batch of tart shells but every time I tried to pull my hand out from underneath the water, the pain was unbearable to the point that I simultaneously mentally accepted, and verbally denied needing medical attention.

Drawn from out of her office by all the commotion, Jennifer pulled rank and insisted that I see a doctor, and I was glad when Tempest volunteered to take me and not Joy. I loved Joy and her irrepressible enthusiasm, but I didn't have the stomach for her brand of rose-colored idealism in that moment.

Tempest was quiet in the car beside me, even though I could feel her burning to say something.

Eventually, she couldn't contain herself anymore.

"You know," she began, her tone uncharacteristically light, "once the doctor wraps up that hand, you won't be able to shower alone. You'll need help."

"Is that an offer, sugar lips?" I asked humorlessly, attempting to joke, but just sounding forced.

"No, dipshit, I was talking about Joel," she corrected glancing over at me in time to see the helpless expression on my face at the mention of his name. "Oh sorry, are we still pretending that we're not one hundred percent, ass-backward, crazy in love with him?"

"Love is a strong word," I stated, not admitting or denying anything.

"I stand by my evaluation," Tempest countered stubbornly.

I allowed myself a moment to consider her words and try to understand her motivation.

"I don't get it, *now* I should seduce and lure him into my shower? I thought I was supposed to stay away from him." Reminding Tempest how she had advised against my getting involved with Joel.

"Yeah, and I was *supposed* to have a baby with a man who turned out to be an adulterous shithead and now I'm with Cage. That's life, honey, things change and we gotta roll with the punches. Sure maybe we misjudged him, but now that I know better, I want to do better, and to start, I'm gonna suggest that you admit, right now in this car, exactly how you feel about him," Tempest demanded obstinately as though she wouldn't accept anything less than unadulterated honesty.

"It doesn't matter," I said shaking my head dismissively.

"It's the *only* thing that matters," Tempest volleyed pointedly.

"You sound like Joy," I said in a cautioning tone, thinking it would rustle Tempest's jimmies enough to get her to drop it, but instead she sighed and looked thoughtfully out onto the road ahead of her.

"How I feel about Cage, and knowing how he feels about me, is the beginning and end of everything. If you and Joel would just admit to each other what everybody else already knows, then maybe together you can find a way out of this mess."

"You make it sound so easy." I huffed a cynical laugh.

"I never said 'easy,'" Tempest countered shaking her head. "But you can bet your ass it will be worth it."

The rest of the drive to the doctor's office passed by in silence as I ruminated on Tempest's words.

When we arrived, I was treated for a second-degree burn and was sent home with instructions on how to replace the dressing and bandages and advised not to use it for up to two weeks which I promptly ignored and insisted on going back to the bakery with Tempest. I couldn't afford not to work, so I wore a latex glove over the bandages, and went right back to making sea salt, caramel, and ganache tarts.

Even after my shift was over, I stayed behind and prepped some items for the following morning.

After the adrenaline and excitement of my medical episode had dissipated, I was left feeling hollowed out and listless. I had learned my lesson about being absentminded at work and decided to combat the fatigue by enlisting the help of coffee. Which only served to make every task even more difficult because, as well as my injury, now I was also a jittery mess.

It took me twice as long as normal to complete the simple task of piping portions of chocolate mousse into white chocolate cups, three of which I broke, and then as I attempted to top them off with passionfruit coulis with my unsteady hand, I ended up spooning more onto the catching tray than inside the cups.

By the time I decided it was time to stop torturing the food, all I could think about was how I wished I could snap my fingers and be home in bed.

Driving along as best as I could with one good hand, I found myself heading toward Joel's garage instead of home.

I had decided quite suddenly that I just needed to see him as soon as possible.

When I arrived, the garage door was open, and Joel appeared from under the hood of a car he was working on.

When he saw it was me, he abandoned his work and wiped his hands on a cloth and began making his way over to greet me.

As he approached, he eyed my bandage covered hand.

"Well ... to what do I owe the pleasure?" was all he had to say, and my muscles instantly unwound themselves as I fell into his chest and wrapped my arms around his body. "Hey there. What's going on? What happened to your hand?" he inquired rubbing soothing circles into my back, but I didn't respond right away.

I just needed him to hold me for a moment. I needed to be surrounded by the reassuring calmness of his presence and the safety of his big, muscular body.

He seemed to understand what I needed and closed in around me as I shut my eyes and focused on the thump of his heart in my ear.

After a few moments and when I was ready, I peeled myself away from him and sighed.

"We have to talk," I said, knowing that I needed to tell him about what had happened at Daisy's with Catfish.

Joel's brow instantly wrinkled with concern.

"Alright." He nodded. "Come on then," he said keeping one arm around me as he led me past the garage toward the office.

I hadn't been inside the office, and though I expected that it would be a mess, it was actually surprisingly well organized.

Everything, including the furniture, was old and run down, and the only thing that looked like it hadn't emerged from the past decade was Joel's laptop, which sat on a cheaply made desk with the laminate beginning to peel off at the edges.

"What's wrong? What happened to your paw?" he asked, pulling his chair around the desk to sit beside me and I smiled at how southern he sounded when said it.

"I had a brain lapse and tried to grab a tray right out of the oven without protecting my hand first. It's nothing, I'll be fine," I assured him as his brow furrowed with sympathy and concern.

"You sure? Did you see a doctor?" he asked me, pulling on my wrist as though he was preparing to inspect it himself if I hadn't.

"I did, it will heal on its own," I assured him, watching the way he tried to peek under the bandages. "Joel."

He looked into my eyes when I said his name.

"Right. What did you want to talk about?" he inquired expectantly, and I looked down at my hand still feeling the residual warmth from where he'd touched my skin.

I decided this would require the Band-Aid approach.

"I ran into that Catfish guy at Daisy's Nut House last night."

It took less than a second for Joel's entire face to change and a cold shock ran through me as his soft, gentle expression frosted completely over and his jaw hollowed out as he clenched it.

"It's fine," I tried to assure him, but Joel was up on his feet agitated and pacing like a bear who'd been prodded in his cage.

"It's *not* fine. Actually, it's the furthest fucking thing from fine. Did you approach him?" Joel asked stopping and pinning me with a hard stare that immediately made me feel like I was being interrogated by the bad cop.

"No, Joel, he approached me. I'm not stupid."

"What did he say to you? Did he threaten you? Was anyone else with him?"

"Aaahhh," my mind went blank as I struggled to keep up with all the questions and considering how to answer them in a way that would stop him from freaking out.

"Listen to me, I mean this," he said pulling his seat closer so that he was just inches away, "if he approaches you again, you make a scene and you get the hell out of there, do you understand me?" Joel ordered, his eyes hard and cold as ice. I wasn't worried, I knew he was just panicking because he thought I was in danger, and maybe I had been, but it was over now, and I didn't want him to worry.

"He thought I was an undercover cop," I explained without context and Joel furrowed his brow in confusion. "Do I give off cop vibes?" I asked attempting to make him smile, but instead, Joel passed his hand over his mouth and down his beard and sighed.

"One time I was in a Starbucks, and a guy came in and tried to steal a bag of coffee beans from the display. As he was running out of the store with the employees in pursuit, I stuck out my foot and tripped him as he went by me. I felt like a real badass," I recounted, not really sure what message I was trying to impart with my story, but figuring it was relevant to my apparent alter ego as an undercover cop.

"I know what you're trying to do," he replied, shaking his head as though it wasn't going to work.

"So, let me do it," I implored him, crossing over to sit on his lap and place my arms around his shoulders.

I knew I was crossing my own self-imposed line in the sand by doing so. I knew I wasn't supposed to be pursuing anything with Joel, but every time he was near me all my rules went out the window and I found myself wanting to risk everything to feel his touch.

"He was just sniffing around to see if I was a cop, that's all. And I think I did a pretty good job of assuring him that I wasn't."

He still did not appear convinced.

"Or that's what he wants you to think. Sophie, these guys are master manipulators. They're experts at getting you to lower your guard so they can have the upper hand if they feel threatened. If Catfish

Hickson went to the trouble of introducing himself to you, then chances are he's feeling pretty fucking threatened," Joel explained, his body still tightly wound beneath mine.

I was quiet as I recalled my impassioned parting words to Catfish and Joel seemed to be able to read my mind as he narrowed his eyes at me.

"You sassed the shit out of him, didn't you?" he asked knowingly, and I removed my arms from around his shoulders and folded them in my lap guiltily.

"Not like ... a lot," I fumbled through my clearly dishonest response which caused Joel to sigh and hang his head when all I wanted to do was kiss him and make everything better.

"Sophie, you can't go around starting fires in front of pyromaniacs," he said with a heavy, frustrated tone.

"I don't like how he talked about you. I got defensive," I replied in an attempt to justify my provocative behavior.

"I don't care if he tells you that I am a goat-romancing, women's-panty-wearing, sludge-snorkeling, Porsche-driving troll from Katmandu, if he tries to talk to you again, do not engage. Do you understand me?" Joel instructed firmly as I lowered my head and nodded in agreement.

"I understand," I agreed as I climbed out of his lap and pulled him to his feet. I lifted my chin to look at him once more before furrowing my brow and asking, "What's wrong with Porsches?"

"Overrated. Every luxury car that ever pulled into our garage with some kind of manufacturing fault was a Porsche. I don't like them," he replied disapprovingly, and I nodded indulgently.

"Okay, I'll take your word for it. Now can you stop yelling at me about Catfishes and Porsches and go back to the part where you were about to kiss me?"

That was bold. Good for you.

It pleased me deeply, to watch the planes of his face shift to a more playful expression and my body began to tingle in response.

"I wasn't aware that I was about to kiss you," he murmured

furrowing his brow as though he was confused, but he'd also hooked his finger into the front of my jeans.

My breath caught as he tugged me, pulling me with ease until I was pressed snugly up against him.

His face hovered inches away from mine and from this proximity, I could taste his breath and smell the dizzying cocktail of clean and dirty.

The smell of grease and fuel was prominent on his clothes, but on the finish, I could make out soap and cologne from his skin.

He continued to linger just beyond my reach, making the moment drag on for an age, until finally I got tired of waiting and thrust upwards onto the balls of my feet to press my lips to his.

There was a fleeting moment where I thought he might not reciprocate, but when he did, all the tension that I had been carrying around shattered and transformed into a flutter of butterflies.

His beard was sharp and prickly against the soft skin of my face, but I loved the scrape in contrast with the softness of his lips and the slow, silky glide of his tongue passing between my lips.

He crushed me closer to him and took my wrists in his hands to guide them up around his neck.

He pulled me along as he stepped back and I'd all but forgotten what it was like to be at the mercy of someone whose physical strength was so commanding that your only choice was to surrender.

I slid my fingers into the coarse, dark fibers of his hair and tugged, sighing at how good it felt as his hands became acquainted with the edges and curves of my body.

We were moving fast, but not fast enough. It wasn't until I tasted the sweet and salt of his tongue that I realized how starved I had become for this.

I closed my teeth around his bottom lip and tugged as I continued my slow exploration down his chest and along the firm undulating surface of his stomach until I reached the button of his jeans.

When he felt me trying to get it open, his hands came around to stop me.

"Hang on a second, wait a minute," he breathed as I withdrew my hand and immediately began to apologize.

"I'm sorry, I shouldn't have done that," I panted. "I got carried away."

Joel closed the gap once more, taking my face into his hands and looking down into my eyes.

"Don't apologize. I want you too," he murmured earnestly and I nodded in understanding as he let go and blew out a steadying breath. "I just can't...here," he explained, his eyes looking toward something that was behind me and I turned to find a framed photo of a much younger Joel with two other men who I assumed were his dad and brother.

I turned back to him and smiled sympathetically.

"It's okay, I understand." Giving him one last kiss, I turned to leave as he pretended to limp behind me and I laughed.

"I have an idea," he said as we walked back out into the garage.

"I love ideas," I said as he held my hand while we walked slowly back to my car.

"How about you let me take you out on a date next week?" he suggested, and I smiled because even though I felt like we were kind of beyond that stage, he still wanted to "do it right."

"I would love to go on a date with you," I said accepting his offer enthusiastically. "Where should we go?"

"Well," he said rubbing the back of his neck. "There's not much choice I'm afraid, but there is the Front Porch restaurant which is kind of nice, I guess." He shrugged, and I laughed at his less than enthusiastic suggestion.

"How can I say no to that? You make it sound so great," I teased, feeling him tug on my hand to bring me to a stop to turn and face him.

"I just know that you're used to much fancier places and—"

"Joel, don't you finish that thought," I warned him firmly before taking both his hands and staring directly into his eyes. "I would choose eating cheeseburgers from McDonald's in the back of your truck a hundred times over some fancy overpriced meal in a restaurant if it meant we could just hang out and have fun together. You don't need to try and impress me, I am already in deeper with you than I promised I would let myself get, so I'm just going with it now." I sighed with resignation and watched as his lips pulled into a smile and his eyes twinkled at my words.

"Glad to know we're on the same page."

CHAPTER 19

I had one dress that had survived my pre-move purge.

A beautiful, dark blue floral midi dress with delicate straps and a suggestive neckline.

While it wasn't quite appropriate for Green Valley's current overcast and blustery weather, it more than made up for it with the confidence I felt when I put it on.

I had been walking past a store when I saw it in the window and given the number of times that a dress literally stopped me in my tracks —almost never—I knew I had to go in and try it on.

The only problem was, once I bought it, it sat in the back of my closet collecting dust because I worked so much that I'd never had the opportunity to wear it.

Tonight, that was all going to change, and Joel was my perfect excuse to finally rip off the price tags and take her for a spin.

Of course, the bandage around my hand wasn't exactly the epitome of chic elegance that I was going for, but I hoped the neckline of my dress would draw his attention elsewhere.

I stood in the mirror admiring the way the fabric curved snuggly around my breasts and laughed when I realized how ineffectual the delicate fabric would be in concealing my nipples once I stepped outside.

Yeah, he's not going to notice the bandage, I asserted to myself confidently as I slid my hands over the full roundness of my breasts.

Ever since our heated embrace at the garage, my desire for Joel had grown out of control. Now that I knew what he was up against, I wanted him even more which was inconvenient considering how complicated the situation was.

I tried not to think about the logistics of this fledgling relationship which seemed to be progressing despite all the caution and good sense I tried to exhibit. It felt bigger than me, bigger than us, and out of our control. Like some overarching force was up there pushing us inevitably into one another's arms.

Every time I thought about leaving him behind, I got a sick, twisting feeling in my stomach and I would have to distract myself or think of something else.

I knew that it was a conversation that needed to happen, but tonight was not the night for that.

Tonight was about encouraging Joel to show himself to me, all of him, the way he was, and not how others saw him. I wanted to go deep with him and not just sexually, but in order to do that, I had to get in a certain headspace.

I watched *Cat on a Hot Tin Roof* on my laptop while I sat on the bed winding my hair around a curling iron and trying to absorb some of the sass and chutzpah Elizabeth Taylor radiated as Maggie the Cat.

One of Anna's favorite quotes by Elizabeth Taylor was, *"Pour yourself a drink, put on some lipstick, and pull yourself together."* And after the week I'd had, that was exactly what I was endeavoring to do before Joel arrived for our date.

When I was done curling my hair, I shook it out with my fingers creating that sexy, tousled, just-got-out-of-bed look, before spritzing with hairspray as a contingency against the less than ideal weather.

Just as I was securing the ankle strap on my shoe, I heard a knock at the front door and glanced at my phone for the time.

He'd arrived at seven on the nose and I leaped off the couch to answer the door the way a kid runs to the tree on Christmas morning.

I swung the door open and the two of us stood silently still, appreciating the clear effort that had been made on both parts to make an impression on one another.

Joel looked nothing short of edible in charcoal-colored suit pants and a baby blue button-down shirt that he kept casual by rolling up the sleeves and leaving the top couple of buttons open. His shoes and belt looked new and he'd made some effort to neaten his hair, though all that did was make me want to sink my fingers into it to get it good and messy again.

He looked so good, I couldn't stop staring at him. It wasn't until he spoke that I realized that I had forgotten to greet him.

"Hey, beautiful," he drawled in that way that by now completely liquified my bones and I knew I was supposed to respond but his presence was consuming, and now that he was in front of me, the last thing I wanted to do was talk. My emotions from the past week were converging with no outlet, and the way his eyes were traveling up and down the length of my body didn't help to slacken the winding tension.

Joel tried to show initiative by taking a step forward and reaching for me, but instead of letting him touch me, I reeled back, causing him to lower his hand and regard me with a look of concern.

"It's just, if you touch me right now, we're not going to make it out of this apartment so ..." Joel smiled in understanding before lowering his eyes to his shirt.

"Well, I had to dust off the old iron for this baby, so I want to show it off," he said attempting to ease some of the tension with humor but all I could see was the way his big hand slid down the solid curve of his chest as he showed off his shirt.

I sighed and shook my head of impure thoughts, reminding myself of the objective for the evening.

"You look so handsome, I want you to show it off too." I smiled encouragingly, hoping to impart with my words that I didn't think Joel Barnes should be hiding in the quiet corners of Green Valley.

I noticed that after having complimented him, he became awfully shy, losing the ability to maintain that intensely focused eye contact that made me feel like I was the only person in the world. Instead, he smiled down at his shoes as though I were paying him lip service.

"Let me just grab my purse, and we'll get going," I said and as I walked across the room to collect it, I could feel his eyes on my back.

"How's your hand?" I heard him ask behind me.

I balled my wrist and felt the tight pull of the healing skin. It didn't hurt anymore, but it still needed some time.

"It's getting there," I said with a smile as I approached him.

I stopped a safe distance away but the way he was looking at me, all heavy-lidded and hungry, was chipping away at my resolve to refrain from leaping right up onto him.

Just as my last threat of self-control was about to snap and I was about to lean onto the balls of my feet to move to him, he took a step back with a smile and turned to the door to open it.

Once we were safely locked out of my apartment, I reached for Joel's hand as we made our way downstairs and outside into the cold November night. I smiled when I saw he'd brought the Camaro, despite shivering as the cold went right through my bones.

The wind sent my hair and the hem of my dress floating around and I had to let go of his hand to keep them under control.

In that moment, I was feeling more Marilyn Monroe than Elizabeth Taylor, but as soon as Joel opened the passenger side door for me and I got in the car, I straightened my dress out, smoothed my hair, and then all was right with the world.

On our way to the restaurant, Joel held my hand for the entire trip, covering my hand with his as he shifted gears. All I could think about was how right everything felt. Like I could definitely get used to this.

I knew those were dangerous thoughts, but I allowed them on the basis that the air between us made them inescapable. After the past week, I needed to feel something pure and good.

When we arrived at the Front Porch, I was struck by how Joel never made a show of his chivalry and how he opened doors and pulled out my chair without even thinking about it. It was a small but attractive behavior that impressed me without him even trying.

After being on dates with guys who leaped theatrically to display their courtliness as though it were a party trick, or currency for getting laid, it was refreshing to note the almost involuntary way Joel went about the same courtesies.

The restaurant was busy despite the weather, but the mood inside was cozy and intimate. All around us, people spoke in hushed tones in the low lighting from dim wall sconces and tea light candles in the center of each table. Soft piano music emanated from speakers in the corners, and the occasional soft clatter of crockery or cutlery added to the warm ambience of the restaurant.

"This place is lovely," I commented, glancing around the room as I got situated in my seat. "My kind of place," I added to allay any worry Joel might still harbor about it not being fancy enough for a "city girl."

"I'm glad you like it," he murmured, his voice low and gruff as he tried to talk quietly, but all it did was turn me on and I knew I had to pace myself.

"Would you like to pick?" I asked sliding the wine list toward him.

"I don't really know that much about wine," he replied regretfully, a hint of self-consciousness clouding over his features, so I offered him a reassuring smile, and commandeered the wine list.

"That's okay, what do you prefer? Red, white? *Pink?*" I inquired, cocking an eyebrow at him from behind the wine list suggestively which succeeded immediately in making him smile.

"Why don't we start with red and see how the night progresses," he suggested with a sexy, lopsided grin which sent a rush through my body as though the ground beneath me had fallen away.

The waiter arrived to fill our water glasses and take our wine order and when he was gone, I folded my hands on top of the menu and looked to Joel curiously.

"Tell me more about Ruby," I requested watching as his brow pinched with confusion.

"Who's Ruby?"

"Oh, I named your Camaro Ruby," I informed him with a casual flick of my hand when I realized I had only ever thought it, but never actually referred to her by name aloud.

He curved his lips and nodded in approval as he leaned forward and began fiddling with the edge of the menu.

"Well, the story goes, my dad had a poker buddy who owned her, but didn't take good care of her and it drove my dad crazy. So, one night during a poker game, he challenged this friend of his to a round for slips, only they were so drunk that they could barely see their cards," he explained, relaying the story to me as I pictured the scene in my mind. "The game had to be officiated by the least drunk member of the party, who was still pretty drunk, mind you. Anyway, my dad won with a full house, queens over threes and worked on spit shining her every night for the rest of his days," he explained wistfully. I noticed that even though he seemed to refer to his dad with affection, there was something behind his eyes that said he had needed to make peace with the past to be able to do so.

"What was he like?" I asked, recalling how Tempest and Joy had talked about him at Genie's. "He sounded like a good man," I inquired wondering if I was right about my hunch.

"He was," Joel confirmed with a somewhat forced smile. "He wasn't perfect by any stretch, but who is? We had our issues like any other family, but I know he tried really hard for us after my momma left," he explained in a solemn tone, his eyes dropping to the table between us.

"Is it hard to talk about him? You don't have to answer any questions if you don't want to," I offered. "I don't want you to feel like this is an interrogation, I just … I want to get to know you better," I explained as his eyes returned to mine and his lips readopted the soft, sexy smile I could have indulged in all day.

"There's not much you couldn't get me to talk about," he admitted, reaching across the table for my hand, and proceeding to brush the pad of his thumb across the back of my knuckles. "Ask me whatever you want, I'll tell you anything."

"Anything?" I asked raising my eyebrows challengingly.

"Anything," he nodded adamantly as though he had nothing to hide and I took comfort in his willingness to be open.

I tried not to be distracted by the stroking of fingers as I peered skyward, trying to think of a question, and decided to start off easy.

"Alright, I got one," I announced. "You said you were born and raised in Green Valley, but have you ever traveled anywhere?" I asked curiously.

"Not farther than Nashville," he admitted, his eyes once again dropping to the tablecloth as I tried to read the thoughts behind his expression.

"Would you like to travel?"

"Absolutely," he replied in earnest, and as though he'd leave right now if he could.

"Where's the first place you'd go?" I asked thinking about what an incredible travel partner he would be.

"Oh man," he said on a breath, leaning back against his chair and letting go of my hand to fold his arms over his chest while he thought about his answer. "Somewhere that couldn't be more different than Green Valley, Tennessee. Maybe Tokyo, that might be cool."

"Tokyo is amazing," I confirmed, my mind instantly recalling the amount of money Anna and I spent on items from vending machines and how I still had an envelope full of photo strips from the strangely addictive photo booths.

"You've been?" Joel asked and I nodded.

"Uh-huh. Anna and I went for my twenty-first birthday." I smiled as Joel reached out to fiddle with his knife.

"Where else have you been?"

"Uh, let's see. England, France, of course. Japan, Italy, Australia, and all over the U.S. and Canada," I replied watching as Joel's smile faded and his expression became somewhat wistful.

"I hope I get to see half as many of those places in my lifetime," he stated quietly. My heart ached for him, thinking about how trapped he must feel here when all he wanted was to be able to experience a handful of some of the amazing things that the world had to offer. "I promised myself that if I got out of this mess, that I wouldn't take it for granted. That I would go everywhere."

"You will," I told him doubtlessly.

"You think so?" He indulged me, though he didn't seem entirely convinced.

"I do. I don't know how or why, but I just do," I stated resolutely even as I wondered if it were only because that was my wish.

"Would I be saying too much, if I said I hoped it was with you?" he asked, watching closely for my reaction.

"No. In fact, say it again, only this time say it like you know I want the same," I demanded, my voice soft and my gaze hungry.

"I hope I get to see the world with you someday, Sophie Copeland," he repeated and all I wanted in that moment was to take his hand and lead him far, far away from Green Valley.

If I closed my eyes, I could picture it vividly. Joel and I sitting together at the airport, handing our passports to customs officers, picking up our rental car and heading off on every kind of adventure.

Still in the background of my impromptu fantasy hung a dark rainy storm cloud in the shape of a Harley Davidson and I deflated slightly.

"I hope we get that chance too," I offered, glancing up just as Joel cocked his head.

He was just about to ask me what I was thinking, when the waiter arrived to take our order and by the time he'd left, the moment had passed.

I glanced at him from over the rim of my wine glass as I sipped and studied the way he looked around at the other patrons. I did the same and noted an older lady sitting in one of the booths to our left, throwing him sideways glances every once in a while.

"Who is that?" I asked, averting my eyes so as not to make it obvious that we were talking about her.

Joel shook his head as though it weren't a big deal.

"Nobody, just … Scotia Simmons. Resident gossip. Just a heads-up that by the time she's done, come Monday morning you'll be a prostitute."

I couldn't help but laugh at his prediction, but he didn't seem as amused by it.

"Don't worry about it, Joel, who fucking cares?"

"It's not me I'm worried about. I'm used to it, but I don't want her talking shit about you," he said with an impatient edge in his voice.

"I'm not going to be around long enough to let myself get hung up on that kind of nonsense." I shrugged indifferently "All I care about are the two people at this table," I said tapping my finger onto the tablecloth.

Joel lifted his eyes to mine, the corner of his mouth hooking upward into a small smile which I considered a victory.

"What do *you* want me to know about you, Joel?" I asked tilting my head to the side as he stared into my eyes while he thought about a response to the question.

"Just you?" he asked, indicating that he was about to share a secret.

"Just me," I confirmed with a nod.

He took a while to answer but when he finally did, he lowered his eyes like he couldn't look at me while he said it.

"I'm...it can be lonely around here. With my brother gone now, and all," he admitted as though he were embarrassed by it.

In that moment, my heart broke clean in two and I wanted more than anything to tell him that I was there for him and would always be, but I knew I couldn't do that. My time in Green Valley was finite and we had no reason to believe his situation with the Wraiths would be resolved any time soon, or ever.

I glanced down at the tea light at the center of our table and wondered if they were as effective for making wishes as birthday candles. I had nothing to lose, so I took the chance and leaned forwards onto my elbows, staring intently into the flame. I made a wish and blew. And I wished harder than I had ever wished for anything in my whole life.

I couldn't make him a promise, but I could make as many wishes as I wanted.

I glanced up to meet his eyes and the soft smile that was on his lips as he watched me.

"Why'd you do that?" he asked softly.

"I made a wish. Don't ask me to tell you what it is because then it won't come true."

He nodded in understanding.

Our food arrived and even though we enjoyed our meal and

227

conversation, including the occasional flirty comment, there remained a wisp of cloud on the horizon from his confession earlier.

I didn't want to let it spoil the evening, so I stretched my leg under the table and slid my foot up the inside of Joel's calf, watching closely to see if he would keep my secret.

Joel's eyes lifted, and his lips curved into a secretive smile just as the waiter sidled up to our table.

When the waiter grasped the edge of my plate to take it away, he frowned at how little I'd eaten.

"Was everything to your satisfaction, ma'am?" he asked, poised to take the offending plate from my sight.

"Oh no, everything was wonderful, honestly. It's no reflection of the meal, it was just … a very generous serving," I assured him, trying to hold back my smile at the real reason.

Actually, I'm anticipating sex with the man seated across the table from me and I don't need a pound of filet mignon bouncing around in there.

Apparently, Anna was able to hijack my thoughts now.

"Will there be anything else for you this evening? Would like to look at the dessert menu?" he asked as Joel and I looked at each other and knew immediately that we were both thinking the same thing.

"Check please," we requested simultaneously.

* * *

The ride home felt weighted with expectation and seemed to extend in distance by a thousand more miles.

There was something slow and bluesy on the stereo and as I slowly came to have enough presence of mind to listen to it, I remembered that it was the same song that was playing the night we slow danced at Genie's.

I remembered the way the fabric of his shirt smelled and the hard, solid press of his body to mine and started to get restless in my seat, impatient with the need to experience those things again, and more.

Turning toward him while his eyes were focused on the road ahead,

I drank in his profile.

The straight line of his nose, the pout of his lips, the small textured spikes of his beard, and the way the hair at the side of his neck curled softly around his ear were all things I wanted to reach out and trace with my fingertip as I committed each detail to memory.

When he finally pulled up in front of our building, I was too eager to wait for him to come around and open my door for me.

I unlatched it myself as he hurried around to take my hand to steady me as I climbed out of the car and onto the sidewalk.

We made our way inside the building, saying nothing as we began to climb the stairs. I had only taken two steps up when I heard the door close solidly behind me and turned around, coming face to face with him.

We stood, eye to eye, close enough that I could smell his scent and feel his breath on my face. My own breath turned shallow as blood began to whir throughout my body.

I could see the rise and fall of his chest and his head bowed just the slightest bit, but I could feel that he was holding back.

He was waiting for permission.

Moving slowly, I lifted my hands and placed them on his sides, bunching the fabric in my good hand and using my grip to pull him toward me and press my mouth to his.

The response was immediate, hot, slow, and deep.

His tongue found mine and I felt the order of things imperative to my survival shift.

Joel. Air. Water. Food. In that order.

His beard was scratchy and harsh on my skin but provided the perfect contrast to the softness of his lips and silk of his tongue as they danced around mine. I felt his hands find my face as he tilted my head, placing me right where he needed me to be.

Pressing forward, I soldered my body to his, and instantly felt the hard line of his arousal at my thigh.

I wanted to tell him we should take it upstairs, but I would rather have died than break that kiss, which grew in urgency as I brought my hand to the front of his pants.

Joel kissed like the end of the world was imminent, his hands grasping and stroking as I curled my fingers around to slowly begin stroking him outside his pants.

The sound that rumbled from within his chest fueled me and I could feel my clit beginning to throb with the need for urgent attention.

Encircling his wrist with my fingers, I guided his hand down my body and used my other hand to lift the hem of my dress until I could slide his fingers inside the front of my underwear.

Our kiss finally broke and our eyes locked.

We both exhaled hotly when his fingers came into contact with my skin and they slipped easily between my folds to find my clit.

I exhaled with relief and gripped his biceps to guide him as I turned us so my back was against the wall.

Joel climbed to the same step and pinned me, tilting his head to watch me as he slowly began making gentle circling motions with his fingertips. My knees buckled.

Using his free hand to hold me up around the waist, Joel guided my other knee to slide up the side of his body to make myself more accessible to him.

"Like that? Tell me how you like it," he breathed on my lips and my eyes rolled shut at his words.

Unable to speak, I covered his hand with mine, guiding his pressure and pace for a few strokes to show him how I needed it before grasping back onto his thick arms.

Everything was on fire and my muscles were failing me as I clawed viciously at his biceps.

I was building quickly to orgasm and tried to peel away from his touch to prolong it, but the grip from just one of his arms was too powerful and I was pinned in by his body as he brought his mouth right to my ear.

"Where are you going, huh?" he teased, the sound of his voice winding my core even tighter. I gasped, feeling myself get right to the brink when he suddenly stopped and withdrew his hand from inside my panties.

I was panting and gasping as he gathered me up against his body and guided my legs around his waist, carrying me up the stairs.

I was weak from need in his arms as we crossed the threshold into his apartment toward his sofa bed, which was blessedly folded out and unmade.

We collapsed onto it and he held himself above me. His arms straight and hard like marble pillars marred only by the fabric covering them. I sought to correct the situation by unbuttoning his shirt.

I refrained from popping them, but didn't have the patience to undo them all, pulling upward for efficiency's sake. I was temporarily appeased by the sight of his upper body, which was work-hardened and solid and I immediately pressed my hands to his upper arms and smoothed my palms down their solid lengths.

He bent his arms to press his body over mine, and my thighs parted to comfortably accommodate his large frame.

"Am I too heavy?" He breathed into my neck as he kissed, licked, nibbled, and sucked at the sensitive spot just below my ear.

"No, you feel really good," I assured him, sliding my hands down to the small of his back so I could lift my hips and pull him to me as I started to slowly grind into him.

He was making that sound again and I was so focused on the vibrations it sent through my body that I almost didn't notice he was one-handedly removing my dress.

I reciprocated by sliding my hands down his hips and between us to unfasten his belt and pants.

When we were both finally naked, Joel tore himself away from me for just long enough to find the condoms that were in his pants pocket. I was pleased with his preparedness as I watched him make quick work of putting one on and moving back over me.

Naked, needy, and becoming impatient, I writhed under him and took a handful of his hair into my hand.

His mouth resumed its slow, deep exploration of my mouth, his hands gripping my hips as I felt him nudging at my entrance with the tip of his cock.

231

I couldn't tell if he was teasing or being cautious, but I needed to let him know that I had waited long enough.

"Joel," I begged him, his name coming out on a breath and his eyes came to mine inquiringly.

"What do you need?" he asked. My response was easy to articulate.

"I want you inside me," I panted breathlessly, pulling my arms tighter around his shoulders. "Please."

He smiled and shifted his body, watching my face closely as he slowly began to press forward and I winced as I felt myself being stretched to accommodate him.

"Do you need me to stop?"

I shook my head though I was holding my breath until I felt his thighs press right up against mine, and then I exhaled.

Opening my eyes, I let out my breath and Joel smiled as he pressed his forehead to mine, giving me a moment to both collect myself and adjust to his challenging endowment.

"You okay?" he whispered, and even in the dark, I could see the glint in his sparkling eyes.

"Yeah." I nodded. "Just start slow," I instructed him before lifting my head up to take his mouth with mine again.

His hands pressed into my thighs, flattening them against the mattress as he slowly began to move.

With our eyes closed, we feasted on each other's mouths, and I sighed audibly as I began to feel him make slow, shallow movements with his hips.

My sighs turned to moans that he drank down as I felt his back and shoulder muscles coiling and releasing under my hands while his strokes started to come harder and deeper.

His lips pulled away and he buried his face into my neck as our audible pleasure overlapped to punctuate the rhythmic movement of our bodies.

I was overcome by his control and strength, enraptured by his sensuality despite his size and wholly consumed by all the little details like the clean, salt of his skin, the sweet tang of his mouth, the resonant depth of his voice, the coarse softness of his hair, and the harsh prickle of his beard.

My feet dug into the bed as that familiar inward winding of pleasure began converging toward my center and the sounds I was making climbed in pitch and urgency.

Sensing my imminent release, Joel's body began to tighten around me, and he lifted his head to fix his eyes to mine.

"I want to watch you come," he stated, his lips moving against mine.

I never wanted this to end, but his words brought me to the brink and it was now outside the bounds of my control. A sharp pinch from his grasp on my thigh sent a spike of pain through my body. My eyes closed and my lips parted as suddenly I was swathed in white-hot heat, coming and clenching around him as I cried out in pleasure.

In the midst of the mind-numbing decadence of my climax, the feel of Joel's forehead pressed to mine and the sounds he was making in the throes of his own release intensified my own.

We moved together, chasing the fireworks that lit up the darkness behind our clenched eyes, grasping, clenching and pulsing, relishing in the release of weeks of built-up tension.

Slowly, we came down together, our bodies refusing to stop pressing and clenching until we'd wrung out every drop of satisfaction to be had from one another.

When it was over, Joel collapsed against me, his cheek pressed to my chest as we lay catching our breath and feeling the throb of each other's pulse gradually returning to normal.

While we basked in post-coital bliss, I slid the tip of my finger around the curve of hair that followed the shape of his ear and along the jagged beard-covered line of his jaw.

"Are you working tomorrow?" he mumbled lazily against the rounded mound of my breast.

"No," I murmured, the word coming out sounding more like a breath.

I felt the prickle of his cheek pull across my skin as he smiled.

"Good. Then it won't matter if we don't get any sleep tonight."

CHAPTER 20

"*J*hate winter," I lamented as I laid across the disheveled surface of Joel's sofa bed on Thanksgiving morning watching an unseasonal flurry descend from the hazy gray above. It wasn't technically winter yet, and the snow wasn't sticking but it was a reminder of what awaited me when I made it north. "Maybe moving back to Boston is a bad idea."

The bakery was closed for the holiday and while everyone was spending time with their families, Joel and I decided to spend the day enjoying pure hedonistic indulgences, such as apple pie French toast, old records, and each other.

Currently, Ella Fitzgerald wanted to know if we had plans on New Year's Eve.

I preferred not to think that far ahead.

"It might be a bit too late to turn back now," I heard Joel approaching behind me.

I turned my head on the pillow to face him, watching as he approached the bed with two cups of coffee, wearing nothing but a pair of gray sweatpants slung low on his body.

A smile immediately pulled across my face as I watched the way he moved, his arms rigid so as not to spill the hot beverage from the mugs.

I loved the way he moved, and the fewer clothes he was wearing when he did, the better.

My eyes followed the defining lines at the front of his torso from his clavicle, all the way down to the waistband of his sweatpants.

He lowered the mugs of coffee to a nearby side table before climbing onto the bed beside me, laying on his stomach, and placing his hand on the small of my back.

I closed my eyes and sighed as he began tracing the tips of his fingers all over and instantly goosebumps pebbled the surface of my skin.

"Mmm," I hummed contentedly at his touch. "Don't ever stop doing that."

"You're just like a kitten who constantly wants pets," he drawled, the bass of his voice near my neck sending vibrations throughout my body.

"I think I just forgot how nice it was to be touched like that," I confessed, trying to recall the last time I'd felt this level of intimacy with someone.

I forgot what I was trying to remember when his fingertips flattened, and his palm began rubbing slow circles all over me.

I was in heaven, but always wrestling with the ever-present knowledge that I was just a visitor.

Every time I started to get comfortable with the idea of how easily I could fall into this thing with Joel, I remembered the circumstances of our respective situations and that put the kibosh on any ideas we might have for longevity.

And back down to earth I tumbled.

"What happened just now?" Joel inquired, feeling how my body suddenly tensed and seeing my eyes flutter open.

I didn't see any sense in lying so I shifted onto my back and pulled his arm to guide his body right up close and alongside me.

He placed his leg between mine, laying his head on my chest as I wrapped my arms around his shoulders, staring up at the ceiling.

Ah, but in case I stand one little chance
Here comes the jackpot question in advance
What are you doing New Year's, New Year's Eve?

* * *

"I wish you could come to Boston with me."

There, I said it.

He took a long time to respond, but while I waited, I ran my fingers through his hair, letting the thick strands slide through my fingers.

"The only thing I've wished for harder than to hear you say that, is to be able to actually do it."

My heart hurt to hear him say that. To acknowledge that it couldn't happen out loud, hurt.

"Can't you just lie and tell me it's going to happen?" I implored, feeling pressure begin to build behind my eyes.

"I wish I could do that too."

The pleasure of his lips moving against my skin was tempered by the words he'd spoken, leaving me to grasp at straws to try and tip the scales back in our favor.

"There has to be something we can do," I insisted, not ready to give up on the idea yet.

A long, hopeless silence followed before Joel lifted his cheek to look up at me, his lips curved in a smile that didn't reach his eyes.

"You know, I could have gone for the rest of my life convinced that there would never be another person who would look at me the way you're looking at me right now. I plan on getting my fill so that once you've moved on, I'll have a trove of memories to look back on and know with certainty there *is* someone out there and she's perfect. If this is all I can have, then I'll take it."

My eyes closed at the straining in my heart and I shook my head gently.

"Not good enough," I stated obstinately. "It's nowhere near good enough. I don't want memories. I want this," I said squeezing my arms around him. "I want your warmth, your taste, your smell, your sexy

237

accent. I even want your beard burn, and your frowny brows. I want ... I need *you*. So, we need to think of a way to make it happen because I won't accept anything less, is that clear?"

I felt his sigh blow over me like a warm breeze and his fingers stroking my skin to soothe me.

"Alright ... okay," he agreed indulgently though it was clear he was just telling me what I wanted to hear.

I didn't need him to believe it. I just needed to keep the possibility of a chance open or my heart would have broken right there and colored the rest of my time with him gray and lifeless and Winter would do a good enough job of that on its own.

* * *

For the next few days, it was business as usual.

The minute Thanksgiving was over, the town put their time and energy into the Green Valley Christmas Market which would run from December fifteenth to the twenty-fourth.

Organizers solicited local businesses to open vendor stalls and the Donner Bakery agreed to participate with a limited holiday-themed menu.

Over the next few days, the team collaborated to come up with five new holiday treats for the stall and four hot drinks.

I was tasked with overseeing the production of the treats, while Bradley, the barista at the bakery, was in charge of the drinks.

Joy petitioned with the fervor of Buddy the Elf to be in charge of staffing the stall once it opened and since there were few other takers, Jennifer was happy to give her the job.

I didn't think there could be a more suitable choice for such a role, so I was glad that she got what she wanted, but wondered if she'd regret it after a few hours standing in the freezing cold outdoor market.

Genie's Country Western Bar really came to the table with their contribution, committing to open an outdoor biergarten where people could come and enjoy a mug of glühwein or a holiday-themed stein of beer.

The market was causing quite the buzz in the local community and even managed to give me moments of fleeting respite from thinking nothing but heavyhearted thoughts about my diminishing time in Green Valley. The fact that the Donner Bakery was entering into its busiest time of year did little to help.

The bakery had been busy over Thanksgiving, but as orders for Christmas started rolling in, I started to panic a little, unable to see how the team would manage fulfilling the sheer volume of additional work, on top of keeping the bakery stocked as usual, and now the Christmas Market in addition.

Productivity was great. I loved it. In fact, to a certain degree, I *needed* that gratifying feeling of accomplishment at the end of a hectic day, but this level of work would mean that time would pass by in the blink of an eye.

As committed as I was to making sure that the families of Green Valley got their holiday indulgences, I couldn't help but think about how Joel needed my time so much more than Scotia Simmons needed her Donner Bakery Christmas panettone.

That, coupled with the fact that John Moxie remained as relentless as ever, was causing me to drag my feet a little more than usual and I felt the weight of my conflicted feelings starting to take its toll.

Even Anna could tell that I was distracted, offering to come to Tennessee and raise some hell with the Iron Wraiths on Joel's behalf, and as tempted as I was to let her, I just didn't think that the people of Green Valley were quite ready for her.

I recalled the time when we were in our twenties trying to get into a bar, and a bouncer with a god complex refused to let us in because her skirt was too short. Cut to one rant about sexism and slut-shaming fifteen minutes later, and the very sheepish bouncer not only let us in but also bestowed upon us a couple of VIP passes. Once inside, I'd had one sip of a drink before Anna demanded we leave so that she could tell the bouncer on the way out that the establishment was not to her usual standards and she wouldn't be back.

Any gumption I possessed was a by-product of keeping company with the likes of Anna who never accepted anything less than respect given and respect received.

I was grateful to her for listening to me carry on about the whole Joel situation when I needed to talk, but the reality was, there wasn't much she, I, or anybody else for that matter, would be able to do to help.

Fortunately, there was one activity Joel and I could depend on to distract us from thoughts of my impending departure. And it worked one hundred percent of the time.

There was at least one aspect of Joel Barnes' life he had a firm command on and that was in the bedroom. Or the sofa. Or a chair. Or the shower. Or on the stairs leading up to the apartment suites.

I wasn't so concerned with how he got his confidence in that regard, only that he seemed to know his way around my body that had me responding in ways I didn't think I was personally capable of, in positions I didn't think I liked.

I didn't have a lot of experience to draw from, but Joel was the kind of lover that you didn't have to be super experienced to know that he was either very gifted, or perhaps we were just extremely compatible.

I was laying on my stomach, my arms stretched out in front of me grasping the wrought iron metal bars of the bedhead. Joel was lying on top of me, rolling his hips against me, his beard pricking into the skin under my ear.

I'd already come sitting in his lap, before we'd switched positions and I assumed he would soon be following until I heard him whisper.

"You gonna give me another one?"

"I can't in this position," I panted, feeling the breath of his laugh against my ear.

"That's what you said the last few times," he asserted which might have sounded boastful if he hadn't been right. I felt the weight of him lift off my back and then the slow slide of his hands beneath my hips. He gripped them and with one sharp jerk, he lifted me up onto all fours. I braced myself as I felt his palm coast up the center of my back and into my hair where he fisted a handful to gently tug my head to the side, so he could lean in and talk directly in my ear.

"You're gonna give me another one," he commanded, as I shook my head in protest.

"No."

"Yes," he breathed, curving all around me and tightening his grip on my hip.

"I don't think I ... ah!"

I gasped loudly as he pressed forward and my hand reached out to seek purchase on the bedhead as the feeling of being stretched and filled by him overtook my senses once more.

I gave myself over to the eye-watering, involuntary-moan-inducing perfection of his pressure, angle, and rhythm as he flexed and pressed deep inside over and over again.

His hot breath in my ear and on my neck, punctuated every now and then by the deep, gritty sound of his pleasured groaning, coupled with the damp slide of our skin across one another's, was just about as close to a spiritual experience as I had ever encountered.

Despite the fact that we'd been awake exploring each other's desires all night long, I still didn't want this to ever end. It felt too right to accept that we couldn't have this feeling whenever we wanted.

Even as I was doubting my own body's ability to climax again, I felt the tide start to pull me off the shore. Each stroke he made caused a wave to crash closer and closer until I could see the one that would envelop me whole and pull me right out to the sea.

"I can't, I can't," I insisted, protesting uselessly against the inevitable.

"Do you want me to stop?" he asked already knowing my answer and sensing that I was close.

Trading the slow, languid curling of his hips for faster, harder, and deeper movements, I clenched my teeth and pressed backward to meet his strokes.

"Don't stop," I begged. "Don't stop, oh my God."

My voice, high pitched and wrenching, cried out, sounding to my ears like some disembodied plea, the bed frame creaking wildly from the weight and motion of our bodies.

Joel's grip on my hip pinched, and that sharp spark of pain triggered a cascading jolt through my nerve endings which set off the blinding sensation of a powerful and consuming orgasm.

The unique experience of pain, relief, pleasure, and the liberation from control all rolled into one paralyzingly blissful moment, was overwhelming. I relished in its otherworldliness, distantly aware that Joel was driving as deep inside me as he could get, lost in the throes of his own climax.

My eyes opened to see his hand had left my hair and was gripping the same iron bar that I was holding onto for leverage.

The sound of his release filled my ears and his beard pricked my shoulder where his teeth caught my skin as we rode it out together in graceless, needful motions until we both slowed but couldn't stop, insistent on chasing the dissipating lights of the fireworks.

Finally, after having wrung out every last drop of pleasure that I could, I relinquished my hold on the bed and fell down flat against the mattress.

A moment later, I felt Joel's chest against my back, his weight coming over me like the most comforting blanket you could ever hope for. Worried that he was too heavy, even though I assured him he wasn't, he took just a few more breaths before finding the strength to reposition himself at my side.

I turned my head to take in the sight of him all disheveled, heavy-lidded, and damp with sweat and smiled at how my body stirred with desire for him again so soon after having just had him. I wanted him all the time.

One of his large hands came to his chest as he draped his other forearm over his eyes while we took several quiet moments to catch our breath and recompose ourselves.

Just as I saw dark clouds approaching on the horizon of my thoughts, Joel sat up and swung his legs off the bed, bringing my attention back to the here and now.

"I'll be right back, don't move," he murmured, his accent thick under the weight of satisfaction-induced fatigue and I nodded, too boneless and spent to protest or question where he was going.

I quite enjoyed the view of him walking across the room, watching his muscles working beneath the sheen of his skin as he made his way into the bathroom.

My eyes had been open for too many hours that day and were starting to protest when he reemerged, and I was treated to the view of his front side as he returned toward the bed.

"You're such a perv," he teased seeing how my lips curved into a smile and the way my eyes shamelessly devoured his impressive form.

I felt the mattress depress under his weight as he climbed onto the bed beside me and placed his hand on my hip.

The heat of his breath warmed my shoulder and I felt the wiriness of his kiss before he whispered, "Turn over for me."

Obliging his request, I shifted my body until I was on my back as per his instructions, noticing the warm, dampened cloth he held in his other hand.

I watched him closely as he placed it between my thighs and slowly cleaned me with gentle, attentive caresses noticing the almost wistful quality of his blue-green eyes while he did it.

I wanted to ask what he was thinking about that made his eyes look so sad, but I refrained on account of the fact that I already knew, and I was trying not to think about it either.

When he was done, he discarded the cloth and lay on his back, pulling me to him with one strong arm. I curled into his side with my hand on his chest and my ear over his heart, listening to the steady sound of his heartbeat.

"You tired?" I heard him ask, the sound of his voice reverberating through his chest and into my ear like a bass guitar.

"Yes ... but I never want to sleep anymore because then ..."

"... it's just another day down," he continued, completing my sentence when I couldn't. I nodded against his chest.

"Tell me what your Christmases were like," he requested apropos of nothing before yawning with a roar.

I thought it was an odd question for the moment, but I supposed it was because he was about as anxious for this day to end as I was.

I sighed, recalling the chaos.

"Oh man, they were crazy. My parents had tons of siblings and every Christmas we'd have a big party at my aunt's place. Now that I think about it, it was probably one of the reasons I moved to the other side of the country."

"You never flew home for the holidays when you were in Seattle?"

"Nope. I was always working," I explained, feeling guilty about how I always wished that time of year away in favor of a break. "What about you?"

"Usually just me, my brother, and my dad. Nothing fancy. Just a roast chicken dinner my dad would fumble his way through and a bunch of beer. Still, they were good times to look back on, we always liked getting together for Christmas."

"You must miss them at this time of year," I stated tentatively, and though I couldn't see him, I felt him nod his head.

"Yeah, I sure do."

"Can I hang out with you this Christmas?" I asked even though I didn't intend on giving him a choice.

"Sure," he agreed, stroking at my shoulder with the pad of his thumb. "Is it okay if we don't do the whole gift thing though? I still don't really feel right about celebrating Christmas ... not with the way things are."

It made me sad to hear him say that. Not out of disappointment, but because it made me realize that he was still in the process of grieving for the loss of his family, the only people in Green Valley who truly knew who he was.

"Of course," I whispered. "We don't even have to do a turkey, we can make a big tray of lasagna, or maybe some tacos. We'll make our own little holiday."

I felt and heard Joel huff a soft laugh under my cheek as he began stroking the long lengths of my hair.

"I can get behind that. In fact, that sounds just about perfect."

CHAPTER 21

 hen Joel wasn't around to distract me from my ever-mounting anxiety over leaving him behind, my emotions undulated dizzyingly between sadness, anger, despair, and helplessness.

I was getting to a place where I was beginning to rationalize care-less ideas, like going to the cops on Joel's behalf, by telling myself that the only thing stopping him from doing it himself was fear.

As much as I wanted to believe that it would be that easy, I knew it was much more complicated and also begrudgingly acknowledged that it wasn't my place to make potentially life-changing decisions for other people no matter how dire the situation or how desperate I felt to help.

Each day closer to the new year, brought me one step closer to being without him until one night, I was an emotional wreck, standing at the kitchen bench crying while trying to talk myself out of what I was about to do.

I tried to dissuade myself by going through all of the inevitable consequences, but even the worst of them didn't seem to be making much of a deterrent.

I needed something powerful enough to dull the cacophony of voices in my head taunting me about my time with Joel running out.

I continued to ignore calls from John Moxie and Joel had started ignoring calls from Catfish, but the two situations were very different because soon Catfish was going to come looking for Joel.

I thought about calling Cletus, but I hadn't seen him since our confrontation which was unusual considering he tended to find any excuse to come to the bakery in the middle of the day to see Jennifer, so I figured he was either avoiding me or trying to convince his wife to fire me.

I didn't want to be fired, because then I'd have to leave Green Valley even sooner which I was already getting to end of my rope thinking about.

Every day, the knot in my stomach pulled a little tighter and shortened my fuse until I found myself irrationally bothered by things that never irritated me before. Like Joy's irrepressible bubbliness for the impending holiday or Tempest's snarkiness toward Joy's glee, even if in jest.

I was barely sleeping unless Joel was beside me, barely eating unless Joel and I ate together, and barely smiling unless I was with him.

I'd reached the breaking point and it had brought me to the moment where I stood in the kitchen in my underwear and a T-shirt with a jar of Nutella with the gold seal still intact and unbroken.

I wasn't proud of myself, but I needed it to take the edge off.

Anna would kill me if she knew, but she wasn't here right now, and I needed something to distract my mind from everything that had happened with Joel as well as my looming departure from Green Valley.

I did resolve to show some semblance of restraint and told myself that I was only allowed to eat the Nutella at the island in the kitchen and not in front of the television.

It was too easy to lose track of how much I consumed under the hypnotic glow of the TV, and my capacity to devour whole jars of the stuff at a time was already pretty impressive. Or disturbing depending on which side of the fence you sat with respect to chocolate hazelnut spread.

I glanced up at the fridge, right into the eyes of a decidedly judgey looking Mr. Newman.

"Don't look at me like that. This is *your* fault. If you had just come through for me one last time and gotten me to Boston instead of stuck here, none of this would've happened," I said gesticulating with both hands to the jar.

I indignantly unscrewed the cap on the jar and slapped it down on the kitchen counter, giving Mr. Newman one last withering glare before looking down at the gold seal right in front of me.

Just one shiny piece of gold paper was all that stood between me and sweet relief.

I acquired a spoon from the cutlery drawer and just as I was about to unceremoniously use it to stab through the seal, my cell phone began to ring.

I glanced up at the sound and my eyes slid toward Mr. Newman, his expression now annoyingly smug.

"You can be a real jerk sometimes, you know that?" I sneered, stomping across the apartment to retrieve my phone from where it lay charging to inspect the screen.

I narrowed my eyes in confusion. I didn't recognize the number, but it was too late for John Moxie to be calling. As relentless as he was, he tended to stick to regular West Coast business hours and only once did he call later than that.

In the end, I was too curious to be cautious and decided to answer the phone.

"Hello."

"Evening," came the succinct greeting delivered with the emotional range of a talking computer. I recognized the voice immediately as Cletus Winston's.

"Hey, Cletus," I replied cautiously. I was also strangely glad to hear from him, even if the motivation behind his call was still unclear.

He cleared his throat and proceeded.

"I wondered if you would be agreeable to a short meeting. I acknowledge the late hour, but—"

"No, it's okay," I interrupted not needing to hear his justification. "I think we need to talk."

"Well, alright then," he replied perhaps sounding a little surprised that I had agreed so readily.

"Where did you want to meet? Daisy's?"

"No, too many people," he replied cryptically, and I wondered at the need for secrecy. "Are you able to come to the bakery?"

I wasn't sure why he wanted to meet there, but I didn't see any reason why I shouldn't.

"Of course. Give me twenty minutes?"

"I'm already here, just knock on the back door when you arrive."

"Alright, I'll be there soon."

I hung up the phone and without time to give too much thought as to what I was going to say to him when I arrived, I hurriedly dressed, gathered up my keys and purse, and left the apartment to drive to the bakery.

On the way, I practiced what I was going to say to Cletus by way of an apology.

He had been nothing but kind to me since I'd arrived in Green Valley and didn't deserve for me to try and guilt him into doing something that would have put him and/or his family in any kind of jeopardy. I was so desperate in my pursuit to try and help Joel that I lost sight of the price Cletus could potentially pay for getting involved and I was a selfish jerk for it.

Great, that's all I need on top of everything else. Guilt, I thought bitterly as I pulled into the bakery parking lot.

I knocked on the back door as Cletus had instructed and waited for him to answer.

I pulled the sides of my jacket together and crossed my arms over my chest to try and bundle up against the cold, peering up as black clouds moved with alarming speed across the sky, feeling that another dusting of snow was likely imminent.

A moment later, the door opened, and Cletus appeared backlit by warm light from inside the bakery.

I shivered, feeling small under the scrutinizing quality of his countenance and for the first time, it crossed my mind that he might have asked me here after having convinced Jenn to fire me.

"Get in here and get warmed up before you catch your death, it's freezing out there," he instructed with the tender authority of a big brother who was pissed off but knew he was going to forgive me anyway. Those few words helped to make me feel more at ease since I wasn't really getting the impression that he was looking for another fight, and I certainly didn't have the stomach for it either.

"Thank you," I replied tentatively, my teeth chattering as he moved aside to let me in and promptly shut the door so as not to let the warmth from inside the bakery leech out.

Inside, Jennifer was standing by a small mixer, and looked up from the bowl she had been peering into to smile at me.

"Hey, Sophie," she greeted looking tired as I slowly made my way toward her.

"Do you ever stop?" I asked her, gesturing toward the mixer with my chin, to which she huffed a laugh and cocked her head.

"One day," she said sounding every bit like "one day" really meant "not really."

"Can I do anything to help?" I offered, knowing what her answer would be, but asking anyway.

"I'm almost done here but thank you. Why don't you and Cletus go into the office and I'll bring you both a hot chocolate once I'm finished."

"Okay," I agreed and smiled at Jennifer as she gave me a wink before Cletus led me through the kitchen toward the office in the back.

Once inside he gestured toward the guest chair for me to sit down and when I was situated, instead of taking the seat on the opposite side of the desk, he perched on the side of it instead.

"Cletus, before you start, can I say something?" I asked, the weight of the apology too heavy to proceed without getting it off my chest.

"Go on," he replied with a nod.

"I just wanted to say that I am *so* sorry about what happened that night. You were one thousand percent in the right and I was being a selfish brat by trying to pressure you into helping Joel. I am usually not such an asshole, but I just—" I stopped abruptly when I felt my voice begin to tremble and pulled my lips between my teeth until I got a handle on the overflow of emotions that had been building with no outlet. "Anyway," I continued. "I made a huge mistake. I'm sorry and I hope you can forgive me."

I swallowed back the tightness in my throat and let out a cleansing breath as I peered up at the ceiling, willing the gathering tears to go back from whence they came.

Cletus slid a box of tissues toward me, but I refused to let tears get the best of me.

"Apology accepted. Let's move on," he said, his tone readopting the straight-to-the-point air that I was more familiar with. "Now," he continued, "are you in love with him?"

I froze at the simple, six-word question and stared at him as though he'd just told me that my croissants sucked.

I had spent so much time avoiding asking myself that very same question that the abruptness of its sudden need to be answered triggered a reaction in my body that I had no control over.

I crumpled inwards on myself and put my head in my hands, resting my elbows on the desk.

"Oh shit," I groaned, faced with the unfettered realization that yes, I was very much in love with Joel and there was no sense in hiding it, especially from Cletus whose range of perception was far too wide for me to evade.

"Well I already knew that, I just wanted you to finally admit it to yourself," Cletus stated with the kind of haughty all-knowing tone that I had no defense against, because he was right.

He stood and walked toward a backpack that was resting on a chair behind the desk.

He unzipped the backpack, reached inside and pulled out a yellow A4 sized envelope before placing it on the desk and sliding it toward me.

I looked up from my hands and eyed the envelope, furrowing my brow questioningly.

"What's this?" I inquired looking up at Cletus, who gestured with his bushy, bearded chin toward the envelope.

"Open it," he instructed placing one hand on the back of the office chair he was standing by and the other on his hip.

I slowly reached for the unsealed envelope and slid my hand inside feeling the stiffness of a stack of cardboard sheets that felt smooth and almost glossy to the touch.

I grasped the stack and pulled them from the envelope, seeing that they were photos.

More specifically, they were surveillance photos.

"What are these?" I asked, until I began sifting through the images and began to understand what I was looking at.

I glanced up at Cletus confused, my mind instantly becoming noisy with questions.

"How did you get these?" I asked returning my attention to the stack of photographs as I flipped through them slowly at first then slowly building in speed as my impatience to see the next one grew.

Cletus hadn't answered my first question yet, when I continued on to the next.

"Why are you showing me these?" I asked looking up at him once more and struggling to make sense of why he'd shared these photos with me.

Cletus maneuvered himself into the chair then and rested his elbows on the armrest.

"To put it simply, where possible, I like to make life as difficult as I can for the Iron Wraiths."

"So, you *are* a vigilante superhero," I nodded as though I knew it was true.

"Catfish as I understand it," he continued, ignoring my declaration, "is making a push to become the club president which makes him more dangerous now because it means he's willing to go to greater lengths to show the club he's capable and worthy of the title ... that coupled with the fact that he kidnapped my brother a few years ago and I'm still not over it, petty as that might seem."

"Petty?" I parroted incredulously. "Cletus, if someone kidnapped someone I loved, I would dedicate my life to getting even with them. I don't think that's petty at all."

Cletus nodded in approval at my response.

"I'm glad we're on the same page, because I can't let Catfish Hickson become president of the Iron Wraiths and these photographs, if used correctly, should work to destabilize his efforts pretty significantly."

"Wait, wait a minute," I interjected holding up my hand while I attempted to navigate the complex network of the relationships involved in this scenario.

"These," I said laying the photographs on the desk in front of me, "are photographs of Catfish getting … inarguably cozy with Daniella Payton." I looked to Cletus who nodded to confirm it.

"That's right."

"And you want us to use these photos of them together, to blackmail him into …" I trailed off, trying to impart that I wasn't entirely sure what the goal was here.

"You can use those photos to blackmail him to do whatever you want…or more precisely to get him to agree that Joel no longer needs to be participating in their illegal activities."

"But what if he forces our hand and we *have* to use them? Isn't Daniella Payton your brother's girlfriend's sister? I can't put your brother's relationship with Simone in that kind of jeopardy."

"First off. Simon and Roscoe are fine, it's Danielle and Simone's relationship that will suffer if Simone finds out that her sister is still cozy with a member of the club that almost killed her and my brother. Trust me, if you show these photos to Catfish, there is no way he's going to let them get out," Cletus said with confidence, but I still needed convincing.

"If Catfish is as motivated as you say he is, then doesn't that make him more unpredictable? How can you be so sure he'll fold?"

Cletus narrowed his eyes at me with a haughtiness that he was too careful to display usually, but something about what he was about to say made the corner of his mouth tick upward in a half-smile.

"Have you ever met Daniella Payton?"

"Yes, I have ... right," I said immediately understanding his point when I remembered Daniella's barely restrained force of a personality.

"Trust me when I tell you, she is not going to let those photos get out. Catfish doesn't know it yet, but these photos are a gun that's pointed right at his foot and one way or another it's gonna go off."

"I'm still not sure I follow." I sighed wearily, unable to keep up with what I'm sure seemed very obvious to Cletus, the vigilante superhero.

"He can't let those pictures of him and Miss Payton go public, which will mean he has to agree to pardon Joel from any future involvement pertaining to their chop shop operations ..." Cletus began to explain. Once he laid down the first section of the track that his mind was on, the picture which had previously been fuzzy in my mind began to take shape until I was able to finish the rest.

"... and letting go of a source of income to the club will make him look weak to the other members!"

"Precisely," Cletus confirmed with a nod of his head.

I was careful to keep a lid on the hope rising within me at the thought of this working even as my mind was busy trying to find any weaknesses in his plan. Cletus must have read my mind, choosing that moment to lean forward and rest his forearms on the desk.

"Sophie," he said, drawing my attention back to him. "This *will* work," he assured me, and it was the first time I'd seen Cletus so earnest about anything other than his wife.

I only had one more question. "Cletus, can I ask you something?"

"Go on," he urged.

"What are you *really* getting out of this? Petty revenge doesn't really seem like your style."

"Au contraire, my friend, petty revenge is exactly my style, but you are correct, it isn't my only motivation."

"I didn't think so ... Well?" I asked raising my eyebrows for him to proceed.

"We're looking to expand the Winston Brother's Auto Shop and we need another location ... I figured if Joel knew I had a hand in helping him get clear of the Wraiths and seeing as how he doesn't really have aspirations to continue on with the auto business, he might be agreeable to selling his shop to me."

In spite of the fact that I still had a voice in the back of my mind cautioning me against becoming too hopeful, the mere idea that there was a way for Joel to be free from the Wraiths and Green Valley was overwhelming and I lowered my face into my hands and started to cry.

"I'm sorry. I'm so sorry," I kept apologizing for my outburst between sobs, fully aware of how uncomfortable my emotional tsunami was making him. "I don't know what to say, Cletus, except thank you."

"It's no trouble just ... please stop crying," he implored, pushing the box of tissues closer.

"Wow you really are a real-life superhero," I declared gazing at him with wide-eyed wonder.

I was just fucking with him now, but it was totally working. He looked horrified.

"Can I have a hug?" I asked for no other purpose than to see the reaction on his face when I asked, and I was not disappointed. Cletus drew in a breath and then paused, trying to figure out how best to politely refuse my affections.

I decided I'd tortured him long enough.

"Relax, I'm just fucking with you," I half laugh, half cried before yanking some tissues from the box and the relief on his face was evident.

A moment later, Jenn appeared with two mugs of hot chocolate and placed them on the desk in front of us.

"I know you must have had a hand in this, Jenn, so thank you. A million times, thank you both for this, I'm sure Joel will be very grateful."

"Don't thank us yet, I still think that you need to be prepared for the possibility, albeit a small one, that this might not work," Cletus cautioned.

"I know, I know." I nodded acknowledging the risk. "It's also up to Joel to decide if he even wants to move forward with this, but at least he has a choice now." I rationalized, hearing the hope creep into my voice again.

"Well then, I think a little drink is in order," Cletus decreed pulling a jar from his backpack and unscrewing the cap.

"Oh Lord," Jennifer groaned when she saw it.

"What is that?" I asked, watching as Cletus poured a nip in each of our hot chocolate cups.

"It's my homemade moonshine," Cletus informed me, and my eyes lit up.

"Ooh I've never had moonshine before," I said picking up my cup and sniffing.

"Miss Sophie, would you like to make a toast?" Jennifer suggested coming around to sit on the arm of Cletus's chair.

I took a moment to think about what I wanted to say before raising my mug. Cletus and Jennifer followed suit.

"To giving, and getting second chances," I said, barely able to make it through the sentence before I started to tear up again.

"Aw," Jennifer offered tilting her head sympathetically as I cleared my throat.

"I'm so sorry, I almost never cry," I hurried to explain. "I don't know what's wrong with me."

"Have a couple of sips of this, you'll feel much better," Cletus advised. I smiled and brought the mug to my lips.

I took a sip and for a moment all I could taste was chocolate, and then a half a second after that, my whole head was on fire.

I immediately began sputtering behind my hand as the burning sensation in my throat spread all the way through me, completely unprepared for the strength of the alcohol.

Cletus took a few big gulps before following up with a satisfied, "Aah, that's good stuff."

I nodded politely, still coughing and tilted my mug to him, "It's really good," I croaked, taking a few seconds and some deep breaths to psyche myself up before taking another sip.

CHAPTER 22

*N*ot so many hours later, I was back at the bakery elbow deep in a pillowy blob of dough that was ready to be formed into French baguettes. I went about dividing, weighing, and rolling each baton on muscle memory while my conscious thought remained fixated on my conversation with Cletus.

I'd be lying if I said that having those photos in my possession didn't make me feel a little like Cate Blanchett in *The Lord of the Rings*, when Frodo offers her the one ring. For a moment, I felt all terrifying, electric, and powerful but just as Galadriel managed to withstand the temptation to use the ring, so did I because I knew that ultimately the decision about whether to use the photos or not was Joel's.

I knew beyond a shadow of a doubt that he would take any opportunity to get out from under the thumb of the Wraiths. What I wasn't so sure about was the part about him selling his shop to Cletus and possibly moving away from Green Valley.

I knew first hand just how hard it was to leave behind everything you've ever known. When I moved across the country to pursue my goal of becoming an elite pastry chef, I did nothing but cry with homesickness for the first two weeks straight.

It wasn't necessarily that I felt Joel would struggle to adapt and make a new life for himself somewhere else, but emotional ties were hard to break at the best of times.

For Joel, there was the added weight of guilt with how things had ended with his brother Nick, the ever-present threat of an unpredictable and far-reaching crime ring, no job to go to, no place to stay, and no guarantee that things would work out between the two of us.

I wished I could give him all the confidence and reassurance he needed to make those breaks, but I knew he had to face those things on his own.

Breaking skin is hard, and it hurts. Perhaps it's because deep down, we know nothing will ever be the same again. And sometimes the worst part is when you come to find that the things you once cherished most are better left behind you. I knew letting go of Green Valley would be hard, but I hoped I could convince him that we could face it together.

Working at the bakery was the ideal place for me in my current state of mind. I mightn't have been able to stop monologuing what I was going to say to Joel in my mind, but the physicality of my job saw that I had an outlet for all that energy.

Deciding that I was better off at the bakery than on my own for the few hours I'd have to wait for Joel to come home, I stayed behind for an extra two hours at the end of my shift, trying to get ahead of the workload for the next day.

When I decided that it was finally time to leave, I stopped at the Piggly Wiggly on the way home, overcome by the urge to flex my culinary muscle and make one of Paradigm's most popular dishes. It was an elaborate dish with lots of little elements and required enough technique to keep me absorbed for the next few hours.

Once I was back at the apartment, I turned on some music and got to work while the photos from Cletus burned a hole in my backpack.

I had in my possession a chance to give Joel a real shot at freedom, but the road ahead was fraught with peril and uncertainty, and I wondered what I would do if he deemed the risk too great.

I simply wasn't okay with just leaving him there, but I knew I couldn't stay.

I'd committed myself to spending the first six months with Anna after the opening of Yeast Affection, and I intended to honor that despite knowing that I was in love with him.

I glanced up at Mr. Newman hanging casually from the refrigerator. Even though I was still directing my ire toward him for getting me stuck in Green Valley and thus, in this situation, I still sought his counsel.

"What do I do, huh?"

Give him the pictures, tell him why you and Cletus think they will work, but let him know that the choice is ultimately his.

"What if he thinks it's too risky?"

Well, it is risky, kid. But it's up to him to decide whether or not it's worth it. You just need to be prepared for the possibility that he might not.

I sighed and turned my attention back to prepping the ingredients for the dinner.

I had decided in advance that beef was the most appropriate theme to accompany a conversation about escaping the clutches of an evil crime organization, and a bottle of Merlot would be bold enough to stand up to the strong flavors I was planning to use.

To start we were going to enjoy a charred winter vegetable salad with a honey and tahini dressing.

For the main course, I made grilled tenderloin with maitake mushrooms, toasted pine nuts, and baby onion rings, scattering each element across a plate dusted with parmesan cheese and dotted with small mounds of horseradish aioli.

I knew Joel didn't particularly care for sweets, so I made more of a palette cleansing lemon and thyme granita to end the meal with. My hope was that by the time the richness of the main meal had been sluiced away by the pairing of citrus and woodsy herbs, together we would have come up with an ingenious plan that we both felt confident in executing before riding off into the sunset together.

I set the tiny dining room table for two, with linens and a candle that I didn't have a candlestick for, so I shoved it into a cleaned, empty wine bottle. I quite liked the effect of the wax melting down the length of the candle before it solidified around the widest part of the bottle and nodded with approval at my successful improvisation. The plates didn't match, and the cutlery was equally as adhoc, but I thought it looked homey and humble and contrasted nicely with the refined food.

I was going more for coziness than romance, given how nervous I was in anticipating Joel's response to the photos, but as I fussed with the arrangement of the charred vegetables on the platter, I felt that he deserved both.

I heard the door open and close behind me, so I picked up my pace to complete the plating before he'd had a chance to cross into the kitchen.

"Smells incredible in here," I heard Joel's drawl greet my ears just moments before his big arms encircled me from behind, one hand grasping my breast and I felt the graze of his beard on the sensitive skin of my neck.

"Hi," I greeted as he placed a line of kisses down my neck and onto my shoulder.

"Hey," he murmured breathing me in and making me unsteady on my feet from the rumble I felt through his chest.

I was getting turned on and so was Joel, so I wriggled free from his hold and tossed him a smile over my shoulder as I headed toward the sink.

"Yergh! I gotta wash my hands," I advised as he stepped out of the way and reached over to turn on the faucet for me.

"What's the occasion?" he asked, picking at a perfectly crisped Brussels sprout leaf while my hands were covered in soap and I couldn't swat him away.

"No occasion in particular," I lied. "I just felt like a spot of stove-side puttering." The truth would be forthcoming once Joel had finished the meal I'd just spent two hours and thirty-six minutes preparing.

I rinsed my sudsy hands and dried them on a dishcloth before handing Joel the bottle of Merlot and wine opener.

"You want to take care of this, while I bring out the food?

"Sure," he agreed watching me as I carried the platter of vegetables to the table and came back for the beef.

"You okay?" he asked narrowing his eyes at me curiously, seeing that I was behaving either nervous or a little more distant than normal.

"I'm fine," I assured him with a nod, carrying the carefully arranged plates out to the dining table.

As I laid the main course down, I heard the pop of the cork and the inviting glug of wine being poured from the bottle. I sat casually in my chair with one knee up to my chest as I watched Joel carry over the two generous glasses of wine in one hand and the bottle in the other.

After freeing up his hands, he bent over the table and tilted my chin up to place a soft kiss on my lips.

An inexplicable sadness came over me which was not the response that I was expecting after a kiss, and I quickly buried it by taking his face in my hands and pulling him back for more.

When I finally let him go, he smiled and brushed his thumb over my bottom lip.

"Thank you for dinner," he offered, his voice once again rolling over me like distant thunder.

"It was my pleasure. Hope you like it because this is the next thing you're learning to make," I only half-joked watching him take his seat.

Joel was a gracious dinner guest who offered constant appreciation and praise throughout the meal. I thought about him alone in his apartment eating ramen noodles and microwave meals and the foodie in me died inside.

Food was an undeniable show of love and affection, and I found myself wishing I could provide him with it all the time as well as giving him the means to be able to provide the same care for himself.

Cooking was an important skill in cultivating independence, not just from family, but from corporations and I couldn't help but make the parallel between Joel, Green Valley, and the Iron Wraiths.

"I ran into Tempest Cassidy," he informed me with a contemplative expression on his face about halfway through the meal.

"Oh yeah?" I replied, urging him to continue.

"Yeah, we were talking about you and this executive producer guy that keeps calling you," he continued, followed by a pregnant pause where my hands halted the cutting motion into the beef for a moment.

"And what did you two decide?"

Joel sipped his wine, eyeing me carefully and I suspected that I knew what was coming.

"You both think I should do it."

"It's three hundred thousand dollars, Soph. Do you know what you could do with that kind of money? You could open your own bakery."

"I know, I do nothing *but* think about it," I sighed, pushing around the food on my plate as I wondered how this turned into a conversation about me. "I think about doing it all the time," I admitted, which was the truth.

"So, what's stopping you?"

"You know why. The thought of losing my shit again will absolutely destroy any chance I have of working anywhere ever again. Trust me, the restaurant industry is a small world."

"Not gonna happen," Joel said with a certainty I had difficulty sharing.

"Yeah everyone keeps saying that, but the reality is that it *could* happen."

"So, let's talk about it, let's break it into smaller pieces, okay?" Joel asked fixing me with an expression that sought my permission to continue the conversation, and I lowered my cutlery in response. "You don't need to practice dessert, you've got that shit on lockdown, this isn't about that. I also don't think it's about the cameras and the lights either."

"Can we talk about something else?" I asked distracting myself by pouring more wine into our glasses.

"No," Joel said with an insistent tone. It wasn't harsh by any means but still made it clear that I wasn't going to get out of this conversation. "I want to know why you don't think you can do this."

I began trying to parse through my thoughts about it for the billionth time and when it was no less clear in my mind than it had been before, I shrugged.

"It's hard to explain, I don't know what it is, it's just ..."

"You," Joel stated, finishing my sentence on my behalf. "The only thing getting between you and winning that competition is *you*," he said jabbing his pointer finger in my direction.

I wilted a little because I knew he was right.

"I don't know how not to," I admitted with a resigned shrug. "I don't know how to stop telling myself that I'm going to fuck up the very next thing that I touch. I am hard on my myself, I know that, but I don't know how not to be. Every mistake I make feels like proof that I shouldn't have tried, and that show was the biggest mistake I ever made."

"Mistakes *aren't* proof that you're not good enough, they're just steps toward wherever it is you're trying to get to," he reasoned encouragingly.

"Not in that environment, they're not." I huffed humorlessly. "In the restaurant industry, mistakes aren't philosophized the way they are for regular people, they're used as ammunition to blow craters in your confidence that you have to spend the rest of your life trying to over-come." I recalled how whole plates of food had flown over my head like missiles for not being plated to absolute perfection.

"So what? You're just going to spend the rest of your life existing in the narrow space that the four or five people who criticized you convinced you that you belong in?"

I glanced up at Joel and watched as he slowly came to the realiza-tion that his question was interchangeable for our current situations.

"Okay, I get it," he said nodding in understanding. "But, at least there's something you can do about your situation," he said, providing me with the perfect segue.

I got up from my chair and crossed the room to retrieve my back-pack and pull out the envelope of surveillance photos.

I walked back to the dinner table and held the envelope out to Joel who frowned as he reached for it.

"What's this?" he asked pulling it from my grasp and opening the flap to reach inside for the contents.

I watched him as he took out the photos and began leafing through them.

"Is that Dani Payton?" he asked, squinting at the photos as though he didn't believe his eyes.

"Yes," I confirmed.

"Where did you get these?" he asked lowering the photos and fixing me with a questioning look.

I took a small breath before responding, knowing that the origin of the photos might surprise him.

"Cletus Winston gave them to me."

I could see the cogwheels in his mind working before asking, "Why would he give you these?"

His tone was already skeptical from the simple mention of Cletus's name, but I had set the conversation in motion, and forged on knowing that there was no going back now.

"Well," I began nervously, "he seems to think that ... they might help you."

It wasn't the clear and concise explanation that I had practiced. Predictably, Joel had questions.

"Help me with what?"

His tone reminded me once more of the night we met. Straight to the point with no room for ambiguity which made me nervous.

"He thinks that these will get Catfish off your case about using you and your garage."

Joel slowly sat back in his seat as he lifted the cloth napkin off his lap and laid it over his plate.

I watched as he snickered, shaking his head then slid back in his chair before getting to his feet.

"Thanks again for dinner," he said coolly and turned away from the table.

My whole body seized, not understanding his response as I scrambled to catch up.

"Wait," I called after him, rising to my feet. "Where are you going?"

"Home."

"Why?" I asked in a panic.

"After asking you not to tell my business to anyone, you went right to the source of this whole mess and decided it was a good idea to share it with them?" he asked with irritated incredulousness and I sighed and lowered my head guiltily.

"I know. I know, you're right. I didn't mean to, it just came out one night when we were talking about you, I got defensive and ... I'm sorry, okay? Joel, he is trying to help. He wants to help," I attempted desperately to clarify but even to my ears, it was a scattered and insufficient explanation.

"Why? For what purpose? Cletus Winston doesn't help anyone unless it serves his own interests."

I dreaded the response, knowing that Joel would only see it as the Winston brother's last nail to hammer in the Barnes Auto Shop coffin.

I took a moment to try and think of another way to lead into the response that focused more on his chance at freedom, but in the end, it all led to the same conclusion.

"Cletus wants to buy your garage," I replied, ripping off the Band-Aid and watching his eyes roll shut as he shook his head and rubbed his brow with exasperation.

"Joel," I appealed to him, taking a tentative step forward. "This is the open door you've been waiting for, what difference does it make how it's opened? Take the money for the shop and get out of Green Valley, like you've been trying to do all along."

Joel's eyes came to mine, and my shoulders fell seeing the hurt that clouded over their vibrancy, making me fully aware that I had said the wrong thing.

"I know that it's just a pile of bricks and mortar to you, but that shop is the only thing left of my dad and brother, so excuse me if I'm particular about handing it over to someone who, as far as I'm concerned, is responsible for putting them in the ground."

"You're right." I nodded in understanding. "You're right, I'm sorry, I didn't mean to imply that this would be easy, I just ... I'm desperate for you to get out of here. I know you don't want to be here," I offered gently, feeling heat springing to my eyes just as a thought occurred to me, "or do you?"

Joel narrowed his eyes at me briefly, as though he were about to argue that it was a ridiculous question.

But then, he didn't.

"I gotta get going," he announced finally, turning to make his way to the door, and then promptly left my apartment.

CHAPTER 23

On the eve of the opening of the Christmas Market, I arrived at the bakery on the Thursday evening for what would be my second to last test kitchen night.

It had been a couple of days since I had presented the photos of Catfish Hickson getting cozy with Daniella Payton to Joel and I'd not seen or heard from him since.

I had considered skipping out on test kitchen night, not being much in the mood for company, but Jennifer had sought me out earlier in the day and expressly mentioned that my presence was required. Seeing as how she was my boss and all, I didn't feel like I had much of a choice.

I pulled into the parking lot and knocked for what felt like forever until finally the door opened and there Jennifer appeared, looking unusually bright.

"Come on in, you're just in time," she said, reaching forward to take my wrist to pull me inside before I could think too much about it.

"Just in time for … what the h—"

My words caught in my throat as I glanced around the brightly lit kitchen.

"What is this? What's happening?" I asked, my words hinting that I might have an inkling, but needing confirmation.

In front of the bench where we usually set up our cake assembly conga line, were two huge box lights and between them, stood two elaborate camera setups.

"What do you think? You ready to start your training?" Tempest inquired, appearing from behind one of the cameras.

"Training?" I asked numbly.

"For *Double the Whisk, Double the Reward*," Tempest replied as though it were obvious.

"Yeah, think of it as stage fright boot camp," Joy piped up from behind the bench where I was presumably supposed to be working.

I was trying to keep up, but I hadn't slept or stopped crying for two days and wasn't much in the headspace to participate in games.

"All the ingredients you need to make Chestnuts Roasting on an Open Fire are on the bench right there. All you have to do is make it," Joy informed me before gesturing toward the bench with game show host hands.

"I don't know if I can really focus on that right n—"

"Sophie," Jennifer interrupted with a gentle, but firm voice that meant business. "We know that the shop has been busy, but think of this less as practicing your recipe and more like practicing being under studio lighting," she advised as she guided me over to the bench with her hands on my shoulders.

"It's not that, it's just …" I started to explain but lost my train of thought.

"What's wrong? You've been weird the last couple of days," Tempest observed in her usual direct manner.

"Nothing." I sighed, aware of how unconvincing I sounded, but without enough energy to care.

"Did something happen with Joel?" Tempest inquired, narrowing her eyes at me. "Do I need to go have a word?"

I glanced at Jennifer whose eyes communicated to me that she had caught on to my reasons for not having answered the question, before making my way over to the bench and began sorting through the ingredients.

I robotically and, completely devoid of any presence of mind, began weighing out flour into a bowl, following next with room temperature butter, yeast, sugar, salt, and finally warm water.

As I began turning the ingredients over in the bowl to combine them, I felt someone's hand come to the crook of my elbow and turned to find Joy at my side with Tempest close behind her, the two of them wearing matching expressions of concern. I realized I was crying.

"Let me finish," I requested, swiping my eyes with my sleeve. "I want to finish."

Tempest nodded, and Joy looked at her over her shoulder uncertain if it was a good idea, but Tempest took her by her arm and gestured for Joy to follow.

Once they were at a distance, I continued forming the dough and then left it in the covered bowl to rest while I started on the crème pâtissière.

Nobody talked, leaving me to work with the understanding that Joel and I were over, so if I could get through this, I could get through *Double the Whisk, Double the Reward.*

I tried to quiet my mind as I went through the steps, but all I could do was think about Joel and how I had once again fucked something up at the most crucial moment.

The tears began flowing more freely then, but I was determined to find some semblance of redemption by seeing this dessert to completion.

I could not have been less aware of the cameras or lights as I heated the cream, milk, sugar, and vanilla in a saucepan and waited for it to come to temperature.

Tempest, Joy, and Jennifer said nothing for the full hour and a half that it took for me to complete the dessert and the second that the last chocolate curl had been placed on top of the mille-feuille, I peeled off my apron to fold it, before gently placing it down beside the plate.

"That looks beautiful, Sophie. You nailed it," Tempest offered, her voice warm with sympathy.

"Thanks." I sniffed inspecting my creation, but unable to see anything but imperfections.

"I need some air," I announced, making my way toward the back door and stepping out into the winter night.

As I was lowering myself down onto the curb to sit, I heard footsteps approaching behind me.

A wisp of white appeared in my peripheral vision and I turned to find Jennifer holding out some tissues to me.

I accepted them as she planted herself down onto the curb beside me.

"I take it that Joel didn't take too kindly to Cletus's offer," she guessed as I blew my nose.

"Nope," I replied. "No, he sure did not," I affirmed before crossing my arms on top of my knees.

"Maybe he just needs some time to come around to the idea," Jennifer suggested kindly, but she didn't see the look of betrayal in his eyes, and I knew that it wasn't the idea of the pictures that bothered him.

"He's upset that I told Cletus about the situation he was in with the Iron Wraiths," I explained. "And I don't blame him, he asked me not to tell anyone."

"You were only trying to help him because you care about him," she reasoned, and though I appreciated her attempt to justify it, I needed to hold myself accountable for my actions.

"It doesn't matter, it wasn't my story to tell," I responded prosaically.

Jennifer sighed and began picking tiny balls of lint from the sleeves of her sweater.

"Cletus feels guilty about the role he and his brothers might have played in making the Barnes' Auto Shop vulnerable to the Wraiths. He hasn't expressly said it, but I can tell," she divulged solemnly.

"It is what it is." I shrugged, not knowing what else I could say that might make either one of us feel any better about the situation.

"Maybe Cletus can talk to Joel," Jennifer suggested. I could only see that making things even worse.

"I'm not sure that's such a good idea," I started to say just as the sound of an approaching vehicle caught both of our attention.

We glanced up as a fast approaching car pulled into the carpark.

"It's Cletus," Jennifer announced, pulling herself up to her feet and making her way to him.

"I'll head inside," I said, leaving to give them privacy, but as I started toward the door, I heard Cletus call out.

"Sophie, wait," Cletus said. "Where's Joel? Is he at home?" he asked with some urgency.

"I don't know—"

"Have you tried calling him, is he answering his phone?"

A cold rush went through my body and I started toward Cletus.

"I haven't seen him in a couple of days, he's not talking to me," I explained as I approached.

"What's going on?" Jennifer asked turning to Cletus, her brow furrowed in concern.

"The fire department and police are on their way to his shop, there's been a fire and nobody can get in touch with him," he informed us as I felt the ground vanish from beneath my feet.

Don't panic. Don't panic yet, there's no need to jump to conclusions.

Without a word, I turned and started toward the bakery.

"Where are you going?" Jennifer called out after me, but I was already inside the door.

I grabbed my jacket and bag. As I was leaving, Tempest and Joy asked me what was going on.

I hastily told them what I knew and exited the bakery, heading toward my car when Cletus called out to me again.

"Sophie, get in," he instructed, referring to his vehicle and I hesitated at the thought of Joel seeing me arrive with the likes of Cletus Winston. "Come now, Miss Sophie, we don't have time to lose," he barked and I relented, running over to join him as he, Jennifer, and I piled into his Geo Prism and peeled out of the bakery parking lot to make our way over to Joel's garage.

I made several attempts to call Joel on the way, but I kept getting his voicemail. With each unsuccessful call, the more frantic with worry I became.

On the last attempt, I let the call go to voicemail and decided to at least leave a message.

"Joel it's me, it's Sophie. I know that you're not talking to me right now and I know that you don't want to see me, and that's okay. But if you could please just send me a text message, just *one* text to let me know that you're …" I almost said the word "alive" and was horrified at the implication. "Okay," I revised, after recovering from the thought. "I need to know you're alright, because if you're not," I continued feeling the tears start to come, not caring if Cletus and Jennifer could hear what I was saying, "I will never be able to forgive myself. I'm already unable to forgive myself for becoming just one more person in this town who you couldn't trust and I'm sorry. With my whole heart, I am sorry. I never wanted to hurt you and … I love you," I whispered unsteadily into my phone and then hung up.

Cletus was diving as fast as was sensible, but it felt like a decade had passed by the time we got close enough to see the plumes of smoke in the distance.

"It doesn't appear to still be ablaze," Cletus said, which was of little comfort to me in that moment.

As we approached, we could see the red flashing lights of the fire department and police and as we neared, I could see Ruby was out of the garage and parked diagonally on the grass clear of any of the structures.

I tried not to assume that Ruby's position meant Joel was there, not having the heart to get my hopes up only to see them crash back down. As soon as Cletus brought the car to stop, I leaped out and began running toward the garage.

My eyes searched for him and I grimaced at the acrid scent of burnt metal and wood.

I stopped just before the parking lot to observe the damage and could see that only one part of the garage seemed to be affected by the fire.

The small garage on the right-hand side, where Joel kept Ruby was scorched and half-collapsed, it's charred edges dripping with water from the fire hoses.

Looking around at the cast of emergency services, I spotted Joel making his way toward Ruby.

"Joel," I called to him. He glanced at me, and paused as I hurried toward him, stopping just a few feet away when the look in his eyes dissuaded me from getting any closer.

"Where are you going?" I asked, just as his gaze zeroed in over my shoulder and I turned to find Cletus and Jennifer cautiously approaching us.

Tiptoeing around the issue was no longer a solution, so I turned back to Joel and moved a couple of steps closer.

"What happened?" I asked gently.

"Catfish. Who do you think?" he responded tightly. "I'm about to pay him a visit," he responded, his eyes wild and unreachable.

"No! Joel," I called his name again, holding out my hands as I appealed to him. "Please don't do that, please stay here with us ... with me."

He shook his head with a growl and pulled open the driver's side door and was about to climb in when Cletus's voice boomed from behind me.

"Joel," Cletus said, appearing at my side and stopping Joel from proceeding further.

"What?" Joel asked impatiently.

"If you want revenge on Catfish Hickson, this isn't the way to go about it," he reasoned, calmly but cautiously. "You have better means at your disposal and some people here who want to help."

"Help?" Joel scoffed. "*Now* you want to help?"

"That's right, we want to help." Cletus nodded emphasizing with his tone, that while nothing could be done about the past, there was a way to move forward.

Joel shook his head like he was about to protest when Cletus beat him to it by making his way toward the passenger's side.

"Well then I'm going with you," he declared boldly as Joel's brow furrowed in confusion.

"Cletus Byron," Jennifer called edgily from behind me, but he ignored her and opened the passenger side door.

"Come on then," Cletus goaded him, and I wasn't sure if he knew what he was doing, but the last thing I needed on my conscience was to have my boss' husband killed alongside the man whose trust I had shattered while they sought revenge over the Iron Wraiths.

"Joel, please," I tried again, moving around the front of the car to come as close to his side as I had the nerve to get. Not because I worried he'd hurt me, but because I was all too aware of the trapped look in his eyes. Like he had nowhere to go and nobody to turn to, and that made him unpredictable.

Joel looked between Cletus and I, before locking eyes with me. I saw his Adam's apple bobbing in his throat.

He opened his mouth to say something, and then stopped himself, lowering his body into the car and closing the door instead.

Cletus cast Jennifer a meaningful look and she nodded to him before he followed Joel into the car.

Ruby roared to life and I moved out of the way as Joel reversed, swung her around, and then pulled her out onto the road.

I turned to Jennifer, who was pulling her phone out of her purse.

"What do we do? Should we follow them?" I suggested.

"No, ma'am, we're waiting here," she replied staring down at her phone while her fingertips flew across the surface of the screen.

"What do you mean, we're waiting here? We can't just stand here and do nothing," I insisted as though she were crazy.

Jennifer glanced up and me and lowered her phone.

"Alright, come on then. Let's go to Daisy's for a slice of pie. We'll wait for them there."

"Jennifer, did you see what just happened?" I asked pointing in the direction that Joel and Cletus had driven off in. "They're going to confront Catfish!"

"Not currently they're not," she said typing out another quick text on her phone.

"How do you know that?" I asked narrowing my eyes at her but also impatient with each passing moment we were losing.

"Cletus is texting me," she said waving her phone in the air. "He's trying to convince Joel to go to the Winston Garage to talk instead."

"He would never—"

"Ooh," she shrieked as she got another text holding her finger up to silence me while she read it. "He agreed. I knew Cletus could convince him not to go after Catfish," she said smiling wickedly to herself as she shoved her phone into her back pocket. "Alright, Miss Sophie, let's go get a slice of pie and then I'll take you home. What do you say?"

I knew she said that Cletus was able to persuade Joel against seeking out Catfish but the urge to find him, to make sure was intense.

"Give him space. I know it's hard, but he needs to be able to say his piece to Cletus. We'll see how things go after that. Okay?" Jennifer implored me, stepping toward the driver's side door and pulling it open.

"Come on," she said. "Let's go get pie. Pie is the answer to everything," she offered, giving me a bright smile before climbing inside the car.

I stood there, part of me unable to share in Jennifer's confidence that Cletus had the situation under control, but the bigger part of me knew that what she had said about Joel needing the catharsis of confronting Cletus was right.

I decided to follow Jennifer's advice and give Joel space while we went to Daisy's to wait out the storm with pie.

CHAPTER 24

When I stepped out of the building the next morning, I could hear the shrill beeping of a truck reversing, men yelling and the indistinct din of what sounded like a construction site.

Peering down the block, I could see people hard at work rushing to complete the assembly of the Green Valley Christmas Market which would be opening later that day.

I had been vaguely aware that something was happening down at the end of the block but had been too preoccupied to notice it taking shape.

Curious, I found myself floating toward it to get a better look.

Had I been more in the Christmas spirit instead of the emotional human husk I had become, I would have felt way more excited about it.

As I neared, I could see the rows of vendor stalls in the shape of rustic log cabins with fake snow drooping over the sides of the gabled roofs. Dotted between them were a variety of Christmas themed novelties such as an elaborately decorated sled and wooden cutouts of Santa, elves, and reindeer with the faces removed so people could poke their faces through for photos.

A carousel was being assembled, as well as a bouncy castle in the shape of Santa's house in the North Pole. There were, of course, reindeer rides (that would likely be a pony with fake antlers attached to its head), a cookie decorating station, and countless other booths manned by local businesses.

I was alarmingly unmoved by it all.

I didn't feel inspired, impressed, or even a fleeting sense of excitement that I was lucky enough to see such a wonderful tradition coming to life right before my eyes.

I sighed, watching my breath form a cloud and sail away in the direction of my car which ...

Oh shit.

I had completely forgotten that I had left my car back at the bakery.

It was 3:30 in the morning, and Green Valley didn't exactly have a local taxi service.

I checked the ride-share app on my phone, but no cars were available either.

I thought about calling Joy or Tempest, but they didn't start until five AM and I didn't want to make them leave early and drive out of their way to come and get me.

Reminding myself of the amount of work waiting for me at the bakery, I tried to mute the voice in the back of my head that was screaming for me to knock on Joel's door, but I genuinely didn't have any other option.

After taking stock one last time to make sure there were no other options, I accepted my fate and headed back toward my building.

I had never walked up a flight of stairs so slowly in my entire adult life.

When I reached the top of the stairs, I took even longer to cross the landing to his door and longer still to knock on it.

My heart was thumping like crazy as I waited for him to answer.

Some moments or possibly a decade later, I could hear him approaching the door and I held my breath anxiously as he unlocked it.

I braced myself, and when the door swung open, there he was in the sweatpants I loved, disheveled from sleep, wearing a *what do you want now* expression.

I took a breath and forced myself to explain the reason behind my presence at this ungodly hour.

"Look, I know it's nauseatingly early and believe me, you're the last person I wanted to ask considering ..." I stopped myself seeing from his expression that he didn't need a reminder of what had just happened to him. "Well anyway, I left my car at the bakery last night and I would never ask but ... I'm kind of stuck here and I need to get to work."

It was messy and barely comprehensible, but the gist of my conundrum was there.

The look on his face, that dark, cloudy expression that brought me back to our first meeting on a confusing mountain road was equal parts comforting and unsettling.

He was so gorgeous, that it made my heart begin to ache all over again.

I didn't want to go to work. I wanted to force myself inside his apartment, shut the door and force him to talk to me and tell me all the ways I'd disappointed him so that I could hopefully be forgiven.

Instead, I held my breath, peering up into his tired face.

I marveled at the way his eyes, which were usually so bright and vibrant, could turn so dark and tumultuous.

I felt like an age had passed without a response and finally I lost my patience.

"Can you stop looking at me like that?" I snapped before realizing that I'd made yet another mistake by coming to him. "You know what, forget it, don't worry abo—"

"Just wait here, give me a minute!" he snapped back. "Jeez." He sighed impatiently then proceeded to close the door in my face.

I drew in a breath and then slowly exhaled, turning away from the door and making my way back to the stairs to wait for him wondering if this was a good idea, but knowing that I didn't have a choice regardless.

About three minutes later he emerged from his apartment fully dressed and avoiding eye contact as he fiddled with his keys.

On the drive to the bakery, I drew a hundred breaths preparing to say something but each time the words caught in my throat and I couldn't bring myself to follow through.

Joel stared unyieldingly at the road ahead and appeared even less likely than me to break the weighted silence.

The only time Joel even came close to acknowledging my presence was when I shoved my hands between my thighs to warm them. Without looking at me, he reached forward and turned the heat higher.

I pretended not to notice.

We pulled up to the bakery and I felt like I had been holding my breath for the entire ride, opening the door just as soon as he pulled up to the curb.

"Thanks for the ride and sorry to have bothered you so early," were the first words spoken between us since the apartment.

"Sure," I heard him respond coolly as I slid out of the car.

I shut the door, leaving the million things that I wanted to say, but didn't have the guts to, behind me in the truck. But then, the thought occurred to me that this might be the last time I saw him.

For some reason, it made me think of Nick, Joel's brother and how things had ended between them.

I knew I couldn't live with myself if I didn't say something, so before I could change my mind I turned back to the truck and opened the passenger side door again.

"I just want to say, in case I don't get the chance again, that ... I love you. I just wanted to tell you in person. You know ... instead of over voice mail. In case you heard it, that is."

I was so nervous that I was rambling, so I shut my mouth and gave him a chance to respond.

The only sign that Joel had heard my confession was the subtle shift of his hand around the steering wheel.

"I'm not saying it to guilt you into forgiving me for what I did, though I really am *so* sorry. I'm telling you because it's the truth, regardless of whether or not its reciprocated."

"I've been thinking a lot about regret lately. And I've come to the realization that there is some regret I can live with, and some that I can't. I *know* I would've regretted it for the rest of my life if I didn't tell you how I felt. I couldn't leave letting you believe that there was nobody out there who loved you and was pulling for you to do all the things you said you wanted to do. I wanted so badly to see you get out of here and get back into construction. To get to travel to Tokyo and meet new people. And since I'm on an honesty kick, I'm gonna admit that maybe there was a selfish part of me that did what I did because I wanted to be with you when you did all of that. That's why I told Cletus. It's not an excuse, I know that, but there it is."

Joel shifted in his seat, but still stared straight ahead unflinchingly.

"Also, for what it's worth, I decided to do the show."

He turned and looked at me then, his expression discernable. I thought he might say something, but when he didn't, I knew there was nothing left for me say.

"Goodbye Joel," I said hating how the word "goodbye" turned my tongue bitter.

Without waiting to see if he had anything to say in response, I swung the door shut and hurried toward the bakery, feeling embarrassed by my word vomit, foolish for how I felt, and inexplicably bereft. Like I was never going to see him again.

* * *

For the next two and a half weeks, all there was, was work.

Donner Bakery staff were asked to extend their hours beyond their regular schedule to accommodate the hundreds of special orders that rolled in from customers wanting a Donner Bakery creation at the center of their Christmas spread. Not to mention the additional responsibility of keeping the Christmas Market stall stocked.

On Christmas Eve, the last day of the Market, Joy fell ill and I volunteered to work the stall knowing everyone else would be anxious to get home and be with their families.

It was a nice change of pace from the bakery and watching all the revelers enjoying the market helped to lighten my heart a little, though I still felt pretty miserable.

Groups of children posed on the sled and poked their little faces into the Christmas cutouts as parents took pictures on their phones and laughed at the silly faces the children pulled.

Couples strolled around, perusing homemade soaps and hand-knitted mittens as they sipped eggnog and ate freshly baked pretzels.

Cheerful Christmas music blared from speakers that were mounted on tripods around the market and a procession of revelers stopped to take selfies in front of the dazzling seventy-foot tall Christmas tree.

By day, it was beautiful but when the sun went down, it was a true show stopper.

At five o'clock every evening, the speakers were silenced, and the local choir assembled at the base of the tree to perform Christmas carols.

I couldn't see them from where the Donner Bakery stall was, but I could hear the stirring harmony of their voices as people slowed or stilled completely in reverence at their performance.

While the market was at a standstill I glanced around, my eyes coming to the cordoned off beer garden that Genie's had contributed to the event.

The beer garden was set up beneath a huge white marquee with picnic style tables, and outdoor heat lamps to warm people from the chilly December air.

I glanced around the patrons enjoying beer, glühwein, and spiked hot apple cider and that's when I spotted Joel, sitting at a bench in the beer garden. Right across from Catfish.

I felt a rush like the ground had vanished from below me as I zeroed in on Joel's hulking figure.

My immediate thought was to assess whether or not he appeared to be in any danger.

While everyone else was focused on the choir, the two men sat staring intently at each other. While they spoke, I watched anxiously from afar, ready to make the scene of the century if I thought for one minute that Joel was in danger.

I couldn't figure out why they would meet somewhere so public until I saw Joel slide an envelope that I recognized across the table to Catfish.

Catfish reached for the envelope and that was the exact moment that the choir chose to finish their performance.

After a short applause, the crowd began to disperse blocking my view of the beer garden.

I stood on my toes trying to get a better look, but I couldn't see anything, and someone was calling my name.

"Sophie! Sophie!"

I turned to Bradley the barista who gestured toward a group of customers whose heads I was looking right over, waiting to be served their Donner Bakery treats.

"Sorry about that," I apologized forcing a smile to the first in line. "What can I get you?" I asked as my eyes kept drifting toward the beer garden.

It was several minutes later when a fortuitous gap in the hoard opened up allowing me a clean line of sight to where they had been seated, but by then, they were both gone.

For the rest of the night, I was sick with anxiety and even when the market closed at nine o'clock, Bradley and I still had to spend an hour emptying the stall so it could be disassembled.

When I could finally leave, I walked the short distance down the street to my building and climbed the stairs to my apartment.

From the top landing, I was reassured by the sound of the television coming from inside his apartment, but there was still the niggling, little voice in the back of my mind that wouldn't be satisfied, unless I saw that he was okay.

Approaching his door, I raised my fist and pressed it to the wooden surface, listening for a sign of something other than the TV.

A minute passed, then two, then three until finally I heard the sound of dishes or glass clattering.

With a sigh of relief, I lowered my hand and turned away from the door heading back inside my apartment.

Fishing out my phone, I saw I had a string of texted Christmas greetings, but I simply didn't have the energy to respond to them.

I cleared the notifications and suddenly came across my text string with Joel.

I stared at it for a long time before slowly tapping out a text that simply read, "Merry Christmas"

I deleted it and-retyped it about four times, before sighing with exasperation and throwing my phone onto the couch.

The man I was in love with, who was right across the hall from me would rather be alone on Christmas than be with me. And with that realization, I clasped my hand over my eyes, turned into the couch cushion and began to sob.

CHAPTER 25

*S*even days later, Joy, Tempest, and I were sitting in Tempest's car at the Greyhound depot in downtown Maryville.

I had decided against buying a new crappy car, to replace my old crappy car on the basis that the prospect of buying a nice, new car if I won *Double the Whisk, Double the Reward* was more of a motivator.

I had assured my friends that it wasn't necessary to drive me all the way to Maryville, but they insisted.

"I want to see you cry when you leave me. So I know that *you* know what a huge mistake you're making by leaving us," Tempest joked, but we all knew there would be tears.

And not just for the friends I was leaving behind.

Despite dutifully putting one foot in front of the other, my heart was not entirely along for the ride and I feared she might never catch up to me again. Opting instead to stay forever in Green Valley, Tennesse with my big, southern man and his frowny brows.

I knew I'd hurt him and betrayed his confidence. A misstep for sure but there was also a small part of me that felt that maybe I was right. Maybe he wasn't ready to leave Green Valley behind quite yet.

Had I been able, I would have waited until he was but I had a promise to Anna to keep, and with that in mind, I forged ahead, Boston bound.

The atmosphere was weighted with anticipation for my impending departure from Green Valley, something nobody wanted to mention until we finally saw the bus pull into the depot.

Joy sighed and poked her head between the two front seats from the back.

"I can't believe you're leaving, I thought for sure you were going to move here and marry—"

"Joy," Tempest interrupted impatiently.

"It's alright," I assured them both, mustering as convincing a smile as I could manage at the mention of Joel and pretending to be brave. "It is what it is."

And what it is, is a bunch of bullshit.

It had been more than two weeks since I had told him I loved him in the Donner Bakery parking lot, and I figured if he had anything to say in return, he knew where to find me. New Year's Day had come and gone, and I was both jobless and homeless after both my employment and rental agreement contracts expired.

I woke up that morning, stripped the bed and left my used towels on the bathroom floor, just as he had requested that first night and gathered my belongings. When I left the apartment, I dropped the keys in the green locked box outside his door and hovered for a minute or two, wanting to say goodbye, but not sure if it was appropriate.

I'd spent countless hours thinking about our situation from every angle only to keep coming back to the same unshakeable conclusion that this wasn't how it was supposed to end. It felt all wrong.

Regardless of how unfinished everything felt, I had to accept that I had taken the risk to tell him how I felt and received no payoff. No answer had been his answer and I would simply need to learn to live with that.

I also had *Double the Whisk, Double the Reward* to prepare for with a filming date set for February eleventh, ten days after the grand opening of Yeast Affection.

Jennifer Donner Winston had graciously agreed to attend the shoot as my celebrity mentor, despite her fervent insistence that she wasn't a celebrity. Of course, Anna would attend as my chosen family member.

"Are you two going to come visit me in Boston?" I asked in an attempt to steer the conversation back to less heartbreaking territory.

"Probably not."

"Eh, I doubt it," they grumbled simultaneously before giggling mischievously.

"You know what? Fuck you both," I smirked shaking my head as I thought about how much I'd miss them.

"Come on, don't be like that. You know we're going to miss you like … like …" Joy cast her eyes skyward as she struggled to come up with a suitable simile. "Like a fat kid misses cake?"

"No that doesn't work … like the desert misses the rain," Tempest chimed in waving her finger in the air.

"Like the sun misses the moon," Joy added, getting the hang of it.

"I miss you like I miss my phone when I forget to take it to the toilet!" Tempest exclaimed proudly.

"I miss you like men miss the toilet!"

"I miss you like I missed the toilet that one time that I puked!"

"Alright! That's lovely, thank you both for missing me as much as you apparently miss toilet activities. I'm honored." I cringed, glancing over my shoulder at Joy who fell back against the seat in laughter.

"Is that your bus?" Tempest asked peering through the windshield and I turned to follow her gaze, noting the approaching vehicle with the recognizable gray and blue logo.

Suddenly, I was overcome with an overwhelming sense of sorrow.

I felt Joy grasp my hand and I turned to find her leaning in between Tempest and I, fixing me with her big, round, sad eyes.

"This really fucking sucks," I admitted looking down at our joined hands. "Why do I feel so … mournful?"

"I think everybody in this car knows the answer to that one, honey," Tempest replied twisting her lips sympathetically.

I shook my head unable to accept the fact that as soon as I boarded that bus, the hope that Joel would show up and tell me that he wanted to work things out would be extinguished.

I leaned my head back against the headrest as we all silently watched the bus pull up to the curb.

"Can you guys do me a favor?" I asked them, my voice soft and drained.

"Sure," Joy agreed before even knowing what I was going to ask.

"Just check in on him every once in a while, to make sure he's okay?"

I wasn't looking at them, but in my peripheral vision, I saw them exchange a quick glance.

"He's gonna be just fine, don't you worry about him," Tempest assured me gently. "You just focus on helping your friend open her bakery and winning *Double the Whisk, Double the Reward* so you can finally open your own. We'll be rooting for you, just remember that if you start to freak out, okay? You've practiced and you're prepared. You got this on lock now, you hear me?"

I nodded robotically, my mind still on the thing I had been instructed not to worry about.

I was as prepared as I would ever be for the *Double the Whisk, Double the Reward* shoot later next month, but being told not to worry about Joel was like being told not to worry as someone reached inside my chest and pulled out my still beating heart.

I wanted to make a grab for it while screaming, "Hey I can't live without that! I *need* that!"

We sat for a few more moments in pensive silence, before I took a breath and turned toward them in my seat.

After delaying the inevitable for long enough, I took in a big breath, slowly exhaled and then looked at my friends.

"Okay, it's time. I better get a move on."

Their forlorn expressions only made my heavy heart sink even further.

Unable to stand it, I opened the door and stepped out to the brisk January air, hoping it would slap some semblance of sense back into me.

Joy and Tempest helped me lug my stuff to the cargo area and I hugged each one of my friends tightly.

"Got your headphones?" Joy asked.

I smiled and tugged on the cord so she could see it.

"Got your Paul Newman?" Tempest teased and I froze.

A bone-chilling rush went through my entire body when I realized that I'd left him on the fridge back at the apartment.

"Oh no, no, no, no!" I exclaimed.

"Uh-oh! Are you sure?" Joy asked crouching down to help me look as we frantically searched my bag.

"It's not here! I can't leave without him. I can't!" I insisted looking around as though it might magically materialize nearby.

"Miss, are you boarding?" the driver asked.

"Uh yes! One minute please, I'm just trying to find something!" I informed him, searching in the zippered pockets.

"You're going to find you've missed the bus if you don't give me your booking confirmation and board this bus! I got a schedule to keep. Do you think I *want* to be making a twenty-three-hour trip on New Year's Day—"

"Alright! Alright! Just *one* minute!" I exclaimed. Having searched every nook and cranny of my backpack to no avail, I looked up at my friend's helpless faces. "I definitely left it back at the apartment, it has to be there," I insisted not knowing where else it could possibly be.

"Aah! Don't panic, it's okay. I'll swing by Joel's tomorrow and ask him to give it to me, and I'll mail it to you," Tempest suggested.

"No! No, you don't understand. That thing is like Thor's hammer to me!" I explained waving my hands in the air in a panic, watching my friends' faces pinch with confusion. "It helps me focus, it helps me think, it helps me make decisions, and *IT HELPS ME STAY CALM!*"

"Miss!" the bus driver shouted at me impatiently. I stopped and slowly spun around to glare at him.

"Do you mind? I am having a *crisis* over here!" I hollered back as he huffed and reaffixed his baseball cap impatiently.

Then, just like in a John Hughes movie, the roar of a beefy engine sounded from behind the bus and we all watched as a very familiar pristine 1969 Camaro Z28 pulled to the curb in front of the bus.

My whole world stopped and my heart right along with it as I watched Joel's familiar shape emerge from the driver's side with my lanyard clutched in his hand.

"Oh my God," I breathed, watching as he came right toward me with that sexy, loose gait that I'd noticed when I first met him.

I was too shocked to think about meeting him halfway until Tempest shoved me from behind.

"Go on. Shoo!" she said flicking her hands to send me on my way.

I turned back to Joel and started, slowly and hesitantly, toward him.

As I looked at him, it was as though the rest of the world had become muted and all I could see in vivid, bright technicolor were those eyes.

We came to a stop two feet away from each other and Joel held out my lanyard with a soft smile that lifted some of the tension I'd been carrying around for the past two and a half weeks.

"Forget something?" he asked, the deep, rumbly quality of his voice and southern drawl making me instantly spark and ignite.

I wanted to respond, but my mouth would not co-operate.

Instead, I bowed my head as he raised the lanyard toward me slipped it around my neck.

"There, that's better," he murmured with the kind of earnestness that only someone who knew what that lanyard meant to me could impart. "Do you have a minute?"

I gestured over my shoulder with my thumb toward the bus and just as I was about to respond, the driver beat me to the punch.

"Oh, what the hell is this now? You blocking me in? Seriously?" the driver complained, gesturing wildly between the bus and the Camaro parked snuggly in front of it.

I sighed and rolled my eyes, turning back to Joel.

"He's going to have a hernia if I don't board," I informed him regretfully.

"Do you have to get on this bus? Can you get the next one or..." he shook his head as though second guessing his words, or what my reaction to them might be.

Or what? Or what, Joel? Please say it.

"Well, yeah. I gotta get to Boston, remember?"

"I know, I know. I just…"

I could see him struggling with what he wanted to say, but it felt important that I gave him the opportunity to say what he wanted.

"I'm on a time budget people!" the bus driver hollered once again, and while I still wanted to give Joel space to say what he needed to say, I decided to help him out a little.

"If I were to pull my suitcases out of cargo…would you have a plan B to get me to Boston?"

Joel regarded me with relief, his eyebrows pinching together as he released a breath and nodded.

"I do."

"Alright. Okay, I won't board then."

"EXCUSE ME!"

"Argh," Joel growled impatiently, "hold on just one sec," he requested before making his way over to talk to the driver.

The two men conversed in hushed tones for a few minutes as I glanced over my shoulder at Joy and Tempest who were huddled together watching and whispering to each other.

I turned back around in time to see the driver open up the cargo compartment and begin offloading my belongings.

With all my earthly possessions now reacquainted with the side-walk, I looked on as Joel picked up them up one by one and began loading them into his trunk.

Of course, we had a lot to talk about but in my heart, I knew all our questions would be answered in due time, and that I trusted him enough to take this risk.

I was also happy to watch him lift heavy things.

With my two suitcases and storage container tucked in the trunk, he got back into the Camaro and moved Ruby far enough forward for the bus to be able to pull back out into the street.

I watched as the Greyhound that was supposed to take me to Boston made its way down the street, the breaks hissing as it stopped at an intersection before continuing on.

My eyes went to Ruby purring idly on the side of the road and I turned to Tempest and Joy who were still standing nearby.

"I think Joel wants you to get in the car with him," Tempest instructed with playful condescension.

"I know." I nodded and gathered up my backpack before making my way over to them. "Weird how he knew I'd be here, any idea how he found out?" I asked wryly.

"Do you really think we'd keep something like this from you?" Tempest asked feigning offense.

"Yes. Yeah, absolutely," I responded without hesitation. Joy covered her mouth as she burst into secretive laughter giving them both away.

"I'm sorry." She giggled, not sounding sorry at all. "I just love a happy ending." She shrugged and then sighed as she clasped her hands to her chest.

I smiled at them and then looked down at my feet as the three of us fell quiet.

In an instant, a flood of memories from my time in Green Valley flashed through my mind and once again, I found myself delaying the inevitable. Luckily though, Tempest was there to rip off the Band-Aid.

"You need to go on and get in that car, you're keeping the man waiting," she scolded me with a nod and raised eyebrows.

"Alright, fine," I conceded. "I'm coming in for a hug though," I said lifting my arms as her face twisted with disapproval.

"Shh shh," I soothed as I wrapped my arms around her. "Just let this happen."

After making her suffer for about three seconds, I let her go but noticed as we parted that she was fighting a smile and her green eyes were glassy with restrained emotion.

"You're the best kind of people, Tempest Cassidy, and I'm gonna miss you."

"I'm gonna miss you too, pastry princess," came her genuine, warm response.

I broke the moment, feeling my eyes begin to fill and turned to Joy.

"My joyful girl," I said holding my arms out and she rushed into them without hesitation.

"You go out there and make television history, you hear me?" she commanded into my shoulder.

"I'll do my best, I promise," I avowed feeling like I really meant it, instead of just offering an empty platitude.

When we parted, Joy took me by the shoulders and sniffled.

"Do you promise to come back and visit?"

"Cross my heart, hope to die," I said crossing my fingertip over my chest and pressing my fingers to my lips before sending my promise heavenward for safekeeping with Mr. Newman.

I took a breath and gave them both a big smile, turning and making my way toward Joel who had been waiting for me patiently.

I approached the passenger's side and opened the door, lowering my head to look inside at Joel.

"So ... about this plan B for getting me to Boston," I said raising my eyebrows at him questioningly.

He smiled softly before gesturing for me to get in and I complied, lowering myself onto the smooth, leather seat and placing my backpack on the floor between my feet.

"So, you're here ... does that mean you don't hate me anymore?" I asked.

"Oh, honey." He sighed regretfully. "I never hated you."

"So, you just let me think that for the past two and a half weeks? Do you have any idea how sick I felt this whole time?" I asked with a humorless laugh.

His large hand came to the side of my face and I peered up at him. If my heart had arms, they would have been making grabby hands across the space between us, but I knew we had some things we needed to discuss.

"I'm sorry," he offered, brushing his thumb across my cheek before lowering his hand and looking out the windshield thoughtfully. "I had some things I needed to take care of."

"I'm aware." I snickered as though his response were the understatement of the century.

"I had to take care of them on my own," he clarified, but I closed my eyes and shook my head impatiently to let him know that wasn't good enough.

"Joel, please don't be cryptic ... what happened with Catfish? I saw you two at the Christmas Market. What happened with Cletus? And why are you here?"

I needed all the information. I needed the facts, not insinuations. I was on tenterhooks trying to hold back the hope that was simmering just below the surface of my heart.

Joel lowered his head sheepishly before shifting slightly around to face me in the car.

"A lot happened, and I want to tell you everything, but first I need to ask you something," he stated, looking nervous.

"Alright," I replied hesitantly.

"Remember on Thanksgiving, we were lying in bed and you said you wished I could come to Boston with you?"

And then it was too late to hold out on that hope I'd been suppressing. At his words, my wishful heart bloomed, and then soared into the stratosphere.

"Yeah ..."

"Did you really mean that?"

Oh God. Oh God. Oh God.

I bit my lips to rein in my smile, but it was hopeless.

"How could you doubt it?" I asked, hearing my voice already starting to crack as I reached for his hand, our fingers immediately tangling and locking together firmly.

Joel looked down at our hands and smiled, before looking right into my eyes and lifting my hand to press his lips to my knuckles.

"I want to come with you to Boston," he said *finally,* and in an instant, I felt the weight of weeks of anxiety, sadness, and helplessness shatter and fall away like a shell of ice that had encased my body.

"The photos worked?" I asked in disbelief on a breath as Joel nodded in confirmation.

"Yeah. Yeah, they worked."

"What happened? Tell me everything!" I commanded, incited by my need for more information.

Over the course of the next few minutes, Joel relayed to me how Catfish had ordered recruits to "encourage" Joel to reopen the garage to the Iron Wraiths by starting a small fire at the shop. The night he had taken off in the Camaro with Cletus, Cletus had convinced him to use the photos to avoid the inevitable collateral damage that would occur if Joel sought out Catfish alone.

"Cletus said it would be unwise to pursue Catfish with a hammer when I had a scalpel at my disposal and as upset as I was at the time, it just made too much sense to ignore... much as I wanted to," he added, though his jibe appeared to be in good humor.

Joel conveyed that Cletus had also apologized to Joel on behalf of the Winston family for not being more sensitive to the fact that the Barnes Auto Shop had suffered as a result of them monopolizing all their clients, explaining that ignorance didn't equate to intention.

"... and then ... he made me an offer on the shop," Joel concluded with a smile like he still couldn't quite believe it.

"I am guessing you accepted."

"Oh, I accepted, I would have been crazier than a dog chasing its own tail if I hadn't."

"How much?" I asked, narrowing my eyes curiously, but Joel just laughed and shook his head.

"Enough to be here with you right now," was how he chose to answer the question which was plenty good enough for me.

Joel tugged my hand and lowered his chin to glance at me inquiringly.

"So back to my question ... about me coming to Boston with you. Obviously, we have some things we'll need to talk about and agree on, but I figure ... we've got fifteen hours of driving ahead of us. What do you say, Miss Sophie?"

I couldn't restrain myself for another millisecond.

I responded by leaping into his lap and wrapping myself around him as best I could in the tight space, crushing my lips to his and initiating a deeply ravenous and enthusiastic kiss that was so over the top, I could feel his resonant laugh vibrating through my entire body. Slowly, I eased the pressure and poured all of my love, happiness, and elation into a long, passionate kiss before finally coming up for air.

When we finally parted, Joel's eyes were glassy and heavy-lidded.

"One more thing," he announced softly, reaching up with his big hand to press to the side of my face.

"What?" I asked watching his mouth while it moved and thinking about how I wanted more of it.

His touch became more insistent and I raised my eyes to his.

"I love you too," he declared, holding me in place with his eyes until he'd said the words. "I should have said it long before you said to it me, because I felt it long before then, but I am saying it now and I plan on making up for lost time."

I smiled as his palm traced the side of my face, and up into my hair and I leaned needily into his touch.

His eyes dropped to my lips before he tugged me in for a long, slow kiss that filled the void that being away from him for the last two and a half weeks had created in my soul.

Adrift in the kiss and our own world of happiness, a loud and obnoxious car horn honked right next to our window. We pulled apart startled, to find Joy and Tempest idling alongside the Camaro waving and making kissy faces before peeling off down the street.

We laughed, and Joel laid on the horn in return as Tempest's car zipped down the road, honking out the rhythm of "Shave and a Haircut, Two Bits" repeatedly until they were out of sight.

"Come on, before we get going, I want to show you something," he announced as I begrudgingly relocated myself back into the passenger seat.

"Where are we going?" I asked curiously as he turned the keys in the ignition bringing Ruby thunderously to life.

"The shop," he replied, offering no more details than that, but I didn't care, reaching out to turn on the radio and find some music that suited my celebratory mood.

* * *

Soon after, we arrived at the Barnes Auto Shop and Joel pulled Ruby up in front of the garage.

I immediately noted his black truck parked in front of the office loaded with what looked like his belongings.

"What would you have done if I said I didn't want you to come with me to Boston?" I asked curiously.

"I still would have left town," he responded without hesitation. "There's nothing left for me here."

I reached for his hand and smiled at him sympathetically as he tightened his lips into a flat smile.

"Does this mean I get to drive the Camaro to Boston and you'll take the truck?" I asked, thinking about the logistics involved with getting two vehicles to Boston.

Joel smiled at me and tossed the car keys up in the air for me to catch. I scrambled forward as they sailed through the air.

They landed in the center of my two cupped hands as I sighed and shook my head.

"You're never going to stop doing that are you?" I asked as I pocketed the keys and tucked myself under his raised arm as we walked toward the reception area together.

As we entered the office of the garage, I couldn't believe my eyes.

"Whoa," I gasped. The space had been recently painted with fresh new signs, framed pictures of classic cars on the walls, indoor plants, and even a little waiting area with a coffee machine and water cooler.

"Greeting, travelers." I heard the familiar sound of Cletus's voice greet us from over my shoulder and I swung around to face him. "Welcome to the Winston Brother's Auto Shop Part Deux," he said holding up two fingers.

"Might take some getting used to," Joel admitted holding out his hand to greet Cletus with a handshake.

"Well luckily that feeling only lasts until you're used to it," Cletus offered in his usual dry delivery. "I see things worked out between y'all," he added nodding his head cordially at me.

"It would appear so. Miss Sophie and I were just on our way out and I wanted to come by to say thank you for …" I watched as Joel's eyes clouded over while he paused trying to come up with how to adequately articulate the magnitude of what Cletus had done for him.

Cletus nodded in understanding and became predictably unsettled at the show of gratitude, holding up his finger to us as he started backing away.

"Wait right there for just a minute, I'll be right back."

A few moments later Cletus returned with two items.

"We found this in the office when we cleared everything out to paint it. We were going to give it back to you, but wondered if you'd let us keep it instead," Cletus asked passing a framed photograph to Joel to inspect.

Joel took the frame from Cletus. It was the picture of him, his dad, and his brother, Nick, from the office.

Joel looked to be in his late teens, early twenties. The men were standing outside the very building we were in, underneath a sign that read *Barnes Auto Shop* and leaning against the Camaro that we'd just been driving in with their arms folded, smiling, and squinting from the light of the summer sun.

"I'm not sure if you ever got a chance to meet Shelly Sullivan, Beau's lady friend. Shelly is a very talented sculpture artist and we asked her if she could help us make a plaque to hang on the wall beneath the photograph if you would be so kind as to let us hold onto it. Or if you prefer, we can make a copy."

The plaque was around fifteen inches wide and ten inches long and simple but striking in its composition. The bronze border and embossed lettering were elegant and tasteful against the black background.

Cletus handed the plaque to Joel who held onto it long after he was done reading the words and solemnly traced his fingers over the inscription which read:

This garage was opened in 1974 by Nicholas Barnes, Senior, (1955-2014) and passed to his sons Nicholas Barnes, Junior (1982 - 2016) and Joel Barnes, who continued to serve the town of Green Valley, TN and its residents until 2019)

"We felt that it was important that people who come here know it's history," Cletus offered reverently as I felt my chest tighten and my eyes start to fill. I stepped away to give the two men space.

For the longest time, Joel stared at the plaque before swallowing back the lump in his throat and offering Cletus a grateful smile.

"That would be …" I could see him struggling to find the right thing to say. "All three of us would appreciate that very much," he said finally, and Cletus nodded in understanding.

"We already put some hooks up on the wall. If you'd do the honors?" Cletus requested, gesturing to a spot right behind the front desk.

Joel cleared his throat and nodded as he walked around the desk, placing the plaque up first and making sure that it was straight before hanging the photo frame directly below it.

His fingers lingered on the photo for a few moments before eventually tearing himself away, overwhelmed by the gesture and the significance of it to the memory of his family.

After a moment, Joel took Cletus's hand and firmly shook it.

"Thank you. Please pass our thanks on to Shelly for the incredible plaque as well, that really means a lot," Joel said finally able to speak before letting go of Cletus's hand.

"Our pleasure, best of luck to you both in the future. Make sure you stop by if you ever come back this way. I'd be pleased if you came to the old Oliver house and tried my sausage," Cletus requested causing me to squint as though I wasn't sure what I just heard.

I didn't feel as though Joel and Cletus were ever going to be the best of friends, but I knew beyond a shadow of a doubt that the hatchet between Joel and the Winston brothers had been well and truly buried and helped to contribute to the newfound light behind Joel's eyes.

The gesture made by Cletus with the plaque provided Joel with the closure he needed to move on from Green Valley and start over somewhere new.

"Looking forward to seeing you win that show on TV," Cletus offered, regarding me with a nod.

"I have a good feeling about it," I smiled confidently as Joel's hand come to the back of my neck.

"We should get going," Joel announced, and I nodded in agreement as we said goodbye to Cletus and headed out to the lot.

Once outside, I encircled Joel's waist with my arm and peered up to observe him to try and gauge his emotions.

"How do you feel?" I inquired gently, placing my other hand at the center of his chest as we ambled along.

Joel sighed and peered thoughtfully up ahead for a moment before turning to me and smiling.

"Free."

EPILOGUE

"*Your crème pâtissière is too tick.*"

"This crème pâtissière is exquisite. It's smooth, it's creamy beyond reason, the density is as it should be in order to support the pastry and add definition to the layers. It's wonderful," Judge Maurice Brockard said after sampling Chestnuts Roasting on an Open Fire in the final round of *No Whisk, No Reward.*

"*More height on ze soufflé, it's flat. IT'S FLAT!*"

"I agree," Judge Krista Chasey nodded. "The chestnut flavor comes through in every element of the dessert, but it's not overpowering. I can taste caramelization from the pastry which is cooked perfectly, I can taste the smokiness from the smoked crème pâtissière and roasted chestnuts, I can taste the praline, I can taste the chocolate. This is going to be a very tough dessert to beat. Well done."

"*What temperature did you temper ze shock-o-lat? It's not shiny. MORE SHINY!*"

Judge Filipe Armand indelicately sliced into the remaining mille-feuille like it was a chore, tearing the forkful away like a savage.

He brought it to his lips and then peered down at me from over his nose, pausing as he held the fork to his lips.

301

"This can't be worse than last time, so I am expecting quite the improvement," he warned as though my life depended on it.

All I could do was swallow and respond with, "Yes, chef."

I held my breath.

As he began to chew, all I could think of was that it was now in Mr. Newman's hands.

Filipe Armand's expression was inscrutable, and it seemed as though time ceased to exist.

I waited for seconds, minutes, hours, weeks for him to be done with his mouthful, but the moment went on for an eternity.

I glanced past the judges to the section behind the studio where our celebrity mentors and family members stood.

Jennifer Donner Winston had her arms folded over her chest and looked as anxious as I felt.

Joel was the picture of cool, calm composure and winked at me comfortingly.

My eyes passed back to Filipe Armand.

Finally, he placed his fork down and licked his lips of any remnants of my dessert that lay there.

"This mille-feuille ..." he began pointing to what was left on my plate, paused for what felt like *a* millennia to gather his thoughts, and once again, I stopped breathing.

"... is not only the best mille-feuille I have ever had, but possibly the best dessert I have ever tasted. Bar none," he declared. The instantaneous *whoosh* of relief that washed over me was so overwhelming that I had to grab a hold of the edge of my bench to stay on my feet.

"It's rich, but not too sweet, the sugar level is as it should be to let the flavor of the other ingredients shine through. There're lots of different textures and interesting ways in which you brought out the flavor of the chestnut," he explained, smacking his lips together as he tried to describe what he was tasting. Fat, heavy tears spilled out of my eyes.

Yeah that's right, I'm that bitch! I'm crying on television.

"The best part about this dessert is that I can see it's a representation of your nostalgia for roasted chestnuts. Is that what you were trying to convey?" he inquired and for a few seconds, all I could do was nod because if I tried to speak, all that would have come out would have been an Oscar worthy sob and snort which would have been immortalized on national television and then the internet for all eternity, and I did not want that to happen.

So, I took a few seconds to compose myself and get a handle on my blubbering before speaking and when I was ready, I wiped my eyes and nodded.

"Yes. Roasted Chestnuts reminds me very much of Christmastime with my parents back home in New York and I really wanted to create something that was symbolic of that."

Judge Filipe Armand offered only four more words after that, but they were so validating that even if I lost this competition, I would have felt okay about it.

"Well," he said smiling at me for the first time ever, "mission accomplished, chef."

"Thank you, chef," I responded respectfully. As the judges began to move to the next contestant's dessert, Judge Filipe Armand stopped and returned for one last bite of my dessert, offering the ultimate compliment, to which even the production team gasped.

I laughed and pushed the plate toward him, encouraging him to eat more. He took it with him and polished it off before moving on to the next contestant. Tears of pride streamed down my face all over again.

When the judges moved along, my attention swung back to Joel and Jennifer off set.

Oh my God! I mouthed to them wide-eyed as they mimed similar sentiments of awe and wonderment at the judge's feedback.

After each dessert was tasted, there was a short filming break while the judges deliberated on the result and we were allowed to spend some time with our support group.

I barely made it off set when Joel rushed to me and lifted me right off the ground, holding me in a tight hug that I could barely breathe through.

"I'm so proud of you," he kept repeating as my tears soaked the fabric covering his shoulder.

I turned my head toward him and kissed him, cradling his face in my hands, sharing our mutual joy for a moment before he lowered me to my feet and I turned to Jennifer.

"What do you think?" she asked, eluding to how confident I felt about winning the competition, handing me a bottle of water which I accepted gratefully.

"I know how this is going to sound," I prefaced, anticipating their response to what I was about to say, "but right now, I don't care if I win or not. No matter what the outcome is, my reward is to finally have this monkey off my back, and I am really proud of myself for taking the risk."

"Amen, sister," Jennifer declared, holding up her palm for a high five, which I reciprocated, but curled my fingers around her hand to hold it there before we pulled away.

"Jennifer, I just want to tell you, that I don't think any of this would have happened if I hadn't have met you and spent time working with you."

"Don't you try and palm the credit off to me," she said in warning.

"I'm not. Like I said, I am really proud of myself, and happy with what I accomplished today, but you have to know this wouldn't have happened if my car didn't break down in backwater Tennessee and I didn't get the opportunity to work with such a wonderful, kind, strong, generous, and inspiring woman. So, thank you. Thank you for agreeing to come and be my celebrity mentor and thank you for … being you."

Joel tapped me on my shoulder and pointed behind me.

I turned and saw John Moxie approaching with his eyebrows raised and his hands held out.

"Huh? Huh?" he said trying to cajole me into telling him he was right.

"You know what? I'm not too proud." I shrugged. "I'll say it, you were right."

At my words, John eased his stance and placed with hands in his suit pockets wearing a wide, almost proud smile.

"I am very happy you agreed to come back, Sophie. No matter what, congratulations."

"Thank you, John."

"I'm alweady thinking about a pitch for the next special. *No Whisk, No Reward: The Best of the Best Edition,* what do you think?" He asked waving his hand through the air as he tried to get me to visualize it.

"Can I see your phone for a minute?" I asked holding out my hand to him.

"Why?" he asked reaching into his suit jacket pocket.

"Because I want to delete my phone number from your contacts list," I said advancing on him as he laughed and backed away from me.

"Oh no, no, no, no," he said removing his hand from his pocket as the production team began filtering back into the studio and John took the opportunity to distract me with their return. "It's almost time to announce the winner. Good luck, kid," he said giving me a wink before walking away from the studio.

I had a few more minutes with Joel and Jennifer who kept assuring me that I had this in the bag, and though I was cautiously optimistic about it, all I really cared about was that I had accomplished something that held real value to me, and that Joel was here with me to see it.

After the break, the cameras began rolling again for the announcement of the winner.

After a long, drawn-out process in which the judges offered feedback on all of the final desserts, host Mickey Flannagan made his way over to announce the winner.

Spoiler Alert. I won!

When my name was called, there was no other way to describe it other than it truly felt like the cherry on top.

I felt that with the support of Joel and my new friends in Green Valley, I was able to overcome my personal struggles and accomplish something that I was truly proud of.

I was now three hundred thousand dollars richer, and putting plans in motion to open up my own bakery, while Joel found work with a construction company based in Boston who had a program called Solid Foundations, in which a team of ten employees where sent on a six week project to underprivileged communities in different parts of the world to build schools, medical facilities or community centers.

Joel would have needed to have been with the company for a full year before being eligible, but we didn't need to wait long for the first opportunity to travel somewhere together, because the first thing I did when I got my prize money from *Double the Whisk, Double the Reward* was book two tickets to Tokyo.

The End.

ACKNOWLEDGMENTS

Thank you to all twelve participating authors in launch 1 of Smarty-pants Romance. This group of women are some of the most talented, kind hearted and generous women, I have ever had the pleasure of working with. Thank you all for your humor, wisdom and advice.

Fiona Fischer. You are a legit Wonder Woman. The grace with which you handled such an enormous undertaking, and to did so with such humor and aplomb was truly impressive and inspiring. Thank you!

Penny. I don't know what else to say except, I love you. I know. Feelings! Ergh. But it's true. You didn't have to open up your precious world to novice writers such as myself and go to all the trouble to guide us through the someties difficult to navigate world of publishing, but I am *so* grateful that you did. I could never thank you enough for holding my hand through my first tentative steps into the world of publishing and I will forever be thankful for you for opening up this new world to me. With your encouragement, I look forward to continuing to learn and grow, and write better and braver stories.

And last, but by no means least, YOU. Yes you! The one who took a chance and read this book. Thank you *so* very much for joining me on this journey through your much beloved Green Valley. I only hope I can continue to earn my place here, in your hearts and on your bookshelves.

ABOUT THE AUTHOR

Ellie Kay is an Australian born living in Vancouver, British Columbia Canada who honed her creative writing skills in the colorful, and imaginative world of Corporate Insurance.

Socially awkward, she loves to respond to theatre ticket vendors who say, "enjoy the movie" with, "Thanks, you too,", but she also likes to cook, travel and spend time with her partner and cat Taako.

Ellie is on a mission to help change the stigma surrounding the Romance genre and hopes to see a day when they are no longer considered "guilty pleasures," but rather, just a pleasure.

Facebook: https://www.facebook.com/authorelliekay
Goodreads: https://www.goodreads.com/user/show/87837596-ellie-kay
Twitter: https://twitter.com/authorelliekay
Instagram: https://www.instagram.com/authorelliekay/

* * *

Find Smartypants Romance online:
Website: www.smartypantsromance.com
Facebook: www.facebook.com/smartypantsromance/
Goodreads: www.goodreads.com/smartypantsromance
Twitter: @smartypantsrom
Instagram: @smartypantsromance

Made in the USA
Monee, IL
10 November 2019